# ASHES ON Ice

## A NOVEL

*Hope you enjoy*
*[signature]*

# ASHES ON Ice

### A NOVEL

## GEORGES LAFONTAINE

BREAKWATER BOOKS LIMITED
100 Water Street • P.O. Box 2188 • St. John's • NL • A1C 6E6
www.breakwaterbooks.com

LIBRARY AND ARCHIVES CANADA CATALOGUING IN PUBLICATION

Lafontaine, Georges, 1957-
  [Des cendres sur la glace. English]
    Ashes on ice / Georges Lafontaine.

Translation of: Des cendres sur la glace.
ISBN 978-1-55081-236-7
I. Title.
PS8623.A359D4713 2007     C843'.6     C2007-901908-0

© 2007 Georges Lafontaine
Front cover photo insert: Passamaquoddy birchbark porpoise-hunting canoe, made by Maine traditional artist, David Moses Bridges © David Moses Bridges

ALL RIGHTS RESERVED. No part of this publication may be reproduced, stored in a retrieval system or transmitted, in any form or by any means, without the prior written consent of the publisher or a licence from The Canadian Copyright Licensing Agency (Access Copyright). For an Access Copyright licence, visit www.accesscopyright.ca or call toll free to 1-800-893-5777.

We acknowledge the financial support of The Canada Council for the Arts for our publishing activities.

We acknowledge the support of the Department of Tourism, Culture and Recreation for our publishing activities.

We acknowledge the financial support of the Government of Canada through the Book Publishing Industry Development Program (BPIDP) for our publishing activities.

Printed in Canada.

## Dedication

In memory of my mother

To my wife and best friend Adela Stryde

For those who believe in love and tolerance

# Acknowledgements

This book would never have been written without two important women in my life. My mother, Fernande Saumur, was the first one to encourage me to write, beginning when I was a young adolescent. This novel is an homage to her. And my wife, Adela Stryde, who inspired this story because of her love for her roots, and made me discover a marvellous place, Newfoundland. I have given her name to the heroine of this novel because, like her, she never has forgotten where she was born.

Special thanks also to the people of Newfoundland who opened the doors of their homes and their hearts. I found the real sense of hospitality and I hope sincerely that this story makes others discover your island.

# One

Sitting on the old wooden stoop, he gazed at the floorboards that had seen so many feet over so many seasons that they were curved, sculpted by the rubbing of a million pairs of shoes and boots. It had been almost seventy years since Achille had built the stoop with his own hands, helped by the woman he was holding today in the little container. His Adela.[1]

Now he regretted that they had never been officially married. The question had been settled long ago for both of them. The churches had rejected them. They had celebrated their union with each day of their life together.

Paul, standing next to him on the stoop, was visibly ill at ease. He was fidgeting with impatience, anxious to leave the place. Yet it was his mother inside the strange funerary urn. Paul had not wanted the ashes to be put inside "the object," as he had referred to the urn throughout the little ceremony that had just come to an end.

"That thing looks like hell. You're not going to put me to shame again, are you? Besides, the urn's included in the price of the cremation," Paul had said when Achille started to put the ashes inside. As if he had any right to an opinion.

The funeral home had put the ashes in a metal urn that shone like the bumpers of a flashy automobile, as did the obituary from the April 2, 1990 edition of *Le Droit*, which had been coated in plastic. As soon as he got home, Achille had transferred the ashes to the urn he had made himself.

It was actually a tree stump. When Adela had first seen it, ten years earlier, on the bank of the river that ran along the edge of their land, she had uttered a little cry of surprise.

"God, it's an iceberg!...It's shaped just like an iceberg!"

Achille, who had never seen a real iceberg, could not picture it. The main trunk had broken off and time had worn the wood down.

---

[1] *Pronounced "Adila"*

Adela had often talked to him about these floating mountains of ice. Moreover, she had an old calendar from 1970 including a magnificent colour photo of an iceberg, which she had shown him several times. Several days after the stump incident, he had taken the famous calendar out of the memento drawer. The ice monster appeared on the July page.

"A glacier for July 1. Kind of strange, don't you think?" he had said.

"*Silly!*" she always said when something foolish came out of his mouth. Icebergs came down from the north and arrived at Newfoundland during the summer months, or the *été mois* as Adela said.

Though she expressed herself correctly in French, Adela still reversed the order of certain words, a habit she had retained from her mother tongue. No one held it against her, especially not Achille. It added a touch of charm, and sometimes humour to what she said.

"The *été mois*, eh?" he had repeated with a twinkle in his eye, still amused after sixty years of living together by this way of speaking that was hers and hers alone.

Often he took one of her most endearing expressions and used it himself. After awhile, he would forget that he had only begun using it to tease her, and it became part of his own vocabulary. People who did not know them had trouble following when the two were talking. Their finest expressions, the ones they most liked hearing each other say, combined to form a new language, a sort of dialect composed of pure Quebecois combined with Elizabethan English, the kind which had been spoken in old England and was still used in certain remote islands around Newfoundland.

Adela had told him a thousand times how the huge masses of ice came down from the north, sometimes running aground so close to shore that she could almost have swum out to them, had the water not been so cold, and had she known how to swim. Each iceberg was unique in volume and shape as well as colour.

"You know, they're not white. They're all sorts of colours. Mostly pale green. They're magic, like crystal," she said.

Achille had gone all the way back down the stream and compared the old stump with the iceberg picture from the calendar. He had to concentrate but finally saw the image that had so struck Adela. When you looked at the stump, blocking out everything around it, cutting it off at ground level and preserving part of the roots, it really did resemble an iceberg. And in the wood, bleached by time, tones of green permeated the grain, created by the lichen and moss that had once grown at the top of the tree.

Armed with his crosscut saw[2] and his bow saw, he had carefully cut the stump and brought it back to the house. He hid it in his workshop. Then, over the winter, he had begun to whittle down the trunk, sometimes referring to the calendar photo for inspiration or listening more attentively to one of Adela's long descriptions at those times when nostalgia got her talking about her native land. First he had removed the bark, then he had begun scraping the roots with a knife, sculpting and changing the shape of the stump to make it slightly larger at the base, like an iceberg. He spent entire evenings sanding it with fine sandpaper. Then he decided to cut off the top of the miniature glacier and hollow out the centre to make a little chest out of it. That took him five years. And even after five years, his creation still seemed to him imperfect. The last year, all he had done was apply the varnish. How many layers? A good twenty of them. Between each layer Achille lovingly re-sanded the object, and by the end, one could have sworn it was made of glass…or ice. When Adela opened the gift, which Achille had wrapped in old newspaper and placed under the Christmas tree, she had burst into tears.

"The stump! *This is it. You're incredible!*" she cried. "You made it into an iceberg!"

Nothing had ever been more precious to her. It sat in the place of honour on the chest-of-drawers in the bedroom, in the middle of a little mat that Adela had braided from tag ends of green and blue fabric. The mat was like a little bit of sea on which the little treasure chest might be sailing.

He had wanted Adela to use it for the small and precious items she kept all over the house. She might have used it for jewellery, but she had none and had never wanted any. Achille was thinking more of all the little objects that awakened fond memories in Adela, which she insisted on piling in the bedroom chest-of-drawers or the kitchen buffet. Sometimes she chose a drawer and completely emptied it, religiously replacing her treasures one by one, saying she had cleaned the drawer up. In truth, she had never thrown anything out, and her dusting served no purpose. This ceremonial cleaning would usually

---

[2]. *A large manual saw of up to two metres long, formerly used to cut down trees.*

take place during the long evenings of winter, and was more than anything directed at awakening the images associated with each object.

Adela had refused to use the gift to keep her treasures in. One evening, deep in thought, while admiring Achille's work of art, she suddenly said: "When I die, I want you to burn me and put my ashes inside!"

Achille almost fell out of his chair. He had so wanted to give Adela a present that would make her happy, and here he had created an object that she associated with death! Moreover, it was the first time she had mentioned such a prospect.

It wasn't that she felt her end was near, but the little box shaped like an iceberg was so real, such a perfect replica of the mountains of ice ever-present in her memory that she had all at once decided to be cremated and have her ashes placed inside.

It upset Achille that his gift had provoked such a morbid thought. The idea of Adela's death had never crossed his mind, or he had pushed it far from his thoughts, for it was unbearable. Adela's eyes filled. As ever, words were useless between them. One's emotions flowed straight into the other's veins. Achille's eyes were red. Adela put her hand over his mouth to prevent him from talking, though he had no intention of doing so. He never spoke needlessly. But the purpose of Adela's gesture had not really been to silence him, but to ask him to listen to her. She was about to say something. It was a serious, solemn moment.

"I want you to listen to me. When I die, I want you to put my ashes in this box. And I want you to send my ashes down the river. I'll let God take my ashes home."

Adela wanted her ashes to be carried off by the Joseph River towards the Gatineau River, which flowed into the Ottawa River. The strong current of the Ottawa would transport her to the Saint Lawrence, and from there, she would return to the sea. She knew that there were hydroelectric dams all along the Gatineau River and they would probably hinder the box's progress, but she told herself that her ashes would spill into the water and be borne that way to the island of her birth.

In the winter as they sat by the fire together, in perfect communion, she told him about her rocky isle. There would be a sparkle in her eyes; maybe it was tears. She had always told him she would take him to see Newfoundland one day.

"It's the sea. When the Rock[3] is covered in fog, you can smell the sea, and that's what I miss so much."

They dreamed of going, and saved every penny, but something had always happened to make them postpone the trip. First it was Paul's schooling, which for ten years they had summoned every effort to pay for. And then in the boy's last year, Achille had borrowed three thousand dollars so he could finish business school. Their son wanted to be rich. Adela and Achille did not understand this infatuation with material goods; but it was his life. Another ten years went by before Paul returned. This time, he was in a tight spot. He had gotten involved in some shady business deal, the details of which Achille and Adela would never learn. He arrived miserable and repentant like the Prodigal Son in the Bible. He wept. He needed ten thousand dollars immediately, he said, or he was in danger of ending up in the Saint Lawrence with cement overshoes. They gave him their entire savings.

Paul did not come back until several years later. He had just turned forty-three and again needed money, this time to finance a big deal that would make his dreams of wealth come true. He promised to pay them back "with interest." Mistrusting her selfish son, Adela would have refused, but Achille made her reconsider.

"You know, we've never had all that much need for money. If it can help him find happiness..."

And so she had relented. That was the last time Paul had spent the night at the house or even stopped by, though he had come all the way to the village for the winter carnival. He disappeared for another few years. He never paid the interest, or even the capital he had borrowed. He was there today, but the old floorboards of the front porch were burning beneath his feet.

"What am I doing here?" Paul asked himself. "She's dead. And what's left of her? Nothing much. An old house made of scantling, a few acres of hilly land that you couldn't get more than a few bucks for, that is, if you managed to sell it." There before his eyes was his mother's entire kingdom. "What misery," he thought.

He remembered this place because he had grown up here. Today he looked at it through the eyes of a stranger, suppressing all thoughts of what attached him to the place, as if it were something shameful. Sainte-Famille d'Aumond was a far cry from Montreal. He felt as if he

---

[3]. *"The Rock" is what Newfoundlanders call their island.*

had been born on another planet when he thought about this hole. For many years, the family did not even have electricity. When Achille and Adela had finally decided to get hooked up, they just took the minimum: a few lights, and then, much later, the refrigerator. That was all in the house that ran on electricity. The electricity bills were so abnormally low that one day, Hydro-Quebec had even sent out a team to make sure the customer had not tampered with his meter to steal their precious current. They had no telephone either, nothing to connect this out-of-the-way place to the rest of the world or disturb its tranquillity.

Achille and Adela had, in a sense, lived on the fringes of society. Of course they were familiar with television, they had even seen a few episodes of the series *Les Belles histoires des pays d'en haut*[4] at the home of one of their neighbours who had a television set. Achille sometimes used the telephone of his friend, the notary, and appreciated its convenience, but they refused to allow this appliance in their home. Nor did they have a car.

At school, Paul became aware that he and his family did not live quite the way others did. It was not so much the lack of electricity that bothered him, but what people said about them. They were considered poor and backward. He had always resented Achille and Adela for forcing this marginal existence upon him. For years, he had pretended and lied. When other boys boasted about their fathers' cars, Paul implied that they owned one too, but did not take it out much due to the poor quality of the roads. When one of his friends unmasked him, he flew into a rage. Over the years he had developed an aversion to this village, this place of shame.

"I have to get back to Montreal, my wife is waiting."

Achille reflected that neither he nor Adela had ever seen this wife. She was Paul's third wife, and he had never had any children.

"I have no time for children," he would say.

Did this woman even know that Paul had parents and that both had been alive until very recently? Achille was broken-hearted. He had often wanted to take his ungrateful son by the scruff of the neck and give him a piece of his mind, but he had never done so. He had loved him as his own child, the child he'd never had. He knew Paul was

---

[4.] *A popular television series from the 1950s-1960s about settlers in the Laurentian region of Quebec.*

ashamed of this milieu, which he considered unworthy of his precious colleagues in Montreal. Born of a woman from Newfoundland and an unknown father, the boy had suffered his schoolmates' name-calling too often to want to talk about his origins. The taunt of "Newfie" irritated him more than all the others.

"Call me if you need to. Here's my new phone number," said Paul, handing him his business card.

All there was on the card was a phone number. No address. Though he had reached retirement age, Paul continued to uselessly and clumsily pursue his dreams of wealth. For several years, he had tried his hand at re-selling merchandise from bankrupt businesses to small itinerant vendors who worked the flea markets around Montreal. This last enterprise had turned into a disaster when the police had seized the lot of designer clothes he had bought from a shady individual.

*Call me if you need to!* That meant: *Don't call for no reason!* Achille took the piece of cardboard and slipped it in his pocket. He had no intention of putting it in a safe place. There was no point. Paul would probably change numbers again in a little while, and there would be no answer at this number but the recorded voice of an unknown operator saying that it was no longer in service.

Paul could take no more. His shiny rental car was waiting for him in the muddy drive that led to the property. There were two kilometres of narrow winding road, gravel-covered and dusty, before he got to paved road. And to call it paved was a bit of an exaggeration. It was more like a strip of tar studded with crude gravel, a dozen kilometres long, leading to highway 117.

"I'll have to get the car washed inside and out when I get to Montreal," he told himself as he walked down the porch stairs. "Otherwise the guys are going to ask me what kind of hole I've been driving around in."

In his mind, he was already gone.

"Your mother and I really loved you, you know. She would have liked to go back to where she was born. She always wanted to go back. I would like you to help me take her ashes back there."

"God damn it!" exploded Paul, who thought all the formalities were done with. "What are you talking about, she's fine where she is!"

"I promised to take her back," insisted Achille.

"Listen up, Pops…"

Achille hated this way of talking, especially to an older person.

There was something condescending about it, and it annoyed him. He was not a child.

"You're making no sense. You're telling me you're going to take that to Newfoundland?"

"*That* is your mother, for the love of God," Achille said to himself.

"But the only way of getting to Newfoundland is to fly or go by car and take a ferry. You don't have a car," said Paul reproachfully. "And to take an airplane, you at least need a credit card, and you don't have that either."

"But *you* have those things. You could make the arrangements," Achille implored.

"Right now, I don't have time, and besides, I need my credit card for work. A return ticket to Newfoundland has got to be six or seven hundred dollars! And I'm not even sure it's legal to throw ashes just anywhere. I don't want to get in trouble over this kind of nonsense. She's fine where she is. Why not bury her over in the corner there, near the garden?"

How could it possibly be illegal to carry his companion's ashes to Newfoundland if it wasn't illegal to bury them in a corner of the yard? There was something in this logic that escaped him. As for Paul's attitude, it left no room for doubt. In spite of all that Achille and Adela had done to help him, he was not going to make the slightest effort to carry out this final request. Money had become his master. It gave him comfort and social status, helped him rise above his origins.

"Forget it, Pops. Anyway, she's gone now. She won't know the difference," said Paul.

"I'll know."

"Besides, you've got to think about what you're going to do now. You should sell this house and go live in the village. They've got housing there for old people."

Paul's sudden concern for his welfare surprised him. He was already halfway to his car. It was over. Achille might never see him again. Even when he died, Paul would probably not come back. Adela was his mother; he had a sense of obligation towards her. Achille had been his adoptive father; he had taken on all the responsibilities without ever claiming the legal title of father. Between Adela and himself, this kind of thing was unnecessary. Adela knew that Achille would always act as a husband to her and as a father to her son. He would never have reneged on his obligations, though legally he had none. Even with a legal document obliging him to do so, Paul would never consider him a father.

All the love he had ever known, everything that had given his life meaning and brought sweetness to his existence was in the box he was holding. Tears ran down his face. What did he have left? Nothing. Even the house and this piece of earth had no more meaning to him, now that she wasn't there any more. He already missed her delicious half-English half-French expressions.

Having left Achille in a sea of sadness, Paul was on the road again. He wanted to flee. To remain there would have been dangerous, for in the house there were also happy and tender memories that could have returned to topple all his certainties. He was overwhelmed by a peculiar sensation. He would have liked to drive faster to get away from the shiver going down his spine, that indefinable sensation. How he had hated his youth and the marginal existence he had found so hard to bear. Yet he remembered sweet moments of early childhood, when others' opinions had no importance and he could feel the warmth of all the love that surrounded him. The trees growing along the road reminded him of this time. He stepped on the accelerator to flee from this sensitive zone more quickly, return to normality and forget, once and for all, his strange youth and his equally strange family. He had arrived at Highway 117 and turned south, towards Montreal. The landscape had changed, and Paul was back in his own world. Finally he could forget the past.

Achille was alone. Alone, at last. At least in the sense of having no one around him. He was not the type to seek out crowds, but Adela's absence weighed heavily upon him. It was as if someone had suddenly muted all the noise of his life. Gone was Adela's sometimes-naive wonder before the small and simple things that made life brighter.

He returned to the house and put the iceberg replica containing Adela's ashes on the table facing the window. That way, she could admire the flowering meadows that she had loved so much, that is, if she could see. Spring had only just begun and the first flowers were poking through the earth in a flurry of colour. Achille swept his eyes over the countryside the urn was faced towards.

"If Adela can see anything, it's through my eyes, I guess," he said to himself.

He went upstairs and entered the bedroom they had shared. The window faced east to capture the rays of early morning sun. The flowered curtains perfectly matched the design of the china water jug. The old chest-of-drawers, which dated from the beginning of the past century, had an oval bevelled glass mirror. It was made of oak and stained an oxblood colour according to the purest cabinet making tradition of the times. This piece of furniture, which both of them had loved, contained only clothing and objects they valued. The rest was carefully stored in the closet near the bedroom door. Adela had cut out photos of well-known Newfoundland scenes, framed them and hung them on the walls. Achille had hung an old painting there too, the only one of his parents' possessions he had obtained after their deaths. No one else had wanted it. He remembered the painting hanging in his mother's room. She was very fond of it, and sometimes he tried looking at it through her eyes to see what she had liked so much about it. The anonymous painter had portrayed a typical Quebec winter scene, with a snow-covered house in the foreground. She had probably been comforted by the warmth that seemed to radiate from this haven in the heart of a cold landscape.

He turned his eyes from the painting to gaze around the room. The walls were made of fine wooden slats, the upper part varnished and the bottom painted bright red. The white-painted iron bedstead, which Adela had always kept in impeccable condition, stood in the middle of the bedroom. It too must have been very old and the metal smith who had made it seemed to have given it special attention. He had added metal rosettes at the joints of the bedposts, making it look like the beds of French aristocrats one saw in pictures. To show it off to its best advantage, Adela had positioned the bed at an angle she had studied long and carefully. In this room, they had spent their sweetest moments. Never had Achille forced Adela to unite with him, and never had she felt forced. Things had happened in their own good time, the way a flower waits for the right moment of summer to open its petals.

Her smell still hovered in the room. No doubt to preserve her light fragrance, Achille had refused to wash the bed sheets. He gently brought her pillow to his face, breathing in the sweetness still trapped in its folds. Up until the last moment, she took care of her appearance, dabbing on the sweet-smelling *eau de cologne* that she made herself from flowers she picked near the house.

A few rare photos were preciously stored in the chest-of-drawers. Among them was a print taken by an itinerant photographer in which Adela was holding Paul, still a baby, in her arms while Achille looked down at them lovingly. It was a black-and-white print, but he clearly remembered that the dress was red. The scene had been captured in front of the house and one could still see the freshly sawed planks of the stoop he had built only few weeks before.

In another photo, Achille and Adela had been immortalised in front of the 1945 Ford recently acquired by Oscar Crytes, the owner of the general store. Oscar was so proud of it that he had gone through kilometres of film, taking photos of all the villagers posing in front of the object of his pride. "Brand new!" he told everyone. Achille could not have said what the car's make was, but he did know that it was "brand new."

And then there was the colour photo taken more recently by Nicole, the village postmistress, who sometimes came by with her son to picnic on Sundays. The photo showed Adela and Achille with Nicole Lyrette's son, Antoine, a very nice little boy whom they adored. By now, he had to be almost twenty-five. He had come to see Achille as soon as he had learned of Adela's death. Antoine had said nothing, but simply sat down beside Achille. He put his hand on his shoulder and they had remained that way without moving, and in silence, for a good twenty minutes. Achille had felt more compassion in this gesture than in all the words of condolence people had offered him.

He mused at how things took on a whole other dimension after a loved one died. Little everyday things that had never had much importance before would trigger so many memories. Like the little hole in the doorframe where a hook had once been. It had only been there a single day. He smiled thinking of it.

Achille walked around each room, running his fingertips over everything that had belonged to Adela or she had even just touched. There were still a few strands of her hair caught in her brush. Achille brought it up to his nose. Her smell was still there, though less than it had been a few days before. It would probably take months, but little by little, her perfume would fade the way water slowly disappears into the sand on the shore after the waves have receded.

He went out of the house and walked around the garden. Every nook and cranny, every plant contained traces of things they had done together. The vegetable garden had been Adela's domain. She was the boss and Achille was her slave, as he often told her. He had sweated and laboured to transport manure and turn the earth each spring. The result was well worth the effort. Adela's hands worked magic, and the vegetables were always plentiful and magnificent.

On the wall of the shed where he stored firewood and gardening tools, the old canoe he had made thirty years before sat up on supports nailed to the wall. He reflected on the way in which this kind of boat had marked his life. The present specimen was the last in a series of canoes he had owned. He'd begun making them in his teens, when old Raphaël Smith, an Algonquian Indian, heir to a thousand-year-old tradition, had taught him everything from the secrets of making birchbark canoes to how to handle them in white water. Later, canoes made of bark had been replaced by ones made of aluminium or fibreglass, far more resistant and requiring less maintenance. Achille considered old Raphaël's boats masterpieces, at once light, robust and easy to handle. Nothing about the new canoes could compete with the Algonquians' thousand-year-old art. Adela loved these escapades on the Joseph River, to which they treated themselves every Sunday in the warmer seasons.

How he would have liked to take Adela back to her island and her native village of Tilting! To see the places she had talked so much about, at last. He could describe them without ever having seen them. He often had to remind himself that he had never been to these places; he had heard Adela describe them so often that he had ended up making her images his own.

According to what Adela had told him, the entire village was built around the port. The Lane house was the richest in Tilting and stood in the middle of the town square. This had been the home of John, who had broken Adela's heart and left her with child. Not far was Dwyer's Premises, located in the heart of Tilting. Achille understood that Dwyer was a man's name, but he had never been able to translate the word "premises." However, he could picture the building as if it were there in front of him. A long barracks made of planks, it housed the general store and the salt fish warehouse. A wharf gave the fishermen direct access to the store when they returned from their fishing expeditions. A trail near the Lane house led to Turpin's Trail. God only knows who this Turpin was, but each time Adela referred to the trail Achille could not help but smile at the French name. Turpin's Trail ran along the coastline, by the waves, and continued up the cliff. From there, one had a spectacular view of the Atlantic Ocean, the mother of all oceans, according to Adela. From April to July, and sometimes even later in the season, in clear weather one could see the icebergs coming down from the north, or the whales performing their ballet near the port. Sometimes one of them got caught by the whalers. Sandy Cove Beach, a little farther down the trail, was one of the rare sand beaches on the island. Adela had walked there, barefoot in the sand, crying out each time a wave washed up and submerged her feet in icy water. Achille pictured these scenes as if he had been there.

Deep in thought, he walked along the water's edge. The Joseph was an old river. Sinuous and lazy, it had jumped its bed in several places, leaving in its wake a terrain that was rich and fertile but easily flooded when the water level rose in the spring. This river had always been very important to them. Often Achille would go there to fish for their evening meal. The river provided water for their household needs and the garden. For Adela, more than anything, it evoked the sea.

"I know it's not the sea, but it's water!" she would say.

He liked to go down the river with her, often letting the canoe slip along in silence, borne by the current. Adela was not a very good paddler, but she liked being on the water, and admired Achille's mastery of the fragile vessel. He frightened her by crossing small rapids, which were not dangerous but made her scream with terror. He roared with laughter. In spite of her fear, she had never failed to follow his instructions, paddling when he shouted at her to do so, and stopping as soon as he gave the order. She did not have a man's paddle stroke but was more dependable than some. She liked to play the great lady, letting her Prince Charming paddle alone while she lounged in the bottom of the canoe, leaning back against the seat and watching him steer the boat with great skill.

"All I need is a parasol to look like *a real lady!*" she would say, bursting with laughter.

Since the incident with the parish priest, they had kept away from churches and devoted their Sundays to these outings on the water. Several times they had gone to the little Anglican church in Maniwaki, but it was a long way by car and they had to beg a ride from someone who was going there. The reception they were given at the Anglican church was nothing as unpleasant as the one they had received from the priest at the little Catholic church when they first arrived in Aumond. But even at the Anglican church, people took a dim view of this cohabitation between a Catholic and an Anglican. The idea would have been acceptable if one of them had converted to the other's religion. The Anglican priest had taken Adela aside after the service to tell her it was not customary for a Catholic to come pray there.

"Especially because you're not married," the Anglican priest had said.

Achille had nonetheless insisted that they go from time to time.

"*No way!* I don't think God is in that place. If you were able to stand up to your '*couré*'[5] for me, I don't know why I would change my ways to obey him."

Achille loved it when she pronounced "u" as "ou." It gave him an opportunity to tease her. He thought of the beach where they used to picnic during their Sunday excursions. It took a good hour of vigorous paddling to get there. There, a bend in the river formed a wide bar of fine sand. The branches of huge trees dangled over the water. One could have sworn it was a beach on one of those beautiful southern islands one saw in magazines. It was their secret place, their little corner of paradise: a place of perfect communion between themselves, the world around them and the celestial spirit they sometimes called God or *Dieu*. They very rarely met anyone, and on the hottest days of summer, Achille like to swim naked. Adela had always pretended to be outraged, claiming that someone could arrive at any minute. In truth, it excited her to see her man emerge from the water stark naked, but she refused to admit it. She often returned home with sand not only between her toes but also down her back and inside all her clothes. Achille took obvious pleasure at this kind of frolic, inciting Adela to dive naked into the cold water to get rid of the sand and the traces of their ardour. What an incredible sensation! She understood why Achille loved these swims. The water slid all over her body like a caress, giving her a feeling of total freedom and original purity. On the hottest days of summer, she often swam in the river in front of the house, but always wore a voluminous bathing suit she had made herself, which covered her body from shoulders to mid-thigh. This could not compare with the incredible sensation of swimming in the nude. What sweet memories! Moments that were tender but intense.

"If I could, my Adela, I would take you down the rivers like a great lady again. I would take you to Fogo Island," he thought.

"If I were ten years younger, I would do it," he said. "But if I were ten years younger, Adela would still be here. If I were ten years younger, I wouldn't even be thinking about this. And if I were ten years older and still alive, I'd probably tell myself I should have done it ten years ago."

It was all becoming clear in his mind.

---

[5]. Mispronunciation of '*curé*,' meaning parish priest.

# Two

The wind was blowing hard. It was still very cold, though the spring sunshine had warmed the water enough to break the ice on the Saint Lawrence. To navigate on the waters of the Saint Lawrence was no easy matter, but Captain Bartlett was experienced. This old seadog, a cod fisherman on the banks of Newfoundland, had seen it all before. He had been sailing his schooner around the island for many years. He had often seen the great sea winds form waves of several metres high which broke with violence against the island's rocky shore.

Bartlett did not like the French. It was in his genes. They were arrogant and always looking to take the best land for themselves. The first fishermen to settle in Newfoundland from England and Ireland had been attacked by the French, by the Indians too, and sometimes both at once. Until 1904, the French had possessed the right to fish and establish their facilities on the northern coast of Newfoundland. The agreement between England and France had come to an end fourteen years earlier and most of the French had left. Some, fortunately not many, had stayed.

In Quebec City, there was nothing but French. Now they called themselves "French Canadians," but to the captain it was all the same. Bartlett felt the country should have continued to belong to the British Crown.

But nowadays, business was business. He got a far better price for his dried cod in the port of Quebec City than what the British merchants gave him in St. John's. Naturally, he did not really have the right to do this, to sell the catch to the highest bidder. It was formally prohibited by the contract that bound him to the rich tradesmen of Newfoundland, and he knew that the sanctions could be terrible. Everything belonged to them, even the fishermen. But one small cargo, loaded on the sly, brought him very big returns. This little voyage also allowed him to stock up on food supplies which he could re-sell to fishermen along the coast at a far better price than what they were forced to pay in Newfoundland to the companies who gave them such a miserable sum for their catch. He looked forward to a tidy profit that would keep him out of reach of those sharks.

The only problem with this particular voyage was the girl who had sneaked onto the boat. She had stowed away in the hold when they had stopped at Fogo Island. He could not get any clear explanation from her as to what she was doing on his boat. He did not know what she was running away from, and clearly she was running away from something. No girl of barely sixteen sneaks onto a boat for no reason. In any case, he did not give a damn what had brought her. The fact was that she had no business on his ship, no matter what she had done. If she had done something reprehensible, all the more reason to get rid of her quickly. He did not want to have anything to do with a criminal.

He had thought of leaving her in one of those little hamlets of French Canadians on the shores of the Saint Lawrence, near Quebec City, but that would have caused a big delay. As it was, he was going to have to invent some new lie to justify a delay of several days to his bosses. He was going to Quebec City; at Quebec City, she would be put off the boat.

Adela Cole was terrified. The past few days had been one drama after another. Her life had been turned upside down. She was on her way to a place that several days before she had not even known existed. She had been forced to leave her native village of Tilting. She had no choice. She had planned to get on a boat that would take her to St. John's, where her friend Norma Brown was going to put her up. Norma had left Tilting several years before, stifled by the narrow-mindedness and rigidity of the little community, which clung to its rock and its immutable traditions. Norma was different. She was flamboyant. Anyway, that was how she seemed to the people of Fogo. Strangely, Norma had never married and no one remembered ever having seen her with a boy; at least not in the usual sense of boy-girl relationships. Norma had prepared her getaway and fled one day by hiding in one of the boats that sailed from village to village around the island of Newfoundland. They all ended up or started out at St. John's, the centre of the former British colony, now an independent dominion. In St. John's, Norma had found refuge in a hospital. She had offered her help as a volunteer to Catholic nuns who cared for the ill. Over time, she had become a nurse. What a feat!

Adela had written her to say that she feared she was pregnant. Norma had asked no questions. When the boat returned several days later, there was a letter for Adela. A few words on a piece of paper, slipped into an envelope. "Come stay with me for the time it takes. I'll be there for you. Norma." Adela had wanted to do as Norma had done, slip onto the boat and get off at St. John's.

Captain Bartlett usually stopped in the ports around Fogo Island. The fishing companies had put him in charge of stocking their food counters in each of the hamlets. These provisions were sold to the fishermen at the price of gold, though the expression was perhaps inappropriate, for there was never any money exchanged, let alone gold. The tradsmen gave the fishermen credit in the spring and deducted the sums they owed from the fish they caught. Generally, their catch did not quite cover the cost of their springtime purchases, so the fishermen went deeper and deeper into debt. Bartlett went around to all the ports again at the season's end to load his cargo of fish.

The captain was a weak link in the company chain. He had his own boat and the English merchants paid him a certain sum for the cargoes he transported. They demanded absolute fidelity from their captains. It was forbidden to transport anything whatsoever besides the goods the company entrusted to their care; it was forbidden to transport or sell merchandise for their own personal gain. Most of the captains were so deeply in debt to the companies that they owned nothing at all. If they made the slightest error, the company would seize the boat and put another captain in charge. Bartlett's boat, however, was not saddled with any debt, and he always managed to pay for what he bought or to reimburse what the company had advanced him. That made him suspect in the eyes of the rich traders.

Bartlett had made a stop at Tilting, a little community in the north of Fogo Island, as he did each time the company asked him to deliver provisions for the fishermen. Generally, he had to bring his cargo of cod back to St. John's, but not this time. As a matter of fact, the captain had set up a lucrative little circuit. Certain fishermen would hide a small portion of their weekly catch. Once per season, Bartlett would sail through and collect the fish they had managed to put aside. With these twenty-odd fishermen accomplices on his circuit, he managed to accumulate a cargo that he would sell in Quebec City. The last stop on his route was Tilting. However, he had to wait until nightfall to load the fish, for it was important that no one find out about it. Though all the fishermen were at the mercy of the companies and up to their ears in debt, there were some who would not have hesitated to denounce those who cheated. That is how jealousy works. And people paid for that kind of information. That is why Bartlett and his associates had to be extremely careful. It had taken him years to build up this network of people he could count on. He had established solid friendships with each person. Certain fisherman had caught wind of the affair and wanted to join the group. But Bartlett pretended not to know what they were talking about, and refused to take on anyone whom he had not approached himself.

For the cargo to be loaded, the boat had to remain in port overnight. The operation took place in total darkness and complete silence. Then, in the wee hours, the boat would haul anchor. An early-rising villager might have noticed that the boat, as it left port, sat more deeply in the water than it had the day before.

Adela had resolved to sneak into the hold of Bartlett's boat, which was supposed to be heading to St. John's. At nightfall, she put her plan into action. The next day, when the vessel had headed out to sea, she planned to emerge from her hiding place. In her pocket she had a few coins to give the captain to pay for her passage.

She groped her way down to the hold. It reeked of fish. Packets of cod were heaped up in one corner. She hid behind them, sheltering herself as best she could with the blanket she had brought. Her suitcase, which was more a kind of bundle, contained only a very few of her belongings.

Adela wept to find herself alone in the dark. She was terrified by the long ordeal that lay ahead. What was her life going to be like? Who would ever want her again? Would she ever be able to return home? Finally she sank into a half-sleep, hiccupping quietly.

She was awakened by footsteps up on deck. It was so dark in the hold that she could not see her hand in front of her face. She saw a star when someone opened the hatch leading down to the hold. Crouched over, Adela crept along the bottom of the ship towards the heaps of dried cod on the other side.

The men were talking so quietly that she could only hear murmurs. First she could just see their feet. They had wrapped rags around their boots, which explained why their footsteps had seemed so faraway and muffled. Who were they? Adela was frightened. If they caught her now, they would throw her onto the dock and she would be a laughing stock. Everyone would know.

The men were loading something into the hold. She slipped between the bundles of cod to avoid being seen, but she saw what they were loading in such great secrecy. It was just more cod! Why? Adela did not understand this little scheme, but she was so afraid of being discovered that she held her breath so the mist coming out of her mouth would not give her away. After a few minutes of this, she almost lost consciousness. Her mind grew dim. Images and sounds came to her through a kind of fog. She closed her eyes.

Emerging from sleep, she heard the boat creaking. They were out to sea. She had not been discovered. She did not know whether she should be happy or not. As she had lost track of time, she resolved to wait a few hours before making her presence known. She recognised the sounds of the sailors going about their business up on deck. They must have removed the rags from their boots, for she could hear their heels pounding against the wood. They were no longer murmuring as they had the night before. She heard Bartlett yelling orders. The captain wanted to advance more quickly. That is what he was saying, and everyone was running. She did not know how many sailors there were, but she distinguished the voices of at least two. The sun entered the hold through crevices in the wood. Now she could see the heaps of cod around her. The odour of salt made her thirsty. She had not foreseen this. She was also hungry. She had thought she would be able to wait it out, but her stomach was topsy-turvy. Was it the sea or her condition that was making her ill? Or maybe it was the odour of fish? She told herself that she had to hold back, to wait.

After several hours, she made a calculation. If she had wakened in the morning, it had to be afternoon by now. The boat was creaking everywhere and had been leaning to one side all day. That was a sign that winds were strong and steady. It was also a sign that Captain Bartlett was pushing his ship to the limit. Now she was afraid of how he would react when he became aware of her presence. She realised that she had seen things that she should not have seen the night before. She had not understood Bartlett's ingenious plot, but the fact that the loading had taken place at night, in secrecy, suggested that something underhanded was going on. She decided to wait for them to discover her. That would no doubt happen shortly, for the captain would soon have to look for a port to dock in for the night. Tomorrow they would arrive in St. John's.

She ended up falling asleep again and did not wake up until the hold was in total darkness. The ship was still moving. At night. So the captain had not given the order to drop anchor in a port but instead kept sailing. It was risky for small vessels to travel in the darkness for they sailed very close to shore. It was only in open sea that one could risk travelling in total darkness.

No one came down to the hold. Then, in the early morning, one of the sailors announced that he was going to sleep for a few hours. The hatch opened and the light hit Adela's face. She grimaced with pain. The early morning sun burnt her eyes, which were already irritated by the salt in the air. Catching sight of her, the man was stunned. He stood there staring with his mouth hanging open, finally managing to stammer: "Captain…Captain…"

Bartlett had seen his sailor's expression of surprise and blocked the helm so he could leave his post and go over to the hatch. From where he was standing, he could not see what had taken the man so much by surprise. Maybe a leak? But his boat was still seaworthy in spite of its age. When he leaned forward to take a better look, it was not a young woman he saw but only the trouble she would cause.

"What in God's name is she doing there?"

He understood none of her explanations, which were punctuated with weeping and moans of despair. Adela held out a handful of small coins that were far from enough to influence the decision he would have to make. The boat had passed St. Anthony and turned before reaching Red Bay, in Labrador. In a few hours, it would reach Blanc-Sablon. He could have put her ashore at St. Barbe on the Newfoundland coast, but obviously someone would question the young girl, and it was clear she could not help but talk about what she had seen. She was a witness, and that could cause problems. There was no question of taking her back to St. John's on their return from Quebec City. She was likely to denounce them.

Ern, one of his sailors, suggested throwing her overboard. Bartlett exploded and grabbed the man by the shirt, holding him precariously over the water.

"Others will go into the water before she does. I run counterband, I'm not a pirate," said Bartlett. Though in fact, one of his distant ancestors had been a pirate who took refuge in Newfoundland.

Ern was right. The girl knew too much. Bartlett resolved to put her quietly ashore at Quebec City. Adela was frightened. She did not know what was happening to her, or where they were. Around them there was nothing but sea. How was it that they had not reached St. John's yet? She had been there once for the wedding of her Uncle Ted, her mother's brother. Uncle Ted was the family's pride and joy. The son of a fisherman, he had gotten an education and become a Protestant minister. Then he had married. Everyone wanted to be at the wedding. It was the only big family gathering she had ever attended. As well as the event itself, which was exceptional, the city had dazzled her. There was activity wherever one looked. The streets themselves seemed magical: horses trotting up and down, women clad in magnificent dresses who seemed to have nothing better to do than roam about with no specific purpose. Never had she seen ladies done up with such elegance, except in old catalogues. None, it seemed, had to clean fish or spread salt on cod fillets. Nor did any of them seem to have to do laundry. She remembered this trip and so knew very well that the boat was sailing away from the more densely populated shores of St. John's, not towards them.

Captain Bartlett came towards her. His powerful voice, angry and menacing, drowned out even the noise of the waves that broke powerfully against the hull of the ship.

"Listen to me, young lady. What you have done is board this ship as a stowaway. That is an act of piracy," said Bartlett, putting the emphasis on the last word.

All inhabitants of Fogo knew what "pirate" meant. The old stories people told around the fireplace were full of poor fishermen robbed and killed by these looters of the sea. To be involved in an act of piracy was to be involved in something very serious. She hiccupped even harder. Bartlett knew she was at his mercy and that what he was about to tell her would frighten her even more.

"At sea, acts of piracy are punished by death. The laws of the sea authorise me to cast you overboard."

Adela panicked. She saw herself in icy water up to the neck, struggling with her heavy skirts. She told herself that she would have to take them off, but then realised how useless this would be when the water was so cold. Death would come in a few minutes, especially because, like most fishermen, she did not know how to swim.

Again she held out the coins to Bartlett. He pretended to reflect, and hesitate between two options, then grabbed the meagre fortune and pocketed it.

"All right, I'll let you off the hook, but you'll have to leave the boat at Quebec City."

Quebec City? She had not the slightest idea where the place was located. Her knowledge of the world was limited to Fogo Island, Newfoundland and, vaguely, England. Was it an island in the south? Desperately she searched for a way to seize control of her life again. She had to get back to St. John's as she had planned to do several days earlier. Norma would be waiting for her, she would stay as long as she had to, then return home to Tilting. This scenario was already complicated enough, why make it more so? Norma would not be waiting for her. She had invited her to come, but Adela had not written back to confirm her arrival. She had preferred to arrive in person and bring her answer that way. Norma would conclude that she had preferred to stay in Fogo Island. And her parents, what would they think? Would they look for her? If so, where would they go looking? No one would think of asking Norma. No one would know that she had stowed away on this boat. And even if they managed to trace her back to Norma, how would Norma know that Adela had taken such a detour? No one would ever find her, of that she was certain.

Ill and weak from not enough food and too much weeping, Adela was on the verge of despair. Quebec City, that unknown place, struck terror in her heart. "The French," Bartlett had said to her. She had heard so many frightening stories about these damned French, their long-time enemies. Over three centuries, her people had been forced to defend their island against the Beothuk Indians, whom they had chased away in order to settle there, and who returned periodically to camp during the summer. Then they had to fight the Portuguese and the French, who wanted to seize their fishing territories. Turpin's Trail had been a favourite place for fishing camps in the summer. There the French had erected "tilts," a kind of communal temporary shelter made of thin branches that they patched together each year. Other than a few permanent establishments, this kind of shelter had long been the only trace of civilisation to be found in Newfoundland. Her own village had started out as a cluster of "tilts" to which the fishermen had not seen fit to give a proper name. Adela had the sombre presentiment that she would never again see the houses of Tilting.

When she saw the long wall of the fortress of Quebec City, for the first time she forgot her sorrow. This block of huge houses, or as much as she could see of them from the port, surrounded by the daunting wall that served to protect them, suddenly made her aware that she knew nothing at all about the world beyond Fogo.

Captain Bartlett ordered her to come up out of the hold, so they could figure out some way of helping her. "Helping her" primarily meant getting rid of her quietly, without anyone asking questions. *The Irish Wind* was moored just across from Bartlett's vessel. This boat was made to sail on the Saint Lawrence. Bartlett greeted its captain heartily and went over to talk to him. Several minutes later, he was back, visibly pleased with his meeting.

"You're in luck, child. You won't be left stranded. The captain of

*The Irish Wind* is looking for a cook for one of the logging camps he supplies. I told him you could do the job."

"No, please! I want to go back to St. John's. I have to go back to St. John's!" Adela begged him, weeping.

"Stop that immediately! Consider yourself lucky that you're still alive! What I'm offering you is a chance to eat. If I leave you here on your own, you'll starve to death in the streets of the city."

He was right, and Adela knew it. In Fogo, you could spend all your time just finding and producing enough to feed and clothe yourself, survive. Here, it was surely worse. Like an animal to slaughter, Adela let herself be led from one boat to the other. Bartlett pulled her along by the sleeve. She would have liked to flee, but where to? This land was not her own. These people were not her people. Worse, she was afraid of them. Bartlett, her last link to Newfoundland, had just cut her loose. Several words were exchanged between the two captains, a few coins quickly changed hands. There was nothing more to say, the deal had been sealed. In spite of her distress, Adela knew very well that she had just been sold like a piece of merchandise, as the blacks whose pictures she had seen in books had been sold to cotton plantations in the United States.

Several hours later, *The Irish Wind* took to sea again, taking advantage of the rising tide to push farther into the mainland. For Adela this too had something frightening about it. All those trees and the narrowing of the river increased the feeling of suffocation that had come over her. She bitterly missed the powerful sea wind that ceaselessly swept over her island. She could hardly breathe.

The captain, a certain McDougall, was employed by companies who harvested the forests of the Northern Outaouais, always on the lookout for precious white pine. There were twenty or so passengers on board *The Irish Wind*, hungry Irish immigrants who had left their country to avoid dying of starvation, hoping to find salvation here. Like Adela, they had been shunted from boat to boat since their arrival.

Though she was happy to learn that they spoke English, she barely said a word to them. She was terrified. Who were they? What kind of shady character might be lurking within each one of them? None of them seemed any happier than she was about this journey. However, whereas they seemed resigned to their fate, Adela was still hoping for the impossible miracle that would take her home again.

# Three

At first Achille rejected the idea, but it kept coming back to haunt him. He wondered if it could be done.

"Maybe it's possible…to Hull, anyway. I've done that trip several times, but after…?" he asked himself.

No matter how hard he tried to steer his mind away from the project, telling himself it made no sense, his thoughts kept coming back to it.

"From the Joseph River, you get to Lake Joseph and then to the Gatineau River. There are the des Eaux rapids, but those are easy if you have a good canoe. After that is Maniwaki. So far so good," reflected Achille.

Three hundred and eighty-six kilometres long, the river was fed by all the bodies of water that flowed into it. Its wild course was suddenly blocked by the mountains, and that was where the real challenge of the Gatineau River began. For a distance of some fifteen kilometres between Maniwaki and Messines there was a series of rapids, each one as difficult as the one that preceded it. The first of them, the Tête-des-Six, was so named because it was the first in a series of six portages that enabled travellers to get beyond the rapids safely. The old man wondered if the portage trail he had used in his youth still existed. Next came the Lucifer, whose name alone inspired fear. Achille knew these rapids, having shot them in the past. There was no point in tempting fate a second time. At this point, the river divided in two. On the turbulent side, in quick and squalling succession, were the Corbeau and du Mur rapids, and the ones referred to as Haute-Tension. This torrent could be partially avoided if the traveller passed on the side of the Kitigan Zibi Indian Reserve, where the current was less vigorous. Achille could shoot these rapids, but would probably have to do a short portage to get around the old Corbeau hydroelectric plant, which had been closed for a long time.

Farther along, the Gatineau River grew calmer, as if it were worn out from fighting so hard. There were one or two rapids after the village of Bouchette, but nothing that could not be tackled by a veteran canoeist. From Gracefield to Low, held back by the Paugan Dam, the river overflowed into the zones below. The current grew weaker and easier to navigate. One could even leave the river and go inland by way of Lake Sainte-Marie. Starting from Low, the river was blocked by three dams that corresponded to as many portages: Paugan to Low, Chelsea, in the village of the same name, and Farmer, at Gatineau. After that was the great Unknown.

Achille took an old map of Quebec from the drawer. Once unfolded, it covered the entire kitchen table. With his finger, he followed the Gatineau River from north to south down to the Ottawa River, which stretched eastwards to Long Sault, where Dollard des Ormeaux was ambushed by the Iroquois in 1660. A navigation canal made it possible to avoid these rapids, which continued for several kilometres. Having overcome this obstacle, one entered the Saint Lawrence River, which grew wider and wider until it reached the Gulf. By staying close to the coastline, a canoeist could surely make his way to Blanc-Sablon. He wondered what it was like to travel on the Saint Lawrence. He had heard that at a certain point on the river, the current changed direction twice a day, moving inland when the tide rose and returning seaward when the tide went out.

Though it seemed to him that this part of the journey could be done, it appeared to be impossible to cross the arm of sea between Blanc-Sablon and St. Barbe, the first village of Newfoundland. On the map, Quebec and Newfoundland looked so close to each other that one would think a bridge could have been built between them. Achille knew that the two shores must be many kilometres apart, maybe twelve. A heck of a distance to cross on open sea and in such a fragile vessel. Achille felt doubtful. He asked himself whether it was possible to travel on the sea by canoe.

"What a stupid question!" he told himself. "The Indians used to go everywhere by canoe."

To cross the arm of sea between Blanc-Sablon and Newfoundland, and go all the way to L'Anse-aux-Meadows would be a perilous enterprise. Next, he would have to get to Fogo by following the coast, which in itself was no mean feat. He was not unaware that winds on the open sea could easily carry his little boat away.

All this prompted Achille to reject the idea once again, but it kept coming back and his mind continued to search for solutions to whatever problems might prevent him from making the expedition. At the age of twenty, he would have been thrilled by such an adventure, but now he was four times that age and he had not paddled for a very long time. It had been years since he had been able to spend an entire day kneeling on the cedar ribs that supported the boat's frame.

Achille put his canoe in the water and set out on a short expedition on the Joseph River to make contact with his old friend. It did not take him long to get the hang of it again. He noted that if he took frequent breaks, his knees could still withstand the effort without seizing up. He remembered how Adela used to attach foam cushions to her knees when she worked in the garden. Over the next few days, he tried them out and saw that they greatly diminished the pain, allowing him to prolong each canoeing session.

The hull was inspected, repaired and waterproofed. Achille remembered how his Algonquin friend, Raphaël Smith, had told him that the Micmacs added higher and more rounded ends to the canoe to jump the waves at sea. These ends, by rounding off the points of the canoe, reduced the quantity of water thrown into the boat by the waves. He made two crescent-shaped reinforcements out of cedar and firmly attached them to the gunwales at either end of the canoe. He applied the bark and started sewing it all together with spruce roots. Each seam had to be coated with a generous portion of pitch[6] to make it waterproof.

He would need two paddles, for one often broke when it was used to push the canoe away from rocks, especially in white water, where the shocks of wood against stone are violent. Did he still have his former reflexes, which had made him master of the rapids? Surely not. He had no illusions about it. When he was younger, he could switch hands on the paddle so quickly that anyone watching who even blinked during the operation would have missed it. Going down a river by canoe, as with log driving, required great anticipation skills and great swiftness. The paddle sometimes had to be passed from one side to the other to prevent the fragile hull from hitting a rock, and then switched back again to help the boat over an obstacle. Made of light wood, it was easily broken. The paddle Adela had used, at least sometimes, was far too short. He needed a new one to firmly attach inside the boat and use as a kind of spare tire. And then there was the matter of transporting his luggage and equipment on his back at certain places to avoid the more violent currents. He made a special

---

[6.] *Mixture of pine and spruce resin, melted and mixed with bear fat.*

harness that he could hoist on like a backpack and that would cover his shoulders with a thick and comfortable layer of padding. That way, he could withstand the rubbing of the portage yoke on his shoulders. When he gave it a trial run, he became exhausted after just a few minutes. He had grown old. He felt as if he had been beaten black and blue.

The most difficult operation, especially with a very full backpack, consisted of lifting the canoe off the ground and placing it on his shoulders. He could no longer lift it and heave it over his head in a single movement, as he had been able to do in the past. He resolved to do it in two movements. First, he leaned the boat's prow up against a tree, a rock or a mound of earth, and slipped underneath. It took him several minutes to find the right point of balance. To avoid useless effort, a portager had to make sure that the weight on his shoulders was slightly heavier towards the back. That way, the canoe was always higher in front, and he could see where he was going. Achille even found the correct portager's walk, which would help him conserve his strength. And he had less and less of that. He judged that he had to focus his physical training on preparing for this difficult part of canoeing. He would also come across banks that were so steep that even a man in the peak of youth would not have been able to scale them. With a light nylon rope, he managed to perfect an ingenious system of pulleys that multiplied his strength. All he had to do was attach the pulleys to a tree and tie the rope to the end of the boat. Achille was able to drag it almost effortlessly over even the steep slopes, though the operation was risky for the very fragile hull. He needed to bring a repair kit, which he decided to fasten to the bow deck.

Achille knew that he had to avoid taking useless luggage. The urn would take up over half the room in his bag. There was no question of transporting large quantities of food. One day's rations, maybe two. No more. He remembered the days when his mother, like the Algonquins, would smoke meat in order to preserve it. She made horrible black strips, tough and dubious-looking. In the midst of working, you just needed to chew on a piece to be revived, or at least think you'd been revived. It took up very little space. He decided to make some for the trip. He would have to find or buy what he needed on the way, in the villages he passed. The villages along the Gatineau were a day's walk from one another, as they had been originally built by lumber merchants to receive the convoys heading up to the forests in the north. It would be easy to get what he needed each day.

He realised he would also need a bit of money, which he did not have; but he had an idea.

A few pieces of clothing, a bar of soap and a washcloth, no towel, that would take up too much space (he would let the wind dry his skin), a razor, a blue plastic groundsheet that he could use as a tent, lighters, a penknife, a bit of fishing line and some spoons. He wondered whether he should bring the little hatchet that he always carried with him. Every extra gram would weigh heavily on his shoulders when he had to portage the canoe, but he admitted that the hatchet would be indispensable. He also had a sleeping bag, which would likely take up a lot of space. He decided instead to bring one of the quilts that Adela had made and wrap it around the urn to protect it. At night, he could use it as a blanket. Adela's quilts could keep you warm even in the small hours of the coldest days of February, long after the last embers in the wood stove had gone out.

"Adela won't mind if I undress her a little for the night," he told himself.

He also took the compass that he usually carried in his pocket when he went into the forest. Achille did not often use it on the water, where all you had to do was follow the path of the river. When canoeing down rivers, even the Saint Lawrence, as long as he stayed close to the shore he would not likely get lost. However, when he had to cross the arm of sea between Quebec and Newfoundland, he would definitely have to keep track of where he was going. On the sea, there would be nothing to guide him. Without ever having travelled on the sea, he remembered how difficult it had been to find his bearings on large bodies of water like the Baskatong Reservoir north of Grand-Remous, where he had often gone fishing. He secured the compass directly in front of him on the rear beam of the canoe so he could consult it at all times. He added a few more articles to his luggage, but was as sparing as he could be. The only excess item he allowed himself was a kettle and tea.

"I don't care if I die of starvation, as long as I have tea," he had the habit of saying after every meal.

In the logging camps, tea drinking was almost a religious act. As soon as work stopped for the short lunch break, they hurried to put water on to boil. In thirty-degree-below weather, the warm liquid was a kind of balm, and the only sweetness they were allowed. Even today, he appreciated tea more for its soothing qualities than for its taste.

He carefully wrapped the urn and put it at the bottom of his backpack; then he put the rest of his belongings on top of it. He had not used this bag for quite a long time. He and Adela had used it for their Sunday picnics, packing the big blanket and their food inside. He adjusted the straps, searching for the most comfortable position. Then he lifted the canoe and carried on with his training. He thought the bag would be heavy on his back, but if he straightened up his shoulders and spine, it served as a counterweight to the boat and made his task easier.

He also had to solve the question of money. He would need to pay certain expenses during his odyssey, and his meagre savings had all gone into paying for the funeral. He decided to consult his friend, the notary Norbert Lafleur. The man of law had always given him good advice and treated him as a friend. He had helped him on a number of occasions, and Achille trusted him.

The next day, Achille went to the village to see the notary. He had been retired for a long time but had kept his title and the right to practise, occasionally helping out friends with his advice. Achille was one of those friends. Norbert Lafleur was from the old school: for him, a person's word had greater value than any legal paper. Achille shared his way of seeing things. He liked what was fair and equitable.

He arrived without warning, but the notary was not surprised by his visit. Achille had the habit of stopping by like this, and the notary was always happy to see him. Norbert had been grieved by Adela's death, for he knew what it represented for his friend. He had gone to offer Achille his support at the time of the funeral, concerned for his health and morale.

When Achille began to explain the reason for his visit, the man of law did not hide his surprise. He needed three thousand dollars and even offered his land as a guarantee. Norbert Lafleur would willingly have lent his friend the money, no questions asked. He knew Achille would do everything to pay him back, and his advanced years were not a consideration. He himself was in his twilight years and had accumulated a nice bundle during his years of active practice. Three thousand dollars more or less would not make him a young man again, and Lafleur knew very well that his money would be of no use to him when he was dead. What worried him was Achille's insistence on pledging his property. Notary Lafleur tried telling him that these legal obligations were not necessary, but Achille insisted, which led the notary to question him about this sudden need for money.

Achille told him about his project. Norbert Lafleur thought his friend had lost his mind. Take off in a canoe, at his age! For the old man of law, a simple walk to the corner store had become an expedition. It is true that he had been living alone for years and had practically ceased to do any physical exercise. He had slowly withdrawn into his home and no longer went out much. Achille and Adela had remained active and enjoyed the benefits of a simple but healthy life on their little piece of land. A much healthier life than his own. And besides, they'd had each other.

Achille talked to him about Adela and how she had wanted to return to her island one day.

"My friend, that's just madness!" the notary said.

Achille reminded him of the days when they were both passionate canoeists, recalling their fishing and white-water expeditions. He told him about his strict training regime and described his plan in detail. Achille had thought of everything. He had thought of every rapid to be crossed, the ones he could shoot and others he would have to portage.

"But why not take the plane?" asked the notary.

"The plane isn't for us. Adela would have wanted to do one last canoe trip. And that's become the most important thing in my life. I want it to be done, but I also want to give myself time to let her go. To take her back to Newfoundland by plane would be like sending her back by mail. I have to do it, and this is the way I want to do it," he said.

Norbert Lafleur was surprised by his determination and admired his conviction. Never had he seen such a strong bond between a man and a woman. And yet they had never been married. In Achille's eyes, he saw an ardour and appetite for life that he himself had lost. He was eighty-eight years old! But what difference should that make? It was Achille who was right.

When they had finished talking, the man of law was convinced that this wild plan was the best idea in the world. On the table he laid out the bank notes Achille would need for the trip. Once again, he tried to refuse his guarantee.

"It's only fair, and I don't know why I would be less fair with a friend than with a stranger," Achille had said, waving away all objections.

Achille was aware that the adventure he was about to embark on could put his life in danger. He was aware of it, as he had been all the other times he had set out on a dangerous canoe trip.

"Listen, both of us know this could be dangerous. You never know what could happen...but I have every intention of coming back to tell you about my voyage," he said, to reassure his friend.

He signed the documents and the notary promised to make a record of the loan. Early the next morning, Achille was ready to go. His luggage had been loaded and tied down to the canoe. He cast a final glance around the house, then closed it up.

As he pushed his frail birchbark boat onto the Joseph River to begin his long journey, Achille turned and looked at what he was leaving behind. It was magnificent. The old house still had a great deal of charm. But without Adela, the idyllic landscape had no life to it, no more than if it were a painting on a wall. A new world was opening up before him, and he was going there...with her.

# Four

Achille was used to keeping his mouth shut. On the farm, his father had no time for fine words or sentimentality. When children reached an age where they could work with their hands, they were put to use. With eleven children in the family, everyone had to help out. Achille, the seventh born, had faded into the background. His father barely noticed him. When he looked at one of his children and could not remember his or her name, that child was usually Achille. When he took notice of him, usually it was to give him a task to do. The last time he had noticed him, the year before, it was to tell him it was time for him to go. The man had decided that the farm would go to his eldest son, Robert. And that was that. The rest of the band had to fend for themselves, as quickly as they could.

"It's time you made a man of yourself, my boy. There's room at the Gilmour lumber camp. I told them you'd be there next week."

That was that. There was no other option offered, no discussion. With a few words, his father had pushed him out of the nest.

The lumber camps were terrible places. Achille knew it from hearing lumberjacks talk. They spoke of the terrible conditions and tyrannical foremen, disturbing and mysterious legends, snowstorms, accidents and deaths. He had hoped there would be some kind of intervention from his mother, but it never came. The little tenderness he had received in his childhood had come from his mother. But being a woman who obeyed her husband's decisions, she knew that rules were rules, however cruel they may be. She knew how hard it was to provide food and shelter for such a big family. She herself had been forced to marry at sixteen to make room in her family home.

When the day came to leave, his father took him to Maniwaki, where the company enlisted workers before heading up to the lumber camps. Achille obediently followed him but felt as if he were being led to the gallows.

The war had just ended, leaving a number of countries in ruins. Even Canada, so far away from the murderous tumult of the old countries, was still recovering. Many families in the Gatineau had lost a young soldier in the trenches of Europe. The time for reconstruction had come, and wood was needed. Maniwaki was the embarcation point for veritable regiments of men armed with axes and crosscut saws, out to conquer the forest.

At sixteen, Achille was considered a man. In his heart, however, he was on the verge of despair. If his father had taken him in his arms, he would have wept his heart out. But his father did not touch him. He did not even dare look him in the eyes, and stared at the ground instead.

"Well, uh, that's it, my boy," he said, handing him his bag.

An empty phrase, the ideal kind for a man who does not want to say anything. Achille would have liked his father to make him feel, for once, that he was his son and that he regretted seeing him go – at least make some kind of gesture. That would have given meaning to everything that had happened in the past sixteen years. But his father did nothing. Achille had the feeling that something had just broken…forever.

They were piled into an old jalopy that took them several kilometres down a muddy road. The truck moved ahead groaning and bilging a cloud of blue smoke. They ended up in a cart that took them even farther north on a road full of bumps and potholes. When the horses had trouble on the slopes and the more difficult passages, the men often had to get out and push.

The leaves on the trees were in full colour now. In several days, maybe several hours, heavy rains and winds would strip the branches clean. The vivid yellows and reds seemed to make the sunlight even brighter. But behind the beauty of this landscape, one could sense winter lying curled in the ice grottoes of the north, preparing to emerge from its lair like a big polar bear. The men were starting to feel its icy breath. Canada geese passed overhead in a big V-formation, crying and squawking. They were fleeing the big bear that was wakening, whereas the men were heading straight towards him.

Sometimes the road veered away from the river so some obstacle could be avoided, but generally it followed the shoreline. The Gatineau River was an incredible mass of moving water. Sitting at the edge of the cart, legs swinging to the rhythm of the bumps in the road, Achille admired the river. Powerful and majestic, it inspired fear and respect. Nothing could stop it. It was a prodigious force. He instinctively felt that his life would be bound to this powerful body of water.

Night had fallen when they arrived at the lumber camp. It was made up of a "sleep camp" and kitchen built with round spruce logs from which the bark had not even been removed. It was surrounded by sheds and a stable for the thirty-odd horses. The stable stood out from the other buildings. Each horse had its own stall with wooden dividing walls. The men who tended the horses, the "barn boys," kept the place very clean and fed the horses generous portions of hay and oats. At the end of the day, it was their job to rub them down. The horses were worth their weight in gold, veritable mountains of muscle, some weighing a ton and capable of hauling several logs at a time. In teams of two, the horses followed the lumberjacks into the forest, bringing out the trees that had been cut down and transporting them to the river. When spring came, all the tree-trunks that had been harvested were pushed into the raging torrent. The company bought the horses at great cost and had to care for them all year round. As for the lumberjacks, the company's obligations to them began in the fall when they arrived at the camps and ended when the season came to a close. It cost nothing to replace a worker who left the camp or died, which was not the case with a horse. A man could be replaced in no time, with no financial loss. If he had no family, or if his wife did not have the wits to ask for the dead man's salary, the company often kept the unpaid wages. The comfort and security of the men in the lumber camps was not considered a priority.

Achille followed the group in silence. The veteran workers immediately headed for the "sleep camp." The construction had been hastily built for the first lumber camp. The doorway was so low that the men had to bend down to enter. It had a dirt floor whose surface was so hard and polished from being walked and spat upon that it looked like a slab of marble. As they entered, the men who had been there the previous winter greeted each other with hearty shouts.

Though life in the lumber camps was hard, some preferred this arduous existence to their sometimes stormy relations with their wives. For them, the call of the forest was a yearly deliverance. But these men were also the first to want to go home when winter, as always, was taking a long time to end. Others would have preferred to avoid this veritable forced labour, but working at the lumber camp was their only way of ensuring their family's survival. These men had souvenirs and sometimes photos hanging on the wall above their beds. Finally, there were the men who were running away from something. Alcohol and gambling, usually. For several months, this cabin was their refuge until spring, when they heard the call of the bottle once more. When spring came, they emerged from the woods only to get drunk and spend, in a matter of days, the money they had accumulated with such difficulty over so many months. Maniwaki had no shortage of what they were after. Though there were no more than two thousand inhabitants, there were twenty or so bars and gaming halls. It was often these reckless characters who agreed to return after the winter camps for the log driving, in spite of the dangers it involved.

In the sleep camp there were two rows of bunks made of crudely cut spruce-wood planks. They were lined up on either side of the room, and each row was two storeys high. In the middle of the room was an immense cast-iron stove, also called "the trout" on account of its shape. It was a kind of big barrel on four stumpy legs. The long black pipe that served as a chimney went up towards the ceiling, then turned at a right angle and ran the length of the cabin. Hanging parallel to the stovepipe was a big iron cord for the men to hang their snow-drenched clothing upon.

Achille headed to the back of the room where there appeared to be a free bed. As soon as he had set down his things, a man sitting on the next bed brusquely intervened. In his hands he was holding an axe whose blade he was whetting with such concentration that he did not even raise his eyes when speaking to Achille.

"Scram, kid. This here is where the old boys sleep. New guys sleep by the door."

Achille wanted to retort that the place did not seem to be taken, but all the men in the sleep camp had stopped what they were doing and were looking in their direction. The camps had their rules, and a newcomer who questioned those rules was committing a capital crime. Fifty pairs of eyes were turned on Achille, and the tension was palpable. The silence was broken only by the noise of the file on the axe blade. The man suspended his activity and pointed with the sharp instrument to the bed right next to the door.

Achille was not the kind to seek confrontation, and it would not have occurred to him to stand up to the man. The lumberjack's axe impressed him far less than the looks the other men were giving him. Without making a scene, he headed to the bed that had been assigned to him, while the others returned to their occupations. Achille wondered why a bunk at the back was worth more than the one he had been given. In the deep of winter, he would understand. It was so cold that the men who slept by the door woke up in the morning with their beards or moustaches white with frost.

Some men slept without getting undressed, removing only their heavy coats. And because they never washed, the place smelled strongly of sweat and urine. When the men came in soaked with snow and sweat after a hard day's work, the iron cables were weighted down with clothing and the wood-burning "trout" was stoked. The air became warm, heavy and humid. This, combined with the strong odours, made the air unbreathable. Later, Achille rigged up a little opening between two spruce logs at the head of his bed, which he plugged up with oakum. When the air became too heavy, he took out the oakum to let a draft of cold air from outside blow over his face.

Achille kept a low profile. In his family, no one had spoken to him except to tell him what to do…or what not to do. He could not remember ever having a conversation with his parents on a subject other than work that needed to be done. But he knew how to listen.

"Hi, I'm Gabriel. Gaby, to people who know me."

Achille looked in surprise at the hand being held out to him. His eyes moved up to the face of the person who had just spoken. Gaby was quite a short man, but straight and slender as a reed. Achille could tell from his accent that he was not from the region. Finally he shook the hand still stretched out towards him.

"And what's your name?" Gaby asked.

"Achille."

It was the first time anyone had asked him his name since he had left home.

"You're new, but you look pretty sturdy. This is my second camp. I just arrived from the west. Alberta, have you heard of it?"

"Ye…yes," replied Achille, searching his memory.

At primary school, "*la petite école*," as country schools used to be called, Achille had learned a bit of geography. For three years punctuated by absences due to farm work, Achille had been in the class of Mademoiselle Leclerc. He had never been one for homework, but he listened carefully. He racked his brain.

"Manitoba, Alberta, Sakatch…iwon," he thought. The other provinces of Canada. On the wall of the village general store, there had been a map of Canada on which he sometimes measured the distance that separated Burbridge[7] from the rest of the world. When he went there with his father, he waited next to the map. He knew what the

---

[7.] *Former name of the village of Messines.*

distance between Burbridge and Hull represented in terms of time. Two to three long days. And on the map, this distance was so small, barely five centimetres, that he could not imagine how long it would take to get to the other side of Canada. Measuring with his fingers, he tried to calculate the number of days it would take to get from one ocean to the other. And to go to the old countries by boat seemed to him an incredible adventure. He loved to travel by canoe. On the water, he was king. But to sail the sea for weeks or even months was inconceivable.

"You come from around here?" asked Gaby.

"Yes. From Burbridge...near Maniwaki."

"I know Maniwaki, I stayed there for a few days when I got here. You should get yourself a couple of blankets. That's where I slept last winter," he said, pointing to Achille's bed. "And I can tell you, you're going to freeze like a rat."

Achille had never seen a frozen rat, and he did not see why Gaby was using this animal as an example. After all, a rat must freeze in the same way as any other animal. However, he did know about cold, and thanked Gaby for his advice.

"Don't count on the foreman to give you a blanket, he's a...a...," said Gaby, thinking for a long moment about what word to use, then murmuring it cautiously, as if it were a mortal sin, "...a...dog."

According to Gaby, Clyde was a real *"tête carrée"*[8] and hated French Canadians. He came down very hard on them. And because of his size, he inspired respect. The worst kind of tyrant.

"Apparently, the men haven't had a cook for weeks. It's the cookee[9] who's been making the food, but he can't even make tea without burning it!" Gaby told him.

The kitchen was a big room built of spruce logs, like the other buildings. There were several tables, and in the middle of the room stood the "trout," which Clyde refused to light before the weather got very cold, "so as not to waste wood." They were surrounded by wood, so much that they were fairly tripping over it, but Clyde maintained that the heat from cooking was enough. At the other end of the building, a wall separated the kitchen from the main room. In

---

[8.] *Literally, square head or block head, pejorative term given by French Canadians to Anglophones who refused to speak or understand French.*

[9.] *Cook's assistant in lumber camps.*

the kitchen, the big wood stove was the centre of all activity. Whatever the time of day, there was always something simmering.

The menu varied little. A lot of baked beans, salt lard, bread and molasses. Around the camps, there were a great many lakes; it was impossible to walk a kilometre in a straight line without coming upon a body of water. Fish were so plentiful that all it took to catch a nice trout was a bent nail tied to the end of a piece of string. During the carp-spawning season, the fish swam up the streams in such great numbers that one could no longer see the bottom. They could be scooped out by hand. And every day, or almost, a deer or moose ambled through the area surrounding the camp, attracted by the noise. They could almost have been killed with a knife. But the company refused to allow the men to add to their menu in this way. Anyone who cheated was dismissed on the spot. And a tyrant like Clyde took pleasure in punishing the slightest offence.

Though afraid to be so far from home, Achille found great comfort in his friendship with Gaby. The slightly older man had taken him under his wing. Gaby had been to school. He had lived in the little city of Falher, near Peace River, where he had been educated by the Oblate brothers of Marie-Immaculée. He was talented, and the brothers had steered him towards classical college, hoping to make a priest of him. But for him, the mysterious call of the forest was stronger than the call of God. He had left Alberta because he wanted to live in a real French-speaking milieu and work in the forest. In Falher people lived in French, but as soon as one left the village, English dominated. Anglophones often reacted aggressively to Francophones. Gaby had decided to leave for Quebec, where his parents came from. On the advice of one of the Oblate brothers, he had chosen Maniwaki. The Oblates were also established in this city in the northern Gatineau, but most of all, it was where the civilised world ended and true forest began. Gaby was not a lumberjack. He was more highly educated than most of the other men, so he had immediately been promoted to bookkeeper.

But what Gaby hoped was to become a scaler[10] and he intended to succeed. He had theories on everything, and Achille learned a great deal about the world over the two winters they slept in neighbouring beds. Each time Gaby expressed his thoughts on something or his

---

[10.] *Person who measures the volume of wood harvested.*

opinion of someone, he did it with great seriousness and due consideration. He weighed all the elements in his head before uttering a word. He could stop talking for an entire minute in mid-sentence. Achille would think he had finished, then Gaby would blurt out the word that represented the sum of his thoughts.

One day when Clyde came down on an old lumberjack for some peccadillo, Gaby had exploded; but it was a slow and weighty explosion. Clyde had the old man by the collar of his shirt and was telling him in English that he could let him go for breaking his axe-handle. Gaby would probably not have intervened if Clyde had not ended up calling him a "stupid French bastard." Gaby was on his feet in a flash. He lifted a finger and held it under Clyde's nose, though the foreman was almost fifteen centimetres taller. He was furious, one could see it in his eyes. His finger trembled with rage.

"Let go of him, you…," said Gaby, stopping in mid-sentence for one of his sudden deep searches for the right word.

Everyone knew what he was doing and waited in silence. Clyde waited too, still holding the poor lumberjack by the collar.

"…you…you big goddamn fag!"

The word "fag" was not often used in the lumberjack camps. Some of the men knew this scornful word for homosexual. Everyone knew that these kind of relations existed, even within the camp, but no one dared talk about it openly. However, rumour had it that Clyde and the cookee had been caught pawing each other. The insult was like a slap in the face to Clyde, who had always believed that his sexual "deviance" had remained secret. He turned pale and immediately released the man, who retreated to a corner of the room. No one knew whether Clyde was going to have a heart attack or hit poor Gaby, who was no match for him. His hand reached out to grab him and he was about to strike him when to everyone's surprise, Achille, the unobtrusive quiet one, stepped to Gaby's side without a second's hesitation. He seized Clyde's hand in mid-air and held it there. All at once, the men surrounded him. Clyde looked around. He sensed that things could turn out badly for him, and all he could do was walk away, grumbling. It was the first time anyone had stood up to the tyrant. Gaby and Achille were given heroes' congratulations. But the victory was short-lived. Achille was assigned to outhouse duty, which in a lumber camp was a revolting job if there ever was one. It was always the new men who were assigned to it, especially those who fell out of grace with the foreman. A new hole had to be dug, the outhouse moved on top of it, and the other hole full of excrement filled in.

Everyone had a good laugh over Gaby's pronouncement. Coming from him, it had the effect of a punch. "*Listen, you, you, big goddamn fag!*" the men repeated in the evening around the "trout," telling and retelling the story, which never failed to make them laugh.

Though he was used to hard work, Achille found the first days of work exhausting. But that was only the beginning. February was particularly difficult that year. It had snowed a great deal and each snowstorm was followed by a cold snap. The men were waist-deep in snow and advanced at a snail's pace. Achille worked with Ned, a real old-timer, as they said. He and Ned formed a good team. Ned had a lot of experience, which meant he could slow down while the young one slaved away. Achille knew it, but did not resent him. The advice of clever and experienced old Ned helped him save time and energy. But most of all, Ned was an expert with a file. He knew how to sharpen almost anything. In his hands, an axe became a scalpel. The teeth of the crosscut saws and the bow saws were so sharp that they had to be handled with great care. To have a good sharpener on hand made it possible to cut more wood, and since everyone was paid by volume, this counted for a lot. A tree was felled with just a few strokes of the crosscut saw. Achille may have been quite skilled in sharpening his saw and axe, but his blades always looked dull in comparison with Ned's. He agreed to let Ned take longer lunch breaks so he could whet the saws.

Meanwhile Achille, armed with his axe, tackled the trees that had already been felled. The operation consisted of cutting off all the branches and keeping just the main trunk. As a general rule, lumberjacks did not like this part of the job. Their feet would get tangled in a maze of boughs, and they were always in danger of injury. The branches on which a tree had fallen were as tense as tight-wound springs. These "spring poles," as the lumberjacks called them, would pop up like the arm of a catapult as soon as the axe blade touched them. Men had been seriously crippled this way.

Achille seized his axe, spinning it around in the air and crying out "Yahoo!" Hitting out right and left, with a few skilful movements he had the log ready to be taken away by the horses.

Gaby was right. It was so cold next to the door that Achille had to sleep with his toque on. Some lumberjacks put on their long johns in the fall and did not take them off until the end of winter. The mattresses rapidly became infested with vermin. Cockroaches, ticks and lice were abundant. Some men preferred to burn their long johns in the spring rather than wash them. Achille had tried to keep his bed clean and maintain an acceptable level of hygiene, but living in such close quarters with the others made it almost impossible to win the battle against vermin.

When spring came, most of the lumberjacks packed their bags. The masses of wood heaped on the riverbank had been pushed along the ice, which only had to melt for the logs to be floated downriver to the factories. Finally the men were returning to civilisation. Some would be returning to wives and children. They dreamed of caresses, and the imminence of their departure heightened their desire. At night they could be heard masturbating beneath the blankets.

Gaby was leaving too. He wanted to enrol in a scaler's course. Achille was sad, for Gaby had been the first person in the camp to treat him like a human being. He had learned a lot from him.

It was also at this time that the company recruited the log driving team. Only the bold and reckless accepted this work. It was true that the pay was better, but even still, some men did not finish the season. Gaby had advised Achille to return to his family, but he knew that his father did not want him back. His father had made it clear that Achille had become one mouth too many to feed. So he agreed to join the team.

The log drivers' mission was to follow the wood's progression on the water. Sometimes logs would wash up on the bank, and the drivers with their long poles, equipped with a hook and spike at one end, had to dislodge them and push them back into the current.

But the most dangerous part of the job was the log jams. When the tree-trunks arrived en masse at a place where the river narrowed and formed rapids, sometimes the wood would pile up. Dancing dangerously from one log to another, spiked boots on their feet and armed with pikes, the drivers had to get to the centre of the jam to untangle it. Pushing and pulling on the pieces of wood, they had to break up the dam. But when the logs started to come free, the jam came apart so quickly that the men barely had time to get back to shore. Sometimes one of them was carried off by the river.

Achille started training near the shore on a little heap of logs. Right from his first step, he took a plunge into the icy water. The others made fun of him, as they always did when a newcomer got his first mouthful of the Gatineau. Discouraged, Achille wondered how he would ever follow the others. It was Pierre who taught him. Grand Pierre was known by no other name. Everyone called him that. And the name suited him well. With his long thin legs, he could make huge leaps. He seemed to be flying when he jumped over open water. It took him several hours to teach Achille how to stay on his feet on the moving tree trunks in the water. The trick was to remain in movement and never remain more than a fraction of a second on the same log. The accomplished log driver gave one the impression that he was just brushing over the surface of the wood in the water. Each time he took a step, his eyes were two or three paces ahead. These men's acrobatics resembled a veritable water ballet. It is not surprising that log drivers were reputed to dance well. It was said that Jos Montferrand, one of the most illustrious drivers[11] had been a skilled dancer. Ladies fought each other for the honour of dancing with him. His exploits were still the talk of the lumber camps.

The strangest part of it was that not one of the drivers knew how to swim, except Achille, who had learned when he was little. They were all scared to death of the water. The use of lifejackets did not become common until much later, so that anyone who fell into the water sunk right to the bottom.

"Why learn to swim?" an experienced driver had once said to him. (One never heard talk of an *old* log driver, as they generally did not live to old age.) "The idea is not to fall in the water," he said.

Achille was still new to log driving when he saw a man die in the torrent for the first time. It was not a big jam, but the men had to intervene quickly, before the heap became too big. Achille, Grand Pierre and two other drivers had climbed up on the pile of wood and feverishly pushed at the pieces that were stuck. Each log that they managed to dislodge was literally sucked into the whirlpool created by the current. Grand Pierre had his pike solidly planted in the end of a piece of wood and was pushing hard when suddenly it slid out of its trap, dragging him along with it. He tried to recover his footing, searching for a solid place to plant his pike, but the log closest to him was so small that it could not hold his weight and sunk. Losing his balance, Pierre fell into the water, just at the edge of the whirlpool. His terrified face appeared above the surface and he grasped onto the treacherous log that had sent him into the churning water. But other logs were

---

[11.] *(1802-1864) Hero of Herculean strength. He worked as a cart driver, log driver, foreman and guide on the rivers of the Outaouais, primarily the Gatineau. Many exploits are attributed to him, including that of beating 100 men with his fists on the bridge between Hull and Ottawa.*

clustering around him, closing in, as he entered the whirlpool. He was propelled around the edge of the funnel formed by the rotating water. Achille, who was near him, saw his face contort with fear and sink into the water, his hand still seeking something to grasp onto. His eyes beseeched him. Then he disappeared into the whirlpool and the carpet of wood closed over his head. The men cried out, running in every direction, searching the water upriver from the log jam, then downriver, hoping to see him come up to the surface again. After a few minutes, everyone knew he was gone. Achille was petrified, rooted to the spot, his hand still stretched out towards the water. He was trembling in every limb. It was the first time that he had seen someone die, and the image of this face disappearing into death would torment him for a long time.

The foreman would not even let the men stop working.

"There's nothing we can do. The river will take him farther down," he said.

And it was true. Often bodies were found farther along, washed up on the riverbank. However, sometimes a body remained submerged for several months before it was found. Some disappeared forever. When the men returned to the camp that night, Achille saw that every trace of Grand Pierre had vanished, his belongings removed as if he had never existed. The rumour circulated that his body had been found downriver, stuck in another logjam. That was the life of a log driver. It was worth less than the logs that floated on the river.

When the men did not succeed in breaking the jam, they used dynamite. And they had to act quickly, before other logs coming down the river got stuck in the heap and made it bigger. This was the most dangerous operation of all. When the river was not very wide, the dynamite cartridge was put at the end of a long wooden pole. The fuse was lit, and whoever was holding the pole had to deposit the explosives in the middle of the logjam as quickly as he could. While he was at it, he had to try and push his dangerous package as deeply as possible into the heart of the blockage. The charge almost always blew up before he had time to remove his pole. Sometimes, the man was hit by chunks of wood following the explosion, if not entire logs.

The ones who handled the dynamite were called monkeys. The monkeys had to deposit the charge in the middle of big jams that were too close to shore for a pole to be used. They would walk along the logs until they got to the middle of the tangle, deposit the cartridges, light the fuse, and head for shelter as quickly as possible. Often they did not have time to duck behind a tree or rock before the explosion sent water and logs flying in all directions.

Cléo Langevin was a monkey, a real devil-may-care type, whom Achille suspected was out to get killed. Cléo liked to shorten the fuse to thrill his audience. He lit his bomb and then, instead of coming back as fast as he could, he would start dancing a jig as a kind of dare on the heap of wood as the fuse burned away. Then, at just the last moment, he would hurl himself onto the shore. It was his trademark. In the camp, his nickname was "Cléo-of-the-short-fuse," a nickname that of course made reference to his strange habit, but also to his sometimes-explosive personality.

One day, Achille was assigned to Cléo's team, and they tried for the whole morning to untangle a heap of wood that had formed north of Grand-Remous. The twisted mass of trees was huge and they had to act quickly, for it was getting bigger with every hour. Upstream from the logjam, the water level was getting higher and they were in danger of losing control. Cléo attached several cartridges together, thinking that one would not be enough. Click, click, click. In several bounds he was at the top of the wood heap. The current was so strong that the logs were sticking out every which way. Cléo climbed down the front of the heap to insert the charge in the right place. The churning water just under his buttocks wet the bottom of his trousers. Achille was fascinated. He saw the smoke from the fuse, which was starting to burn. As usual, Cléo started doing his little dance instead of returning to shore. He smiled broadly to show that he was afraid of nothing. But when he finally made the leap to shore, he lost his footing and fell head first between two logs. He struggled like the devil to get out of his perilous position, but each time, his hands slipped on the wet surface of the wood. All the men started to yell at once, it was a veritable cacophony, but no one dared go to his rescue. It was too late.

When Cléo finally managed to get his footing, he knew he had no time to get to shelter, so he retraced his steps to the place where he had put the charge. He plunged his hand inside the logjam and brought it out again, holding up the bundle of smoking dynamite. He turned to hurl it into the distance. His arm outstretched, his hand opened to release the dynamite, but just at that moment it exploded. Achille saw Cléo's arm disintegrate.

Luckily the man was thrown back onto the logs. The others rushed to help him. He was covered with blood from head to toe. Incredibly, he had survived the accident, but his right arm had been completely torn off and the noise of the explosion was the last sound he ever heard.

Achille was shaken by the episode. The foreman gave them a fifteen-minute break to take the wounded man away and pass around a bottle of moonshine. Alcohol was forbidden at all times, but when this kind of thing happened, certain foremen were more understanding than others. Immediately after, the men resumed their work. Another charge was deposited and the jam was finally blown up. The current carried off the logs that were red with Cléo's blood and flesh.

Achille's stomach heaved. For a long time, the mere mention of this difficult experience was enough to make him nauseous.

Whereas the other men feared water, Achille adored it, the river especially. He sometimes went to the foot of the rapids to watch the tons of water crash down with a deafening roar. He was fascinated by the river's power and beauty, and respected it as if it were a living being. Sometimes he even spoke to it as if it were a woman. But at the same time, he would have liked to tame it. It was old Raphaël Smith who had taught him to love the river. Smith was an Algonquin guide whose services were often called upon to lead fishermen to spots where fish were plentiful, and hunters towards the finest game.

Though he could not understand a word of English, Achille had often gone with his father to meet parties of tourists from the United States. They were rich and sometimes came to hunt and fish in the north. It was an incredible journey of several days by train, horseback and canoe, all in order to kill a moose, of which they would bring back nothing but the antlers, or to fish an unbelievable quantity of trout and keep only two or three of the biggest. Achille's job was to carry their luggage. That was how he had met Raphaël Smith.

Raphaël had been adopted by a colonist who had settled near the Indian reserve. It was said that the Oblate brothers of Marie-Immaculée had given this colonist a plot of earth in exchange for his adopting two young orphan "savages." Smith had given his name to the two young Algonquins, but Raphaël had returned to his traditional way of life as soon as he came of age. Achille and the Indian immediately became friends. By nature, the Algonquins were a reserved people, and this was probably what Smith liked about Achille. He mistrusted white people. He had seen them invade his territory, and his people had been reduced to living on a little parcel of earth between the Désert and the Gatineau rivers.

The Algonquin had inherited the traditional technique of making birchbark canoes, and he was also a past master in the art of manoeuvring this kind of boat. There was science in even the simple gesture of putting the canoe on his shoulders for portage. Every one of his movements was studied. Achille had watched and listened to Smith.

"Let the others leave. Take your time to position your supplies and your canoe properly. You'll catch up with them later," he said.

And he was right. Sometimes the American group got ahead of them, eager to get their lines in the water, but after two kilometres they were exhausted, and Achille and Raphaël overtook them. They arrived at the lake long before the troop and were already ready to leave again.

But it was not enough just to know how to put the canoe on one's shoulders.

"You have to know how to walk," Smith told him the first time. It had made Achille smile.

Walk. He had known how to do that since early childhood. But the man had taught him that a *portageur*'s walk was different.

"You have to find a balance between small steps and big steps, between lifting your feet and sliding them," he said.

Most of all, Raphaël had initiated him in the art of white-water paddling. Achille remembered the first time he had made him "shoot" the Devil's rapid.[12]

The Devil's rapid was a man-eater. Rare were the men who had got through it and lived to tell the tale. That day, Raphaël had to take a group from Kensington[13] to a very exceptional little trout lake. The truck that transported the group had passed by the Algonquin reserve to get to the Gatineau River at a place called Le Corbeau. Here the river was wild, both upstream and down, except for a short stretch between the two rapids, where the current grew calm and allowed canoes to cross from one bank to the other. The group had crossed the river without difficulty, and then the canoes had been carried to the fishing lake.

They returned to the shores of the Gatineau mid-day with a nice string of trout. They had to portage to get by the rapids safely and reach the bottom of the rapide du Mur, where the fishermen hoped to catch sturgeon and yellow pike. At the end of the day, they had planned to go downriver to the Bonnet Rouge rapid, where the truck

---

[12.] *Better known today by the name of "Lucifer."*
[13.] *Former name of the municipality of Déléage, near Maniwaki.*

that had brought them that morning would be waiting.

The trail from the lake to the Gatineau River was in no way difficult. Achille and Raphaël were transporting all the equipment. The men followed in single file, avoiding the rocks and numerous fissures. One of the rich Americans was clearly not in the habit of walking in the forest. His shoes would have been fine for the luxury hotels of New York, but here they were as suitable for walking as a pair of skis. His foot got stuck in a fissure and the weight of his body was thrown forward. Achille heard a sharp crack and thought at first that someone had stepped on a branch, but the cry of pain that followed left no room for doubt. He set down the canoe and turned around to see the American lying on the ground, writhing in pain. His anklebone had been fractured in two places and a blood-smeared shard of tibia was sticking out of the flesh. His cries tore through the air. Raphaël rushed over to the wounded man and, without asking his opinion, with a single sharp movement set the bone back in place in its envelope of muscle. He hurriedly applied a tourniquet to stop the haemorrhaging. Raphaël ordered Achille to find him some big pieces of bark from a quaking aspen so he could make a splint. Achille quickly found one and removed the bark with his axe.

The man was shouting and cursing, at least from what Achille could understand. The others were standing around, not knowing what to do. They had to return to Maniwaki, but at this part of the river they were between two major rapids. They would have had to carry the man in order to avoid the du Corbeau and the Tête-de-Six, then get back on the river and travel against the current all the way to Maniwaki. This was a laborious expedition, which would take several hours. Too many hours. All the more so because it was getting late, and the man had to be transported on a stretcher.

There was also the possibility of carrying him downriver until they finally got to the truck at Bonnet Rouge. But to portage would take even longer, and they had to act quickly. All there was left to do was to shoot the du Mur rapids one after the other, then the rapide des Cèdres, to get to Bonnet Rouge more quickly. There, the truck would be waiting and could rush them to Maniwaki.

"Do something, I don't want to die here!" the man cried. He was still losing blood.

And he was in danger of dying if they did not act. His companions begged them. Raphaël explained the different possibilities and the risks of each. To shoot the rapids was very dangerous, but the man continued imploring them to do something to end his pain. The old Algonquin expressed his fears, but the wounded man's friends pleaded with him, promising him a generous bonus if he succeeded.

"Your bonus won't be worth much if we go under," he replied.

Raphaël exchanged glances with Achille. Despite his fear, he nodded. He agreed to take the risk. It was decided that only he and Achille would ride in the canoe with the wounded man. Quickly, they constructed a crude stretcher and set it in the middle of the canoe. The man's companions had given him bourbon for the pain, and the alcohol was beginning to take effect. Smith got in the back and pushed the canoe while Achille paddled hard.

"Listen, my friend, what we are about to do, few men have done before and lived to tell the tale. You are going to see the river roar as you have never seen it do, and may never see again. When you see the water monster in front of us, you are going to be afraid. I'll be afraid too. But if you want us to come out of this alive, you're going to have to listen to me at all times and do exactly as I tell you. And when the monster looms up in front of you, you must never stop listening to my voice, otherwise we'll be done for."

Never had Raphaël said so many words to him at the same time, and Achille had registered the seriousness of the message. The Algonquin had warned him: "We have to go down the middle and never leave the current until we get to the Rapide du Mur. You'll get the impression that it's less dangerous on either side of the river, but that's an illusion. The canoe would become uncontrollable. We have to enter the jaws of the monster. So don't resist and let me guide us into the heart of the storm."

Achille was not sure he understood his friend's picturesque language, but he trusted him. Soon, at a bend in the river, the current quickened. When the canoe got around the bend, Achille discovered what Raphaël meant. Before them, the river had gone wild. Tons of water were trapped in a narrow passage. In the centre, the rapids must have been almost two metres high and the noise of rushing water was deafening. Raphaël shouted orders at Achille. Though frightened by the spectacle, which surely spelled death, he followed the old guide's commandments down to the last detail. Raphaël yelled at him to paddle hard, sometimes left, sometimes right, then suddenly ordered him to stop, and plunged his own paddle deep into the churning water to steer the boat onto the right course. The monster was drawing nearer, growing bigger as they gained speed. The canoe mounted the mass of water formed by a wave in the middle of the river. Achille could no longer hear Raphaël clearly, but he paddled with desperate vigour. The wounded man was shouting too, in terror. He was sure that they were going to die. The frail vessel stood almost upright, then nose-dived. Achille leaned backwards to compensate. As the boat fell back again, the end entered the torrent. Achille heard shouts of "Row, row, row!" He paddled faster and harder, pushing himself to the limit. He was completely submerged and almost went overboard. Suddenly, his face emerged from the veil of water. They had passed through the jaws of the monster, but Raphaël still bellowed at him to paddle. He was right. They were not out of danger yet. Other treacherous rapids awaited them. Smith directed the boat between the rocks, keeping it in the middle of the current. Several minutes of hell, then the canoe, half filled with water, entered calmer waters. Achille was completely soaked, but he had never felt so hot. He had been so frightened that he was trembling all over, and his hands could barely keep hold of the paddle. He wanted to cry and laugh at the same time. They made a short stop to bail water from the canoe.

Bonnet Rouge was in sight, and the truck was at the designated spot. When Achille and Raphaël took the wounded man from the canoe, they realised that he'd been so afraid that his bowels had let go. Achille and Raphaël said nothing, but they had been just as frightened as he. The man was transported to Maniwaki and survived.

Achille had never forgotten this first and last voyage over these rapids, the biggest in the Gatineau. He had been terribly afraid but at the same time experienced an incredible sensation, an incomparable surge of adrenaline. Later he would try to re-live this sensation.

The following year, he worked in a logging camp where the previous foreman had left a magnificent cedar canoe. Achille had eyed it longingly until the new boss noticed and invited him to use it. The man himself was too afraid of this kind of boat to want to keep it for his own use. Achille took it out each Sunday and every time he had a free moment, trying his skills on the rapids near the camp. After shooting the rapids, he came back along the shore, paddling against the current, until he reached the foot of the waterfall. Then, turning sharply, he shot into the rushing water and descended the wild and powerful current again. Each time, there was a look of great joy on his face. It was like being on the back of a wild horse. The other log drivers, flabbergasted, gathered at the river's edge to watch him. Achille had won the respect of his companions. All the more because he did not always succeed in mastering the river, and ended up overboard, his canoe upside down. The others held their breath until he reappeared, uttering a loud "Yahoo!," his face joyous.

They admired his prowess, but also envied his talent as a swimmer. This was how Achille won the esteem of his confreres. For once, he was someone special. He was the river-tamer and people remembered his name.

# Five

At twenty-five, Martin Éthier had few illusions about life. As a public observer, he was a privileged witness to the events of his region, both great and small. Especially the very smallest. Over five years of working for the regional press, he had seen everything from dogs hit by cars to pre-electoral visits from ministers on the decline. But most of all he had listened, often against his will, to the inanities of the Joe Know-It-Alls who lurked in every café and restaurant in the world. They went on and on, telling him their stories, which were usually outlandish, just because he was a journalist.

Yet he had aspired to great things when he had started out writing. Fresh out of the Cégep de Chicoutimi, Class of 1985, he had accumulated a mountain of noble and courageous principles that he felt must guide a free press in its search for information. He hoped to become a kind of defender of the widow and orphan, an upholder of the truth. However, when the search for truth consisted of wondering whether to believe the man who claims his pumpkin weighs one hundred kilos, it was a far cry from grand debates on journalistic ethics. What rubbish! And that's how it went every autumn in the Vallée-de-la-Gatineau. Happy Sunday gardeners exhibited monstrosities from their gardens, hoping to get their picture in the paper.

There were also the endless celebrations for this, that and the other thing, which he could not miss because he had promised to be there. To start with, there were the winter carnivals. Martin dreaded them. Because the carnival organisers had paid for a bit of advertising in the paper, he was required to cover the event. What event? Saturday morning, thirty degrees below zero, three participants, and somehow he had to take a photo showing the highlights of the activity. Even the carnival queen, who was barely out of diapers and had been chosen through the drawing of lots, would not go outdoors.

Yet Martin had written some wonderful articles and done excellent interviews with political personalities of the hour. But who was interested in that? He rarely received any comments, positive or negative, when one of these pieces was published. Yet each time he published the photo of a gardener standing next to his obese tomato, he would hear about it for weeks.

However, those he had dared go after with his pen had long memories and a lot of clout, and several times he had been called into the office of the newspaper's owner, who had harshly reprimanded him and even threatened to fire him. Muzzled, he now had to make do with traffic accidents, corn shucking contests and society pages to fill the pages of his paper. Writing had become mechanical. In fact, he could have copied and reused some of his stories one year to the next, changing only the dates and names. His initial enthusiasm had lost its edge.

Entering the Rialdo restaurant, where he usually went to read his paper and drink his coffee, Martin was greeted by jokes from the other regulars.

"Hey, newspaper-man, you got a tomato story this week? Because if you don't, you can have my wife's photo," called the eternally unemployed Collin, making one of his stupid jokes.

It was true that Collin's wife could have beaten all the records for roundness. She must have weighed one hundred and fifty kilos. And she was short, what's more. "With a green hat and a red dress, she really would look like a giant tomato," thought Martin.

"If I were you, Collin, I'd watch my tongue. Because if your wife finds out what you're saying about her, you're going to be in deep trouble," answered Martin, heading to his table.

The comment provoked general hilarity, for everyone was familiar with the matron's girth and scalding temper. Martin never sat with the others but always chose a table off to the side. Maybe it was his way of keeping a "necessary journalistic distance," as they used to say in school, but at the same time, their familiarity did him good. He felt accepted and respected by the group. Quite an honour.

With Collin, you were always bound to see Réal, a trucker who was just finishing his night shift. Réal transported logs to the factories. He had been working from nine o'clock the previous evening until seven o'clock that morning. He gave himself an hour's break before he started the day shift. He had no choice if he was going to pay for the damn truck, which was worth a quarter of a million dollars.

There was also Jacques, the night watchman. He had to be at least sixty-five years old. No one knew exactly, and he skilfully avoided all questions on the subject. He had started working as a night watchman at the age of seventeen for the International Paper Company, the I.P.C.

He had been doing it ever since. He had remained single and lived in a miserable trailer that he had made into a permanent home. It was said that Jacques was rich. He had saved almost all his paycheques, and his greatest luxury was his morning coffee.

And then there was Oscar, the taxi driver. Oscar was an inexhaustible source of news for Martin. He spent the night at the taxi station. Though the term "taxi station" was a bit of an exaggeration, as there was only one taxi. He kept his ear glued to his radio, which was tuned to the frequency of the police cars and ambulances. He was always first with the information about accidents, fires and human dramas. Each time he met Martin, he always started the conversation in the same way.

"Hey, Mr. Reporter, I guess you know what happened?" he would ask, knowing very well that Martin, unlike himself, did not spend his evenings listening to the police radio band.

Martin found this kind of greeting quite exasperating. There was always sarcasm in Oscar's voice, as if he were gloating over the fact that he had a scoop that even the town reporter did not know about. Today was no exception.

"Hey, Mr. Reporter, you must know about the drunk guy the police arrested on the road last night?"

Someone had been arrested in a state of inebriation at the wheel? It couldn't be just anybody for Oscar to be mentioning it.

"Not yet," replied Martin, who seconds earlier did not even know there had been an arrest. "But it must be someone important, because I'm having trouble finding out who he is."

This way, he did not completely lose face, letting on that he already knew about the story while giving Oscar the pleasure of revealing the person's name. And Martin was burning with curiosity, now that Oscar-the-chatterbox had gotten him interested.

"Well I can tell you, my friend, tongues will be wagging tomorrow. The guy is the president of the Regional Committee on Industry, Dagenais. Seems he was out with some exotic dancers. He's liable to lose more than his licence and his president's chair," said Oscar, referring to the man's wife, who would not appreciate his escapades being exposed for all to see.

Pierre Dagenais was a greedy businessman who always put his own interests first. On every board of directors of every organisation for which he had worked as a volunteer, he had been able to turn the situation to his own advantage. He managed to occupy strategic positions, which enabled him to grant contracts to his company without making submissions. Martin had denounced the situation, but everyone trembled before the businessman, and so in spite of his detailed articles, nothing had changed. Dagenais' misadventure did not displease him. "Maybe divine justice strikes the bad guys, after all," he thought with satisfaction.

Oscar's news had the effect of a bomb. Everyone at the table added his two-cents' worth. Today everyone recognised big Dagenais for the bag of dirt that he was, whereas only the day before, no one had dared criticise him. He reigned like a monarch over the town, and now that he had fallen from grace they were having a great time putting him down.

"Seems big Dagenais didn't go quietly. One of the cops got punched in the nose. He had to go to hospital," added Oscar.

The last cups of coffee had been drunk more quickly than usual, each man wanting to be the first to spread the news. Just as he was leaving, Oscar leaned over to Martin: "Oh yeah, I almost forgot. You who like strange stories, last night around suppertime, I heard a strange message on the police band. Seems they arrested a guy at Low because he was canoeing down the Gatineau River."

"I don't see why they'd arrest him. There's nothing illegal about canoeing down the river. Okay, it's dangerous, but not illegal. Dozens of kids do it each year," insisted Martin.

"Kids, yes. But not eighty-eight-year-old men! And do you know where the old guy was headed in his canoe?"

"No. To Hull or Ottawa, I suppose," suggested Martin.

"Get this. The guy told them he'd left from Sainte-Famille d'Aumond by canoe and that he was going to Newfoundland. Jeez! If you want my opinion, he's another Alzheimer case who's lost it!"

It was incredible. Oscar had to be mistaken. Or else he had heard wrong. Martin found them pitiful, these stories about elderly people who wandered in their heads the way they wandered around their neighbourhoods. This kind of story often made the tabloid headlines. But for the moment, the Dagenais affair was the one that was making him salivate.

He hurried back to the office and contacted the police, who at first refused to answer his questions. He had to wait for Captain Lapierre, the only person who could give him the details. There was no point in trying to find out more. The officer kept repeating the same message: it was too big a catch for him to talk about. The captain would not be back until early afternoon, he told him.

"Like hell!" thought Martin. Lapierre was probably in his office looking for a way to hush up the affair or water it down. He and Dagenais were great buddies. They went fishing together, and the president of the Committee on Industry made it a point of honour to participate in the yearly police golf tournament, whose profits went to sick children. The businessman did not give much of anything to the sick children; however, he handed out several thousand dollars' worth of prizes for participation. Most of the golfers in the tournament were policemen, and each remembered the personal gift he had received.

How was it that Dagenais had not managed to get off the hook this time? Martin decided to go hang around the Four Stars strip club. There was only one of its kind in the area; it would have had to be that one which Dagenais was coming out of when the incident occurred.

At nine in the morning, this kind of establishment is usually closed. In fact, the Four Stars only opened at five p.m., when office employees emerged from their cages and the "forest guys" returned to civilisation, still smelling of pine gum and chainsaw fuel.

Martin knocked at the door of the bar. The guy who did the cleaning came to open it. He was a bit simple-minded and would not have been able to give him a valid eyewitness account even if he had been in the police car when the arrest was made. Still, Martin took advantage of the opportunity to slip inside, despite the sweeper's protests. He took a look around, and was happy not to see the owner, Simone. She would have thrown him out without further explanation. Simone was an intelligent woman and she would have known before he opened his mouth that he had come about the Dagenais affair. Dagenais spent a lot of money in her establishment, and it was not in her interest to kill the hen with the golden eggs. He often brought clients with him, or politicians whose favour Simone sought to attract. After a few drinks, he would pay one of the dancers to spend the night with his client, ensuring the latter's future loyalty via blackmail, especially if the client was married.

"There's no one here. Come back later," the sweeper kept droning.

"I hear noise in the kitchen. There's got to be someone there," insisted Martin.

"It's one of the girls. She's eating."

"Well, okay, I'll come back later. But before I leave, do you think I could use the washroom?"

"Of course," the man said trustingly.

Martin headed for the washroom, glancing inside the kitchen. Christine, one of the dancers, was making herself a peanut butter sandwich. Christine was around thirty, but ten years of taking off her clothes in bars all over Quebec had taken their toll. She had been at her peak at seventeen, but had abused drugs and alcohol, stayed up so many nights and sold herself for a few dollars to so many men that her beauty had quickly faded. She had started out as queen of Montreal's top strip clubs. Money flowed…through her fingers. Then other, younger beauties had replaced her, and she had been forced to dance in suburban bars. Now she was reduced to seedy establishments in little towns in the countryside.

"Hi Christine," said Martin, who knew her well.

Though not a habitué of strip bars, Martin often accompanied friends there for a drink. Half the time, the guys chose to go to a strip bar. Sure, the girls were pretty, but Martin found his friends' behaviour a little strange, to say the least. Usually so reserved, there they were, drooling over these girls like dogs in front of a bone. The girls represented all the fantasies they would never dare suggest to their wives.

"So, was it a good night?"

"Not really. The thing that happened was kind of a downer."

"And that's just what I want to know – what happened?"

Christine lifted her head and looked at Martin sidelong.

"I figured if you were here so early it wasn't just to see my pretty face. What's your problem? No one want to tell you about it?"

"That's about it," admitted Martin.

"If Simone heard me, she'd show me the door, but I don't give a damn. I never liked the great Dagenais. He's disgusting. He takes us for whores."

That's what she was, and Martin knew it. But he also knew that the president of the Committee on Industry had used their services on several occasions, and by "disgusting," Christine meant that he treated the girls like animals. Martin did not dare imagine what Dagenais might have required them to do.

"The big guy was here with another guy. They drank, and then Dagenais paid a few girls to dance at their table. Around two, he sent the other guy off with little Julie, then he split the way he usually does after snaring someone. But he didn't get very far because we saw the lights of the cop cars go on as soon as he left the parking lot. It wasn't my set yet, so I went out to see what was going on. It was two young cops, fresh out of college. You have to think no one had told them about their chief's list of 'friends,' because when Dagenais started yelling at them and telling him he'd make them lose their jobs, they didn't waste any time. They went to cuff him and drive him to the station. The big guy was furious, he even hit one of them in the face. Next thing you know, he's face down on the hood of the car, his hands cuffed behind his back. They had him blow into the balloon and it almost exploded. Three times the allowed limit."

"How do you know all this?" asked Martin.

"I know because the young cop came back later to question me. He wanted to know if I saw the arrest and told me: '2.4 milligrams.' Seems they don't see 'em drunk like that too often."

So it was true.

"Thanks, Christine. You can count on my discretion."

The affair was going to make waves. But he would have to be careful. Dagenais might have been brought to his knees, but he was not dead yet. And there were still a lot of people whose strings he pulled.

Martin returned to the office. While waiting for a sign of life from police captain Lapierre, he wanted to find out the names of the officers involved. Dagenais was right. This could do their careers a lot of damage, even if he was found guilty. And since they would probably be under Lapierre's command for a few years yet, the captain would have plenty of opportunity to make them pay. He had to find out the officers' names before the press conference, for he was convinced that the captain would try to suppress the information. The best way of finding out more was to go to the place where the officers took their breaks.

The policemen in Maniwaki took over from each other, and the La Pizzeria restaurant was where they gathered. Everyone knew why. During the daytime, the officers paid like anyone else, but at night their pizza was free. The owner benefited from incomparable police protection.

Martin arrived at lunchtime. There were a few customers, but the "wolfpack," as they were called, had not yet arrived. The big round table was always reserved for them. He looked around at the other tables and recognised Serge Auger, president of the local Optimists Club. Auger was what was known as a nice guy, one of those people who do volunteer work for the pleasure of doing good. He never looked for recognition and the journalist had great difficulty convincing him to let him take his picture when he was covering the club's activities.

"May I join you?" asked Martin.

"Of course!" replied Serge Auger, offering him a seat.

And of course they began talking about the subject of the day until the first policemen arrived. Martin recognised several of them, who politely nodded at him in greeting. The police avoided journalists like the plague. Everything they said could be turned against them, and that is generally what happened. Laflamme, the last to arrive, was a great nitwit. Caricatures of policemen could have been done using him as a model. The cop despised Martin and had a hard time hiding it. He immediately fired off an insult.

"Something smells bad around here," said Laflamme.

"Must be the dead bodies in your closet," replied Martin.

He had no regrets about making Laflamme look like a clod. That's what he was. In any case, Martin was not sure he was smart enough to understand that he was being made fun of. But he did not want the wolfpack to close ranks around Laflamme, either. He had to play it cool, not go straight to the point.

"I know what you want. You want to know what's going on with the president of the Regional Committee on Industry. Don't count on me to tell you anything," Laflamme shot back, proud of himself, thinking he had been shrewd.

In fact, the fool had just confirmed there was police business involving Dagenais. His colleague, Officer Fortin, who was brighter, recognised the blunder.

"Anyway, we don't even know who's involved and we don't have to talk about it. You can talk to the chief," said Officer Fortin.

Martin sensed that he had to redeem the situation; otherwise he would never learn anything.

"The Dagenais affair is old news. Everyone's talking about it," he bluffed. "At this point, the only thing I don't know yet about last night is how many litres of urine he pissed."

Martin suddenly remembered the story of the old man who had been intercepted on the Gatineau River, and he turned the conversation to the subject.

"What I'd really like to know is, who are the heroes who saved the old guy from drowning? Someone told me it was the two new officers – what are their names?"

"Gauthier and Morin? Come off it, they weren't even on duty!"

Bingo! Martin had their names, their last names anyway. They were the only two new guys at the station, and from what Christine had said, rookies had made the arrest. Given the right decoy, tongues could sometimes be loosened up.

"Actually, no one saved that old man from drowning. In fact, I've hardly ever seen a guy of his age in such good shape. When we got to him, he was portaging around the Paugan Dam and was just about to get back on the river. And I can tell you, it took all we had to keep up with him," explained Fortin.

"But tell me it's not true that he wants to go to Newfoundland," said Martin, this time with real interest.

"It would appear that he does," replied Officer Fortin.

"Another old guy who's losing his marbles?" suggested the journalist.

"I'm not sure about that. I talked to him for an hour and I wouldn't say he has Alzheimer's…or that he's crazy. How can I put it? You'd almost think he comes from another world, another time, or something between the two. An original, but definitely not crazy."

The officer's tone surprised him. It was obvious that the old man had made a big impression on him. He was still moved by their encounter.

"But if he didn't do anything illegal, why did you arrest him?"

"We didn't arrest him. We put him into preventive detention," said Fortin.

The second sentence was almost a murmur, as if he did not want anyone to hear it.

"The other day, they published a photo of a killer in Montreal. He was put into preventive detention too. What's the difference?"

"Uh…it's a family matter, it'd be better if you asked someone else."

The policeman was suddenly ill at ease. Martin told himself that it was over and he was not going to learn anything more. And indeed, no one in the group said a word to him during the meal. Then, just as he was about to leave, Officer Fortin let the others go ahead and leaned over Martin's shoulder.

"Listen, there's something that bugs me about this business with the old man. There's something not right about it. You should look into it." There were people on every corner telling Martin he should "look into" something. Usually, the person who said it had a vested interest in the news being publicised. But Martin sensed that the officer was truly moved. And it was no easy matter to move a policeman who had spent ten years on the force and seen so much human drama.

For the second time that day, the story intrigued him. Even more than the affair of "King Dagenais" and all his underhanded dealings. The businessman's arrest in a state of inebriation had not surprised him. On the contrary, the bastard had been driving drunk for years. It was common knowledge. But the case was much bigger than the story of the old canoeist, which would have to wait.

※

Three journalists from the local press were in attendance for the police captain's press conference. The Ottawa daily *Le Droit* had even assigned their legal affairs reporter to the case. He sat solemnly at the front of the room like a great journalist. The young woman journalist from the community radio station fluttered around him admiringly. And he was probably asking himself whether he would let himself be tempted by her or go straight back to Ottawa. Martin arrived a few minutes later and nodded to his two colleagues in greeting. The young journalist nodded back, but the journalist from the Ottawa daily did not deign to reply.

"What a pretentious bugger!" thought Martin. "Real journalism is a humble task." But truth to tell, he would not have spit on a better salary and decent working conditions, which a job on a daily newspaper could have offered him.

Captain Lapierre finally arrived, accompanied by the regional liaison officer, a kind of publicist whose job it was to water down information so it no longer meant anything.

"Madam, gentlemen…"

It was a rare moment in the life of Lapierre. Someone from the regional office had to be there for him to pompously address the journalists as "madam" and "gentlemen."

"Madam, gentlemen, as you perhaps already know, last night we carried out the arrest of an individual at the wheel of his car. The individual, Mister Pierre Dagenais, fifty-two years old, of Maniwaki, was taken to the police station, where he underwent a breathalyser test conducted by an officer duly trained in the procedure. The test revealed 0.09 milligrams of alcohol in the blood, whereas the allowed limit is 0.08 milligrams. The case has been referred to the Crown Prosecutor, who will determine whether there are grounds to charge Mr. Dagenais with impaired driving. That is all I can tell you at the present time without jeopardising the inquiry."

Martin was astounded. This did not at all correspond with his information. So Lapierre had not succeeded in saving the day for his buddy Dagenais, but he had managed to get him off lightly.

The reporter from *Le Droit* asked what time the event had occurred, and when the court appearance would take place. The young community radio reporter asked if he was alone at the wheel, which made Lapierre laugh. She blushed from head to toe, realising her blunder.

"Yes, of course he was alone at the wheel, but if the object of your question was to find out if he was alone in the vehicle, the answer is also yes."

Martin raised his hand, Lapierre pretended not to see him. "Three journalists in the room and he can't see me raise my hand," Martin mused.

"If there are no other questions…."

"I have a few questions," said Martin.

Lapierre glared at him.

"Yes, Mister Éthier, but keep it short."

"Tell me, at what address did the arrest occur?"

"I don't have that information with me. It's on rue Principale," said Lapierre, scowling.

"Was the address not 124 rue Principale?"

"It's possible. Anyway, it could have happened around there."

"Was the car driving in the street or had it just left a parking lot?"

"A parking lot, I believe, but I couldn't say for sure."

"So if I say the arrest took place in the area of 124 rue Principale, I'm not making a mistake?"

"No."

"Isn't 124 rue Principale the Four Star strip club?"

"Do not attribute statements to me that I have not made," said Lapierre. His voice grew a little louder with each of the journalist's questions.

"No, but the Four Star bar is the only place on the street that has its own parking lot, and it's located at 124 rue Principale. So if Mister Dagenais was coming out of a parking lot, it would have to be that one, wouldn't it?"

"That will be revealed in court," was all he answered.

"Could you tell us the names of the officers who made the arrest?"

"That information will be made public when the officers testify at the trial. For the moment, I can't tell you anything."

"Is it true that officers Morin and Gauthier, from the Maniwaki precinct, have been put on desk duty as of this morning and forbidden contact with their union representative?"

It was a crude bluff, but Martin had heard that the two young policemen had been given a good talking-to and been separated from the "wolfpack" to do administrative tasks. In other words, they had been shelved. Martin was not sure about this information, but it was his only chance of making Lapierre talk. Here, in front of the journalist from the only daily paper and the officer from the regional detachment office, he could not play too many tricks. Lapierre came close to exploding, which made him lose his cool.

"We never stopped them from contacting their union representative, that is incorrect."

Bull's eye! Martin had guessed right. Lapierre had more or less confirmed the names of the agents involved.

"But they're on desk and not patrol duty?"

"I don't have to answer that. That is an internal matter. Any other questions?" he said, looking over Martin's head.

He was clearly addressing the other journalists, who did not dare add anything.

"Yes, I've got another question. Will there be any charges of assault or resisting arrest laid against Mister Dagenais?"

"Not on your life! There was never any question of that."

"But didn't Mister Dagenais resist arrest?"

"No," replied Lapierre stoically.

"Then tell us about the injuries one of the officers sustained during the altercation with Mister Dagenais. How serious are these injuries?"

Lapierre was fuming. He felt cornered. He hesitated, and then reiterated his lie.

"No, there was no resistance."

"Yet an eye-witness saw a police officer arrive at the hospital emergency with blood on his face only a few minutes after the reported time of Mister Dagenais' arrest. I also have a witness who was at the scene and saw Mister Dagenais hit one of the policemen in the face."

"This press conference is terminated," the liaison officer said hastily, seeing that the meeting was getting out of hand.

The local journalists were pushed towards the exit while Lapierre and the liaison officer took the journalist from *Le Droit* aside. They were obviously going to try to repair the damage Martin had done. If the story were only reported in *La Gazette*, it would quite possibly die of its own accord.

But it was a big story, and Martin was in the middle of it. He was alone in contesting the official version, and his questions all tended to reveal a despicable attempt at a cover-up on the part of the chief of police. But there were still a lot of loose ends to be tied up before he could publish a piece contradicting the official version of events.

Arriving at the office, Martin started typing frantically on his keyboard, looking for his lead, a single sentence in the first paragraph which would sum up the facts for the reader and put the story into context. Therein lay the art of journalistic writing. Some of his leads were true gems. He could concentrate for twenty minutes, sometimes more when there was no deadline pressure, sitting deep in thought in front of his computer screen. When inspiration came, the piece was written in several minutes.

He did not hear his boss come in, and when he looked up was surprised to see him standing there. There were only two occasions when the boss came down from his second-floor office: at Christmas, when he distributed their meagre bonuses, or when a leading citizen called him to say that one of his employees had done a bad job. Martin understood that this time it was the second option, not because he had done a bad job but because Christmas was a long time away. His boss had no doubt received a call from Lapierre, with whom he shared a passion for golf.

His boss was visibly ill at ease. He did not quite know how to broach the subject. Martin was a good journalist, and he knew it. He also knew that his journalist's suspicions were probably well founded and that it would be difficult to steer him away from the truth.

"Listen, Martin, I don't think we're giving enough coverage to what's happening in the south. The mayor of Lac Sainte-Marie complained about it again. So I've decided we're going to do a series of in-depth reports, a kind of portrait of those municipalities. You'll go meet everyone in each municipality, the mayor, the parish priest, the president of the seniors' club, and put it all into a nice story, as only you can do. After that, the publicist will come by and we'll do a special feature. Two pages per municipality," he said.

Martin was not fooled. He was getting him away from the Maniwaki bureau and most of all, from the Dagenais affair.

"I have to finish these articles first."

"Just leave them with the student intern, it'll give him a chance to write about something other than dogs hit by cars."

The intern? He could not tell the difference between a seniors' item and a top story. Martin remembered the first time that the cub reporter had arrived in the office, claiming he had a scoop. Martin hastened to question him, only to learn that his scoop was the name of the new president of the Optimists Club.

To give this story to the intern was a good way of detracting attention from it. Sick at heart, Martin called Benoît on the in-house line to prep him. He did not want to abandon the story but had no choice. He had to get young Benoît working for him, snooping around in his stead.

"Listen, Benoît, the boss wants it to be you who covers this story. Big Dagenais is in up to his neck and the chief of police wants to protect him, or at least reduce the charges that could be held against him. I want you to try and find out more. That's our job. We're not mouthpieces for the police, or the Regional Committee on Industry, or even the boss. Our job is to investigate, understand, find proof and report the truth to keep the readers informed."

"I understand," said Benoît, who seemed to grasp the significance of Martin's message. He did not have a lot of backbone, but he possessed the fervour of a true journalist.

"You have to find out what happened with Officer Gauthier. Go hang out where the cops do. They'll end up spilling the beans, because they don't like it when one of their own gets roughed up and someone's trying to protect the perp. Also try and find out what happened in the strip bar and who Dagenais was there with. If someone agrees to talk to you, record it for backup and keep the information to yourself until we've spoken."

Benoît agreed. He trusted Martin, but he also feared the boss's fury, which could lose him this first job, obtained with such difficulty. Martin brought the conversation to an end, and took care of a few last details.

The big boss paid him a visit and put a cheque for $500 on his desk.

"To pay the expenses for your report," he said.

Martin would have liked to be in a position where he could throw the cheque in his boss's face, demanding whether it was his money or Dagenais', but he preferred to hold his tongue. His pay was meagre and he needed the cheque. It was useless to play Mr. Virtuous. He put the cheque in his pocket.

❧

Martin left Maniwaki the next day and went to Lac Sainte-Marie, where he began his first report. He met with the mayor, a kindly man who talked about his village with great feeling. The man was delighted to finally see a journalist in his municipality, and he gave him the grand tour. To play up to the journalist, he invited him to dinner at the Centre Mont Sainte-Marie, a prestigious ski and golf resort that had been established in his municipality fifteen years before. The dinner was accompanied by several bottles of excellent wine. Martin had reserved a room in the hotel of the ski centre, stipulating that the bill should be sent to the newspaper.

"I won't hear of it, the municipality will pay," the mayor had said, only too happy for the free publicity.

"Thank you very much, but my boss is absolutely intent on leaving some money here. After all, Lac Sainte-Marie is part of our territory," replied Martin, smiling to himself.

"In that case…"

The room had to cost around $120 a night. Martin wondered how the boss was going to take it. Too bad for him!

From his hotel room, he managed to reach Benoît at home.

"It's kind of strange," said Benoît.

"What do you mean, strange?"

"Well, I wasn't expecting the office of Mister Dagenais to return my calls, but he ended up calling me back in person."

"What…? He returned your call?"

"Yes, and what's more, he seemed to be in a very good mood. I wanted to ask him a few questions about his arrest, but he answered that he had much bigger news, and that in any case, his lawyer had advised him not to talk about it."

"But what exactly did he want?"

"He wanted to talk to me about a plan for a billboard factory. He said that very soon he'll have big news to announce, a piece of news that'll bring hundreds of jobs to the region. What do you think?"

"A good way for him to shift the attention, when everyone wants to know more about his little tantrum the other night."

"As a matter of fact, he said that once people knew, they would understand why all that happened, and that he was just working for the good of the region."

"Generally when Big Dagenais works for the good of anyone, it's himself…or to take away someone else's."

"But it sounded serious," insisted Benoît.

"Did he give you the details, the name of the business, or where they'd set up this famous factory?"

"No, but he said that we'll know very soon. There are just a few details that need ironing out. He said it was 'almost in the bag.' That's how he put it," emphasised Benoît.

"You could try finding out more from the industrial commissioner. If there's a project underway, they'll be in the know. If the story's true, I wouldn't mind seeing them cut the grass under his feet, otherwise he'll use it to make himself out to be a saint. Did you get the details of his arrest?" added Martin.

"I talked to the police union representative. He wasn't in a very good mood. I don't think he likes Mister Dagenais too much," said Benoît.

This way of always calling the shady businessman "Mister" irritated Martin. But Benoît tended to call everyone "Mister."

"Did he tell you anything?"

"Not much, just that his union was investigating the circumstances of his arrest. He could file a complaint if it were proven that someone intervened to reduce the charges against Mister Dagenais, but he was being very cagey. I got the feeling he'd been instructed to discuss it as little as possible, which goes against his nature."

"Yes, he's got a damn big mouth when it comes to defending police officers, even when they're in the wrong. Did you do any other checking?"

"I went to the courthouse to see if any official charges had been laid. Nothing yet, but apparently that's not unusual. Weeks can go by before they institute proceedings. However…," said Benoît, hesitating.

"However, what?"

"There were quite a lot of people at the courthouse. Lawyers I've never seen before."

"Lawyers? For Dagenais?"

"I don't think so. At least that's what they told me, but obviously they know him, because when I asked the court clerk if there were any new developments about charges against Mister Dagenais, their ears all perked up and they asked me if I was talking about the president of the Regional Committee on Industry."

"You're sure they weren't there for Dagenais?"

"Yes. According to the clerk, they were there for another case. Some story about mental incompetence."

"That's strange," said Martin.

Martin said he would contact him later and gave him a few leads for continuing his inquiry. Then he turned on his computer and started writing his piece about the municipality of Lac Sainte-Marie. Though he would have preferred to be probing the Dagenais affair, Martin did not dislike doing this kind of reporting. It gave him the opportunity to be around nice people, like the mayor, for example. He might be a little awkward and make mincemeat of the language of Molière, while treating him to a lavish dinner to get good coverage, but he was very pleasant. He talked about his municipality and its people with respect and affection. He made you want to listen. And Martin chose to write about the human side of what he had seen that day, the people he had met and spoken with. He wanted these people's love for their village to come through in his article.

The next day, he decided to go to Low to start his second report. Low is a small municipality with deep Irish roots. The village was founded by the Irish immigrants who came to work in the lumber camps. At this spot on the Gatineau River, the surrounding mountains blocked the flow of the water and forced it through a narrow passage, where it descended several metres over a short distance. The first inhabitants made their homes down by the foot of the rapids and the place was simply called "Low." In 1928, the Gatineau Power Company constructed a dam on the formidable rapids. At the time, it was the biggest hydroelectric dam in the world. At the height of its construction, close to fifteen hundred people lived in the village. For a brief time, Low had the appearances of a real city. Then the last brick was laid on the dam and the population rapidly dwindled. Today, there were no more than five hundred people living there. They had kept to their old Irish roots. Stubborn and proud, that is how they were, clinging to the memory of a time that was gone forever.

The best way of taking the pulse of the area was to go to the village *dépanneur*.[14] *Dépanneur*? The word was poorly chosen. *Dépanneur* – post office – liquor store – head office of the Lion's Club – town hall – barber – all would have been a more accurate way of describing the true vocation of the place. People went there to buy things of course, but also, and most especially, to talk, shoot the breeze. If there was something to know about the village, this was where you would find out about it.

He entered. As in the old general stores, a little bell over the door tinkled to announce the arrival of a customer. Five people were there, deep in discussion. Martin greeted the owner behind the counter and went to get a soft drink from the refrigerator. He paid, opened the bottle, and asked the owner what was going on around town.

"Nothing ever happens in Low. You get the feeling the government's forgotten us," he said, grumbling.

It was always the government's fault when something happened... or did not happen. No one got offended when someone railed against the government. Martin pretended to be concentrating on magazines in the stand next to the counter. Most were issues from the previous month. He did not want to enter the conversation uninvited, or without having found an opportunity to make a contribution that the others would welcome. One learned much more from letting people talk than from firing questions at them.

"Apparently the guy is crazy," one of them was saying.

"I wouldn't be so sure of that, young fellow."

The man talking had to be seventy or eighty years old and the "young fellow" to whom he was speaking had to be sixty. Martin smiled.

"Anyway, it's rare we see police in these parts. Most of the time, they completely forget about us. Even when Widow McNeel had her accident, they just asked if there was anyone hurt. When we told them no, they told us to make an 'unofficial statement' because they wouldn't be coming by."

"Then they show up for a little old man in a canoe."

Martin was startled. The old man again! Clearly he was making people talk, even here, a hundred kilometres from Maniwaki. Forgetting his reserve, he asked the person who had just been talking:

---

[14.] *Quebecois word for a corner store.*

"Did you see the man yourself?"

"Not personally, but the dam guy did."

"Dam guy" was what they called the only person still working at the dam. Since Quebec's nationalisation of electricity in 1963, there remained only one permanent employee to take care of the immense dam. Sometimes maintenance employees came to make repairs, but the "dam guy" was entirely in charge of supervising the premises, checking the dials, and all in all, doing very little with his days. People in the village would joke when they met him with his wife: "Hey, there's the dam guy and his *dame*."

Forgetting the main objective of his visit to the municipality, Martin went over to the hydroelectric dam. The structure stood less than a kilometre from the village. A steep little road led up to the top. It was a strange sensation to see the water's surface only a metre below road level on one side of the road, with a drop of almost one hundred metres on the other. At the foot of the dam, the river resumed its course.

When Martin got to the top of the dam, Jack Saint-Jean, the watchman, was there. He appeared to be conducting an inspection that was as futile as it was artificial, spurred by the sudden arrival of a visitor. Very few people came around the dam, even though it was the only place for kilometres where one could cross the river. Hardly ten vehicles passed each day, but every time one did, he made a point of looking as if he were hard at work. French Canadian by birth, Jacques Saint-Jean had married a woman of English origin. Her family had come directly from England and she felt this gave her a title of nobility and a superior social status to the natives of the country. She had so often and so thoroughly denigrated the "French frogs" that Jacques had decided to stop speaking French, or at least pretend he did not speak it whenever the occasion arose. He had shortened his name to Jack and his last name was now pronounced "Saint Gene."

"Hello, Monsieur Saint-Jean," said Martin, pronouncing his name the French way and introducing himself as a reporter from *La Gazette*.

"Sainte-Gene," corrected Jack, insisting on the English pronunciation.

"I've come to see you about the man who apparently arrived here by canoe."

"Are you going to take my photo?" the "dam guy" asked, a smile of delight on his face.

This was not Martin's intention, but he knew very well that there was nothing better for getting people to talk than the idea of seeing their photo in the paper. Ordinary people never got talked about in newspapers, and for them it was probably a once-in-a-lifetime opportunity.

"But of course, that's just what I came for," lied Martin, taking out his camera. After all, the story about the *old man in the canoe* was starting to interest him more than anything, and he would need photographs to illustrate an eventual article.

Jack thrust his chest out and asked the photographer if he could see the whole dam behind him. He suggested a few other poses, "to better illustrate the article," he said.

"Take a photo here, this is where it happened. I'll point to the place on the ground while you're taking the photo."

Martin found it ridiculous. This photo made him think of a photo he had seen on the front page of one of those strange American magazines that report on extraterrestrial invasions each week. And this story was not about a Martian any more than it was about a murderer. Nevertheless, he took another photo.

Jacques Saint-Jean seemed satisfied by the range of photos that had been taken.

"So tell me," said Martin. "Did you see this man?"

"As well as I can see you," he said. "He was coming from the north, and waved to me. Then he got out of the canoe and we talked a bit. After that, he loaded his canoe and his pack on his back, and continued by road."

"He took the canoe on his back?" asked Martin incredulously. "The man has got to be eighty-seven or eighty-eight, if I've got my facts straight!"

"He was no youngster, that's for sure, but he looked like he was in pretty good shape. And most of all, he seemed to know about canoes. Me, I've never trusted those boats, they tip like the devil."

"Did he tell you where he was going?"

"Well, he said he was going down to Hull and from there he intended to follow the current to Montreal, and even farther, to…I can't really remember the name…I think it was Pogo or something like that…"

"And he seemed all right to you, this man?"

"A guy who can carry a canoe on his shoulders at the age of eighty-eight can't be sick."

"No, I mean, did the man seem disturbed, crazy?"

"Not a bit. He even taught me all sorts of things I didn't know about the dam. He came through here by canoe before it was built, you know, and he described how it was back then. Seems there were quite the rapids. Then he came by again during the construction. You know, there may be one of my ancestors in this dam, a Saint-Jean," this time he pronounced it the French way, "who apparently fell into the cement while it was being poured. He sunk, and they left his body in the foundation. That man knew about it," he said proudly.

"Did you see the police when they came to pick him up?" asked Martin.

"I sure did. Not that I don't have better things to do," he added, to justify his curiosity. "But I was in the middle of my rounds. He was heading down with his canoe on his back when they came by. They drove up here to turn the car around then went back down. They had to chase him down that little trail you see there," he said, pointing down at a path that was barely visible. "One of the policemen even fell flat on his back."

"And did he go with them quietly, or did he put up a fight?"

"From here, I couldn't hear what they were saying, but I don't think so. They talked, then he went with them."

"And they left the canoe there?"

"Yes, yes, but he came back to get it later that day."

"Who, the policeman?"

"No! The man. He came back late afternoon."

"How? In a truck?"

"No, no, he came by foot and got back on the river with his canoe. He even called out and waved goodbye. Lucky I was here, because I could have been busy somewhere else on the dam," he said, once again justifying the way he used his time. Clearly, the man had a lot of free moments in which to watch what was going on in the general area.

"Did the police come back?"

"They sure did, they even came up to ask me some questions. I told them what I just told you. They didn't look too happy."

Martin thanked him and promised to let him know when the article was going to be published.

Decidedly, this story was becoming more and more interesting. It seemed the old man had slipped through their fingers and carried on with his voyage. Martin already had more material for this story than what he had gathered in the past two days.

Back in his hotel room at Mont Sainte-Marie, he phoned Benoît to find out what was happening with the Dagenais affair.

"Not much. Nobody's talking," Benoît told him.

"Well anyway, we may know more in the next few days. I'd like you to find out about the old man the police picked up on the river. It seems he gave them the slip."

"Funny you should mention that. You know, the lawyers I told you about yesterday were here about him. And they weren't cheapies, either. Lawyers from Montreal."

"From Montreal? Listen, Benoît, I want to know everything about this man: his name, where he comes from, who his neighbours are, what he used to do for a living. Also try and find out if anyone was in the know about his strange expedition. Too bad the lawyers aren't here any more, you could have grilled them," said Martin.

"They're still in Maniwaki."

The information astonished him. Lawyers from Montreal for a story like this! It didn't make sense. Clearly the man was hiding something interesting. If he couldn't go after Big Dagenais, he reflected, this might be his chance to write a very nice article.

# Six

The boat sailed to Montreal where it made a stop. The human cargo changed to another means of transport. Adela only caught a glimpse of the city, for they were quickly herded to a train station and onto a train bound for Ottawa. Loaves of bread were distributed, and eating calmed her stomach a little. What else could she do but follow? Escape? But where? She felt as if she were on another planet. A lot of the people around her were speaking French. Adela had learned to mistrust these people, remembering the stories she had been told about them.

    The train slowly made its way to Ottawa, which older people still referred to as Bytown, though the city had long since become the capital of Canada. The man in charge of the convoy made them get out, and another man came to meet them. He told them they would be leaving the next day for the lumber camps in the northern Gatineau. Shelter had been provided for those who did not have the money to pay for a room, that is to say, everyone. In fact, the shelter was a stable and each person had to make a mattress out of hay. But that was more comfortable than what Adela had been sleeping on since leaving Fogo Island. In what looked to have been a horse's stall, Adela made a pile of hay big enough so that she would be warm and comfortable. The people around her were doing the same. She literally buried herself in the hay. She could smell the odours of the stable, the smell of horses and hay.

    She was deeply asleep when she felt a hand touch her ankle, then grab and pull on it. She instantly woke up, but it took her a few seconds to realise where she was. She felt herself being dragged from her bed of hay while another hand clamped down over her mouth. She could now feel fingers rooting under her skirt. She tried to cry out, but her attacker held her down firmly, preventing her from uttering a sound. She was trapped, and she knew what this man wanted. She did not know who he was, but his intentions were clear. In spite of her struggles, she was not able to push him away or get out from under him. He yanked at her underwear and tore it. Adela was seized with panic. The man's free hand moved down to unfasten his trousers. Adela felt the cold touch of his belt buckle against her thigh, and a few seconds later, the hardened member. She could feel his breath and his whiskers against her cheek. Her legs started to thrash in every direction. It seemed that she had touched a strategic point, for suddenly the hand over her mouth fell away. The one rooting under her dress withdrew at the same moment and the man uttered a stifled cry. She sat up in a single bound and retreated, panting, to the back of the stall. Her hand made contact with a hard object. It was a piece of wood partly covered in metal, with loops. It was part of a horse team's harness. Though she could see absolutely nothing in the darkness, she took hold of the piece of wood and lashed out in front of her. The second time she swung it around, it hit something squarely. She heard a thud, like someone falling on the ground.

"I'll get you, bitch!" a man's voice yelled.

Adela was ready to hit him again, but she heard the sound of footsteps retreating. She spent the rest of the night awake, sitting on the floor with her back against the wall of the wooden stall, holding the piece of harness. She was trembling from head to foot. The touch of her attacker's member kept coming into her mind and made her stomach turn. How could the same act be so revolting, when it had been so sweet the first time she had been with a man?

Anyone who came near would have been struck with the piece of wood, no matter what his intentions. When day broke, Adela was still terrified. She still did not know who had attacked her. She had not seen him. She did not even know if he was tall. But she had smelled him, and it made her stomach heave to think of it. He smelled of sweat and dirt, the accumulated grime of weeks. His breath smelled of alcohol and his shaggy beard had touched her face. She knew he was probably in this stable, but did not dare look any of the men in the face for fear of provoking a new attack. Who was he? Where was he? She wanted to flee, but where could she go? She was trapped and could not imagine how she would ever return home. She thought of her two sisters and two brothers who remained at home, all younger than herself. She also thought of her parents. Her mother and her father would die of grief if they knew why she had left.

Everyone around her was gathering his belongings without paying any attention to her. They could not have helped hearing what had happened, yet everyone was acting as if the attack had occurred miles away. She held on tight to her bundle of possessions, still holding the weapon, which she was reluctant to abandon. She threw it away almost regretfully, and followed the others; she did not know where they were going, but resigned herself to following them to whatever hell they were all being led to.

The air was permeated with the odour of freshly sawn wood. It was a good smell. A man came up and introduced himself as Reed. He explained that they had to cross Hull and from there, wagons from the Gilmour and Hughson Company, for whom they would be working, would take them up the Gatineau River. Carts full of foodstuffs formed the procession, which set out on the mud road that ran along the river bank. The caravan crawled along for a long time. Passing Wakefield, they saw railway men doing the last bit of work on the new tracks. The two groups barely noticed each other.

Adela might have been frightened by everything that was happening to her, but the beautiful, oppressive landscape took her breath away. The white pines were immense, gigantic, much taller than the masts of the biggest boats she had ever seen. Never, in Fogo, did a tree grow so big. The trunks of certain trees were so thick that one could have cut a hole in them big enough for a cart to pass through, a cart like the one she was riding in, without the tree falling down.

She felt caged in by this horizon that stopped at the forest. In Fogo Island, the horizon stretched as far as the eye could see. Here, the view was limited to a few metres on either side of the road. The only places one could see farther were gaps in the trees through which the river could be glimpsed. After a day on the road, the troop reached a "stopping place" where they could finally eat a hot meal of pork and beans and bread. Adela, who had always hated the fish that made up practically every meal at home, started to dream of a meal of pan-fried cod, which her mother prepared so well, served with "scrunchions," little pieces of streaky bacon that had been cooked at high heat until they were almost dry. Her mouth watered just thinking of it.

When night fell, once again the group had to make do with a barn to sleep in. In this stable, there was not much difference between the animals and themselves. In a way, they were all slaves of the company.

Adela was discovering all this from one minute to the next. It occupied her mind and stopped her from thinking about her family. Sitting in the hay, she nibbled at her piece of bread, staring into space. She looked at the magnificent field that stretched out on a gentle slope in front of the farm. She had never seen such a large stretch of arable ground, at least not one that was owned by a single tenant. In Fogo, they grew vegetables between the stones. There was always a barrier of rock that limited the size of a tract of land. They planted in spots where there was enough earth between the boulders to grow something. Each handful of arable soil was precious. Several centimetres below the surface, the earth was rock. But here, she had seen a big hole being dug for the foundation of a house. The hole had to have been two metres deep and there was still no sign of rock.

"The Lord may have given us fish to eat but this is where he put all the soil," she said to herself.

Gazing off into the distance, she did not notice the man passing through her range of vision. However, she noticed that he slowed down and was looking at her from the corner of his eye. Coming out of her reverie, her eyes slid over to him. She wondered why he was looking at her so aggressively. When he turned, she noticed that his ear was bandaged.

"It's him," she thought, horrified.

The man had red hair. His eyes frightened her, perverse, wicked eyes, close-set on either side of a nose that was curved like the beak of a bird of prey. Adela was on her feet in a second, looking around for help, for someone to whom she could yell for help, but the man was coming towards her menacingly. In an English that left no doubt about his Irish origins he said: "Listen, chickie. I don't know where you come from, but here you're exactly like the rest of us worthless immigrants. So if you're thinking of opening your trap, I suggest you start saying your prayers."

Adela was chilled. She wanted to cry out, but no sound came out of her mouth. She wanted to run, but her legs were paralysed. The man still smelled of sweat and his breath reeked of the alcohol he had consumed the day before. He walked away, giving her a murderous glance.

Terrified, not knowing what to do, she went out of the stable and headed for the adjoining house. As she arrived, a lady came out on the stoop, about to draw water from a well with a hand pump. On the island some people, though not many, had this type of pump, which enabled them to draw enough much water as they needed in just a few seconds.

"May I help you, young lady?" asked the plump woman in French.

Her smile was inviting and she seemed nice. This was the first friendly gesture anyone had made towards Adela since she left Fogo. Unfortunately, she did not understand a word of what the woman was saying. It was her first real contact with someone who spoke French. Of course, she had heard a lot of people speaking French when she was transferred from the boat in Quebec City. She had also heard it in Ottawa and when they had crossed the bridge to get on the cart, but no one had actually addressed her.

Adela started to speak to her in English, but she realised that the good lady, who still had a big smile on her face, did not understand a word of what she was saying. She almost fled with no explanation, but the woman's smile was so hospitable and friendly that she did not want to leave. She would have very much liked to wash, for since leaving Fogo, her toilette had been minimal. But most of all, the memory of her attacker made the odour of sweat rise to her nostrils. She felt unclean. Adela pointed to the pump and tried to mime someone washing.

"Ah, you want to wash? Well, of course, go ahead," she said, with an inviting gesture. "Water is for everyone. And I've always said that to be clean is the best way of keeping illness away."

Adela understood nothing in this deluge of words rattled off so quickly, but the tone of voice and the smile spoke volumes. When she rolled up her sleeves to wash in the cold water, the lady gently took her sleeve and invited her inside. Adela thought of running away. The woman was the lady of the manor. Her husband, Jeffrey McConnery, son of an Irish immigrant, liked the French-speaking Catholic milieu in Quebec much more than that of the English landowners, who were just as scornful and domineering as they were in his native Ireland. The cold and distant temperament did not suit him. The French Canadians were a nation of humble people. They liked to celebrate. So did he. They were Catholic. So was he. They hated the English. So did he.

He had met Marie and had immediately loved her. For her smile, especially. Perhaps also because of her lovely plump figure, which gave her a look of health, life and joy. In the Lafrenière family, no one was happy seeing her go around with an Englishman. "English speaking" meant Englishman, with no distinction made as to where he came from. And even though they knew the Irish were Catholic, religion did not excuse everything. But Jeff had decided to make himself accepted at all costs, and had immediately adopted the language of the people. In any case, Marie spoke her husband's language very little. Jeff had insisted that she speak to him in French so that he could learn it. This prevented him from getting a foreman's job on the company farm, as he otherwise would have done due to the fact that he spoke English. He was well aware of it.

Adela was torn between the lady's inviting smile and everything she had been told about the French. The people who attacked the fishermen's colonies in her island's legends could not be of the same race as this woman who had such a nice face. Was it possible she might drag her inside and give herself over to the baser instincts of her people? Adela followed her inside, ready to cry out and fight if the woman attacked. The woman's hand was holding her arm, not firmly or roughly, but with a great deal of warmth. The young Newfoundlander was hypnotised by this woman who continued to say words she did not understand. She pulled aside a curtain that concealed a magnificent bathtub with feet. Adela looked at it, incredulous before such hospitality. She had never used a real bathtub. At home, they washed, of course. Her mother was very strict about cleanliness, but they washed themselves with a bar of soap and a washtub.

The bathtub was hidden in the corner of the kitchen so that water boiled on the stove could be easily poured into it. The lady had her sit down in a chair at the end of the kitchen table while she put the water on to boil. She said all sorts of words, pointing to this and that, but Adela could not understand her. The lady came to her and leaned down. Her radiant look had been replaced by a melancholy smile. Her voice too became warmer, gentler, almost a murmur: "I don't know what happened to you, but you look like a wild cat caught in a trap. I don't know where you come from either, but obviously it's not from around here. And you're not Irish. How on earth did such a young girl end up here with this pack of wolves? You need a little bit of warmth, child," said Marie.

Her hand stroked her cheek as she was talking. Adela was no longer afraid. She did not understand anything, but it was the first time anyone had been kind to her since she left Fogo Island. Like a beaver dam that bursts in springtime when the waters swell, all the emotion built up over the past few days was suddenly released. She cried her heart out and Marie did nothing to stop her. Adela rested her head in the warm hollow between the woman's ample breasts. There, the child she remained found the maternal affection she had thought was lost for good. Marie held her, stroking her hair for several long minutes.

"Cry, darling, it will do you good."

This woman had understood everything about her without any words being exchanged. Her voice was gentle and comforting. Marie went to close the two doors that gave access to the kitchen and bolted them, making sure Adela took note and felt reassured. She also pulled the curtains and poured the water in the bathtub. Adela let herself slide into it. What sweetness! She felt the dust of the last days melt from her body. She wanted most of all to get rid of the filth of the man's hands, his sweat and his odour, which she thought she could still smell. She rubbed hard at her skin with the bar of soap, trying to erase all trace of her attacker. And the fact that she was able to be alone like this did her good, protected by this matron who was big enough to knock a man over yet who was so gentle too. When she got out of the bath, shy about sharing such private moments with a stranger, she saw that the lady had slipped some clean clothes onto the chair. Her own clothes had been rolled up in a ball and put on the floor.

"I've prepared you some clean clothes. They belonged to me when I was more…when I was younger, let's say. I am not sure they'll suit you but they'll give you time to wash your own clothes. I was keeping them for the day when I would recover my youthful figure. But I've given up on that," said Marie, bursting into laughter.

Adela understood nothing, but from her laugh, she guessed she had just said something funny. She wanted to protest when Marie handed her the clothes, but the woman said: "No! Don't say anything. This is the way it is."

Adela did not have enough bosom to fill out Marie's dress, but otherwise it fit. Most of all, the dress smelled nice. When she came out from behind the curtain, there was a plate of stewed meat waiting for her on the table. At first suspicious, Adela noted that it strangely resembled the "Jigg's dinner" her mother made, except in Tilting, the recipe included salt beef. She ate heartily, sometimes looking at Marie sitting beside her and overflowing with words. Adela would have liked to know what she was saying, for she liked this woman. Marie sometimes touched her hand with her fingertips as she talked. So much warmth in a single touch. Adela told herself with regret that she had to leave her and go back to the stable. She got up, addressing the woman, though knowing she would not understand her: "Thank you for everything. You have been so kind. I'll bring your dress back tomorrow before we leave."

Marie accompanied her out of the house, but did not seem ready to let her go. Adela started heading for the barn, but Marie shook her head vigorously and held her by the arm. She hailed a man who was passing and spoke to him for a few minutes. The man addressed Adela in English.

"You're lucky, child. The boss lady wants you to stay for supper and sleep in the big house. She thinks someone in the stable is scaring you."

So it was true. She had read her mind. It frightened her.

"What's her name?" Adela asked the man, pointing to Marie.

"You've got an odd accent, there. Where are you from?" the man asked.

"*He's* the one with the odd accent," thought Adela. "I come from Fogo. What's her name?" she repeated, more insistently.

"Madame Lafrenière…Marie Lafrenière. And yours?"

"Adela Cole," she said, hesitantly.

"Adela! Where'd you come up with a name like that?"

Adela was certainly not going to tell him that it was the name of a Portuguese boat that her father had seen moored in the port of Tilting. He had found the name charming and decided that was what his newborn daughter would be called. She would have liked to tell Marie the story.

Marie was still waiting.

"So?"

"Tell her thank you," mumbled Adela.

The man seemed to be reporting the words they had exchanged. Marie's face lit up when the man told her Adela's name. She tried to repeat it.

"Adzila," she ended up saying.

Marie accompanied her to the stable. Adela still understood nothing of her flood of words, but recognised her name each time it resonated like a song in the woman's mouth. She inwardly thanked Marie for coming with her, for she would not have liked to be alone in the same room with that man. The young woman hurried over to her bundle of possessions and picked it up without looking at anyone.

Marie led her to the kitchen and offered her a cup of tea, continuing her running monologue. Adela had decided not to remain inactive. Though the floor did not seem to need cleaning, she seized the broom and started a painstaking inspection of every corner, looking for the slightest grain of dust. She felt indebted to this woman.

Her hostess's husband arrived a little later. Adela did not know what to do with herself when he entered, but the man did not seem surprised to see her and greeted her as if it was quite usual for her to be sitting there in the kitchen. He talked with Marie for a few minutes then turned to Adela.

"My wife, Marie, doesn't speak English. It's a bit my fault, because I've always spoken to her in French. She tells me you arrived with the group of Irish. She believes you had problems with the big redheaded fellow. I can make him think twice about doing it again, you know."

"Don't do anything, I beg you, he'll just take it out on me," said Adela, remembering her attacker's threats.

She was happy to talk to someone, especially someone friendly. At least, she supposed he must be friendly. If this man was married to Marie he could only be good. She realised with surprise that in just a few minutes, Marie had managed to dissolve centuries of hatred against the French. But how had this woman managed to guess everything without Adela saying a word? For Marie had immediately understood everything. Her irrepressible need to wash, the distress in her eyes, all this had made Marie understand that the young woman was in desperate circumstances. No need to be a mind reader to understand that a young and pretty girl put in the middle of a group of men risked being the object of sexual violence. When Marie entered the stable, she immediately saw the murderous look of the tall red-haired man and his wounded ear. Marie knew that he was the one as soon as she laid eyes on him.

"Where do you come from and how old are you?"

The question had not yet been asked of her, and Adela was about to tell her everything, but she remembered the words of Captain Bartlett. Would she be hanged if she admitted to being a stowaway? And what about the fact of her illegal entry into Canada? Would it get her thrown in a cell?

"I...I don't come from around here," was all she finally said.

"You don't come from around here, that's obvious. And you're not Irish either, but you speak the old English. Here, in this house, you have nothing to fear."

Adela did not know what to do, but her eyes met Marie's and her last of her fears vanished.

"I...I come from Newfoundland. I got onto Captain Bartlett's boat at Fogo Island to go to St. John's, but he got mad at me and wanted to throw me overboard. In Quebec City, he told me I had to get off and take another boat to go work in a lumber camp to pay for my passage back to Newfoundland," Adela told the story between sobs.

"You mean you were a stowaway?"

"Y...yes," she said weakly.

Jeff knew what it could cost to stow away on a ship. Captains transported many people illegally, but those who did not pay had better beware, for their voyage often ended at the bottom of the sea. He explained to his wife what Adela had just told him. Marie kept her eyes on her, smiling affectionately.

"Ask her how long she's been pregnant," she asked, with no other explanation to her stunned husband.

"Come on, Marie, I can't ask her that, I'm a man."

"Oh, drop the 'I'm a man' business. I can't speak English and have no time to learn. Later, maybe, but for the moment, I want to know."

Visibly ill at ease and not knowing quite how to begin, Jeff reflected on the most acceptable way of broaching the subject.

"Go on!" repeated Marie.

"My wife claims that you are pregnant and wants to know when you're going to have your baby."

Jeff could not understand how Marie could guess these things. The young woman before him seemed no bigger than a doe and there was no thickening around her middle that would have led one to make such a conclusion. Adela's jaw dropped. She could not find the words to reply. Marie had read her like an open book. Again she burst into tears. The lady had also understood that the child had probably been conceived out of wedlock, which would explain why the young woman would want to leave her home in secrecy.

"I haven't had my period for two months," she told Jeff, who hastened to translate.

Marie came to sit down next to her and took her hand. Her eyes were full of compassion, her voice even warmer, more understanding. She talked to her a moment, then turned to her husband, putting on her most persuasive smile.

"This child can't go up to Ottawa Lake in her condition, can she, Jeff? I know you can do something," she said, laying on all the charm she could muster.

She knew Jeff had difficulty resisting her, and she did not take advantage. But sometimes...

"Marie, you're incredible. You think that just because I'm a foreman, I can do whatever I want. But if I don't send her up to the camp at Ottawa Lake, the company will come down hard on me."

"I know you can do something."

Jeff was furious and rushed out of the house. Adela did not understand what had been said, but sensed she was the cause of the dispute.

"Don't you worry, dear, he'll be back for supper and in a good mood again."

She was not wrong. Jeff came back to the house at suppertime and sat down at the head of the table. As Marie started to serve, he scratched his head as if in thought. Marie had won. She knew it, but she also knew that she could not ask him any questions. He would announce it as if it had been his own decision. She was especially eager to see what solution he had come up with. He was pigheaded, as the Irish were, but oh, how she loved her Jeff! Her eyes and her smile were constantly saying so.

"I think I've found something a bit less rough for her," he said, first of all in French. "There's old Latour, who I wanted to send to the Castor Blanc camp as a cook and who'd be more than willing to switch places, since he doesn't get along with the foreman. I think I could send him to Ottawa Lake, and she could replace him at the Castor camp. That way she wouldn't be so far away and she'd be close to the doctor in Maniwaki when her time comes. What do you think?"

"Are you sure this Latour will agree?"

"At Ottawa Lake, Latour can hope to fool around with the Indian women, whereas here there isn't a woman who'd want anything to do with him."

Marie did not like certain men's attitudes towards Indian women. These people had another way of thinking, and such men took advantage of it to get the women pregnant or pass on shameful diseases. But in this case, she was happy about the proclivities of old Latour.

"Well, what I think is that you are wonderful!" she said.

Jeff explained the situation to Adela. He would have liked to help her return home again, but that was impossible. He did not see how he could have done so, especially now, when Adela had to work especially hard at surviving. The Castor Blanc camp was only a day's cart ride from Maniwaki, where she could find a doctor. At the Ottawa Lake camp, Adela would have been far from everything, subjected for eight months to a horde of louts, in conditions so difficult that even certain lumberjacks refused to go there.

Adela did not see how this option was any better than the other. She felt she was a prisoner of a destiny not her own, a destiny she had not chosen.

In the space of several days, Adela had lost her family, her island, her country, and ended up in a place so far away that she would never have been able to find it on a map. She was stranded on the "mainland," as people said. In Fogo, safety was the coastline. All the villages were built there and people rarely ventured into the forest. The forest was mysterious, dangerous, far more so than the sea. There lurked "the savage." Now they were going so deeply inland, so far into the forest, that it was difficult for Adela to imagine finding her way out again. The trees represented the mesh of an inescapable net that was closing behind her.

For a few small coins, she had been traded like common livestock and led across an unknown land. But one day, she would return to Tilting. She made a promise to herself.

# Seven

Achille did not understand what the police could possibly want from him. They had arrived just as he had set foot on dry land and started to portage around the Paugan Dam. No easy matter, for he had to transport both his canoe and his baggage. At first view, it looked as if he would have to do a detour of about one kilometre before getting back on the river farther down, especially since the current moved very quickly at the foot of the dam. He had done this route a very long time ago. At that time the dam had just been built, but the road that led there was not paved as it was today. He had wrapped the strange iceberg-shaped box containing his Adela's ashes as carefully as if it were an egg. The bundle attached to his backpack lovingly tapped against his buttocks with each step he took, and he could not help but smile. Adela was with him and was encouraging him to keep on going. Sometimes he murmured to her: "Stop pushing, you know I'm not twenty any more."

He must have been halfway down the long slope leading to the dam when he met the patrol car coming from the opposite direction. He barely paid attention. His head was buried under his canoe, his range of vision limited to the ground in front of his feet. He noticed that the car was moving very slowly as it passed him, but he did not look up. He was counting his steps. Achille found it encouraging. Each step he took meant one less step to take before he got to where he was going. It was a habit he had adopted while portaging with his old Algonquin friend. Of course, he did not know the exact number of steps that separated him from the place where he would put his canoe in the water, but he would soon find out.

"I'll know for my return trip," he told himself, smiling.

"Just look at the crazy old guy!" Officer Laflamme said to his partner.

Michel Fortin did not care for the company of his colleague. Laflamme was so narrow-minded and was of such limited intelligence that two ideas could not meet in his head at the same time. But he had to accept the partner who had been assigned to him. Though no one wanted to be teamed up with Laflamme, Fortin would have attracted the others' animosity if he ever had the poor judgement to protest.

Fortin was expecting anything but to see this old man with a canoe on his back. He had to be in exceptional shape. Fortin estimated the weight of the boat and paddles to be about twenty-five kilos, and the man was also transporting a backpack with an odd package tied to it. He continued his route while the patrol car slowed down as they approached him.

"Go turn around at the top of the road on the dam, we're going to park behind him," commanded Fortin.

Laflamme, who seemed to have become a policeman for the sole pleasure of activating the siren and flashing lights, was about to put them on when Fortin ordered him not to.

"It's not necessary. Did you see the speed he's going at?"

The car drove up the steep hill to the top of the dam. There, the road curved and became so narrow that there was room for only one car at a time to pass. Laflamme turned the car around and started to make the descent. The two officers expected to see the canoe and the old man struggling with his burden, but to their great surprise, he had disappeared. The policemen were stunned. He had gotten away.

"I knew I should have put on the siren," Laflamme said stupidly, stepping on the accelerator as if Jack the Ripper were getting away from them.

Suddenly between the branches of the trees they saw the bottom of the canoe moving down a winding trail towards the river. Achille had decided to take this path to save steps.

"One or two hundred steps less are worth a bit of extra effort," he told himself.

Moreover, the little trail was better adapted to this expedition than the asphalt of the highway. On paved road, every step gave his joints a hard knock, whereas here the earth and vegetation absorbed the shock and made walking less difficult.

Laflamme locked the brakes and made the car skid on the shoulder of the road, and at the same time activated the siren.

"Stop that Laflamme!"

"We're going to be stuck running after him!" grumbled the officer.

Clearly Achille had no intention of stopping. They could see the back of the canoe moving to the rhythm of his footsteps. Measured steps. He was rediscovering the art of forest walking that he had learned in his youth, always making sure to put his foot in the right place, with no wasted efforts.

Officers Laflamme and Fortin had no choice but to take the path to catch up to the old man. Wearing their bullet-proof vests, weighed down by their gear of pistols, ammunition, clubs, handcuffs and radios, unlike Achille, the two policemen seemed far less at ease than they had been on paved road. Moreover, Laflamme put the sole of his shoe on the wet grass and his feet went out from under him. He fell flat on his back like a package of old laundry. Fortin, who was running down the slope so as not to slip, had to jump aside to avoid him.

"Goddam, I just know I've knocked my back out! I'm going to be stuck in bed for two weeks…if not more!" groaned Laflamme.

Officer Fortin doubted the seriousness of Laflamme's injuries. Lazy as a mule, the policeman seized every possible occasion to be put on sick leave. Fortin could not contain his laughter.

"Don't laugh, damn it, I almost killed myself!" groaned Laflamme, who nonetheless accepted Fortin's extended hand.

The seat of Laflamme's pants was soaked and streaked with long grass stains. Meanwhile Achille continued walking. The two officers proceeded more carefully in their pursuit. In a few seconds they had caught up with him. Laflamme was still furious.

"Hey, old man, don't you listen when people tell you to stop?"

Fortin had passed the canoe and arrived at the man's side. He leaned over to look at him. Achille saw the policeman's face appear at the right side of the canoe. The man seemed nice enough. Achille gave him a big smile, but without slowing his pace.

"Sir, you'll have to stop. We have to talk to you."

"Four hundred and fifty, I'm up to four hundred and fifty steps, my friend. In another fifty steps I'll stop and then we can talk. You have to understand that at my age, lifting the canoe on and off my shoulders is no small thing."

Michel Fortin did not quite know what to do.

"Okay, we'll follow you," he said.

Laflamme exploded

"What do you mean, 'we'll follow you'? It's up to him to follow us! We're not going to keep walking down this cow path!"

"Ha, ha!" laughed Achille under his canoe. "You don't know how right you are! The first time I came here, it really was just a cow path. It should be less steep once we get past the rock over there."

The image made him smile. The old man with the canoe led the march, nimbly sidestepping obstacles and climbing over rocks and roots. The policemen followed, stumbling on every obstacle. After a few minutes, they had arrived at their destination. There, the trail opened out onto the river, which resumed its turbulent course after being re-routed by the huge human construction. Achille turned the canoe over. It landed gently in the grass, a few metres from the water. He took off his pack and sat down on a dead tree trunk. His back hurt and his legs were painful, as if he had walked for dozens of kilometres. The heat under the canoe had made him sweat profusely, but he had succeeded. The two young men, who were just arriving, seemed as out of breath as he was.

"Well, what would you like to talk to me about?" asked Achille, who was giving himself a few minutes' break before getting back on the water.

He allowed himself a plug of chewing tobacco. He had gotten into the habit of tobacco chewing in the lumber camps. It was not really the taste he appreciated but what he associated with the activity. In the forest, the men chewed tobacco during the lunch break or in the evening. For Achille, chewing tobacco went together with taking a break after very hard labour. And this portage had been a tough exercise. He was no longer young and his muscles needed a few moments' rest.

"Sir, you're going to have to follow us. You shouldn't be doing what you're doing."

"I know, my Adela used to tell me the same thing. But I don't chew tobacco all that often."

"No, not that…," said Fortin, a little disconcerted. "I mean the canoe, going down the river like that, all alone, paddling."

"And why would that be?" asked Achille, intrigued by what the policeman had said.

"Well, come on, it's just crazy to go down a river like the Gatineau by canoe, Pops," said Laflamme.

Achille hated this way of speaking. And he did not understand it. He was not this man's father.

"I'm not your father," Achille simply said.

"He's obviously off his rocker," Laflamme said to his colleague under his breath.

"Why? *Is* he your father?" asked Fortin, amused by the old man's reply.

"Well, of course not!" Laflamme hotly retorted.

Then, addressing Achille again: "Sir –" he had suddenly changed his tone. "What I mean is that it doesn't make sense for a man of your age, it's dangerous, and besides, carrying a canoe like that, you're going to kill yourself."

"You know, young man, age is not the question, it's experience. You have to know where to put your feet," Achille said mockingly, pointing to the officer's clothes that were smeared with grass and dew.

Laflamme reddened, while Fortin once again had to restrain himself from laughing.

"Besides, I didn't know there was a maximum age for canoeing. You know, over my lifetime, I have probably spent more hours in a canoe than you have lived."

"I'm sorry, sir," said Fortin, "but we have a court order and you're going to have to come with us."

"An order?"

"Yes, an order from a judge."

"I don't know any judge and I am sure no judge knows me either. I have never had any dealings with the law," proclaimed Achille, who was just starting to understand that the two officers were not boy scouts come to give him a hand.

"Listen, I'm only carrying out the orders of the court. You'll have to come with us and fight it out with the judge."

The officer explained that he would have to leave the canoe where it was and that someone would come the next day to take it to the Maniwaki police station. The Maniwaki station? So that meant he was going all the way back up the route he had taken two days to cover, and end up almost back where he started?

Laflamme had wanted to handcuff him, but Michel Fortin glared at him, and he had not insisted. The officer was ill at ease before this man, who was venerable due to his age and dignified bearing, and who did not seem to have lost his mind. Achille talked little during the trip, replying succinctly to the questions of Officer Fortin, who seemed interested in him. But maybe he was only doing his job as a police officer. Achille had always believed the police were there to defend good people against villains. He could not understand why they were interested in him, for he had always led a very quiet life on his land in Aumond. He paid his taxes without protest, though he had never really understood what his municipality gave him in return for such a large sum. Never had he complained, except to Adela, who, each time, had heard him out religiously then said: "Well, why don't you go tell them?" which usually shut him up. Then she would give him a big smile and go back to what she was doing.

The procedure, in cases such as this, was to take the man to the hospital emergency for a first evaluation that would ultimately serve as justification for holding him. Moreover, the hospital had been warned that they were bringing in a "psychiatric" client.

James Whiteduck had been on duty in the emergency for sixteen hours with barely a moment's rest. Between a baby with a fever and the victim of a highway accident, he had choked down some food of not the best quality, and a lot of coffee. He did not really like so-called psychiatric cases, like the one whose arrival had just been announced. The person usually arrived in a crisis state. He had to do a physical exam and evaluate the patient's mental state so the law could take charge of him. This did not pose much of a problem except that the patients were often incoherent and uncooperative. Many of them were even violent.

James had seen it all. After he graduated, he had to move to the far north to practise, because it seemed that all the positions in the regular hospitals in the province were closed to him. The people of Quebec judged that the north was a perfect place for an Indian. An Algonquin from the Maniwaki band, now called Kitigan Zibi,[15] he had attended primary and secondary school on the reserve but had to bend over backwards to be accepted into medicine at university. He was denied access because university authorities balked at recognising diplomas issued by the Kitigan Zibi Board of Education. It was an old conflict that had exploded when the Algonquins decided to set up their own schools. The young Algonquins' departure from white schools also meant the departure of millions of dollars that the federal government was paying for their education. Hence, the Ministry of Education had decided, a little vengefully, not to recognise the band's system of education or the diplomas it issued. After three years of fruitless attempts to be admitted to university, he had been obliged to re-do all his exams before he could be issued a "real" high school diploma. Once he had finished medical school, he had been shown the door to the far north as the condition of admission to jobs in hospitals located elsewhere in Quebec. Now he had come back home again.

The man he saw coming through the door of the emergency room

---

[15.] *Garden of the river.*

did not at all correspond to what he had imagined. Usually, this kind of patient was handcuffed and literally carried by the police. Sometimes the patient screamed and struggled so violently that restraints had to be applied immediately to avoid putting the staff in danger. But the man who entered was not handcuffed. The officers followed him. He stood straight and was about one metre eighty. His eyes met the doctor's and gave him a penetrating look. They entered one of the offices without going through the nurse who did the triage between the urgent and less urgent cases. That was the rule with psychiatric patients. James took care of two other people whom he had already begun to treat, then went into the office where they had taken Achille.

He had expected to find the man on the examining table, but instead it was Officer Laflamme sitting there while Achille sat in the chair. Laflamme, whose pants were still smeared with grass and mud, got up quickly, like a child caught doing something he shouldn't.

"Mister Roy. Achille, I believe? Like in Greek mythology?"

"Except I don't have a weak tendon," replied Achille, amused.

James was surprised by the reply. The man knew the Greek legend. He asked him several questions to check if the patriarch knew who he was, where he was, and if he had a sense of time. Achille replied directly and clearly to each of the questions.

"So what's wrong, Mister Roy?"

"Absolutely nothing. You tell me."

"I see here that you were picked up at Low going down the Gatineau River by canoe. That's quite strange."

"I don't see what's so strange about it. You can only go down the Gatineau River by canoe. You should know that, it was your people who taught us how to use the canoe."

The remark surprised and amused the doctor. "Touché," he said to himself. "I've just been put in my place."

"Still, Mister Roy, at your age it's dangerous."

"Listen, Doctor, I read the paper once a week, on Saturday. Sometimes I collect old magazines. Do you know that I hear about deaths on the road far more often than deaths on the rivers?"

James saw a sparkle of mischief in Achille's eyes.

"Mister Roy, if my information is correct, you are eighty-eight years old?"

"Your information is correct. Mine must not be so good because I didn't know the canoe was forbidden after a certain age."

"All the same, it's dangerous. You're not being very reasonable."

"For me, Doctor, what's reasonable is what I have to do. And I have to do it by canoe. Because that's how I want to do it."

"But to go to Hull by canoe isn't all that common."

"I'm not going to Hull," replied Achille.

"And where are you going?"

"To Fogo."

"Fo…what?"

"Fogo."

"Where is this place?"

"In Newfoundland, Newfoundland."

Laflamme burst out: "You see? I knew it! Pops is going to Newfoundland by canoe. It's crazy."

Achille cast him another irritated glance.

"I would like you to stop saying I'm your father, it's very annoying."

"And I would like you to leave the room during the examination," said Doctor Whiteduck, giving him a look that left no room for argument.

The doctor continued with his medical examination while Officer Laflamme sheepishly left the room to look for his colleague. The old man may have been considered crazy, but he did not seem very dangerous.

"Come now, Mister Roy, no one has ever gone to Newfoundland by canoe."

"Your ancestors did. I read it in a book. Anyway, Adela read it for me."

Again, the old man was taking him back to his roots.

"But why not take the plane or the bus?"

"I don't know anything about the plane, it seems complicated to me. Seems you need a credit card, and I don't have one. And the bus, well, I don't like it. It's too shut in, and Adela wouldn't like it either."

"Who is Adela?"

"Adela is my… my companion," replied Achille.

He was about to say "my wife," but he did not like this way of referring to his life partner. Everyone had always considered them man and wife but the fact that they had never married had always prevented him from using the term. And besides, to call someone *my husband* or *my wife* had something possessive about it that did not correspond with their relationship or Adela's character. Something shocked him about this way of talking. Adela belonged to nobody. He remembered their meeting at the Castor Blanc camp, those brutes who had thought they could make her *their thing*, and how he had put them in their place.

"But where is this Adela?"

"She died recently," he said with a look of sadness. "But she never leaves me. Anyway, except today, for her ashes are in the backpack that the police took from me. I'd like to get it back, because we're never apart."

"And why Newfoundland, do you know someone there?"

"The only person I know who comes from Newfoundland is Adela, and I promised one day that I'd go back with her to the village where she was born on Fogo Island. But we never got to do it. So now I've decided to take her back to her island. You know, for almost seventy years, she talked to me about this island without ever being able to go back there. I don't think I'd be much of a man if I didn't do the impossible to make her dream come true. And anyway, I promised."

Doctor Whiteduck continued his examination in silence. After asking his patient to wait, he left the room and went to find the two police officers. He chided them for having separated Achille from his precious backpack and ordered them to give it back to him immediately.

"This man doesn't seem to have lost his mind to me," he said to the policemen. "And I don't believe he is affected by any illness that reduces his mental capacity. He's an original, that's for sure, but no madman."

This time it was Michel Fortin who spoke: "We have a court order, Doctor. There's nothing we can do about it. It's not our decision to make."

"And besides, we have to get back to the station," added Laflamme, anxious to be done with this affair, which was boring and drab for a *real* policeman like himself who had dreamed since childhood of shootouts and wild car chases.

A court order left no room for discussion, James had to agree. Against his will, he signed the report confirming that the patient was to be held for forty-eight hours. This gave the army of social workers, psychologists and lawyers time to prepare the case they would present in court. He felt like an accomplice, in the wrong sense of the word. In the space where he had to indicate the measures to be taken by the psychiatric team, he wrote: "minimal measures, no restraints." Still, he thought it best to go tell the man what was going to happen.

"I have no choice, sir, the court is asking me to detain you and I have to obey the law."

"I don't know the law, but I believe I've always obeyed it. I've never hurt anyone whatsoever except that tall red-haired man who wanted to attack Adela. He really deserved it. I've always paid my taxes, and I thought that a man was free as long as he didn't cause harm to anyone around him. That's what I know about the law."

"It seems that someone thinks you might harm yourself."

"I think it's now that I'm being harmed."

The reply touched Doctor Whiteduck. This man did not know very much, that was clear, but he was full of the implacable common sense of simple people. *Good Québécois common sense*, one of his Francophone friends would have said. Common sense, period. The kind that comes from the earth. He had a sense of justice and the goodness of a simple man, uncorrupted by vanity, jealousy, or the desire for personal gain and power. A life philosophy that could be summed up in a few words: be good and just towards yourself and others. That was all. Achille applied this simple rule to everything and everyone.

The doctor returned to his patients while the policemen left the premises, and the orderlies from the psychiatric unit accompanied Achille into an isolation room. *The hole*, it was called by patients who had been in prison. And indeed, apart from the fixtures, the decor and the instruments, it looked very much like prison.

Achille noticed the strangeness of the place. In his entire life, he had slept only in three places: the room he shared with his many brothers, the bunkhouse of the lumber camps where almost an entire legion slept in the same confined space, and the room he had shared for the rest of his life with Adela. The memory of this room brought back images. It was simply decorated, but the room exuded happiness, warmth and love. It smelled of the sweetness of their lovemaking, the thought of which still excited him, in spite of his eighty-eight years. Each time was an offering. Not an act, but a gift that each was giving the other. It was almost a form of religious ceremony. Each gesture was a moment of happiness and grace.

But the room where he was now was nothing like that. It was more modern than anything he had ever seen or imagined. And he was alone there. That bothered him even more than sharing a confined space with fifty men, as in the lumber camps of his youth. And its appearance put him off a thousand times more than his family's tiny dormitory with its torn wallpaper. A big window looked out on the nursing station where Achille could see the medical staff buzzing around like bees in a hive. Nobody seemed to give him a second thought. One of them glanced at him briefly from time to time, but never for long. As for the old man, he looked at them intently, trying to figure out, during these brief eye contacts, who he was dealing with and why he was shut up here. But each time he looked, it seemed to disturb them and they preferred to bury their noses in paperwork rather than return his inquisitive gaze. Achille saw their lips move but heard no sound. Only the faint hum of the neon lights over his head broke the silence.

The bed was of a very strange design. The sides made of bars could be lifted, with straps in certain places used to restrain patients. The heavy green door had to be made of metal and possessed a lock that opened only on the side of the nursing station. A mechanism closed it automatically, and anyone inside the room was imprisoned unless someone outside opened it or pressed on the red button under the reception desk. Each time someone pressed the button, a noisy and annoying hum could be heard, like the sound of the doorbell you pushed when you entered the Maniwaki office of old Doctor Besner, the only doctor Achille had ever gone to.

Time here was hell. "It's enough to drive a person crazy," thought Achille.

James Whiteduck had to administer a few stitches to a young reveller who had fallen on his bottle and cut his hand open, then give a shot of adrenaline to a young man who was allergic to beestings and had arrived at emergency with a hand swollen to the size of the Michelin man's. He had also seen a slightly overprotective mother whose little three-year-old girl had a light fever. Finally, calm was restored to the emergency room and he could take a few minutes' break. He should have used the down time to sleep, but the image of the old man kept coming into his mind. Almost without thinking, he made a detour through the psychiatric unit. He arrived during the four o'clock change of shift. During these few minutes, the wheels of the hospital care machine seemed to stop turning. The employees waiting to leave could no longer concentrate on their work. Their thoughts were already far away, at home, at the cottage or someplace else, but not within the walls of this establishment. The ones arriving at work were still at home, in their minds.

Lisa, the nurse at the reception desk, recognised James and gave him a big smile. He was appreciated for his competence, but women were also sensitive to his physical appearance. They were attracted by his dark complexion, typical of American Indians, his athletic built, his ebony black hair. Most of the young and even less young nurses openly gave him the eye. What a catch for the woman who managed to get him in her clutches! They confessed their feelings frankly to each other during coffee breaks. But James, though polite and flattered, always kept his distance. Now he returned the nurse's greeting with a smile that he meant to be as persuasive as possible.

"I've come to see your patient," he said.

The nurse showed him the door with a glance that seemed to say, "You know the way."

"We're going to make him take his clothes off to put on a hospital gown, and we'll have to give him a sedative," the nurse added.

"I'll take care of it," said James, taking the medicine and the horrible gown with him. Often patients had to put on their gowns without assistance and could not tie them it up in the back. Drowsy from the medicine, they sometimes wandered down the corridor with their buttocks exposed for all to see. There was something disrespectful about it, even for the ones who were no longer aware of what they were doing.

When James entered, Achille was admiring the view from the window, which looked out over the city of Maniwaki. James thought he saw his eyes directed towards the river.

"Well, Mister Roy, how are you?" asked Doctor Whiteduck, a little sheepish at the banality of his question.

In fact, he did not quite know what to say. He did not himself understand what he was doing in Achille's room. The old man made him think of the bear that a crafts seller on the Indian reserve had captured and put in a cage to attract tourists. The tourists had come en masse and bought the bad imitations of drums and little tomahawks the man sold, but a year later, the bear died. He died of captivity, of lost freedom and of what people had wanted to make him into.

James sat down on the bed. Achille turned to him with a sad smile. His bag was at his feet and before him, on the windowsill, was the sculpture in the shape of an iceberg. Achille's hand, weathered by time, was gently stroking it. There was such tenderness in the gesture that tears came to James's eyes.

"You loved her very much, didn't you?"

"You know, Doctor, I don't think a lot of people really know what it means to love. You can love chocolate ice cream, but if you eat too much of it you won't be able to stand it any more. That's how you see love, from the way you're talking. That wasn't how it was between us. She was a part of me, and I think I was a part of her. When I was sick, she felt my fever before I even knew I had one. As if my blood ran in her veins. Same thing for me. I wasn't myself, she wasn't herself. We were us."

James had never heard such a profound and simple definition of love. The real thing. Poets had struggled for thousands of years and with millions of words to define Love, and this man had summed it up in a few short sentences.

"I envy you, you know. Very few people are lucky enough to experience that."

Achille's blue eyes looked deeply into his and he put his hand on his arm.

"I know. And I truly hope you'll meet a woman like Adela, doctor. That's why it's so important for me to go to Fogo Island."

James was touched but also tormented.

"I can't let you go," said James, who knew that a doctor, a Native Doctor what's more, who defied a court order was looking for trouble. "But sometimes there are situations when even a doctor can commit an error, with the help of fatigue," he added.

Achille obviously did not understand what James was trying to tell him.

"This door, for example, it could happen that a garbage can keeps it from closing and, through carelessness, I don't notice it. It could also happen that the nurse at the reception desk gets so busy that she doesn't see a man leave this room and take the emergency exit to the left. After that, the man would just have to go down three stories and push the door open to find himself outdoors. But the law prevents me from telling you this. Am I making myself understood?"

James knew that if anyone managed to trace this back to him, the job that he had obtained with such difficulty would be at risk. He also knew that his conscience would torment him if he simply closed his eyes, as other doctors would have done, and which he probably should have done too. He recommended that Achille put on the hospital gown over his clothes and get into bed, as if he were about to fall asleep.

Achille understood. He did not know why this stranger wanted to help him, but he was the first person to have done so. He lay down on the bed and James covered him with a sheet. Just as he was about to leave, Achille put his hand on the one the doctor was resting on the side rail that prevented patients from falling…or escaping.

"You don't have to do this, Doctor. I've had seventy years of happiness. That's a lot more than a lot of people. But I thank you and wish the same for you."

"Me too, but I'm already thirty-six and it hasn't happened yet. I doubt I'll live to a hundred and six so I can be happy for such a long time. I'm not doing this for you, I'm doing it for myself."

James went to the door and turned off the light, plunging the room in darkness. He hastened to hide the pill in his pocket while with his foot he pushed the garbage can into the doorway. He held onto the door just as it closed to avoid making noise. When he passed by the reception desk, Lisa held out a form on which he had to record the time when the medication had been administered. He wrote it down and added his signature, reflecting that it was the first time he had falsified a report, something of which he would have never thought himself capable. Then, contrary to habit and to the nurse's great surprise he struck up a conversation with her. She fairly purred with pleasure. James, usually quite reserved, was openly flirting with her. He leaned over the desk, almost right over her, his face only a few centimetres from hers. For Lisa, the world had stopped. The entire universe outside the bubble in which she found herself in the company of Doctor Whiteduck had ceased to exist. The world could fall to pieces for all she cared, as long as nothing happened to break the spell. She did not see the shadow passing along the wall of the hallway and through the emergency exit. Nor did she hear the click as the door of the room closed, or the door of the emergency exit. As for James, he heard both loud and clear, a real hubbub, which prompted him to flirt even harder.

Achille went down the three floors and found himself outside, his precious backpack in hand, not quite knowing what direction to head in. He went down the road leading away from the hospital and found himself on Boulevard Desjardins. He headed south, aware that he had to find a solution. A light rain had started and he looked for shelter. Sunny's gas station, with its big roof over the gas pumps, offered him temporary shelter. As he stood watching the rain, a truck driver who had just stopped to fill his tank and have a coffee spoke to him.

"Not a very nice day for a walk, sir."

"No, but I won't melt. If it lets up, I'm going to get back on the road."

Albert Gagnon had been a trucker for over twenty-five years, driving across Canada and the United States from one end to the other several times a year. He sometimes took hitchhikers on board, but only rarely, for one never knew whom one might meet, especially in the States. When he picked up someone thumbing a ride, it was usually a young and small student. Though size would not have changed anything if the person had a weapon. He kept a kind of cudgel next to his seat, just in case. But this man seemed nice enough and gave him no reason to fear.

"If I can be of any use and you're going in the same direction as me, I'd be glad to drop you somewhere," he said.

"I'm going to Low, that's where my canoe is."

"Your canoe?" said Albert, surprised and amused by his reply. "I'm going through Low. Come on, get in, we'll chat along the way."

Achille had often seen these huge trucks hauling one, and sometimes even two, trailers of wood. He had always been impressed by them…and also disturbed. A machine that transported so much wood could not be good for the health of the forest. There were so many of these monstrous machines on the highways that Achille did not understand how the forest could produce so many trees without being in danger. He had never seen the inside of one of these trucks and could not open the door. Albert was amused and went to open the door for him, expecting to have to help him up. But the old man seized the handle and quickly hoisted himself up, without apparent effort.

In the hour that followed, Albert had time to ask his passenger all the questions he wanted. Incapable of lying, Achille told him everything, from his canoe expedition to his arrest, then his internment and escape. Albert was bowled over by this man. At first, he thought he was dealing with a madman, and told himself he would have to alert the police as soon as he let him out. But the more he talked to him, the more he realised that there was nothing deranged about Achille. The idea of going to Newfoundland by canoe seemed crazy, but little by little, as Achille explained, it simply seemed unusual. Like himself at eighteen, deciding to hitchhike to Peru. Everyone had tried to stop him. His mother had even gone to see the police to find out if they could do something. Unable to obtain their assistance, she threatened to close the door of her home to him forever and even disinherit him if he went ahead with his plan. He had stood up to her and made the trip anyway, in spite of his mother, in spite of the danger it represented and in spite of what other people thought was sensible. And he had never regretted it. Of course, he was eighteen when he had gone off on this adventure. This man had reached the age of wisdom. But he admired the strength, even the youthfulness of Achille's determination. When he dropped him off, he resolved to say nothing. And even later, when the police launched an appeal in the media to find the old man, whom they claimed was suffering from insanity, he took care not to contact the authorities. Nor when he read that the man had got a ride with an unknown trucker whom they were also searching for.

Achille got out of the truck. He quickly walked to the place where he had left his canoe, fearing someone had already taken it. As he passed, he waved at the dam keeper who was looking down like the lord of the manor from his watchtower. As he headed down the trail where he had met the policemen, he was happy to find the boat exactly where he had left it.

Though the sun was about to go down, he decided to resume his journey right away, and pushed his boat into the current, paddling quickly to get to the middle of the river. The current was strong and the canoe took on speed. He continued on his way until dusk forced him to stop. He found an ideal place, where the shore formed a surface that was flat enough for him to bivouac. A wide and sinuous stream flowed into the river after crossing the surrounding farmland. There was a big pine growing there, which would shelter him if it rained.

Achille got out of the canoe and looked around at the surrounding landscape. The river had grown calm again after its turbulence, and the mountains in the Wakefield region, majestic, cast their reflections in the water. On the opposite shore, here and there through the trees, he could see Highway 105 and its incessant flow of traffic. People who passed this spot every day surely no longer saw the magnificent view.

Adela would have liked this panorama dominated by boulders and rock face. It would have reminded her of Newfoundland, that was certain, except for the spruce trees and giant pines, of course. In any case, she saw Fogo Island in everything around her: in wild strawberries, blueberries, a heap of rocks, a thicket of spruce trees reduced to the size of bonsais all along the edge of a cliff, the fish he caught in the river. Here was the perfect marriage between the rock of her island and Achille's forests. Giant pines, magnificent maples, cedars of an impressive diameter, "clinging to the rock by the tips of their fingernails," he used to say. Just as he and his Adela had clung to their little piece of earth.

But he was worried. He had gone over what had happened to him that day and still could not understand who would want to lock him up, or why. Achille had the feeling that his run-ins with the law were not over yet. The law does not like anyone who slips out of its grasp, even if that person seems to have every good reason for doing so. He knew that. There was a man, for example, who had bought a piece of land near his place, had lived there for five years before it was discovered that he was wanted by the Ontario police for fraud. It was better to be careful. This little creek would provide him with good shelter for the night, but the next day he would have to play it safe on the river, because it ran through most of the villages. The villages had been established on the river's shores at a time when it was the only line of communication. Curiously, modern life had made people turn their backs on the river. The new villages faced the highway. From the river one could only see the backs of the houses. It is true that for a long time, the Gatineau had been the property of the lumber companies. The logs that were always floating down the river made it dangerous for boats. In the spring, there were so many trees floating down the river that it was blocked all the way across. A skilful log driver could easily have crossed it, running from log to log.

Achille thought of all that, realising how much the world had changed since the time that he was king of the canoe. The world had also changed a lot since his Adela had gone. Over all those years, they had created their own world, admitting only what they really wanted and rejecting whatever they did not consider necessary to their happiness. It was their world, a world of tourtières and Jigg's Dinner, and *Frenglish* and *Ench*, of deep forests full of giant pines on the background of an ocean stretching as far as the eye could see.

That world no longer existed. But for one last time, Achille wanted to communicate with Adela and finally see the place he had known for such a long time without ever having seen it. Nobody was going to prevent him from doing that. "Never," he said out loud, as if to make the vow official.

# Eight

The log driving had been finished for some time, and Achille had remained at camp to do a few other jobs. In the two years he had been at the lumber camp, he had returned to Burbridge for just one two-week stop at harvest-time, in July. His father grumbled when he saw him return, but Achille's strong arms had proved so useful for farm tasks that the patriarch started griping once again when his son announced he was going back to the camp.

Since his departure, life had changed on the family farm. His older brother Robert had taken over. At least he thought he had, but in truth, their father still made the rules. And things were probably better that way, because although Robert was a big talker, he was also a bungler. For Achille, this had become intolerable. Now, when he went back home, he had two bosses: his father and his brother. What's more, there was some question of Robert marrying Madeleine Potvin. A date had not been set, but it was obvious that Madeleine would come live at the farm, though there would be even less room. Annette and Yolande, his two older sisters, had left the previous fall for the Grey Nuns' convent in Ottawa. His parents' pretext for sending them was that they would get an education and maybe become nuns themselves. "It would make us so proud," his mother repeated. But most of all, thought Achille, it was a way for his parents to arrange to have two fewer mouths to feed while assuaging their consciences. Annette and Yolande had spent their first summer at the convent. They would not be allowed to return until the next year during the summer holidays. By then they would almost be nuns.

Achille preferred the life of the lumber camp for other reasons too. There, he was considered a man, not a boy. On the farm, all he was paid was the food he was given, but in the forest he received a real salary. It was a modest remuneration, considering the work he had to do, but a salary nonetheless.

Before the men returned for the new season, there was always a great deal of work to do at the camp. Few lumberjacks agreed to rush back to do these jobs. Most of them owned a little plot of land, not enough so they could entirely live from its revenues, but perfect for producing what they needed to eat. And feeding their family was often their sole preoccupation. The seasons were marked by a series of tasks that required their presence on the farm: seeding in the springtime, then cows or pigs giving birth, haying in the summer, harvest in the autumn and woodcutting before the big cold spells came in winter. Another baby to get started, too. Often the child was born during the winter, and the man returned from the lumber camp just in time to get to know the baby before he or she was baptised. Thus the cycle continued.

Achille had returned to the lumber camp in time for the firewood cutting. Numerous cords of wood were needed to keep these big camps warm during the winter, and he had worked for several weeks to build up an adequate supply.

It was already late autumn and the lumberjacks were beginning to arrive for the big winter camp. That day, the carts were bringing a new batch of workers. Achille recognised the faces of lumberjacks who had been there the previous winter. His friend Gaby had also come back, after training as a scaler. Some were newcomers, Irish immigrants mostly, as well as one Pole. "One of them will get the bed of ice," thought Achille, who had moved up in the ranks by participating in the log driving. His seniority gave him the right to choose a bed that was closer to the "trout."

Then she appeared. Her long tousled brown hair was tied back and she looked around terrified as she got out of the cart. On the road to the camp, everyone ended up talking to each other. Even the French managed to jabber a few words in English to their travelling companions, with whom they were going to have to live for the next few months. She got into the cart alone and was every bit as solitary when she got out again.

Achille only glanced at her and retreated into his usual shyness, staring at the ground in front of him as he walked to the "sleep camp." At the same moment, she backed away from the group, as if she were afraid of something. She tripped on a root and fell against Achille, who had arrived at her side at just that moment. Reacting quickly, he caught her and held her against him. His face was a few centimetres from hers. All he could see were her terror-stricken eyes. Adela recovered her balance, just as embarrassed as Achille by the physical contact. He blushed. The two excused themselves at the same time, he in French and she in English. She quickly moved away.

Clyde, who had come out to meet her, took her directly to the kitchen. Finally the men would be able to have real meals. No more inedible *gibelottes* made by the "cookee." If they'd had to judge the cookee on the basis of his culinary talent, the men of the lumber camp would have surely strung him up. Lucky for him that he was under the foreman's protection. Not a single evening went by in the sleep camp when someone did not suggest cooking him on a spit to punish him for his incompetence.

"Clyde would be happy to eat him on a brochette," someone said.

Without fail, one of the veterans would get up and cry out: "…you…you big goddamn fag!" and everyone would burst out laughing to recall the altercation between Clyde and Gaby. At the end of the winter, the newcomers would know the story so well that they would tell it as if they had been there to see it happen.

The newcomers settled into camp life, each doing what he had to do. In the evening, one could see the alliances that had been forged.

Achille was now one of the "old guys," though he was not yet twenty. He had become friends with a lumberjack who possessed a very particular sense of humour. Omer Lafond was a *bon vivant*. He was quick with a joke, talked loudly and was the life of the party. He was a leader, one saw and sensed it. When the group had an opinion to express, it was always through him that they spoke. His big mouth got him into trouble, too, for he was often known to slip a few jokes about the *têtes carrées* into his inexhaustible repertoire of funny stories. Generally, his jokes were not mean, and most of the Anglophones in the camp laughed at them heartily. They always found a joke about "French frogs" to come back at him with, and Omer was the first to find it funny.

But the McHammond group did not much like this kind of humour. McHammond did not like anyone. Tall and thin, he inspired respect with his size, but he felt especially strong in the presence of his sidekicks. McHammond hung around with a certain John O'Brien, a recent arrival to the lumber camp, and another man whom everyone called Pat. If the group of lumberjacks felt linked to each other by a common fate, McHammond and his acolytes were not part of it. On the other hand, they had immediately got in good with Clyde. This friendship made them suspect in the eyes of the others. McHammond was the resident boot-licker and had no qualms about reporting everything that happened in the sleep camp.

The company formally forbade the possession and consumption of alcohol in the camp. Certain foremen tolerated a bit of moonshine from time to time, as long as it was not consumed in excess. Sometimes one of the boys drank too much and the others covered for him, unless it became a habit. But McHammond hastened to talk about everything he saw in the sleep camp.

One night Omer Lafond decided to have one over on McHammond. He got hold of three one-gallon jugs, the kind that owners of small clandestine distilleries used to bottle their alcohol. Two were full of water while the third was filled to the top with a strong mixture of moonshine. That night, Lafond displayed the two gallon jugs.

"Anyone want a little shot of the strong stuff? I've got some good hooch, and lots of it," announced Lafond.

Right away, four men volunteered. These were men with whom he often played reprehensible jokes, and whom he had let in on his plan. All five abundantly drank what was actually just water and feigned drunkenness. McHammond had not missed a thing. Bright and early the next morning he reported the incident to Clyde, who decided to catch Lafond red-handed. While the men were still in the sleep camp, preparing to go to the kitchen for breakfast, Clyde entered, accompanied by the big boss and another foreman.

"Lafond, we want to see your things," said Clyde, sure of what he was going to discover.

The two bottles, which Omer had slid under the bed, were in plain view.

"You're done for, Lafond," he said, holding up the bottles.

"I didn't know it wasn't allowed," said Lafond with his most innocent look.

"Come off it, Lafond, you know alcohol is forbidden in the camp. I've always said you were good for nothing."

"I know about alcohol, but I didn't know that water was forbidden too," retorted Lafond, making a great effort not to burst out laughing.

Clyde grew purple while the big boss seized one of the jugs himself to smell its contents.

"It's water. Just water!" he said.

Using the little English he knew, but with a particularly marked French accent, Omer continued, addressing the big boss.

"But if you are looking for alcohol, Mister, I saw some last night," he said, glancing over at McHammond's bed.

It did not take long to find the third bottle, which indeed was full of alcohol. Clyde was both furious and disconcerted. Losing face in front of the big boss, he risked a lot. The boss, an intelligent man, immediately recognised McHammond's role in the group and the trap he had fallen into. He lectured Clyde for having disturbed him for no reason, and assigned McHammond to latrine duty. As soon as the "temperance committee" had left the room, everyone laughed except McHammond, who was scarlet with rage. This made for another story to fill the long winter nights.

※

Having only just arrived, Adela, docile, followed Clyde, trying to memorise everything he was telling her. There were too many things to understand, see and assimilate all at once.

The place where the meals were served was divided into two sections. There was the big room that one entered through a door located at the end of the building, across from the sleep camp. Crudely built tables were lined up on either side with the "trout" in the middle, as usual. At the end of the room, a door gave access to a much smaller space that was used as a kitchen. There was a big wood stove with two ovens, and beside it, a smaller range used in the morning or afternoon for stovetop cooking. All around the room were shelves where foodstuffs and kitchen equipment were piled up according to no particular order. A narrow high table in the middle of the room was used for meal preparation. Adela noted the bread bin with its wooden top smeared with flour, the only piece of furniture that seemed familiar to her. Light came in through a window on the south side.

In one corner, behind a partition, was a room hardly bigger than a broom closet. Inside was a little wooden bed with a straw pallet. There was just enough space between the bed and the wall to put one's feet on the floor, but not enough to stand up and walk around. The door to the room was a burlap-bag curtain on which one could read the words "Robin Hood Flour."

A second door opened onto the summer kitchen and the area behind it, where an outdoor wood stove had been set up. There, food was cooked on the hottest days of summer and during Indian summer in the fall.

Adela was desperate. She was a stranger in a strange land. Here she was, in the middle of a forest that she had no idea how to locate on the map of the world, and what's more, she had to cook. She had of course cooked at home. Her mother had made a point of teaching her the traditional recipes of her country and the art of food preparation, but between cooking for six or seven people and making meals for sixty-odd men, there was a big difference. Moreover, these people did not eat the way they did at home; there was no fish, no wild fruit, no vegetables, and lots of salted meat.

❦

This man Clyde had given the young cookee, Luc, the job of helping her.

"You take care of him," he had told her.

She wondered why he was insisting she take care of the cookee when she was the one who most needed help. Luc was lazy as a mule. Adela gave him tasks to do, but he took his time over them, yet was quick to report to Clyde every detail of what happened in the kitchen.

The first meal was a disaster. She had tried to make a stew, but it had gotten overcooked. She was not really familiar with the wood they used for cooking here, and had filled the stove with logs of dry fir. The food had a slightly burnt taste, and the men in the camp had trouble getting it down. She had not had time to make bread, and lazy Luc had not peeled enough potatoes. The meal had been a catastrophe and the lumberjacks' recriminations added to her distress.

"There's no way we're going to spend a whole winter like this! We were eating bad enough with the cookee in charge, and now it's even worse!"

Adela was desperate after her first day. She would have given anything not to be in this place, but knew she had no choice. She had nowhere else to go. Clyde came to see her after the meal and delivered a serious threat.

"You'd better make something good next time, otherwise you won't be staying," he said.

She was terrified. Luc, who was usually indifferent to everything that happened in the camp, was touched to see her crying after Clyde's visit and decided to give her a hand. He hated cooking, but he did not want Clyde to dismiss her, for then he would have to take her place. And he did not want that to happen.

However, Luc showed interest in the few feminine objects in Adela's possession: her hairbrush and a little mirror. Also in her meagre luggage she had brought a bottle of toilet water she had made herself from wildflowers. He loved the smell of this perfume. She had understood that he was what, at home, they called a "man-woman." The men never called Luc by his first or his last name and treated him with disdain, as if he were not man enough to have a name. Adela had noticed this. She had also noticed that other than Clyde, no one spoke to Luc and he was on his own. But he was her only companion and she quickly developed a good rapport with him. They had their femininity in common.

Adela finally managed to pass the test. After her initial failure, she put into practice what her mother had shown her and followed the advice of the cookee, who was more attuned to habits in the camp and aware of how the men wanted to eat. She was up at four in the morning preparing the bread, brioches and desserts, stoking the fire, cooking the pork and beans and cutting the ham. The men ate the second meal in silence. No compliments, but no complaints either. This was the equivalent of praise. Clyde came to the door again and said to her simply: "That was okay."

Achille had been discreetly watching the newcomer. There was something about her that made her different from the women he knew. Sometimes she glanced over at a particular group of men whom she made a point of avoiding. She seemed very frightened whenever they were around. He had followed her eyes a few times to try to understand what could be causing such terror. Each time, her eyes went to the McHammond band. She only spoke English so she could have conversed with this group, but instead she seemed to want to avoid all contact with them. On the rare occasion that she had said a few words in his presence, Achille had noticed that she did not speak the same English as the others. Of course it was the same language but the intonations were different. He knew the *English people from England* who had conquered New France, and the *English of the famine* who had fled Ireland to try and survive the great drought that had afflicted their country, and the *English from the States*, who all seemed rich and came to hunt and fish in the north. Was it possible that there was a fourth kind of English?

Adela had taken refuge in her kitchen like a wild animal wrenched from its natural milieu that rolls up in a ball in a corner of its cage. When work was finished, she sat by the window, looking out beyond the horizon, endlessly calling up images of her village. It was the sea she missed most of all. Walking barefoot on Sandy Cove Beach, she would count the waves and recognise the seventh, always stronger than the others. This one would touch her feet, breaking on the shore. And then there was the wind off the sea with its sweet saline odour. There was no fragrance she missed more since being shut up in this prison. Here the odours that dominated were those of freshly cut wood and the men's sweat. Yet she had come to like the aroma of pine needles, especially when a warm breeze blew through the tree branches, becoming saturated with the perfume of sun-warmed resin.

Then there was the man who seemed fated to follow her everywhere. The big red-haired man with the eagle nose was here. Every morning and evening, he gave her a lustful glance, making sure she noticed him. Sometimes he pretended to kiss her or stuck out his tongue as if to lick her. O'Brien liked to feel her fear. At night in bed he masturbated thinking of her and her fear. It excited him unbearably and he did everything he could to maintain it.

"One day she'll be mine," he told Pat, who always followed him around.

The first time he had gone into his routine, she had gone back into the kitchen very shaken. She did not know whether it was the horror of the thing that made her stomach lurch or whether it was her condition, but this man repelled her. The very sight of him left her frozen with terror. He was not alone in ogling her. Other men also pursued her, more or less discreetly. This made her ill at ease. Some of them spoke French and she understood nothing of their advances, but the look in their eyes and their tone of voice left no doubt as to their intentions. In spite of everything, most of them inspired no fear in her. Their innuendos were mostly jokes, and they did not insist beyond words. However the routine was repeated daily, and she knew it would get worse when winter confined them to the lumber camp and time made them forget their own women.

Every day, Adela felt life growing within her. The child was taking up more and more space. She tightened her belt so nothing would show, but sooner or later this would no longer be possible. She had seen her mother pregnant and knew that soon she would no longer be able to hide her round belly. Her breasts were swollen, and in the morning sometimes she was nauseous when she woke up. She had hoped the child would disappear. He was the origin of her despair and her exile in this hostile milieu. But at the same time, she considered the child her most precious possession. He was her last real tie to Fogo Island. He was conceived there and was a real Newfoundlander, like herself.

Adela made sure she was never alone, except at night when she finally went to bed. Though her young assistant was an idler, she appreciated his presence. He helped keep the O'Brien group away from her, for O'Brien was aware that the cookee would immediately have reported him to the foreman. Luc was also the only man who felt no attraction to the only woman in the lumber camp.

One night, after the men had finished supper and retired to the sleep camp, Clyde had come into the kitchen. He had not spoken to her but stuck his head in the door for a second, looking for the cookee. Luc had seen him coming and had apparently ducked out, as he did when he wanted to elude the man's caresses. Everything had been put away and Adela was starting to wash and get ready for bed. She poured water in the metal tub used for washing potatoes, then picked up a piece of fabric that she used as a washcloth. Suddenly the door between the kitchen and the main room opened. O'Brien was there. He looked at her with his vulture eyes as if she were prey. She wanted to cry out, but with two quick strides he had his hand over her mouth. This time, she would not escape. The monster was not alone. Pat, his eternal companion, was with him.

"Watch to make sure no one's coming. I go first."

Several days before, at O'Brien's suggestion, the two men had made a plan to have their way with the cook. All they had to do, he said, was wait for night-time, when Clyde invited the kitchen boy to his room and she found herself alone. He would take her first, and then it would be his companion's turn. Pat went to stand guard by the main door to make sure no one interrupted the party. He salivated at the idea that his turn was coming soon.

Adela fought like a devil in holy water. Her nostrils were filled with the noxious odour of her rapist, the same one she had smelled in the stable when he had attacked her.

"This time you won't escape," he told her, his nose pressed a few centimetres from hers.

She wanted to cry out, but his powerful hand was holding her so tightly that she could barely breathe. The thing she had most feared since her arrival was about to happen. The man pushed her down on the middle of the table where she prepared the meals. She fell on her back, overpowered by his brutal strength. Keeping her firmly pinned, he lifted her skirt and underwear. He undid the buckle of his pants and displayed his erect penis. He smelled of old sweat and of an animal in heat.

Desperate, unable to cry out, Adela flung her foot out in the direction of the pots and pans hanging on the wall. The falling utensils caused a hubbub, however it did not seem to diminish O'Brien's ardour. He was now on his knees on the table above her, holding one hand over her mouth and another on his penis. Adela tried to turn from one side to the other, but he prevented her. She felt his hard member about to enter her. She wanted to vomit. Her throat filled, the liquid sprayed between the rapist's fingers, but she had to swallow the acid contents of her stomach and started to choke. She could not breathe and her strength was giving out. Spots of light passed before her eyes. The light grew dim and she lost consciousness. It was all over. The monster had won.

O'Brien was so excited that he was going to ejaculate even before penetrating her. The touch of the soft young thighs on his penis gave him a foretaste of pleasure that he felt was imminent. He did not hear the kitchen door open behind him, but he felt the hand that seized him by the collar, a big hand like a bear trap that went almost all the way around his neck. In a fraction of a second, he found himself up in the air. Suspended between sky and earth, he saw that Adele's lovely frightened face, which had been before him a moment ago, had been replaced by the eyes of Achille, mad with rage. O'Brien saw such hatred and violence in them that he felt with equal intensity the fear he'd had such pleasure provoking in the young woman.

Achille held him at arm's length, his legs flailing around in mid-air. What he had seen had enraged him and he could no longer control himself. O'Brien started struggling and hit him several times before Achille reacted. He started hitting the man in the face with his other hand. How many times? He did not know. Until the other's face was just a mass of blood. O'Brien had been unconscious for some time when Achille recovered his senses and opened his hand. The body fell to the floor like a sack of flour. It was an absurd spectacle. O'Brien's face was unrecognisable, covered in blood, his pants down around his ankles and his long underwear open, exposing his penis. It had lost its ardour of moments ago and hung flaccidly.

Pat, who had been standing guard at the other end of the room, had heard the commotion of the pots and pans falling and gone to see what was happening. He had seen O'Brien dropping his pants and climbing up on the table. He had returned to his post, eager for his turn to come. Meanwhile, Achille had walked around the building and entered by the back door without Pat noticing. When the tumult started up again, he had believed it was caused by another struggle between O'Brien and the woman. When he heard the thud of a body falling, he came back to take a look. Seeing Achille, he seized a big cast-iron frying pan that had fallen from the wall and was about to hit him over the head. Achille moved aside at the last moment and the frying pan had touched his head, but it was his shoulder that absorbed most of the shock. Pat was terrified by what he saw in the man's eyes. Sheer fury. He tried several times to hit him, but Achille parried each of his blows with his arms. Each time the heavy pan hit him, it should have broken his bones but he seemed to feel no pain. Achille advanced towards Pat, who backed up as fast as he could, hitting him repeatedly with the frying pan. When Achille managed to seize the hand holding the heavy instrument, he squeezed so hard that a distinct cracking of bone could be heard. Pat could not suppress a cry. Achille caught him by the shirt and threw him across the room. Pat hit the wall and collapsed to the floor. He did not have time to get up before Achille was upon him again. He could not contain his rage. He threw him with such force against the other wall that the wallboards gave way and his body went right through. A wood splinter pierced the left side of his stomach. He found himself on the ground outside the kitchen, skewered like a chicken and screaming at the top of his lungs. Alerted by the noise, the men emerged half dressed from the sleep camps to discover Pat writhing with pain like a worm.

Achille returned to the kitchen. O'Brien had not budged. Adela lay still on the table. She was in an altered state. When O'Brien's hand had left her face, she had started breathing again and spit up what was blocking her throat. The contents of her stomach were smeared in her hair. Achille put her skirts back in place and started to carry her to her bed. She emerged from the fog and looked at this face that had replaced O'Brien's. The anger in Achille's eyes had been replaced by great gentleness. She was reassured, but the memory of the attack returned to her mind and she started to retch again. Sheepish, not knowing what to do, Achille slowly rubbed her back.

Men had come running from everywhere. Clyde, who was still looking for the cookee and had not had time to get undressed, arrived before the others. When they saw Pat, no one understood what had happened. First they thought it was a simple fight between lumberjacks. Scuffles were frequent in the camps. However, they had seen Achille through the window and could not believe this gentle man was capable of such violence. Pat was seriously injured and would be out of commission for the rest of the season. Clyde was furious and was going to let Achille have it. When the group of men arrived at the kitchen door and saw O'Brien covered with blood and half-dressed on the kitchen floor, everyone understood what had happened.

Achille paid no attention to any of them. He wanted to get Adela's would-be rapist out of her sight. He gripped him by the shirt and dragged him across the floor to the adjoining room. The men stepped aside to let him pass and no one tried to intervene, not even Clyde. A trail of blood marked the place where the body had been dragged. Like a zombie, Achille returned to the kitchen, where he clumsily began picking up what had fallen on the floor, as if this was the most important thing to do under the circumstances. He seemed to be in a trance. Luc, the cookee, who had suddenly reappeared amidst the commotion, understood better than anyone what had happened. He knew. He entered the kitchen and put his hand on Achille's, looking him in the eyes and wordlessly indicating that he would tidy the kitchen.

Gaby, Achille's eternal companion, had arrived too and had taken him by the arm to lead him away. The room was in complete silence. Sixty men, usually as noisy as a herd of buffalo, were making no more noise than a housefly. One of them bent over O'Brien to see what kind of state he was in.

"He...he's dead," he whispered.

The other man would survive, but had to be taken to Maniwaki to be treated. In any case, even had he been in better condition, it was no longer possible to keep him on at the camp. The men hated rapists and he might not have survived the winter. There was no law in lumberjack camps except that of the men, and it was implacable. No one would want to work with him or talk to him. It would not be surprising if he were the victim of an "accident" if ever he remained at the camp.

Omer Lafond, who as usual spoke on behalf of the lumberjacks, stepped forward and looked at everyone present.

"This man died because a tree fell on him," he said, pointing to O'Brien's body.

The other men nodded their agreement. Clyde wanted to protest, then changed his mind. He might like young boys, but rapists repelled him. He could not defend what was indefensible.

"Put him somewhere else. Tomorrow we'll make him a box," Clyde simply said.

Thus the law of the forest was applied. O'Brien had gotten what he deserved. Achille had only been defending himself. And besides, thought Clyde, this Achille was a good worker. It was enough to lose two lumberjacks at once. The law would have deprived him of a third one. When the big boss was informed, he told Clyde that he did not want to know anything about what had happened. He did not want any problems with the law either, and he knew there were things that the men had to resolve between themselves. Pat was isolated until he was taken down to Maniwaki. He too had been told that O'Brien had officially died crushed by a tree. Everyone knew he would hold his tongue, otherwise he would risk being accused of participating in the rape.

The next day, no one was talking about the event any more, though in each man's head was the image of the disfigured O'Brien. He was buried near the lumber camp. No one was present at the burial, except the two men appointed to dig the hole. A little wooden cross without an inscription marked the spot.

Nor did anyone protest when it was noted that the cookee was momentarily back in charge of the kitchen. But twenty-four hours later, Adela was at work again. However, things had changed. These crude men, hard as nails, showed her sympathy in their own way. Having ignored her for so long, now they greeted her politely and were very friendly towards her.

Adela looked for Achille. She had not seen him again. He had been led to the dormitory after the incident. Lafond had taken out his jug of moonshine and carefully knocked him out with alcohol to put him to bed. Achille did not show up for work the next day, his joints were swollen like a glove filled with water. And the blow he had taken on the head from the frying pan had left a huge goose-egg. His friend Gaby did not want Achille to find himself among the others right away. He would realise the gravity of what happened, and Gaby was aware that he would need help. He was supported by Omer Lafond, and Clyde had agreed to turn a blind eye.

When Achille woke up the next day, he was black and blue. In a few seconds, he relived the incidents of the day before. The vision of O'Brien, half naked, holding his organ and assaulting the young woman, had driven him mad. The rest was just a series of images that had no connection with him, like pictures in a book. He had hit the man in a rage and after that, he remembered nothing. Then he had heard: "He's dead." The words gave him a shock, as if he had received a hammer blow in the middle of his forehead. He had killed a man. The most terrible thing one can do before God. He had not wanted to…anyway, he had not really wanted to, but a dam had suddenly broken inside him, the one that normally held back his anger. To stop it would have been the equivalent of trying to stop the water in a river with his bare hands. And as for the other man he had hit, he had made do with throwing him in the air. He did not yet know that Pat had several broken ribs and that the side of his stomach was pierced right through. Luckily, the splinter had touched no vital organs. Achille expected to be fired and rejected by the others, but in the morning all the men passed by his bed, giving him a little nod in greeting. Gaby remained with him.

"I know what you're thinking, Achille Roy, but get that out of your head. That guy didn't deserve any better. Maybe he didn't deserve to die, but he deserved every one of those blows. And I don't think you really meant to kill him. For everyone here, he died crushed by a tree. Even Pat, the guy you roughed up, is ready to swear it on the Bible. He knows too well what would happen if he admitted that he and O'Brien were in the process of raping the little Newfoundlander. You've got to forget about it."

Forget, forget. It was easy to say. Each second, each minute that passed brought back images. It was all very well to keep telling himself it was just an accident, the fact was, it had happened. A murderer, him? In reality, this kind of thing frequently occurred. A lot of men died in the forest, far from the eyes of the world, in fierce clashes between bands of rival companies. The men fought and sometimes one of them died. His friends would swear vengeance, but first everyone would agree to keep quiet about it. What happened in the forest, remained in the forest.

Since the beginning of her misadventure, Adela had felt abandoned and rejected by everyone except for kind Madame Lafrenière, who had offered her lodgings, a dress and a bath. It was the only show of sympathy she had received. When she woke from her nightmare, she had seen Achille's face and fear had left her. The next day the terrible images returned, of O'Brien, who had threatened her from the beginning and had again tried to rape her, but also the face of the man who had rescued her.

Adela was grateful to him but at the same time feared that his only motivation, like that of all the others, was to obtain her favours. But over the following days, when Achille came into the kitchen for dinner, he barely met her eyes. No, that was not what this man was after. However one evening, to her surprise, he came into the kitchen. He remained standing there, not knowing quite what to do or say. O'Brien's death weighed on his conscience. He was haunted by the image of his bloody face, and to him it seemed that only Adela could share his distress.

Luc was still in the kitchen. He too was astonished to see Achille. Luc had instructions to watch over the woman and warn Clyde immediately if a man approached her. He glanced at Adela, who gave him a nod to signal that there was nothing to fear. From being around Clyde, Luc had learned a few words of English. Their conversations were limited to a few common words designating a pot or an ingredient used in food preparation. Adela signalled to him that he could leave. He left, but not without casting a glance behind him. Clyde, who'd had an earful from the big boss after the attempted rape, would not forgive him if something else happened.

Achille remained there a long moment, incapable of saying anything. Adela was as ill at ease as he was. Then he began to speak. The words poured out. She did not understand anything he was saying, but listened attentively. Achille explained, and she understood from his gestures that he was referring to the moment when he had seized the man and struck him. Suddenly, he buried his head in his hands and when he raised it again, she saw big tears running down his cheeks. She would not have been able to repeat a word of what he had said, but she understood his meaning. He suffered from having this man's death on his conscience. He had felt the need to talk about it and curiously, he had chosen the only person in the lumber camp who could not understand a single word of his pain but who felt it as if it were as palpable and visible as Pat's gaping wound.

While Achille was talking, Adela had remained immobile before him. He collapsed on the chair by the vat where the cookee usually peeled potatoes. This man who had been capable of such violence inspired not the slightest fear in her. Adela was touched. She moved forward and bent down, taking his still battered hand. She started to wash his wound before applying a new dressing, and this time she was the one who did the talking. It had been such a long time since she had communicated with anyone. She said as many words as he had several minutes before, her eyes riveted to the hand she was nursing with such gentleness. She told him about her life, her affair with the spoiled brat of the village, John, his refusal to accept the child they had made together and her escape to St. John's, where she was supposed to have hidden while waiting for the baby to arrive. Finally she told him about her voyage to Quebec City and the lumber camp.

Achille listened to the words without understanding them, but found her voice's intonation beautiful. There was something musical and sweet about it. He also felt her pain and distress. He noted that Adela had put her hand on her stomach twice while talking, but he did not understand what it meant. When she finished, she remained silent for a few minutes, still holding his hand. Achille did not move either and was careful not to break the spell. Finally, with reluctance, he got up, said goodbye and thanked her for listening to him. She found herself alone, but never, since her departure from Tilting, had she felt less abandoned.

※

Each morning and evening, at mealtime, Achille had the impression that his portions were bigger than those of the others, and that the pieces of meat he was served were always the best. Even Gaby noticed.

"One gets the feeling the little Newfoundlander wants to thank you," he said, pointing his fork at Achille's plate.

"There's nothing to thank me for," he replied, embarrassed as ever by attention from others.

Sometimes, in the evening, after Luc had left the kitchen, Achille came back. Adela greeted him with a big smile. He talked to her. She listened in silence and waited for him to finish. Without understanding the language, it was hard to tell when he had finished, but Adela guessed it from the tone of his voice. Then it was her turn to talk and confide in him.

The secret she had so wanted to hide was becoming more and more obvious. Her belly stuck straight out. Already the first snow had fallen and the cold of winter had settled over the camp. She did her best to hide her condition, sucking in her stomach so hard that she could barely breathe. It was Luc who first noticed. He said nothing about it, but watched Adela in secret. He was well aware that she was sometimes nauseated in the morning, but as he had no experience in the matter, he had not recognised the signs. However, he had seen pregnant women before and this stomach looked a lot like the ones he had seen in past. He confided it to Clyde on one of his nocturnal expeditions into the foreman's bed.

Clyde's first thought was that the child was the product of O'Brien's rape, but he had apparently not had time to penetrate her before passing from life to death. Then he thought it might be the child of Achille, who had become Adela's protector, but the pregnancy clearly dated from before her arrival. The presence of a pregnant woman could not be tolerated in a lumber camp. Especially because one day she would have to give birth. No one there was in a position to deliver a baby. They barely knew how to take care of minor wounds. Clyde went to inform the boss, who seemed in a very bad mood to learn the news. The woman would have to leave, but since it was the middle of winter, it was difficult to get down to Maniwaki. And most of all, to find someone to replace her would be an impossible mission. He gave Clyde the duty of notifying the woman that she would have to leave, which the foreman proceeded to do without mincing words.

Though Adela had felt like a prisoner at the lumber camp since the moment she arrived, she had no other place to live. She did not see how she was going to manage. She wept and pleaded, but Clyde, enjoying his authority, showed her no sympathy.

"You've been screwed. It's not my business," was all he could say.

She would have to leave with the next convoy leaving for Maniwaki. Luc felt guilty hearing the verdict. He had developed a certain affection for Adela and because of his indiscretion, she was being sent away. Not knowing what to do to repair his mistake, he went to Achille and told him what had happened.

Achille was stunned to learn that Adela was pregnant. Not that he was shocked, but he felt stupid for not having noticed it himself. Even more so because she had quite possibly told him while talking to him. Only at this moment did he remember her putting her hand on her belly and understand the meaning of the gesture. She was going to leave without him knowing who she was or where she came from, and especially, without having understood a single one of the thousands of words she had been saying to him for weeks. He decided to ask his friend Gaby to act as his interpreter. In Alberta, Francophones had to be able to speak English to survive, and Gaby had learned the language as a child.

Adela was in great distress after Clyde's announcement. She could not return to Fogo Island, for she did not have a penny. She was going to be left without resources or even a roof over her head in an unfamiliar city. She had been through Maniwaki on the way up to the camp, just as she had passed through other villages, but she could not remember it. And how was she to take care of the child who was going to be born?

She felt shy when she saw Achille coming with Gaby, even more so when the man explained that Achille had asked him to translate what she had been telling him over the past weeks. Thus he finally learned about her island, her escape, how she had been sold, and her arrival at the lumber camp. He was astonished, and understood her great despair. He left her, asking Gaby to tell her that everything would be all right.

"Poor little thing, she's had a hard time and the future doesn't look any brighter for her," Gaby said.

"You told me once that in life, there's what's fair and what's not fair. And this isn't fair," said Achille, heading over to see Clyde and give him a piece of his mind.

"A pregnant woman in a lumber camp? It's just not done. It's indecent!" cried Clyde, unmoved.

Gaby, who had followed Achille, could not help but reply: "And a man who paws young boys, is that indecent?"

Clyde's face became crimson, but he did not back down.

"All right then, tell your boss to get my pay ready, because I'm leaving too," said Achille.

Gaby was surprised to hear Achille, usually so docile, talk this way. He did not find the decision fair either, and knew how insensitive the forestry companies were towards their workers.

"You can do mine at the same time," said Gaby, "and I think you're going to have to do it for a few others too."

Clyde did not believe them. Men did not leave their jobs in the lumber camps, they were dismissed. Gaby decided to inform the others. Omer Lafond, who was a man of heart, sensitive to the fate of his fellow men, immediately announced that he too would ask for his pay the next day.

"And any man here who has a heart should do the same," he said, intending for the others to hear him.

The next morning, about twenty men were waiting in front of Clyde's office. One after the other, they asked for the money that was owed them. Clyde could not believe his ears. He had a mutiny on his hands. And none of these men leaving could be replaced, at least not this year. It revolted him to have to back down, but he had no choice. And he knew that his bosses would hold him responsible if the camp did not meet its quota. He agreed to keep on the Newfoundlander until the snow melted, but she would have to leave when the lumber camp ended. He saw fit to add: "…And I don't want her having that baby here!" As if she could have dictated the course of nature.

When winter grew weary and slowly shed its white mantle, Adela arrived at the end of her pregnancy. Her back curved to support the weight of her belly, which had become so heavy that she had trouble walking up the stairs from the front stoop to the kitchen.

In spite of pleas from Clyde, who had to form the log driving team for the season, Achille refused to take part this time, and asked for the wages he had accumulated over the year. For the past weeks, he had thought a great deal and made certain decisions. On the day of his departure, he went to the kitchen early and signalled for Adela to follow him. She was happy, for she had feared that Achille might remain at the camp for the log driving. The horses had been hitched up to drive the group to the next stopping place, where a truck was to pick them up and take them to Maniwaki. The voyage was difficult for the young woman and when the group moved from the cart to the truck, it was even worse. The truck rocked from side to side along the road and bounced them up in the air each time they drove over a pothole or a rock, of which there were many.

The pain arrived like a knife through her belly. It began low down, but soon it was spreading through her back. Adela uttered a hoarse cry. It sounded like nothing that the men had heard before. A cry of pain mingled with a superhuman effort.

"I…I think he's coming," she said in a tense, strained voice.

The waters broke just before Maniwaki and her cries of pain grew louder. In spite of the relatively cool weather, she was perspiring profusely. She sought the hand of Achille, who grasped it without really knowing what else he could do to ease such suffering. He leaned over to murmur into her ear. She did not understand, but his voice was reassuring. She pressed his hand.

The men sitting in the back of the truck began to knock like mad on the cabin, demanding that the two passengers in front give her their place, which they hastened to do. When the truck finally arrived in Maniwaki, it passed the forestry company office without stopping, heading straight for the nun's hospital located next to the Eglise de L'Assomption. The sisters were surprised to see twenty-odd men emerge from the truck, some of whom were lifting the young woman out with care to take her into the hospital.

Between two contractions, Adela looked up at the big three-storey building. Her stomach weighed on her, ripping her entrails. She wept, searching the group for Achille's face. She could only see the cornette of the nun who had come out to meet her. She thought of how her life had been turned upside down since her departure from Fogo. Here she was, a young girl strictly raised in Anglican tradition, suspicious of Catholicism, in the arms of a Catholic nun and about to give birth to an illegitimate child.

Once again she had been thrown into the arms of strangers.

She thought: "I'll never see Tilting again."

# Nine

The affair had the police working overtime. How could the old man have slipped through their fingers? What's more, it had taken the hospital several hours to even notice he was missing. The hospital director was unable to explain how the man could have escaped. Police captain Lapierre had trouble containing his rage and decided to take matters in hand. A description of the missing man had been sent to the media. Unfortunately, the provincial police force, the Sûreté du Québec, did not have a photo of him. Nor did Achille Roy exist in the files of the provincial auto insurance bureau, which issued drivers' licences.

"How is it possible for a man to live so long without ending up in someone's files or anyone having a photo of him?" Lapierre asked himself.

The "Wanted" notice read: "Caucasian man, 88 years old. Could be travelling by canoe on the Gatineau River." The newspapers were treating it as a case of Alzheimer's disease. Most had simply recopied what the police had written, softening the blunt, minimalist style that is typical of official police documents. Other journalists, seeking a more sensationalist effect, made their own speculations, citing cases of elderly people suffering from Alzheimer's who had been found too late.

However, the more Martin learned about this story, the more it interested him. Benoît had gathered information here and there, but the man remained a mystery. He had been living on a little farm in Sainte-Famille d'Aumond for almost seventy years, yet no one knew him very well. From what Martin had learned from people such as Oscar, the taxi driver, faithful eavesdropper of police radio conversations, Achille Roy had decided to take off by canoe to transport his wife's ashes to Newfoundland. Why Newfoundland? He still did not know. Maybe the lady had always wanted to go to Newfoundland. "Odd idea," thought Martin, trying to recall what he knew about Newfoundland, which was not very much. He knew it was a big island where people lived from fishing, and which had made the headlines during the cod crisis. A former British colony, Newfoundland had been the last province to join Canada, in 1949.

Martin decided to go to Sainte-Famille d'Aumond to talk to the villagers. His first stop, as ever, was the village store. It was obviously an old building, and had not aged well. It was a former general store, the kind that used to be found in every village, and there must have been a time when it sold a bit of everything: food, hardware supplies, construction materials and even clothing, all the vital necessities of village life. Once, the store's façade must have stretched some fifteen metres on the village's main street. But with the improvement of roads, and the rise of the automobile, which made it easier to get around, the people of the village found a wider selection of goods and often better prices in Maniwaki, Mont-Laurier and even Hull.

Gradually, the store had reduced its floor space. Clothing was one of the first things to go, followed by hardware and construction supplies. Finally the grocery section had been reduced to that of a *dépanneur*, with a few jars of jam, a cold room filled with beer, a counter where cigarettes and lottery tickets were sold, and of course, a large wall of videos for rent. A little snack bar, only open during the summer, had been set up in one part of the old, near-empty building.

Hanging on the wall by the front door were old photos of the store and the village. Looking at the photos, one could see how the little village had declined since the photographer had taken them. The handsome storefront, where one could see the words *Crytes et fils, magasin général* written in big letters, had been replaced by a nondescript fluorescent sign, three-quarters covered by the name of the multinational Pepsi company, with the words *Dépanneur Crytes* written below in smaller letters. This newer sign had a lot less panache.

There was a man behind the counter who looked as if he were part of the furnishings. He quickly butted the cigarette he was furtively smoking. For several years, non-smokers had been applying more and more pressure to get smoking outlawed in public places. Smoking behind his counter, as he had always done, was becoming difficult. Particularly fussy customers had threatened to take their business elsewhere if he continued smoking in his store. Edgar Crytes knew his customers and knew which ones could tolerate the smoke of his cigarettes without protest, and those he had to hide from. Men were generally less adamant than women, but with strangers, one never knew.

Martin introduced himself, but waited before bringing up the reason for his visit. The idea of doing a series of articles on the southern municipalities had served him well so far. He resolved to proceed in the same fashion this time. Edgar Crytes was flattered and showed him old photos of the village and store, talking effusively about the good old days when the store had been the centre of the community. Edgar had acquired the store from his father, who had run it all his life. He knew everyone in this village, which he had never left except for two years when he went off to pursue his education.

Martin took a few photos of the owner in front of his store. The photo made both look better than they did in reality. In the photo, one could only see the remaining section of the old and sumptuous storefront. Martin had insisted that the owner put on his white grocer's apron, which he had not worn for years. In the photo, he had his arms crossed across his chest, which camouflaged the yellow stains that countless cigarettes had left on his fingers, while giving him a more dignified bearing.

Just as Martin was about to leave, pretending he had just remembered an unimportant detail, he broached the subject that interested him most.

"Oh, yes, incidentally, do you know that man who supposedly took off in a canoe?"

"Old Achille? Of course. There are a lot of things in this *dépanneur* we keep in stock just for him. I'd say he's the only customer we have who buys everything here. When we closed the hardware section, I kept on supplying him. He'd come here with his list, and I'd go get what he wanted from Maniwaki."

"Seems he's a bit off his head?" Martin dared to ask.

"Achille? He's definitely an original, especially in this day and age, but he's got more spunk than you and I put together," said Edgar.

Lowering his voice confidentially, though he and Martin were alone in the *dépanneur*, he added: "You know, I value his opinion on almost everything. He's pretty amazing. During the last elections for mayor, I didn't know who to vote for. I talked to Achille about it, even though he didn't know any of the candidates. I asked him: 'Who do you think we should vote for, Mr. Achille?' You know what he said?" asked Edgar, without waiting for reply. "He just said: 'I'd vote for the one I can believe, and the one I can believe is the one who can look me in the eye when he tells me why he's running for mayor.' And you know what? He was right, pure and simple. That's how Mr. Achille is. So when someone tells me he's off his head, I say he has more sense than a lot of other people I could name."

"Did you know he'd decided to go to Newfoundland by canoe?"

"No, but it doesn't surprise me. Well, yes it does a bit, but on the other hand, young man, they were the most remarkable couple I've ever seen."

"Remarkable? How?"

"You know, in a small village, everyone knows everyone else's business. We know everybody's stories, the ones we want to know and others we'd prefer not to. We know who's slept with who, and when. We know when couples are fighting and can even predict the moment they'll split up. There are couples that last, but most of them find it hard. That couple was another story. You know how they say you can see a current pass between a man and a woman? Well with them it was always like that. They'd come in here and I'd see it. He'd look at her and I could see it in his eyes. It was like that all the time. And she was the same. When she died, I went to see him. So if he's off to Newfoundland in a canoe, that doesn't surprise me."

"But why Newfoundland?"

"That's where she was from. But around here, there weren't many people who really knew them, besides the old notary, Mr. Lafleur. I mean, we saw them around, but not a lot. Their life was each other. They even had their own sort of jargon, a way of talking to each other that we didn't always understand. It was a mixture of French and English, but it wasn't really English because people who spoke English couldn't follow what they were saying. Old McCloud told me it was a kind of old English from England that isn't spoken any more."

"But you must have met them at social activities or at church?"

"Church?" scoffed Edgar. "Anywhere but there! My father told me a story once; it's part of the local folklore. Seems that Achille and his wife, and their child as well, went to church one day. At that time, the village was under the thumb of Father Perras. He tore strips off them from the pulpit like you wouldn't believe. My father said his hair stood on end to listen to that sermon. It made you ashamed to be Catholic. Two days later, Father Perras went to see Achille at his home. Apparently Achille kicked him on the backside all the way off his property. It was quite a big deal at the time."

"You say there was a child?"

"Well, I never knew him very well. I saw him at school, and after that he left. We never saw him much after that."

Martin thanked him. He was intrigued by what he had just heard. He decided to go visit the notary. Lafleur greeted him suspiciously. He answered his questions about the village of Aumond, but when he brought up the subject of the man in the canoe, he could not fool the notary as he had the owner of the *dépanneur*. The notary stiffened and showed him the door.

"I have nothing more to say to you, sir, and I would like you to leave."

"Listen, I'm sorry, that was clumsy of me. The truth is, I want to know more about him. I've heard he's not right in the head, but from everything I've learned about him up until now, he doesn't seem to be as feeble-minded as people say."

"You and the other journalists who've made him out to be a crazy old man are despicable. Most of the media made up their minds about him when the Sûreté du Québec put out a bulletin saying he was disturbed, and that's how they've been treating the case ever since."

"That's true, and I agree with you, but if no one corrects that information, he'll continue to be thought of as a crazy old man. That's why I've come to see you," urged Martin.

The notary hesitated. What the journalist was saying was true, but could he trust him? Too many times, journalists asked seemingly innocent questions and people replied trustingly, only to see their words misrepresented and quoted out of context in the paper, giving them a meaning that had nothing to do with reality. Sensationalism reigned supreme.

Martin knew that journalists had a bad reputation, and he could not blame the man for being on his guard.

"You know, sir, I don't know this man. And the idea of going to Newfoundland by canoe seems…strange, to say the least. But I also find it very strange that people are making such an effort to stop him from doing what he wants," emphasised Martin.

"That's just the point!" said the notary, suddenly realising that he had just divulged a piece of information. "Listen, I'll agree to talk to you, but there is certain information that I would ask you not to use."

Martin agreed, and for once he even offered to show the notary what he had written before publishing it. The notary looked him warily in the eye as he spoke. He was sizing him up. There was a long silence. The journalist held the old man's gaze without flinching. The notary's face relaxed, indicating to Martin that he had decided to trust him.

For almost two hours, Norbert Lafleur told him about the man and woman who lived on the land on Concession Road IV. He told him what he knew about Achille and Adela, how the man had arrived out of the blue one day seventy years before, and on the spot, had bought a little farm for a woman who had just had a baby. He talked about their strange and moving love. He also said that the child was not Achille's. Martin saw there was a drama here that he knew nothing about, something having to do with this child. The child, Paul, had left the region when he was quite young and had almost never returned. According to the notary, people said the boy had had a lot of trouble at school, where he was often a laughing-stock. When he was of an age to make his own decisions, he had disowned his family. Achille had been very hurt by this, for himself, because he considered him his own son, but especially for Adela, the boy's biological mother, who had suffered so greatly from his birth. He also told him about the scene with Father Perras, who had treated them like pariahs because Adela was not Catholic, and especially because the couple was not married.

"I know that must seem strange today, but at the time, it created a scandal. Achille stood up to everyone for her," the old notary told the young man.

Martin also learned that the woman's name was Adela Cole and that she had come from a little island off Newfoundland. But he did not learn much more. However, the notary told him, the postmistress could give him more information, for she used to visit Achille and Adela quite often. The lady's name was Nicole Lyrette. One day Nicole had left the village and returned a year later with a baby. Everyone knew that the child was not a creation of the Holy Sprit, but no one knew anything more about it.

"Did he talk to you about his project?"

"Of course he talked to me about it! I even helped him out," the notary replied.

"Why do it by canoe?"

"You'd have to know Achille Roy to understand, my young friend. Come, I'll show you."

The two men left the room where they had been talking, crossed the kitchen and went outside. They headed for a little building, a former garage whose doors were barred shut with a plank of wood. Martin helped the old man remove it and the two big doors swung open, revealing the room the notary wanted to show him. The object was sitting up on trestles. It was a real collector's item, this canoe, which had to be six metres long, built according to the traditional method of the Algonquins. The frame was composed of slender cedar ribs, the bottom meticulously covered with the bark of a big birch. The ends had been sewn so as to create a nice curve and joined at the gunwales with slender roots of white spruce. The seams had then been waterproofed with a light sealer, a mixture of resins whose secret recipe Achille had learned from Raphaël Smith. Patient scraping had created unusual patterns in the bark. Notary Lafleur admitted that he used it very rarely, first of all, because he considered it a work of art. He liked fishing, but had long since replaced the canoe with an aluminium boat. The two men stood admiring the treasure in silence. It was perfect, and so light that it could be lifted with just one hand. Achille had given him this remarkable present to thank him for helping him buy his house.

"I turned down five thousand dollars from an American collector who saw it one day when I took it out to wash it."

Norbert Lafleur told him Achille had acquired a solid reputation as a canoeist, both in the lumber camps and as a guide for American fishermen.

"You know, he once shot the Devil's Rapid on the Gatineau River to save a man's life," he told Martin, who had no idea what this "devil's rapid" could be. The notary explained to him that these were long and dangerous rapids, terrifying and practically impossible to navigate by canoe. He was the only man in memory, at least the only white man, to have accomplished such a feat and come out of it alive.

"So you see, canoeing down the river is not a challenge for him."

He also told him about the couple's canoe rides. The story was starting to make more sense. But to go to Newfoundland by this means of transport still seemed odd to the journalist. Just as he was about to leave, the notary told Martin that he was not the first person who had been asking questions about Achille. Martin was surprised.

"Who else – another journalist?"

"No, not a journalist," he said hesitantly. "Three men came to see me shortly after Achille's departure. I think it was the day after. There was a lawyer from Montreal. A young know-it-all, in my opinion, dressed like a businessman. He was with an Anglophone who didn't say much, but from what I could tell, he was the boss. At least, the chauffeur driving the limousine opened the door for him and not the others. And then there was Achille's son, Paul."

"His son? His son came to see you? I thought he'd left the region?"

"Yes, and it's even more surprising when you consider they had to call him several times before he would come pay his last respects to his mother. I know that because Achille used my phone each time he needed to make a call, which was once or twice a year. Paul finally came, but he stayed just an hour then hurried back to Montreal. Achille told me he didn't think Paul would ever be back, even to bury him."

"May I ask you what they wanted?"

"They wanted to know about the transactions Achille made on his land."

"On his land? What do you mean?"

"Well, you know I'm bound by professional secrecy, but if you go to the registry office, you'll see that I registered a three thousand dollar mortgage on Achille Roy's land. It was he who insisted I do it. I'd have lent him money on his word alone. The son also wanted to know what's in the will. They threatened to take legal measures to find out. I didn't tell them anything."

"Amazing," said Martin.

"Not really. As far as I know, Paul has become a rather miserable human being who worships money and his own interests above all. But what's most astonishing is the offer they made me. The boss mumbled something in the lawyer's ear, and he offered me double the amount Achille owed me if I'd just hand over the mortgage."

"Double the amount? Well, that is surprising. May I ask what you told them?"

"At my age, you know, money has little importance. I'm not rich, but I have enough money to live peacefully and eat three times a day. And besides, Achille Roy's friendship is worth a lot more to me than their dollars. Paul was furious. I have to say that I got more pleasure from seeing how put off they were than from any profit I could have made," said Norbert Lafleur with a mischievous smile.

"I know Mr. Roy is your friend and I won't hold it against you if you don't want to answer me, but I'd like to know what that money was for?"

"To finance his trip."

"But with that money, he could have taken the plane!" exclaimed Martin.

"Achille has never left the region. He has never taken a plane and he wanted to do things his own way. I admire that," he said.

Martin left, thanking the notary for his confidence. He noted that everyone who had come into contact with Achille, whether recently or in the past, had a great deal of respect for him. He was a kind of hermit, but one who seemed to possess many fine qualities that touched everyone who knew him. But what could have suddenly interested the ingrate son and most of all, his ultra-rich and mysterious companion? Certainly not Achille's fortune, for he had only the money the notary had lent him, and his little piece of land.

He went to the post office next. Nicole Lyrette was a woman of forty-seven. She had worked as postmistress since the age of twenty-four and would soon be able to retire. When Martin started to question her about Achille Roy and his wife, she clammed up. The journalist tried in vain to explain that he did not want to harm Achille and in fact was looking to help him, but to no avail. However, just as he was about to leave she blurted: "If anyone tries to say he's crazy, they'll have to answer to me!"

Clearly, she too had a high opinion of the man. Martin decided that he would pay a visit to the registry office later to verify the notary's information. That day, when he got back to the office, Benoît was busy writing at his computer. He greeted him and asked him how the Dagenais inquest was going. The intern, obviously ill at ease, did not know where to begin.

"The boss bawled me out," he said. "He knew I was inquiring into Dagenais' arrest on your behalf, and since this morning, no one can lay a finger on Dagenais. He's the new Messiah. Didn't you listen to the radio?"

Martin had no idea what he was talking about. He had been concentrating on his article and had not listened to the news.

"Dagenais held his press conference this morning," said Benoît.

"His press conference? About his famous factory?"

"Yup! Dagenais announced the opening of a billboard factory in the region. A hundred million dollar investment that's supposed to create two hundred jobs. A really big deal. He even managed to insinuate that, at the time of his arrest, that was what he was in the middle of negotiating."

"Obviously he's going to use that to get himself off the hook or at least excuse his behaviour: 'I was drunk, Your Honour, but look, I'm working to create two hundred jobs!'" fumed Martin. "But is this project serious? I've seen and heard about a lot of projects that never came to anything," he continued, suspicious as ever when it came to Dagenais.

"Very serious. The Forestech Company has even proposed to build the factory. All the high rollers were there to make the announcement," he said, showing Martin a photo of the group taken at the press conference.

Martin naturally recognised the president of the Regional Committee on Industry, all smiles, and stage centre. Standing around him were the Commissioner of Industry, old Ovide, big Dagenais' official snitch, as well as two other people he did not know who were representing the Forestech Company.

"In pocket they've got the contract to supply the wood, as well as a letter from the forestry minister," continued Benoît. "In my opinion, this time it's for real. But I got the feeling a few things are still missing. When I brought up financing, they said there were 'still some loose ends to tie up' but that it would be done soon. The minister himself is supposed to come here in person in a month or two to make the official announcement and launch the construction."

"Obviously, Fatcat Dagenais had to put pressure on someone to get the announcement made before his trial. Have you checked with the arresting officers?" asked Martin.

"I managed to see one of them without him seeing me. I hung around the police station watching the officers come and go. I saw one who was sporting quite the raccoon mask. Both his eyes were black. When he saw me, he did an about-face and disappeared into the police station. Two minutes later, the boss called me on my cell phone and told me to get over there on the double. That's when he told me about the press conference. He also threatened to give me my walking papers if I dug for any more dirt on Dagenais. It's a dirty business!" he said.

"Very!" muttered Martin.

"It was the boss who told me there'd be a press conference this morning. I wanted to warn you but he stopped me. That was when he warned me that I couldn't investigate Dagenais any more."

Benoît was making progress; he did not call Dagenais "Mister" any more. Maybe he would end up being able to say "Fat Dagenais." Talking to Martin, Benoît recovered his journalistic ardour. But when faced with the boss, he gritted his teeth and toed the line. Martin advised him to keep a low profile so the boss would forget about him. He knew the boss and his terrible rages. Benoît was in danger of getting himself fired if he did not bend to his will.

It was hard to get people to talk. Everyone kept his or her mouth shut. The police had been told "mum's the word," and assault charges would probably not be laid against Dagenais. He could always get by on an impaired driving charge. Many political, artistic and sports personalities were regularly stopped for drunk driving. Their driver's licences were suspended for a year, and people forgave them, especially when there were no victims. Though socially, driving under the influence was condemned, people could still remember a time (and it was not so long ago) when a drunk driver's only punishment would be the confiscation of the bottle he was holding between his legs. Besides, Dagenais had the means to pay a chauffeur for a year, an idea that did not displease him. It would make him feel important. But to face charges of assault with injuries was risky. Dagenais, who had the ambition of running for Member of the National Assembly one day, knew this. Not only did he aspire to a life in politics, he considered it his due, but a criminal record including an act of violence was a serious matter and the doors of politics would forever be closed to him.

But was Martin going to find the information, to get the officers involved to talk? And then there was the mystery man whom Dagenais had spent the evening with. Today he had affirmed that he had been "working" on the factory dossier on the night of the incident. So who was this stranger who had spent the evening with him? It had to be one of the men who appeared on the official photo that Benoît had shown him. Maybe Dagenais had bought him a night of sex to incite him to go ahead with the project. That was Dagenais' usual *modus operandi*. Maybe the method was morally questionable, but who was going to complain now that he had announced a hundred million dollar investment? Most people would have been outraged by such practices before the factory's construction had been announced, but today they would surely be ready to pitch in and reimburse him for what he paid the girl.

Martin headed for the Rialdo. The usual quartet of resident gossips was sitting there working on their fourth cups of coffee. As usual, the journalist sat down at the table next to theirs. Naturally the discussion revolved around the big factory whose construction Dagenais had just announced. Collin was in the middle of saying that at last he would be able to find a job, but everyone knew that he would keep his distance from the place. Collin would never apply, for fear that he would be offered a real permanent job. He would only work as long as it took to accumulate enough hours to qualify for unemployment insurance. Those who knew him avoided giving him work for too long a period. As soon as he had accumulated the required number of hours, he ceased to be productive, failed to come into work some days and set about getting himself laid off.

"You get the impression that Dagenais has just prettied-up his image again with his factory announcement. What do you think, Martin?" asked Oscar.

"I'm sure he has. He can't erase his breathalyser reading, but I was surprised there was no mention of his fight with the police officers. It looks as if it's been suppressed. Maybe, after all, that fight was just a bit of a tussle," said Martin.

"A bit of a *tussle*? No way!" exploded Oscar. "That guy was really bleeding, damn it!"

Oscar seemed to know more than he was letting on. Martin decided to meet with him later. After all, Oscar had heard the conversations on the police radio band. He was sure that Oscar would not say more, there at the restaurant.

"Anyway, with that announcement, Dagenais went from asshole to hero," grumbled Réal, the trucker. "I wouldn't be surprised if he makes himself a bundle of cash, that's what he usually does."

"Not counting the little contracts he'll negotiate under the table once the factory's built," added Jacques.

Despite their lack of education, they saw things the way they were. They constituted a representative sample of the general population. While eagerly putting Dagenais down, and fully aware of his dishonesty, they were ready to forget everything for the sake of the famous factory, which they had been promised for so long. Martin left them, not without murmuring in Oscar's ear that he would stop by the taxi station later to have a word with him. Then he dropped by the registry office where he asked to look at the registers for Lot 4, Concession Road IV of the township of Aumond.

"It's a popular lot these days," the woman employee commented, surprised. "You're the second person who's asked to look at the transactions on this lot."

He did not learn much from the register. Since Achille had bought the property in 1920, nothing had happened except several days earlier, when the notary Lafleur had registered his possessory lien, as he had told Martin. When he had finished, he asked the woman if she could tell him who else had looked at the register.

"He asked for a copy. The signature on the receipt belongs to a Maître Robert Blanchette, a lawyer from Montreal."

"Probably the same lawyer who went to see Lafleur," thought Martin. Though he did not yet have all the information, he was feverishly excited at the thought of writing his story on the *old man and the canoe*. Sitting at his computer, he smoked two cigarettes and gulped down his coffee, then started typing the first lines. He thought about the old man, who was unique, to say the least, and the justice system that was pursuing him because, so they said, he did not have all his faculties. Inspiration struck:

### TO NEWFOUNDLAND BY CANOE AT THE AGE OF 88
*An astonishing act of love or madness?*

*Is it madness to strike out on an adventure at the age of 88 to fulfil a promise made to the woman you loved for seventy years, or is it an extraordinary act of love?*

*Love is what inspires the exceptional story of this man from Sainte-Famille d'Aumond, Achille Roy, who the Sûreté du Québec have been searching for since he escaped from the psychiatric ward of the Maniwaki Health Centre, where he was being held.*

*Achille Roy is a man who has lived quietly in the region for his entire life. For almost seventy years, he shared his life with a woman from Newfoundland, Adela Cole, who died last month. An unassuming couple, always full of love for each other, they were known in their village as the most striking example of what a united couple should be.*

*Having left Newfoundland when she was only sixteen, Adela Cole never returned to Fogo Island, where she was born. It seems her husband promised to take her back to her native land one day. Using the means of transportation that he knows best – and he is said to be an expert canoeist – Achille Roy set out on a very unusual expedition ten days ago: on the Gatineau River, in a canoe, with his wife's ashes. His destination: Fogo Island, Newfoundland. A voyage of 2500 kilometres by canoe, which will take him through a stretch of open sea.*

*But now the Quebec provincial court has judged that the man is no longer in his right mind and ordered that he be placed under observation while it decides whether he should be permanently confined to institutional care. Several hours after his arrest, the old man took leave of his jailers and resumed his astonishing voyage to Newfoundland.*

*For the Sûreté du Québec, the man's escape has given rise to a veritable manhunt. Moreover the police have issued a province-wide alert. However, according to the people of the village of Aumond, Achille Roy is not as crazy as some say.*

*"He's definitely an original, especially in this day and age, but he's got more spunk than you and I put together," declared Edgar Crytes, a citizen of Aumond who knew him well. Owner of the village dépanneur, Edgar Crytes says he has never hesitated to consult Achille Roy on all sorts of matters because of Mr. Roy's unshakeable judgement. The village postmistress, Nicole Lyrette, claims that if anyone tries to make Achille Roy out as crazy, they'll have her to answer to. For the time being, the old man and the ashes of the woman he loved are out there somewhere on the waters of the Ottawa or the Saint Lawrence River, heading for Fogo Island.*

The story was accompanied by a photo of the house where Adela and Achille had lived. He had also included the photo of Edgar Crytes in front of the half-storefront of his establishment. The article read well and the illustrations were inviting. Satisfied, Martin put the finishing touches on the story and sent it off to the layout department. Then he wrote up the reports he had done that week and recopied a series of small, socially oriented items.

His deadline was approaching. As usual, he finished his last piece barely two minutes before zero hour. Every week he told himself that this time, he would write his articles ahead of time, but something always came up to upset his schedule. The day before his deadline, he usually sat up most of the night writing his articles and telling himself he would never make it on time. But two minutes before his time ran out, he would finish his last piece. Life in a weekly newspaper was no joyride.

When five o'clock arrived, he was exhausted and started putting his things away. Friday being the only day when Martin could officially say that he finished at five o'clock, he had got into the habit of having a beer with friends at Chez Martineau. Chez Martineau was a strange place. The establishment had been built just across from the railway station. The railway linked Maniwaki to Hull. In the earlier part of the century, everyone who got off the train went there to quench their thirst. Workers on their way to lumber camps in the north also spent the night there. Then the train stopped running, the station closed its doors and was demolished, but Chez Martineau had remained the same, except for the hotel rooms upstairs which had been closed for good. Of course the clientele had changed, but the place was still a tavern. No one knew why, but everyone preferred this bar to all others. Entering it, one felt as if one had stepped into another time zone. Maybe it was because in this place, you could still order quart bottles of beer, and there was no music, as there was in other bars, to prevent you from talking to your neighbour. You were just as likely to meet a politician, nurse, or logger, as you were to meet the local wino, sometimes all at the same table.

Martin liked this atmosphere. Here, no one could put on airs. From four o'clock, the place started to fill, first with civil servants, then, gradually, with other workers. From five to seven on Fridays, the establishment was filled to capacity, buzzing with hundreds of conversations going on in the room from one end to another, each competing with the ones at the next table. A joyous weekend atmosphere prevailed. Then at seven, after filling up on beer, everyone suddenly remembered a wife, husband or children at home. The place emptied. Only the regulars remained, serious drinkers who had been there before everyone arrived and would be there until late in the evening, when the waiter announced the traditional last call.

For Martin, it was also an excellent place to learn the news of the day, items he already knew about and others he would never have learned if alcohol had not loosened people's tongues and numbed their brains. Of course the talk of the tavern was the big new factory. The two local radio stations had saturated the airwaves with the story, broadcasting Dagenais' pompous declarations all day long. One week before, when people were talking about his arrest, Dagenais was considered a bastard. This week, the tone was different: "Goddamn Dagenais. He may be crooked as hell but he's tough, you gotta give him that," said one of the regulars who the week before had announced for all to hear that he had always considered Dagenais "a big fat-arse no-good."

Martin had soon had enough. As he was leaving the bar, he remembered he had promised to drop by the taxi station, which was strategically located close to the bar. Oscar did not often take time off. Martin wondered how he could stay married. He was at the station practically seven days a week and spent almost all his nights there. He had brought in an armchair, where he spent most of his time, as well as a sofa where he dozed off at night. A little television on a shelf in the corner was always on.

Martin found Oscar sitting on his usual chair. Next to him, the radio that picked up the CB band emitted a crackling sound from which words would occasionally emerge. Oscar was watching an old film on the television, leaning towards the radio when a sound came out of it. That way he would know before everyone else when a fire was reported. By listening to the ambulance drivers, he learned who had just had a heart attack or an accident. And of course, he eavesdropped on even the slightest conversation between police officers.

He was not surprised when he saw Martin enter.

"I was wondering when you'd come. Not easy for a newspaper man to admit that an old taxi driver like me could know more than him, eh?"

He was right, but Martin also knew that it was often from the most humble and retiring people that one learned the most. However, Oscar was not always a reliable source. He was so proud of being the first to broadcast his little bits of news that sometimes he got carried away. Before his usual audience at the Rialdo restaurant, Oscar added details, embellishments and drama to the stories he had heard. When he reported a fire, he would frequently say that there were four or five trucks at the scene, whereas the fire department only owned three. Or that the fire had burned all night whereas it had only taken an hour to get it under control. Or that such-and-such a road accident victim was at death's door, whereas he only had contusions. These embellishments guaranteed him an interested and admiring audience.

"That's true, Oscar, but I have to say, I don't spend my nights listening to the radio. Maybe I'm not as well informed as you about the police, but I do have a sex life," he replied with a touch of humour.

Oscar ignored this reply, even though Martin was right. Oscar's wife had never much liked sex. In fact, to say that was far from the truth. She hated it. She considered men monsters with one-track minds. The rare times he had obtained her favours, she was almost glacial, submitting "because she had to." She counted the minutes until her husband attained orgasm, and then returned to her beach novels and magazines. He had ended up preferring the solitude of the taxi station to the chill of home.

"Listen, Oscar, seems to me that Fat Dagenais is getting off easy, especially because, unless I'm mistaken, he had a run-in with the cops," said Martin.

"He did, no doubt about it, but you know how chummy-chummy he is with the police chief, so it's not too surprising the case died."

"Yes, and it seems the officers have been ordered to keep their mouths shut. Even their union rep, who's a big-mouth, seems to have clammed up."

"The chief must have promised to take care of a few litigation files with the union in exchange for his silence," Oscar concluded with a lucidity that astonished Martin.

"I think so too, but it pisses me off to think Fat Dagenais can get off so easy when if you or I had slugged a police officer, we'd have been on the front page of *Allô Police*."

"That's for sure. And I can tell you, we'd have been in deep you-know-what. But Dagenais has got a lot of clout. And now that he's made the announcement about his factory, you're going to have even more trouble finding people to talk to you."

"As a matter of fact, I'd like to know what you heard on the radio that night."

"I heard everything," said Oscar, letting Martin stew in his curiosity.

"…And?"

"Listen Martin, you're a good kid and I like what you write. I think you're the only one trips them up from time to time and stops them from doing what they want, but…"

Martin had heard this before. It was the kind of preamble people used to tell him they couldn't talk to him.

"You know, Dagenais can get heavy-handed and I don't want any trouble with him. He could bar my taxi from all the local businesses. Just to do me in, he could decide to start his own taxi service…He told me so himself."

"He told you that? You mean recently?"

"Yup, he heard about what I said at the Rialdo the other day, and he had the message passed on to me. If I so much as talk about it, I'll be crossed off the call-list at the hospital. The big guy has friends on the hospital board and strongly hinted there'd been complaints about me, which is false. He told me he'd defend me so I can keep doing transfers, as long as I keep my mouth shut."

Oscar made most of his revenue from these transfers. The hospital often required his services to transport a patient who had to go to Hull for an appointment with a specialist. The taxi was a lot more economical than an ambulance when the patient did not need a stretcher and was not in danger of having an attack. Each trip brought in $400. For Oscar, it was manna from heaven, and Martin was well aware of it. To cancel the transfers would be a typical Dagenais tactic. He ran over anyone who stood in his way. Dagenais owned most of the board members in all the public services and used his influence to get contracts or banish anyone who might threaten his dictatorship.

"I understand," said Martin, who was preparing to leave with regret when Oscar hurriedly added: "I won't tell you anything, but if you heard it yourself, you could use it, couldn't you?"

"Well of course, but the problem is that I didn't hear it myself, like I just told you."

"You didn't hear it *then*, but if you heard it now, you could use it…"

Oscar reached towards the CB receiver and showed him a little tape recorder. It was a cheap machine with a built-in microphone, the kind made twenty years earlier.

"You know, Martin, we're not even supposed to listen to conversations on the police channel, to say nothing of recording them, but for years I've used this little tape recorder because sometimes they talk so fast on this radio you don't have time to understand. So I record it and play it back when I want to hear it again. And that night, when I heard the officer, I turned on the tape recorder. So now I'm giving you the cassette, but I've never heard anything about it. That cassette is not mine, and I don't want anything to do with it."

"You taped the conversation?" Martin asked, astonished.

"No, I didn't tape anything. You did," he repeated, holding onto the cassette until the reporter confirmed it.

"Of course, of course," said Martin, overjoyed.

He would have liked to listen to it immediately, but he knew that Oscar was uneasy and wanted to get rid of this burden as quickly as possible.

"Here, now go, and don't talk to me about it again."

"Thank you," Martin simply said. He almost wanted to kiss him.

Just as he was going out the door, Oscar said to him through his teeth: "Try not to let the son of a bitch get away!"

"Don't worry, I won't."

Martin could not believe his luck. The cassette contained the information he was looking for. He was so eager to listen to it that he could not wait to get home, and put the cassette in the tape player of his car. But after a few minutes, he had had enough, for the first recordings were about all kinds of events that had nothing to do with the subject of his research. Ambulance drivers talking to their dispatcher to confirm the address of a patient they had to pick up, then policemen communicating with the station to verify the identity of a driver in a bit too much of a hurry.

When he got home, he immediately turned on his tape player. The quality of the recording left much to be desired. Oscar's tape recorder was far from being a high quality device, but Martin could make out snatches of conversation. In the background the television could be heard, as well as Oscar's chair, whose springs creaked painfully with each of his movements. Martin had to listen to almost forty-five minutes of this cacophony. He was starting to give up hope when the recording got to the part that interested him.

"Car 12 here, we're about to intercept a beige Ford Taurus. The suspect vehicle pulled onto the road from 124 rue Principale. A suspected case of impaired driving. Proceeding to intercept."

The tape recorder had kept on, but for several long minutes there was nothing but the faraway noise of the taxi station television and Oscar's chair emitting little creaks with the slightest movement. Then the radio conversation resumed.

"Car 12 to central. Identity check for the name Pierre Dagenais, licence number DAGP12045002. Over!"

A new silence, then the voice spoke again even before the requested information was given.

"Officer Morin here. The individual seems to be under the influence of alcohol and is threatening Officer Gauthier. We're going to try to subdue him."

Again the tape rolled for several minutes, then the distraught voice of Officer Morin could be heard.

"Car 12 here, I need backup immediately. The suspect attacked us and Officer Gauthier is wounded. He was hit several times and is bleeding heavily. I repeat, requesting backup to subdue the suspect."

The rest was a jumble of jittery conversations between the station and the second patrol that had been despatched to arrest Dagenais. Martin could not discern who the other two officers were, but he understood they were from Car 7. He stopped the tape. So now he had proof. There had in fact been an altercation and one of the officers had even sustained blows to the face from Dagenais. He had also obtained confirmation of the names of the officers, Morin and Gauthier. Gauthier had been injured. But how was he going to use this information? The boss would never let him release a piece of news like this one. Dagenais was an octopus and his tentacles reached all the way to Martin's desk. He studied the cassette and resolved to put it in a safe place.

# Ten

It had been a difficult birth. The baby, a handsome boy weighing eight pounds, took over sixteen hours to be born. The doctor who finally showed up reeked of alcohol. Things had not gone well and Adela had lost consciousness.

When she finally woke, she was so weak that she could barely move her arms and her body ached as if she had been beaten. She had wept when she saw the child. This baby, so innocent and fragile, had turned her life upside down. She found him magnificent and took him from the nun who brought him in to her. The sister tried to speak to her, stammering a few words in English, but Adela did not understand very much. "Milk," the sister said, pointing to her breast. Adela understood that she had to feed the child. She had seen her mother do it, but her breasts were so painful and swollen that she could hardly touch them. When the baby managed to grip the nipple and suck, pain spread through her body right from the tip of her breasts. But gradually, as the baby drank, the pressure diminished and the pain with it.

The doctor finally made an appearance.

"So you're awake again. You were lucky," he said.

There was still a trace of alcohol on his breath.

"Unfortunately, there were complications and I don't think you'll be able to have any more children," he bluntly announced.

The verdict had been pronounced. This illegitimate child would be the only one she would ever have. She began to weep again at the bad luck that seemed to follow her everywhere.

Over the next few days, Adela recuperated a little. She answered the questions of the sister who had come to inquire after her and check whether the child had a father. When the nun asked if she wished to receive communion, Adela told her that she was Anglican, which made her grimace with distaste. She left the patient without another word. But the next day, the sister who was hospital director came to tell Adela to pack her bags and go.

"In any case," she informed her, "we don't accept the needy for more than a few days."

The good sisters' generosity seemed to vary according to the patient's religion. Where could Adela go with a newborn baby in this strange and hostile world? The sister recommended she go knock at the door of the Anglican Church. But just as she was leaving, Adela saw a profile she recognised, a face in the shadows by the front door of the hospital. The man was there…again.

Achille was talking with the Mother Superior, fidgeting with the toque he had removed when he had entered the hospital. His face lit up when he saw Adela coming towards him, slowly and painfully. He hurried to help her. She did not understand. What was he doing there? Even if he had told her, she would not have understood. No doubt Achille was trying to explain as he walked with her. The daylight irritated Adela's eyes as she emerged from the hospital. The child, whose face was uncovered, started to cry. Adela pulled down the blanket the sisters had given her, to create a screen between the sun and the newborn's eyes.

In front of the hospital, a horse and wagon were waiting.

"They're not mine. I borrowed them from the notary and I have to take them back this evening."

Adela listened without understanding a word, but she followed him like an automaton. What else could she do? They drove slowly for over two hours. Achille was talking, but stopped each time he saw the young woman's face twist with pain. Finally they left the main road and entered a smaller one. All one could see of it was a trail made by cartwheels. Grass grew down the middle, between the two furrows, forming a bushy line. They headed into a tunnel of tree branches, some of which hung so low that they had to lean over or brush them away. Finally the cart arrived in a field. On the left, a river flowed lazily, tracing a wide curve before disappearing a little farther along. By the water's edge grew a bank of luxuriant flowering vegetation. The perfume of the blossoms, borne by a light breeze, could be scented at even this distance. About fifty metres from the water was a little two-storey house. Its wood-shingled roof, which had grown almost black over time, stood in sharp contrast with the walls made of huge pieces of pine, which had been many times whitewashed. The light entered through big windows. Even the two bedrooms, upstairs, had windows.

Achille got out of the cart. He was smiling and talking volubly, pointing to his little domain. He was almost running back and forth, describing what they would do in each place, what still needed to be built, where the garden would go. Adela, still sitting in the seat of the cart with the baby in her arms, followed each of his gestures attentively, trying to glean information from them. He opened the door of the house, then ran back to help her out of the cart. Adela let herself be led inside. Her eyes were round as marbles, exploring every corner. She hesitated a moment when he showed her the staircase and invited her to go up. Her mother would have never let her go upstairs with a man who was not her father, her brother...or her husband. "But that didn't stop me from getting pregnant," thought Adela. Finally she followed him up. The stairway led to a little corridor that was no more than two metres long. There was a door on either side. He opened the first, but it was a short visit. Adela saw there was not very much inside. A single bed, a little chest-of-drawers was all. Completely Spartan. Achille touched his chest to show her that this was his room. Then he opened the door of the other room, the one that looked south. This room was much bigger. In the middle was an old double bed made of metal, whose mattress was covered with a magnificent quilt. In one corner stood a big chest-of-drawers with a pivoting mirror on top. Next to the bed was a little night table on which a water pitcher and porcelain basin stood. On the other side there was a little cradle and rocking chair. One could tell by the colour and the smell of wood that the cradle had just been made. The rocking chair, however, must have put generations of children to sleep. This time, Achille pointed to her and then the room. As if he had understood that she might have fears about his intentions, he showed her that there was a hook on the door. He even closed the door and hooked it, pulling on the doorknob twice to show her the hook was firmly planted.

Adela had tears in her eyes. Once again this man she did not know, or whom she knew so little, had saved her. He had made her a room and built a cradle for her son. Yet everything ought to have pushed him away. He knew that this child was a "bastard," as children born out of wedlock were commonly called. He was also aware that she was not of his faith and that this situation was likely to invite public disapproval. Not only did he accept her and her child, but he was asking for nothing in return...not even her body.

Achille left her alone with the baby in her new room and went down to make a fire to reduce the humidity that had invaded the house. It had not been inhabited for over a year. The man who had owned it had died with no heirs and his widow had wanted to sell it right away. When Achille returned from the lumber camps, he had visited the neighbouring villages to look for a property to buy. His father had put him in contact with Norbert Lafleur, a young notary who had decided to settle in the region. The young man, he said, seemed trustworthy. Lafleur had immediately inspired his sympathy, and the feeling was mutual. Achille had shown him the eight hundred dollars he had in his pocket.

"To be frank, it's not much, and I doubt anyone's going to give you financing, but there's a widow who's been looking to sell her house for a year. She might decide to trust you," the notary said, after talking with Achille.

At first, she had refused, but let herself be persuaded by the young notary to meet Achille. What more could he say to convince her, other than the simple truth? He told her his story, even about the death of O'Brien. She was touched and agreed to finance the purchase. She handed over the property for three thousand dollars, which he had to repay over five years. The papers had been prepared and signed, the money had changed hands. Norbert Lafleur had also agreed to lend him his cart to drive to Maniwaki the next day.

Achille had slept alone in his new house while Adela was in the hospital. He could not believe it and had not slept for the entire night. He got up twice, lit a candle, and walked around the house to convince himself it was all true.

At the first light of day, he had hitched up the horse and wagon and left for Maniwaki. Was he hoping to find a companion? He did not know. This woman with a tragic destiny attracted him like a magnet. The fact that she was so different made her all the more attractive. She was beautiful. Her long hair tumbling free over her shoulders made her even more beautiful. He desired her. But maybe she would reject him?

Achille thought of all this, leaning on the kitchen table. Upstairs he heard the floorboards creak beneath Adela's feet, then the noise of the chair rocking on the floor. The movement lasted for several minutes then stopped. He heard the sound of a screw turning in the dry wood.

When she came downstairs, she threw the hook on the table.

"It won't be necessary. I trust you," she told him.

She had also decided that she would have to learn to speak his language. Achille would have liked to understand what she was saying, but her gesture was worth a hundred words. He had won her trust and the hook on the table was the proof.

"*Confiance!*" he said, insisting on the word's pronunciation, as if he had read her mind.

"*Confiance*," she repeated. "So trust is *confiance*." With words and gestures, he managed to explain that he had to return to the lumber camp the following day to pay for the house. The season for river driving was not yet finished and he knew the company was in need of able-bodied men. When he took the horse back to Lafleur, he invited the young woman to go with him and stop by the general store. He put twenty dollars on the counter and told the storekeeper that Adela wanted to buy food in his name. She took advantage of the occasion to buy seeds for the garden. Holding the baby on her hip, she looked at the merchandise, occasionally flashing a little smile at Achille.

When Achille left the house the next day, she was sad but at the same time happy. She was sad thinking of her native island, but just as everything was about to fall apart, this man had come to change her life. She had only learned his last name when she went to get flour at the village store.

"Ah! Madame Roy," the storekeeper said, presuming they were man and wife.

Thus she had learned that Achille was Achille Roy. She realised she had never asked him his last name. Adela decided he would have to know who she was. She found a big map of Eastern Canada. Thus for the first time she was able to trace the voyage that had brought her to Aumond. The distance on the map that separated her from Tilting seemed very slight, no longer than her forearm. But she remembered all the days it had taken her to get to the lumber camp. This place was very different from all that she had known, and she felt a pang in her heart each time she thought of Tilting. But it seemed more and more unlikely she would ever go back. In any case, how would she get there? By foot? She was no longer alone. There was a child. He needed care. And then there was the man. He was big and strong, but his eyes were so gentle. She had resisted, but her images of him and the things they had done together had come to be included among her happy memories. When she thought of Tilting, Achille's face also came into her mind. She did not want to admit it to herself, but his absence weighed on her.

Adela had thought of writing to her family. But to tell them what? She was too ashamed. Better that they think her dead. Maybe one day she would write them, but for the time being, it was better to get on with her life.

Achille returned with the first hot weather of summer. Adela saw him the moment he arrived, coming up the drive with his bundle of belongings slung over his shoulder. She ran towards him, but stopped a few centimetres away, no longer knowing what to do. She had instinctively run to him, but now the gesture seemed inappropriate. She blushed. She showed Achille the garden she had planted and from which she had already started to harvest green onions, radishes and lettuce. A large part of the garden was devoted to growing potatoes, and already the plants were abundantly leafy.

She prepared a delicious supper with a magnificent trout she had caught in the nearby river. After the meal, she rocked the child while telling Achille that she had decided to name him Paul.

"It's pronounced the same in both English and French," she explained.

She had brought down the little cradle and decorated it. She took it with her everywhere, laying little Paul inside when she needed both hands to work. When supper was finished, she settled Paul comfortably in his cradle. After a few minutes of rocking sleep overcame him.

On the kitchen table, Adela unfolded the big map she had found. She showed Achille where they were on the map. Sainte-Famille d'Aumond did not appear, but "Maniwaki" was written in tiny letters that were hardly visible. Next her finger traced the path of the Gatineau River, turned onto the Ottawa then followed the Saint Lawrence to Quebec City. She stopped at Quebec City, trying to explain how she had happened to end up there. Then she continued all the way to Newfoundland and finally to Fogo Island. The names of the villages did not appear on this map, because Newfoundland was not yet part of Canada. A line separated the two land masses. "British land" was indicated on the part of the map showing Newfoundland. She put her hand on her chest and repeated the word "Tilting" several times, pointing to the island on the map. Then, making an effort to reproduce the sounds she had heard in his mouth, she showed him the place where they were, and said "Sainte-Famille d'Aumond."

Next she pointed at Achille's chest and said "Achille Roy." The word sounded like "Roua" when she said it and he smiled. She pointed at herself and said "Adela Cole."

They had so many things to tell each other. It was a game of discovery. For the entire evening and the days and weeks to follow, the two learned to speak to each other, one memorizing English words, the other learning the difficult pronunciation of French expressions.

They laughed uproariously at their own mistakes. Achille loved her laugh. It sounded like the joyous rippling of a waterfall in spring.

The summer was all sweetness. Little Paul became more and more aware of his environment. His happy gurgles filled the house. Achille could have listened to him for hours. Sometimes he leaned over the cradle and started to reproduce Paul's babbling and other noises, which made the baby laugh with delight. Watching the scene, Adela could not help but burst out laughing to see this big strapping fellow playing the fool over the cradle. Achille would blush, realising how ridiculous he looked, but ended up laughing too, for Adela's joyous laughter was contagious.

Slowly, subtly, during these moments of happiness, something in the house changed. Though attentive to Adela's every need, Achille was so shy that he dared not make the slightest gesture that could have been considered out of place. Sometimes their hands touched when they were working together, or when Adela took the map out to tell him about her country. With every bit of contact, a current passed between them, and it was growing stronger and stronger.

Achille had taken advantage of the summer months to initiate Adela in the art of canoeing, so she might discover the world around her via the river. These outings on the Joseph River made her happy. Though the current was calm, she always worried about the baby. She had noticed how unstable a canoe was, and feared what would happen to Paul if it overturned. Achille had traded a knife for a kind of backpack, made of wood and buckskin, in which Algonquin women carried their babies, called a *tikinagan*. The bag, he told her, could float even with a child inside it, as well as being very comfortable and practical.

Then autumn and the harvest arrived. The garden had produced a large yield. Achille had been obliged to get some burlap bags in which to put all the potatoes that Adela had managed to make grow. The big cabbages reigned like kings over the garden, where they remained until the first snowfall. The turnips and carrots were stored in the cold room, waiting for winter.

Achille told Adela with regret that he would soon be joining the men to go up to the lumber camps again. He still had to reimburse the widow who had sold him the house. The lady had trusted Achille, and he did not intend to disappoint her.

In the days before Achille's departure, the young woman became sadder and sadder. She loved the sweet evenings she spent with him as they learned the words of each other's language, talking and laughing about everything and nothing. She had not realised how much she valued Achille's company and it was painful to think of the long winter ahead. What if he did not return? What if something happened to him?

The night before Achille's departure, when he was savouring the end of one of the last warm days of the season, Adela came to him and took his hand. It was the first time she had made this gesture since the moment in the truck coming back from the lumber camp, when she had needed to feel him near. She stroked his big calloused hand as if it were a precious object. She spoke, mixing up her own language with the words she had learned in French. She thanked him for everything he had done for her. She thanked him for having saved her from the clutches of O'Brien, for protecting her against Clyde who wanted to send her away, for not rejecting her though knowing she was pregnant, for providing a roof for her son and herself when he had no obligation towards her, for giving her his friendship, affection and a reason for living. Achille was moved and his eyes misted with tears that he tried to hold back.

"Thank you for that too," she said, wiping away with her finger the tears that had started to trickle down his cheeks. Then she reminded him of the first word he had taught her: "*Confiance*" – trust.

That night, Achille was the last to go up to bed. He was still shaken by what she had said to him. Just as he entered his room, the door across the hall opened. Adela was there in a white nightgown that he had never seen. He did not even know if she'd had one when she first arrived. She signalled to him to be quiet and pushed his bedroom door open. The baby and the cradle were there.

"This will be his room now," she said in English. "*Sa chambre*," she repeated. Taking his big hand in hers, she pulled him towards her own bedroom. He had desired this moment for a long time, but now he was ill at ease, not quite knowing what to do. He thought of fleeing.

"I...I've never...," he stammered shyly.

She put her finger on his lips. She knew. Slowly she helped him take off his shirt and then his trousers. He found himself sitting almost naked at the edge of the bed, clumsy and red with embarrassment. Should he lie down? His near nudity made him uncomfortable. She sensed it, and took off her nightgown. In the candlelight, Achille admired her firm and voluptuous breasts, her hips, which in the semi-darkness resembled the curves of a violin. He would have liked to hold back his excitement, but his member had already grown hard. Even though she was no longer a virgin, Adela did not have much more experience than him. She slipped between the sheets, inviting him to join her.

Achille quickly removed his underwear and slid under the covers, trying to hide his excitement. She had washed the sheets and hung them outside. They smelled fresh and exuded the fragrance of wildflowers. When the skin of his thigh touched hers, he thought his faculties would fail him. He did not know where to put his hands or how to position himself in the bed. He was paralysed. But his embarrassment left him when she took his arm, put it around her neck and lovingly huddled into the hollow of his shoulder. He felt not only her thigh but also her breast against his chest. After a few seconds, he bent his arm, which had remained rigid as a board, to put his hand at the hollow of her back, just above her buttocks. She arched her back and murmured with pleasure. She searched for his mouth, their lips joined. Achille was no longer himself. His penis touched Adela's belly and he could feel his member in the hair of the young woman's pubic mound. He was so excited he thought he would ejaculate immediately. Adela's hand moved gently down Achille's chest, then his stomach, and finally touched his penis. She guided him into her. He felt the sweet damp warmth inside her sex. At this stage, his lack of experience no longer mattered. He no longer controlled his body, which had only one goal: to take this woman he so desired. For weeks, he had tried to imagine the nudity of the woman sleeping only metres away from him. Adela moaned with pleasure, which brought Achille to the peak of excitement. He ejaculated after only a few thrusts. Ashamed and remorseful at having brought this moment of happiness to an end so abruptly, he wanted to pull out, but Adela held him back, keeping him inside her when he made a move to withdraw. There he was, on top of her, madly in love, utterly fulfilled, stroking her hair, kissing her eyes, her nose, her mouth, her forehead. Nothing and nobody was so beautiful or precious as this woman, and before he realised, his member had recovered its vigour. Adela felt him swelling inside her and she grew very excited again. Their hips began to move together, slowly at first then more and more rapidly. He caressed her neck, touched her breasts, and felt her climax just as he exploded inside her. Their cries of love mingled in the night. If Achille had discovered the joys of lovemaking for the first time, she was discovering the ecstasy of female pleasure. Her mother had expressed only disgust for sex, saying that she could not see how "anyone could like such a thing." Never had she told her that pleasure could make her body vibrate like that, make her lose her head.

    They slept little that night, remaining in each other's arms, their bodies fused together. Adela wondered if it was not a sin when one's partner grew excited again during the night. But she did not refuse him her love. They were discovering their own and each other's bodies. Never would Achille forget that night. For him, that bed could never be anything but paradise.

# Eleven

If it had not been for François Poulin, the affair would probably have been passed over and filed away with all the other stories of senile old people who wandered off and were never heard from again. Poulin was from Maniwaki, though he had left the village of his birth thirty years before. His career in journalism had begun almost by accident, for he was far more suited to working in finance than to writing up the news. He had just graduated from college in Administration and was jobless when the owner of the local weekly offered him the job of sportswriter. Anyone who had the slightest interest in sports and a bit of knowledge could do the job. It was not even necessary to write well.

"What people want here isn't literature," his boss told him. "The name and photo of their son or grandson in the paper is better than any article, no matter how good it is."

But François Poulin did know how to write, had a sense of image and a knack for sensationalistic wording. A player did not just shoot the puck into the net when Poulin described a hockey match. The article took on the flavour of guerrilla warfare, cannonballs whistling from all directions around a fort protected by such and such a pit bull. He also had an instinct for what paid. François was not only a newsman, he knew what kind of news brought in profits. He designed the advertising himself and explained to the advertisers without mincing words that an ad in his paper could earn them good press at a later date.

"You know," he told them, "we don't bite the hand that feeds us!"

The message was clear. Especially because François Poulin had a mordant style. He had damaged a number of politicians with his corrosive commentaries. In less than a year, he had gone from covering general news to being Editor-in-Chief of the paper. Several months later, he obtained the job of journalist on the Ottawa daily, *Le Droit*, and had left Maniwaki for good. There too, Poulin had made rapid progress and made sure his bosses took note of it. They had not hesitated to give him the job of Chief-Editor. Now all that remained was to land the job of Editor-in-Chief and his joy would be complete. This would probably not take long, as the person who currently held that title had reached retirement age. Out of respect, top management had not yet shown him the door, but the general feeling was that the job had become too much for him. Poulin was not unaware of this, and he never missed a chance to point out the old man's failings.

Though he had left Maniwaki, François still kept tabs on what was happening there. Each week, he combed through the weekly newspapers to check the latest subjects of interest in the region. Especially to see what had escaped the attention of his team of "bureaucrats," as he called his journalists on the daily. He remembered the time he had spent working for the weeklies, sixty hours or more per week and exhausting weekends on the road covering the activities in each village. He never missed a chance to remind his journalists that work on a weekly newspaper was the real thing. Not only did he like to keep up with what was happening in the regions covered by his paper, but in the weeklies he also found numerous subjects that his journalists, who covered the Ottawa region, never heard about. Or if they had heard about them, they were careful not to mention them so as not to get stuck with a trip to the *outback*.

Thus, every Friday morning, François went through the dozen weekly newspapers that had accumulated on his desk over the week. He would scan each one, skipping over the unimportant stories about giant tomatoes and the like. He glanced at the piece on the Dagenais affair to see whether the article his journalist had written corresponded to what had been reported locally. He noted that the weekly alluded to a possible altercation, which, it seemed to him, his journalist had not mentioned. Then he read an article announcing the big factory opening. He tossed the paper on top of the ones he had already read and started on another. He had leafed through several pages when the title of an article he had skipped over suddenly came into his mind.

"To Newfoundland by canoe? That rings a bell!" he thought.

He had noticed the search bulletin the police had published in his newspaper, but it was only five or six lines. They only mentioned they were looking for an old man, apparently senile. The man had purportedly canoed down the Gatineau River to Low. Poulin was impressed. He remembered that some of the rapids in this river were exceptionally dangerous. He picked up the paper again and went back to the article that had captured his attention. He read it attentively from beginning to end.

"This would make a damn good story!" he said to himself, cutting out the article.

During a meeting of the editorial committee that afternoon, he did not miss the opportunity to make fun of the journalist who had covered the affair.

"A little village journalist manages to make something out of this story, and you guys find just four lines to write about it! Four lines, it's unbelievable!" he exclaimed, assuming an air of righteous indignation, carefully rehearsed.

"Listen, this is just some elderly person who's wandered off," replied one of the journalists being accused.

"*Just some elderly person?*" fumed Poulin. "Listen, in ten years from now, half the population will be of retirement age, and do you think this doesn't interest them?"

There was no room for discussion. Everyone on the team knew the ambitious news editor and also knew he did not tolerate any back talk. Several journalists were assigned the item.

"I want all the dirt on this. I want you to talk to anyone who might know this man from close up or far. I also want you to meet with associations for the elderly, the commission of human rights... everyone! And try to find out more on that place... Togo Island. But most of all, find me a photo of that man!" ordered Poulin.

The journalists from *Le Droit* had a great deal of difficulty making people from Aumond talk to them, but they managed to get enough information to write a report. The photographer took photos of all the people in the community who had something to say about the man, "from close up or far." He had also photographed the little house by the Joseph River. Poulin had even prepared a map showing the presumed trajectory of the old canoeist, all the way to Fogo Island.

When the news appeared in the daily, it was reprinted under the heading of *Believe it or Not* by several other newspapers. In *The Gazette*, from Montreal, the item was translated and placed well in evidence. The story was then picked up by a journalist from the Associated Press, who wired it to English newspapers who subscribed to the service. Several days later, the story of the old man had made its way around Quebec, crossing linguistic and national borders. Several English-language newspapers had given the item precedence over the major news stories of the hour. Certain television networks had also mentioned it.

When the chief editor of the St. John's *Evening Telegram* read the article in the Toronto *Globe and Mail*, his attention was captured by the mention of Newfoundland. It was so rare that Newfoundland was mentioned in the big Toronto newspaper that it was an event in itself. He decided to report the story, highlighting the fact that the ashes the man was transporting were those of a woman from Newfoundland. He asked his journalist to thoroughly research Fogo Island and the woman. The reporter went to Tilting, where he was able to locate a descendent of the Cole family.

The man had not known the woman herself, but had heard of her from his grandfather. If they were talking about the same person, she had mysteriously disappeared when she was only sixteen. All this time, she had been believed dead. Back then, no one had known she had been planning to go to St. John's, nor that she had never arrived at her destination. People believed she had been killed, and the prime suspect was the son of a leading citizen of the village, John Lane, whom the girl had been in love with.

The *Evening Telegram* published the story and was literally flooded with calls from all over the island. Every Newfoundlander had been profoundly touched by the affair. Their love of the mother country, or the mother Rock, rather, was stronger than anything. Though many had been forced to leave the island to survive, the island had never left them. Everyone who left hoped to return one day. Newfoundlanders were very upset to learn the story of this woman who, for seventy years, had lived away but remained so attached to her native earth that she had transmitted her passion to a stranger who had never seen "The Rock."

In the days to follow, one of the members of the Newfoundland legislature introduced a resolution whereby the government would absorb the cost of repatriating the ashes of Adela Cole. In Tilting and the entire territory of Fogo Island, people had decided to take action and create a fund to finance the return of the lovely exile. They had even planned to build a monument to the memory of Adela and all children of the island who had left and were never able to return. As soon as the people of Newfoundland had been informed of the plan, and despite their modest means, almost fifty thousand dollars was raised in only a few days. The gifts came from everywhere. Even the premier of the province had contributed five hundred dollars from his own pocket, to earn himself a little political capital in view of the coming elections.

A committee had been formed in Tilting to organise the procedures. But for the time being, no one knew where these precious ashes were, or the man who had made it his mission to return them.

The press revealed that he was on the run and considered mentally unstable for having undertaken such a big voyage by canoe. Indeed, the operation did seem a little strange.

"It's true, you'd have to be a bit crazy to take off on an expedition like that by canoe," admitted the president of the Tilting committee, Rose Leate.

Everyone agreed and added his or her two cents' worth, until an old fisherman from Fogo, James Eneligh, called for silence.

"My father and grandfather fished on a dory to feed their families. But it was no bigger than a bathtub. Would you say *they* were crazy?" he asked, causing embarrassment among the people who had been the most outspoken. "I've seen everything there is to see about the ocean, and to me, a guy who takes to the sea in a canoe to bring home the woman he loves deserves my respect…and he should deserve yours. If this man had been a man of the sea, if he hadn't been a Frenchman, you'd have built a statue to him," said Eneligh.

Everyone realised what an immense task this Achille had taken on, and was ashamed of having spoken out against him minutes earlier.

"You know, we can erect all the statues we want, but that's not what makes us what we are. It's the sea, the rock, and everything around us. Today there's no more fishing, nothing to do here any more, and suddenly because of this man people are talking about us so much, they're sending television cameras by ferry to Fogo Island for the first time. Seems there are even tourists who've asked to see the house of this Adela Cole," added James Leate, the captain of the ferry that ran between Fogo and the island of Newfoundland.

The journalist of the *Evening Telegram* reported the story in great detail. "The Adela Affair" had taken on unexpected dimensions. The newspaper *Le Droit* in Ottawa had also been flooded with calls and François Poulin was happy to see that his instincts had served him well once again. First the people from Aumond called in, some to add a detail or two, others to claim that they were "close friends" with this Achille. All of them wanted their hour of glory in the newspaper. Then it was the Outaouais Canoeists League who called asking for the details of the old man's itinerary. The group was particularly impressed by the courage of this man, who seemed to have stepped straight out of the days of the *coureurs des bois*. A team of canoeists had been formed to accompany him on his journey, and there was even talk of making him honorary club president. Several hours later, the Quebec Seniors Association called a press conference. This organisation for the defence of the elderly had decided to side with Achille Roy. The journalist who covered the event reported the item as follows:

> Along with some twenty representatives from golden age clubs in the region, the president of the Quebec Seniors' Association, Blanche Bouchard, made a point of denouncing society's infantilising of the elderly. Citing the case of the "canoe man," Blanche Bouchard predicted it would be held up as a example in the defence of the elderly's right to autonomy.
>
> Madame Bouchard declared that society gives itself the right to decide what is good or bad for the elderly. "They are ready to start shouting about 'senility,' when all their parents want is to fulfil their dreams," she said and was met with applause from numerous senior citizens in the audience.
>
> The president affirmed that the case of Achille Roy had become a symbol of the elderly's fight for autonomy. "Society is ready to give us the right to euthanasia because it suits their financial agenda for the elderly to die, but it refuses us the right to live the way we want!" exclaimed one of the ladies present, who admitted to being eighty-five. The lady explained that she had always dreamed of visiting Africa. "My children prevented me because they said it was dangerous. Now it's all decided, I'm going to Africa next month!" she said.
>
> The Seniors' Association had been inundated with people phoning in with extreme cases of this kind. Madame Bouchard also pointed the finger at social services, who sometimes join forces with the system to limit the freedom of the elderly.

The affair did not stop there. Inflamed comments flooded into call-in shows. Even the celebrity host of the TVA television network, whose commentaries were always laced with vitriol, had devoted an entire show to the story. He had tracked down several people who had had similar experiences. Certain politicians from Quebec City and Ottawa were called to comment by human rights associations. The affair had been taken to the tribunals so they could not comment, the politicians replied, thus avoiding having to make a statement on a subject that threatened to lose them the precious "grey-hair vote." But the movement was not limited to seniors' groups. The Quebec Students' National Association launched a campaign with the slogan "Don't mess with my granddad!" The students had organised a petition and collected 20,000 signatures in support of the rights of the elderly. One of the press photos showed the surprising image, taken at the entrance of a metro station, of an old hunched-over man asking passers-by to sign the petition, a young woman at his side sporting chains, multiple earrings and mane of day-glow green hair.

Poulin was happy. *Le Droit* was being quoted everywhere. On the television, radio and even in the *Le Devoir* newspaper, which prided itself on being Quebec's top journalistic reference, the article in his newspaper had been mentioned. It was his story and he was happy with it. At least, it was the story of some unknown little hack in Maniwaki, but Poulin was going to take care of him. This young fellow had clearly done his time in purgatory and it was time for him to move on to the major leagues. He intended to offer him a job.

"That way, the story will remain in the family," the editor thought, smiling.

But they had to stay on their toes. Journalists from various media were tripping over each other trying to be the first to find the old man who had escaped. Several Ottawa River canoeists had literally been mobbed by curious bystanders and the media, who believed they had finally discovered Achille. It was out of the question to let some other newspaper or medium get all the attention. Poulin summoned his team.

"You have to question the locals, patrol the riverbanks from the air with a helicopter if you have to, but find me this man!" he exclaimed. "This guy is ours!"

In Maniwaki, the affair had made a lot of waves. It was hard to explain how a patient in preventive detention could have escaped so easily. Hospital management could not explain it and the regional health department had ordered a committee of inquiry.

"Another committee that'll die from accomplishing nothing," thought Poulin.

Then there was the Sûreté du Québec, whose image had been tarnished. How could an old man of eighty-eight, carrying a canoe on his back, have escaped from the province's finest? The police had despatched the helicopter they used to search for missing persons to fly over the river. Patrol cars were constantly cruising down the river roads. Nothing. The man seemed to have vanished into thin air. Poulin wanted the *old man in the canoe* to be caught. If he weren't, the readers would lose interest.

"Let's just hope he hasn't drowned," he said to himself. "Or at least if he has, I hope the body will be found."

If Achille was not apprehended, the balloon would deflate. The affair would lose its edge, but for the moment it was *Le Droit*'s baby, and it had to be pumped with air to keep it aloft in the firmament of current events.

# Twelve

Achille had lost the habit of sleeping outdoors. Every morning, his aching body cruelly reminded him that he was no longer of an age to do this kind of exercise. But he had no choice. Now that he had succeeded in escaping, he was fairly sure that they would come looking for him. Maybe when he got farther away from Maniwaki, the police would give up searching. With this hope in mind, he decided to leave quickly and discreetly, for highway 105 ran along the river for quite a distance. He skilfully guided his boat towards the shore below the highway. It would be difficult for even the police to see him. Several patrol cars cruised by without noticing the little boat, gliding along in silence beneath the branches overhanging the water. When he got near Wakefield, he decided to stop. He could not go under the bridge without being seen from the highway, especially because a police station, overlooking the river, had been built on the right bank.

Once again he entered a stream that flowed into the river, but was surprised, after only a few paddle strokes, to find he was approaching a house. It was made of pine planks painted red and was getting on in years, but what a delightful dwelling! The two-storey building had character, and had probably been inhabited by several generations. A stable made of weather-beaten grey boards hid a magnificent garden in which plants were already shooting out of the earth beneath the rays of spring sun. Without really thinking about it, Achille pulled on his paddle to direct the canoe towards the shore. He lifted the boat out and turned it over on the riverbank. The man sitting on the front steps of the house was very surprised to see Achille emerge from the bushes. Since he had been living there, John McTavish had seen many things change, not always for the better, but it had been a long time since he had seen a *voyageur* on the Gatineau. Of course canoeing had become a fad over the past few years, but the canoeists were back-to-nature types, fleeing the city to invade his territory. He looked down on these fair-weather canoe buffs, especially since they had sent around a petition to prevent him from spreading manure on his land. It polluted, they said, and prevented them from taking advantage of the pure, fresh air.

"If they think it smells like shit here, they should just stay in town," he had told the municipal inspector who had come by to report the complaint.

Irish on his father's side and Scottish on his mother's, McTavish had enough character to stand up to the intruders. He had acquired his little plot of land sixty-five years earlier and had made his life there. He had married and fathered five children. All of them had left, drawn by the benefits the Ottawa public service could offer them, and no one had wanted to take over his land. His wife had died several years earlier, but he had decided to stay on the farm. His children had wanted him to follow them to the city, but he had refused. The man was stubborn as only the Irish can be. His children stopped harassing him about it, and in the end they stopped coming to see him entirely.

It had been so long since he had seen a birchbark canoe that at first he had thought Achilles boat was an imitation. He addressed Achille in English, and Achille replied in the same language. McTavish found his accent amusing. Of course, he was French, that was obvious. But his English accent was different. There was something of the old English in his way of speaking. Achille asked him if he could spend the night on his land. Only too happy to have a companion, McTavish suggested that he have supper with him. As for sleeping, there were enough bedrooms in his house to open an inn, and he invited him to spend the night in one of them.

The two men became acquainted. Achille was happy not only to have found shelter, but also a table to eat at and a companion to talk to. Since he had been living alone, McTavish kept his little television set right on the kitchen table. He sat at the opposite end and watched it as he ate. Achille told him he had never had a television. The old farmer was astounded. Thinking that Achille had told him this because he wanted to watch television, he turned it on. Achille had seen televisions in the past and watched a number of programmes, but neither he nor Adela had ever felt the need to own a set.

John jumped from channel to channel, as if to allow Achille to get a look at what television could offer. He suddenly realised that if this man had never had a television, it was useless flipping through the channels hoping he would choose one. He stopped at the Radio-Canada station, which was presenting the local news. The newscaster rattled off the items in a monotonous series of words and images. The two men paid no attention until the moment Achille's name was mentioned. They immediately stopped talking and listened in silence. John turned to him.

"Now, tell me what all this is about," he said, intrigued.

Achille explained why he had left and about his arrest then the escape that had brought him to this farm. When he heard the search bulletin, it occurred to John to call the police. After all, the man might be a criminal. McTavish knew that appearances could be deceptive. But after he had heard Achille's story, going to the police was out of the question. The man had the right to go to the ends of the earth if he wanted to, just as he himself had the right to remain where he was and die on his own land. Later, when he had gotten into bed, McTavish thought about what he had learned from this odd man.

The next morning, when Achille was about to leave, John detained him. There was no question of letting him leave just like that. He was aware that Achille would have trouble getting past the village of Wakefield without being seen. His old 1957 Dodge pickup was brought out and they put the canoe in the back, carefully covering it with a groundsheet. The strange couple effortlessly crossed the Gatineau River on the Highway 366 Bridge. A police car was stopped on the bridge, the two officers leaning over the guardrails on either side, looking upriver and down in search of the canoe. The two men greeted them with big smiles as they passed, to which the two young officers replied with courtesy but without paying them much attention. Once they had passed the bridge, Achille and his companion burst out laughing. John took a little side road and followed the river for one kilometre. The place was well camouflaged and Achille was able to head back onto the water without being seen. He thanked John.

"Don't thank me. Just do it!" McTavish said with a smile of complicity.

Achille was back on the river, stopping as he approached the more densely populated sectors. At those places, he would travel furtively, at dawn or dusk when everything was grey. Twice he managed to pass Hydro-Quebec dams and portage his canoe without being seen. At the Chelsea Dam, the plant growth was abundant and the operation had been easy. At the Farmer Dam, he had waited until the day's end to portage, for there, by the river, traffic was heavier. Now he had arrived in Gatineau and felt it was going to be tough going. He had heard his name on television. He, Achille Roy, had been presented as a lunatic. There was no doubt they would try to nab him when he passed through this city.

Just before the rapids by the Alonzo-Wright Bridge, Achille decided it would be best to stop on the island of the Collège Saint-Alexandre. This magnificent island was part of the *château* Wright, which had been ceded to the fathers of the Saint-Esprit in the beginning of the century to be used as a classical college. At the time of the *voyageurs*, people would stop on this island before resuming the voyage north. Now it was used only for students' natural science field trips. Achille could take refuge there, but making a fire was out of the question. He camouflaged his canoe under the foliage and settled himself on a rock where he could take advantage of the last rays of sun. He was happy that John had given him a few provisions. While he ate, Achille evaluated his situation and judged that he would have to leave after nightfall. He did not know if the helicopters that kept passing overhead were looking for him, but he did not want to take any chances. At twilight, he slid his boat into the water and attacked the rapids. The rapids themselves were not big, but there were a lot of rocks. He had to proceed with caution. The current, which was strong, made him gain speed and helped him get over this section of the river without being seen.

Achille glided in silence under the bridge while the motorists passed overhead without noticing his presence. In no time, he had reached Kettle Island. Night was falling, but he decided to keep on going. It was not his habit to travel at night, but he had no choice. He had to get past the urban sector before finding himself a safe place to sleep. It had to be one in the morning, maybe later, when he approached the shore again. He had passed by the city of Gatineau and was now in a less densely populated area. He paddled to the shore and looked for a place to disembark. It was so dark that he could not see a stream or a dip in the shoreline where he could stop. Finally there was an opening in the branches and he entered a narrow body of water. The stream was barely wider than the canoe. He moved ahead and finally realised that the stream was nothing but the run-off from a ditch. The water flowed under the highway towards the river through a pipe. It was impossible to go any farther. Impossible to hide, too, for the riverbanks were not sufficiently wooded and he would be visible from the nearby houses. He was afraid that the police would be contacted as soon as he was spotted. He got out of the boat and climbed up to the edge of the road. On the other side there was a more densely wooded area where he could probably hide, but he could not leave the canoe at the edge of the river. He put on his precious bag, lifted the boat and hoisted it onto his shoulders. The slope that led to the road was steep and he had trouble climbing it.

That evening, Maurice Latour was finishing a long run in his truck. Twice he had driven to Grand-Remous to pick up loads of wood chips and transport them to the factory at Gatineau. Now he was returning to Buckingham to rest up, until it all started again the following day. His huge truck was barrelling down the highway and he savoured with anticipation the pleasures of being at home again. In twenty years he had driven millions of kilometres and he had seen pretty much everything. At first he did not notice the shadow moving out of the ditch. When it caught his eye, his mind started scrambling to figure out what the object could be. Suddenly, as the old man made one last effort to haul himself up to the road, Maurice saw that it was a canoe he was carrying. Though the person transporting it was standing on the shoulder, the canoe was jutting out into the highway. Maurice applied the brakes so suddenly that there was long strident shriek of tires skidding on asphalt. He veered left, hoping that his long trailer, now empty of wood chips, would follow without overturning. The trailer tipped dangerously to the right during the manoeuvre and for a moment, the wheels on the other side lifted off the ground. Maurice cast a brief and nervous glance in his rear-view mirror, and immediately pointed his front tires to the right to regain control. The trailer fell back on its wheels and missed the canoe by just a few inches.

The heavy vehicle came to a stop fifty or so metres farther. Maurice Latour immediately jumped out and ran towards the man. Achille realised that he had almost caused an accident and expected the man to be furious.

"It's you!" he said. "You're the canoe man, aren't you?"

Achille was stunned. How could this man possibly know him? He remembered the police alert and was afraid the man would turn him in.

"Listen, sir, I'm sorry but I don't want any trouble with the police."

"Oh, I know," said Maurice, thrilled to be the first to find the *old man in the canoe*.

When the news had first appeared in *Le Droit*, he had picked up the message from a Maniwaki trucker, entreating his colleagues to assist the old man if ever he turned up on one of their routes.

"We can't stay here. A police car could come by. I'm going to help you. We'll put the canoe back in the trailer."

Achille did not understand. This man who he did not know was ready to assist him. At first he was suspicious, but let him go ahead and help load the canoe into the trailer. In any case, he was exhausted. Maurice helped Achille climb up into the truck.

"Well, I never thought I'd see the day when a celebrity would be climbing into my truck. So there she is, your beloved Adele," said the trucker, pointing to Achilles' bag.

Achille nodded, surprised that the man knew so much about him. How could that be? He asked Maurice, who eagerly showed him the article that had appeared in *Le Droit*.

"We're on your side," said Maurice, giving him a wink.

He was "on his side." His side of what? Achille did not understand, nor could he understand how his story had ended up in the newspaper. They were talking about him, his Adela, their love, the woman's Newfoundland origins. There was a photo of his house. A distant relative of Adela's had even been tracked down on Fogo Island. He was flabbergasted. How was it that he, who had spent the greater part of his life quietly living on a little piece of land in Aumond, could have attracted everyone's attention like this?

Maurice saw that the man was not aware of all that had happened in the past few days. "You've become a star, you know. Because of you, the old folks are pretty up in arms. According to what they say on TV, you've started a revolution among the grey-haired set. There are a lot of middle-aged kids in deep shit today because you've woken up their parents and they're saying no!" explained Latour.

"No to what?" asked Achille.

"No to what people want to do with them. Here, look at this article. The provincial president of seniors' clubs says you're 'a symbol of resistance for the elderly.' Even young people have got on board…your canoe! 'Don't mess with my granddad!' is what they're saying, and they've gathered 20,000 signatures to back you up. The police are looking for you everywhere, did you know that?"

Achille nodded.

"Well, they're not going to find you with me, that's for sure!"

They met a police car slowly cruising down the river road. As they passed the cruiser, Maurice cheerfully greeted the officers, and when the patrol was out of sight, he gave them the finger.

Achille fell asleep on the back seat, rocked by the purring vibration of the motor. Latour had to shake him awake when they arrived at their destination. He did not live right on the river, but one could see the water from the dwelling. Achille, still half asleep, started towards his canoe but the trucker held him back.

"Let the kids take care of it."

He entered the house and woke everyone up. His sons of sixteen and eighteen were the last to get up.

"Come on, guys, we've got big company!" Latour announced to his troupe.

"Who, Céline Dion?" said one, who was still half asleep.

"Almost. Get dressed and go get the canoe out of the trailer, then hide it carefully in the garage."

"I can't believe it! Don't tell me this is the canoe man?" asked his wife Maryse.

"You got it! And we have to make him a bed."

Achille protested. He would have been quite content with the garage, he said, or even the Latours' living room couch.

"Don't even think about it," said Maryse. "I'd die of shame."

Every two minutes, she asked him if he was hungry. Every time he said no, she would insist again, and ended up concluding that he was hungry and had to eat. Anyone who passed the Latour house that night would have been surprised to see the lights burning at such a late hour. Achille slept deeply for the rest of the night and part of the next day. When he woke up it had to be five o'clock and he had no idea where he was. He came out of the room; the Latour family was glued to the small screen, following the adventures of Achille Roy. A Wakefield man was being interviewed, a certain John McTavish who claimed he had lodged the canoe man for the night.

"It's the best thing I've done since my wife's death, and I'm happy to have been able to help him," he said. The report continued, emphasizing that *Le Droit* was offering a reward of $2,000 to anyone who could provide information leading to the man's discovery.

"It's incredible!" said Maryse. "You'd think this man was Jesse James when he's only doing what he thinks is right!"

Everyone was happy to see Achille and that he'd been able to have a good rest. Maryse resumed her monologue of "You must be hungry" until Achille gave in.

"They're closing in on you, Mister Roy," Maurice Latour told him. "For the moment, I don't think it's wise to get back on the river."

But Achille was adamant. He had decided this was how things were going to be and had no intention of changing his plans. Since making his decision, he had done this trip a hundred times in his head. He had seen himself paddling on the Saint Lawrence, trying to make sense of the tides so as better to navigate them; he had imagined himself on the sea in his frail boat. For him, the canoe had been an instrument of work, a means of transportation and sometimes even a kind of toy. It was everything to him, and of course he could not have accepted Maurice's proposal to build a secret caravan to take him and the canoe to Halifax. Latour was also sure he could find a trucker willing to drive them to Newfoundland on the sly. But for Achille, this option would be tantamount to failure.

"Adela wouldn't have wanted it. She agreed with me…and still does," he said.

"Well then, I'll drive you to the other side of the Carillon Rapids. Because of the canal, people would notice you. After that you can get back on the river."

Maurice respected the man's decision. To some it might seem like futile stubbornness, but he understood. That day, he had launched an appeal among his trucker colleagues and found more volunteers than Achille would ever need. One proposed to take him to Quebec City, another to the border of New Brunswick, and finally, another to Halifax. The story had made such a stir in the press that there was not a single trucker from Newfoundland who would have hesitated to lend a hand to the man who was bringing his wife's ashes back to the Rock. But things had to be done as Achille had decided to do them, or not be done at all. Latour understood, and he admired the old man's determination.

He called a colleague who agreed to pick up Achille and his canoe a few kilometres outside of Buckingham, and drive him to the other side of Carillon Rapids. Maurice gave him instructions as to the best place to let him out. The meeting happened at the break of dawn. The *old man and the canoe* switched vehicles in a matter of seconds. The two Latour boys had insisted on being there. At first they, like many others, had believed the old man was a little disturbed, but they had come to realise that he was just different. They followed their father's truck in the older son's pickup, and once the transfer was accomplished, they agreed to escort them to the foot of the Carillon Rapids. When they arrived, they took care of everything and gave Achille a big hug before pushing the canoe into the water. The old man was touched by the young men's gesture of solidarity.

"See all these wonderful people we're meeting, Adela, and everyone knows you by name. Isn't it strange?" murmured Achille, resuming his voyage.

He paddled for a long time, staying close to the shore to avoid being seen, but things were becoming increasingly complicated. When evening came, he looked for a place to spend the night. As he guided his canoe towards the shore, he caught sight of a little cabin. It was a hut used for ice fishing. The tiny house had been hauled to this place in preparation for the following winter. It was equipped with rails that allowed it to slide across the snow. It did not look as if the hut had ever been used on the river. Achille doubted that the ice ever became solid enough for a long enough period of time for anyone to install a fishing hut on the river. It was probably used on one of the nearby lakes. Inside was a bench that ran along three of the walls. The floor had a hole in it where the fishermen could put down their lines. This shelter gave him a place to settle for the night. He slept lightly, waking up at the merest sound. He understood how a hunted animal must feel.

When he got back on the river the next day, the current was not as strong as it had been the day before. He was probably starting to feel the effects of the tides. Farther along, at Quebec City, he would probably have to pull his canoe up on the shore and wait until high tide had passed. If not, he would start going backwards. He was paddling hard when a speedboat full of tourists raced by. One started shouting: "It's the canoe man, I saw the canoe man!" Several pairs of binoculars were turned in his direction. Everyone said they had seen him. The captain of the speedboat, the *Breaker-Jumper*, veered around and started heading in Achille's direction. Completely exposed, he looked around for a place to hide. The speedboat passed close to his canoe, generating big waves and a powerful gust of air. The old man negotiated the waves as best he could, but the blast of the big motors set his boat to turning dangerously. The passengers saw the danger and started to protest. The captain had to speed away.

The captain thought about the two-thousand-dollar reward and contacted *Le Droit*. The information was thought suspect at first. The newspaper had received calls from numerous cranks who claimed they had seen the canoe man. But after checking, François Poulin saw that the informer seemed credible and despatched a helicopter to the site.

"I hope this time it's for real," thought François Poulin as he gave the thumbs-up to the crew of the helicopter, which the newspaper was paying for.

In less than twenty minutes, the aircraft was on the scene, flying low over the shoreline until the photographer's camera stopped on a shape below. There he was, the mysterious man in his canoe. What sensational photos! The helicopter hovered while the photographer shot a rapid-fire series of photos of Achille, who was trying to get to shore to escape their attention. François Poulin, in radio contact with the crew, was following the operation, second by second. He could not let the goose with the golden eggs get away from him again. As soon as the pilot informed him that they had found the man, he had alerted the Sûreté du Québec, and the police helicopter was on the scene in no time, behind the one *Le Droit* had hired.

Next it was the television networks' turn to arrive, having heard the call that had gone out to the police. This entire aerial circus circled the frail canoe while the officers attempted to proceed to an arrest. Difficult to intercept such a little boat from mid-air. It was finally a Canadian Coast Guard boat that succeeded in halting the canoe and its passenger. They made him get on board their boat. When it entered the port of Montreal, it was followed by three helicopters and preceded by dozens of flashing lights from the patrol cars on the dock. The handing over of the prisoner into custody was straight out of a Hollywood cop show, except the "bad guy" looked anything but tough.

The news of Achille's arrest took precedence over an important announcement that the Ministry of Education had made the same day. The new school policy was to be found at the bottom of page two, while the front pages of all the newspapers were emblazoned with the photo of the old man on the Saint Lawrence. The most sensational image was a close-up of Achille in his canoe and the Sûreté du Québec helicopter flying at low altitude in the background. The effect was quite striking. Other photos, showing the man surrounded by coast guards as he was handed him over to the police, added to the drama of the scene. Poulin had devoted four pages of the newspaper, including the front page, to the arrest of Achille Roy. It was an excellent story, and what happened in court promised to be even better. "That crazy old guy is a gold mine," he mused.

Achille was taken to a psychiatric unit and put under close surveillance. As soon as he arrived, he was given a strong tranquilliser and soon began to sink into darkness. His will began to wane.

"Why resist? I'm tired and there are so many of them."

The flying machines, the cameras, photographers and policemen, they were all too much for him. He could not hide from everyone.

"I can't do it, Adela, I can't," he murmured before falling into a deep sleep, firmly clutching the bag that contained the ashes of his beloved.

## Thirteen

Paul's childhood on the banks of the Joseph River had been filled with sweetness. He had been cherished by a mother who had made him the centre of her universe and a father who showered him with love and attention. Almost all his memories of his first six years of life revolved around these two people. They often went to do their errands in the village, and he got to know the general store owner as well as the man who ran the post office. There was also the man in charge of maintaining the roads who came by sometimes to chat with his father. But in general, they received very few visitors.

Shortly after the Paul's birth, Achille proposed that the three of them go to church in the village. After all, Achille came from a religious family for whom it would be unheard of to miss a Sunday mass. Therefore he felt they ought to pay a visit to the church in their new village. He talked about it with Adela, who was reluctant at first. She had learned during her childhood to be wary of Catholics, though the majority of people in Tilting were Irish Catholic. There were only a few families in the community who were Anglican like her own family. Meeting Achille, and Marie Lafrenière before him, had changed her way of thinking. If a man could be so good, so fair and was Catholic, it meant that this religion could not be as "terrible" as people said it was. And besides, the God of her church had to be the same as the God of the Catholics, for both groups founded their beliefs on the same book, the Bible.

"If God is in this church, he must surely be present for anyone who believes in him," she concluded, and agreed to accompany Achille the following Sunday.

From the clothes cupboard they took the only clothes they considered appropriate for such an occasion and Adela had dressed little Paul in an outfit she had sewn herself. Achille swept the straw from the back of the cart and curried the mare before putting on her harness.

The bright white church stood on top of a little hill in the middle of the village and on their way, they could hear the church bells calling the faithful to worship. Achille was proud to have Adela on his arm and to be able to present her to everybody.

Father Perras was waiting for his flock on the front steps of the church. He had a commanding appearance, which gave him authority over his parishioners. Even the mayor of the village had less hold over the citizens of Sainte-Famille d'Aumond than Father Perras did. In the three years he had been in this parish, Perras had come to know everyone. He knew all their little defects, all the sins they had confided in the secrecy of the confessional. He did not miss a chance to remind them of it, either. He liked the feeling of power his position gave him. When he was younger he had dreamed of becoming a lawyer, but his parents had promised at least one son to the priesthood, and that fate had fallen on his shoulders.

His prayer book in hand, he donned his Sunday smile. He was shaking hands with the head of the ladies' auxiliary, Madam Délicia Saint-Jacques, when he caught sight of the strange family coming up the steps. At first he took them for strangers, but the rumour machine works quickly in a small village. He had heard about this unusual couple who lived on the farm of the widow Hébert and the atmosphere of sacrilege that prevailed in that place. There, a Catholic fornicated with an Anglican outside the bonds of marriage. Moreover, this couple had a child of unknown origins. It was said she had been "knocked up" even before she had met him and that the child had been born of rape.

"Not surprising for an Anglican," Father Perras had said when this malicious gossip had been reported to him.

He was outraged that such people could be living in his parish. When he understood that the couple coming up the steps was the very one people had been talking about, his prayer book dropped from his hands.

"Sacrilege!" he said.

He did not know quite what to do. The mass was about to begin and he could not afford to make a scene on the church steps. He turned on his heel and stalked up to the altar, in a hurry to get the scandal over with. He genuflected, but remained in front of the cross, hands joined, praying to heaven to chase these heathens from his house of worship. When he turned around again, he saw them behind him, waiting for the mass to begin, and understood that his prayer had not been granted.

The face of Father Perras was red with anger and he was having trouble containing himself. His state of mind was revealed by his tone of voice as he read from the Holy Scriptures. When the time came for his sermon, he put the speech he had prepared back in the pocket of his cassock. This outrage could not be allowed to pass in silence. His authority over his community obliged him to say something.

"Dear brothers, today I had intended to talk to you about the epistle we have just read, but certain events force me to address another subject. As you know, the Catholic community that is ours has always been preserved from misfortunes such as those that have afflicted the Old Countries. I think of our Irish brothers who have been fighting for an eternity against the forces of evil that oppress them. So far we have been very fortunate in having been preserved from these bad influences and the evil they bring. But today, evil is on our very doorstep. How can I tell you the sorrow, the immense pain, even the shame the Lord feels upon seeing the relations that exist among us, heinous examples for the youth of our community. No, my friends, I am not speaking of an evil we cannot see. I am talking about visible evil. I am talking about promiscuity. I am talking about the unnatural relations between people of different religions. I am talking about people who are living in sin, outside the sacred bonds of marriage. I am also talking about a child born in sin who has not received the sacraments that might once have saved him. My brothers, this cannot be tolerated!" shouted the *curé* from up in his pulpit.

Achille had understood that the priest was referring to himself, his woman and their child. Adela was praying in silence and had paid no attention to the sermon of which, in any case, she would not have seized a single word. But when he firmly gripped her hand and pulled her from the pew, she understood that something had happened, something serious. He stood in the centre aisle, standing very straight and looking the priest in the eyes, then around at the entire congregation. Everyone lowered his or her eyes. They may have been ashamed, as the priest had said, but it was what Father Perras had said that shamed them most of all. For all the parishioners, a denunciation from the pulpit was almost tantamount to excommunication. Yet no one dared defy the harsh extremity of the *curé*'s words. Achille was furious, but turned back slowly and, as if to defy the man of the cloth, took the child from Adela's arms and held him out, almost at arm's length, to show him to everyone. He was not ashamed of this child the priest had just ostracised. He hugged the child to his chest. There was a weighty silence in the church and the noise of the couple's footsteps echoed like drumbeats. No one moved, except the young notary, who had just arrived in the village. He too got up to leave, looking disgusted by this public lapidation.

"That spineless young fellow needs to change his ways," the *curé* said to himself, still furious, "otherwise he won't be notary in this town for long!"

Achille returned home without saying a word, and Adela, though she was anxious to understand what the *curé* had said, respected his silence. When they arrived at the house, all Achille said was: "We're never going to that church again. The God I know is a just God. He wasn't in that church."

The days passed and he did not speak of the incident again, though it was still on his mind. One day as he was working around the house, some visitors appeared. He did not see them arrive. Adela, who was working in the garden, was the first to hear the car drive up the road to the house. It was one of those Ford Model-T vehicles that ran on gasoline. Automobiles were still rare, but this model was the one most people knew. The engine loudly backfired in the direction of the house. The young woman recognised Oscar Crytes, the owner of the general store, at the wheel. He seemed uneasy and his gaze was evasive, which was most unlike him. Someone was sitting in the passenger seat, but from where she was, Adela could not identify him. The car stopped in front of the house and Oscar got out, still wearing his white grocer's apron. He greeted Adela with a polite but embarrassed smile, then went around the vehicle to open the passenger door. Achille had heard noise of the motor too, and was wondering who had come to visit. It was the first time a gas-operated car had come to his house and he was curious. He recognised Oscar and gave him a big smile and a hearty wave just as Oscar opened the passenger door. First Achille saw the flap of the cassock, then he recognised Father Perras getting out of the car. He felt rage ignite inside him, the same rage he had been holding back since the church incident. Once again he swallowed it down. After all, the man may have realised how cruel his words had been and was coming to make peace with his new parishioners. Looking at him, Achille mused at how closely he resembled a crow with his cassock and black hat.

Curé Perras did not so much as glance at Adela, probably considering that her religious affiliation justified his ignoring her. He headed towards Achille with a determined gait. Achille greeted him with a curt nod. The priest cleared his throat and coughed a couple of times before he spoke.

"Mister Roy, I know you're new to this village, but you cannot be unaware that there are things we cannot tolerate. This creature you are living with and this illegitimate child –"

In those days, it was common in conversation to refer to women as "creatures." But Curé Perras had pronounced the word with disdain, as if he were talking about an animal. The anger that Achille had been holding back rose up in his throat. He heard no more of the *curé*'s speech. He cut him off in the middle of the great lyrical oration the priest had been preparing for several days and rehearsed for the whole trip in Oscar Crytes' car.

"That's enough!" said Achille, putting up his hand to make him stop.

The order had been shouted and the priest was so surprised that he stopped short in mid-sentence. Achille's tone left no room for discussion.

"Now you listen to me, *Curé*," he continued.

Oscar noticed that Achille, who was so polite by nature, had suddenly dropped the polite form of address normally used when speaking to a priest.

"Look around you. What you see here is the work of God, the One I know and the One she knows too. This woman who you talk about as if she were less than nothing, is worth more than you will ever be. So look around you because what you see here is God, and it's the last time you'll ever set foot here. Get out, and never come back again," said Achille, pointing towards the road by which the *curé* had come.

Father Perras was outraged by the tone Achille had used. "That is not how things are going to be, my friend. God –" he started to say.

"Do not say the name of the One you don't know!" interrupted Achille. "Things are going to be this way, and you are going to walk down that road and off this property."

Backing up his words with actions, he grabbed the priest by the scruff of his cassock and gave him a firm kick in the buttocks, forcing him to keep moving. Each time the man opened his mouth to protest, Achille's foot on his backside forced him to start walking again. Never had Curé Perras, who was accustomed to complete submissiveness from his flock, been put to such shame. No one had ever dared contest him, much less raise a hand to him. He was indignant and wanted to shout insults at Achille, but each time he opened his mouth, a firm kick was planted on his posterior, raising him off the ground a few centimetres. He walked and protested, both at once, like a naughty boy who has just been spanked.

Oscar Crytes stood with his mouth open. The *curé* had come to see him and ordered him to drive him to the "the place of sin." He could never have believed such a thing possible. Dumbfounded, his hand clasped over his open mouth, he watched the incredible scene. He did not know what to do. He thought maybe he should intervene, but after the incendiary sermon that Perras had delivered at church, he felt that Achille had every reason to resent him. Once his astonishment had passed, he started to laugh uncontrollably.

"Well, I have to give it to you, my friend. If anyone had told me Curé Perras would be put in his place like this, I'd have never believed him!"

He let Achille accompany the priest to the edge of the property before cranking up his car motor. He met Achille coming back up the road and gave him a big wave and a mocking grin. When the priest got into the car, fuming, Oscar was still having trouble containing his mirth.

"Did you see that?" the priest cried. "You saw what he did! We have to go to the police. You'll be my witness."

It was anyone's guess what suddenly gave Oscar the courage to do it, for he had never dared confront a religious authority, but his reply was a sharp one.

"I didn't see anything. I saw a good man defending his wife, his property, and his child. And if anyone asks me, in my opinion, you fell flat on your ass…Monsieur le Curé. And if you intend to go to the police, you should tell me now because I'll let you out of my car right here."

Oscar's tone was firm, leaving no room for argument, and Father Perras, slowed down by his generous girth and unaccustomed to physical effort, had no intention of walking the five kilometres that separated him from the village. His voice went down a notch.

"I hope this incident will remain between us."

The case was closed. Few people ever knew this story. Sometimes Oscar Crytes would tell it at Christmas time to a handful of close friends after a few glasses of cheer, and every time, he laughed so hard he almost had a seizure. When Achille came into the store, Oscar always found a way to slip a joke in.

"So, Mister Roy, still chasing crows off your land?"

Achille would smile but say nothing, embarrassed at having let himself get carried away.

The child grew up surrounded by love. Achille taught him what he knew about the world they lived in. He often took him fishing in the canoe and patiently answered his many questions. Adela loved seeing them together. The child had even learned their special dialect. Paul was a happy child who grew up in a vale of beauty.

Then it came time for him to go to the village school. His mother sewed him a magnificent outfit, as her mother had shown her how to do when she was still a child herself. Achille had bought some material at the general store, and she had worked several days on the clothes he would wear to school. He had also bought two little scribblers and pencils. The previous autumn, Achille had put aside the hide of a Virginia stag he had caught, carefully tanning it to make his son a schoolbag. Adela had sewn it and decorated the skin with drawings and porcupine quills. The little boy had been overjoyed by his presents. He was eager to go to school, especially to meet other children. He sometimes met one or two when he went to the village with his parents, but had established only brief relations with them. A few minutes here and there at the general store or post office. With envy he watched them play with each other and would have liked to share in their moments of pleasure.

Achille and Adela were aware that their child needed contact with others and were happy to take him to school. Though the distance between their home and the village was something of an obstacle, they made it their duty, each morning at six, to hitch up the mare to the old carriage and take Paul to school. They went back to get him at the end of the day. When Achille went off to the lumber camps, Adela took over, though sometimes they were snowed in for several days at a time. At those times, the sled would replace the cart, and as soon as the roller had gone by to press the snow down, she would get out the horse again and drive the child to school.

There was just one class. Each morning, twenty or so pupils of all levels would crowd in to the classroom. There were five or six children of Paul's age, but the others were older. Some were twice as old as him.

The desks were lined up in rows. The lucky ones had their desks near the woodstove where they could take advantage of its gentle warmth during the winter. Mademoiselle Lévesque, the teacher, usually had the youngest children sit near the fire and the older ones near the walls. But this privilege was not to everyone's satisfaction. That was the case with big Roméo Fortin, who sat in the back in the coldest corner of the room. Mademoiselle Lévesque was a good teacher. She took a lot of pleasure in her work, but could not discipline her class. She had tried to maintain order, but she feared students like Roméo. He was taller than her and had a violent temper, and most of all, big Roméo had "connections" that the others did not have. Madame Fortin, his mother, was on the school administration commission. One day, the young schoolmistress had enough of Roméo and sent him home, saying he could not come back except if he came with his parents. And that is what happened. Madame Fortin, far from being furious with her son, went after the schoolmistress, threatening to make her lose her job if she dared reprimand her child again. The young woman knew very well that being fired would put an end to her teaching career. She would never find another position. So she decided to forget Roméo. He disappeared from her mind, but not from the classroom.

The overgrown boy was in no way a model student, on the contrary. He was the oldest child of the family of Herménégilde Fortin, and his mother had promised that the first child would become a priest. Roméo showed as much aptitude for the priesthood as a wolf did for the job of shepherd, but she pushed him to stay in school despite his disastrous marks, blaming her son's failures on the inexperience of the young schoolmistress. She had spoiled and protected him so thoroughly that she could not see, and even less so admit, that her son was a spoiled baby who risked becoming a good-for-nothing. Herménégilde was not fooled, but his wife totally dominated him. He never would have confronted her, but when she was not around, he administered severe punishments on his wayward offspring in the hope, he said, of teaching him obedience.

It may have been for this reason that big Roméo had developed the unpleasant habit of picking on the younger children. He derived a devilish pleasure from his physical domination of the small children in the class. And if one of them presented any special characteristics, Roméo made him the target of his persecution. Donat Morin was a nice little boy, but in place of ordinary-sized incisors he possessed two huge paddle-shaped teeth. Even when his lips were closed, the two teeth were always visible. Roméo had nicknamed him "Beaver." All day long he taunted him across the room, telling stupid jokes, making fun of him, shoving him or throwing objects at him. The others in the class were only too happy to laugh at his jokes, though they were never funny. Better to be one of the ones who laugh than a victim of that laughter.

When Paul arrived at the school, big Roméo already knew who he was. The family from Concession Road IV, the "fiends," Curé Perras called them. The Devil's family.

"Hey, there goes the De-e-e-e-vil," Roméo would say, putting emphasis on the "e."

In class, he would always sit behind him, throwing little pebbles at him then feigning innocence when Mademoiselle Lévesque looked over in his direction. If Paul dared complain, Roméo would be waiting for him after school and give him a serious beating. The kicks and punches were painful, but what really pierced his heart were the insults.

"He's a bastard, everyone knows it. The child of the De-e-e-e-vil is always a bastard. Go near him and you go to hell," he said.

In the face of this harassment, Paul had come to wish that he really did resemble the picture of the Devil he had seen in the Bible, an enormous snake with the head of dragon. He would have made Roméo burn on the spot with a single breath.

There was also another story Roméo told everyone about Paul, that Achille was not his father.

"Achille Roy is like Joseph in the holy family," he said, "except in their family it wasn't the holy spirit who made the baby, his mother slept with the Devil."

"Liar, liar!" cried Paul.

All this jeering cruelly wounded him, but when he asked his mother about the story, Adela felt it was important not to lie to him. Achille felt the same way. Though the subject had never come up, Achille had never really hidden the fact that he was not his "real" father, but joyfully let him call him "Papa."

"It's true, Achille is not your real father. But at the same time, he's more than your father. He loves you more than a father and considers you his son."

None of that mattered to Paul. So what Roméo said was true! His insults cut him even more deeply.

"Those people don't even go to mass. It's obvious they're the family of the De-e-e-e-vil," taunted Roméo.

Roméo was right about this. Paul had never been to church, and when he asked his parents why, Achille told him the priest had insulted his mother, though he avoided telling him about the *curé*'s visit. Paul was too young to understand. What the child understood, however, was that this special status made him suspect in the eyes of others, and he became a target of cruelty. In the schoolyard, he was usually alone. For awhile he was friends with little Donat Morin in the "rejects' club," but the boy soon left the school, unable to bear Roméo's harassment any longer. Paul tried to make himself invisible, but his torturer would not let him be. Especially because the Roys were considered strange by the entire village.

"A backward family," Roméo said.

More and more people were proudly displaying an automobile in front of their house, even those who did not really have the means to buy one, and everyone had water pumped into the kitchen. Some homes that were located near the sawmill even had electricity, the height of modernity. The village sawmill, built by a stream of the Joseph River, was run on water power. A generator activated by the big paddlewheel allowed surplus current to be distributed among the surrounding houses. But at Paul's home, there was nothing like that, and he felt different from other people. Even the clothes made by his mother and the schoolbag he had at first been so proud of made him a laughingstock among his schoolmates.

Time passed slowly in class, and each day Paul dreaded recess, when Roméo would pick on him. He had developed a strategy. If he managed to get out of the school building quickly and hide behind something, he sometimes managed to avoid getting hit or otherwise attacked. He took refuge behind the school and waited anxiously for the bell to sound the end of recess. At lunch hour, he bolted down his food alone, behind a little cedar hedge that hid him from the others. But this did not always work. When Roméo had no one else to pick on, he went looking for Paul... and found him every time.

It was a spring day and Mademoiselle Lévesque had told her students that they had to be on their best behaviour because an important visitor was coming. Every spring, before harvest time emptied the rows of desks, the president of the local school commission made his annual visit with the parish priest.

"It's a very big day," said Mademoiselle Lévesque.

The purpose of the visit was to judge the quality of her work. Based on the results of this inspection, the school board could decide to dismiss her. But it could also give her grounds to request a raise in salary, if she could find the courage to ask.

Alexandre Poirier, the president of the school commission, was a man of influence. A farmer, he had had a little more education than some and was also on the municipal board. Mademoiselle Lévesque had all the children take their places, the desks had been washed and she had personally examined everyone's clothes. When Monsieur Poirier entered with the *curé*, all the students rose from their benches and chanted in unison: "Hello, Monsieur Poirier. Hello, Father Perras."

Curé Perras adored these visits. They allowed him to meet the young people and establish his authority for the years to come. After several demonstrations of what the students had learned, carefully prepared by Mademoiselle Lévesque, the priest went around the class, questioning each student individually. The children knew him well and also knew they had to make a good impression, for if they didn't, the priest would not hesitate to complain to their parents. Even big Roméo behaved like an angel. Curé Perras greatly enjoyed this demonstration of power. The mere sight of his cassock was enough to inspire fear in the youngsters.

When he got to Paul, he was taken aback by the beauty of the child's features and reached out to take his chin in his hand, the way one would cup a flower in the palm of the hand. His surprise was all the greater because he was usually able to recognise the parents' features in the faces of their children. But this child was completely unknown to him.

"And who is this lovely little boy?" he asked the schoolmistress.

"That's Paul…," she said uneasily. "Paul, the son of Achille Roy," she added.

Curé Perras had done everything to forget this man, though he never missed a chance to bad-mouth him and his woman. Never would it have crossed his mind that this boy whose angelic face he was holding in his hand could be a child of the damned. His reaction was immediate and spontaneous. He brutally slapped the boy, who started to cry. Curé Perras had lost his cool and regretted the gesture, but did not let it show. The other children were stunned. He quickly brought his visit to an end, without going around to see the other children. In a matter of minutes it was all over and he had left. Everyone turned to the still-suffering child. The others thought he must truly be a child of the Devil to have provoked such a reaction from a man of the Church. Even Mademoiselle Lévesque glared at him, aware that this incident could tarnish her record for good. Paul resented his parents. They were the cause of this nightmare. Everyone hated him because of his mother and a man who was not even his father.

The years passed and Paul became more and more isolated from the mother and father he was so ashamed of, and from others too.

He even joined in on the jokes of Roméo's group, who constantly made fun of his parents. The others were surprised by his attitude, but it succeeded in reducing the harassment he received. The more he put his parents down, the better he was accepted by the others.

"The old man," he said, referring to Achille, "he's crazy."

Achille and Adela noticed the change in him. Paul no longer wanted to go fishing with Achille, though it was a pastime he loved. Once a talkative and enthusiastic child, he no longer spoke to his mother. And when he became a teenager, he fled the house more and more often, only returning late at night.

They did everything they could to understand the child, who was growing up fast. When he turned sixteen, he announced he was leaving "this rat hole." Adela and Achille tried to stop him from going, but in vain. He left one day in July, leaving his mother in a state of deep despair.

"I'm never coming back here," he said.

And he almost kept his word. For four years, Adela and Achille heard nothing of him. At first, for Adela the pain was unbearable. She woke up in the middle of the night to weep. Her only child, the only one she would ever have, was gone. To see children leave the nest was normal, but Paul in some sense was dead. He had disowned them, and they did not even know where he was. Adela continued to fear for him, imagining him in the worst kind of situations. Achille had also wept, in silence, out of Adela's hearing so as not to add to her despair. And yet this trial made them stronger as a couple, each finding comfort in the presence of the other.

## Fourteen

A social worker came to see Achille. "*Social worker*," thought Achille, "that's a strange name for a job." He did not quite understand what she was doing there. She had wanted to take his backpack from him, but he had strongly objected. After all, he did not know her. And in fact, his pack no longer really resembled a backpack. There had been a quite a fuss about this bag. The police had taken it away from him, saying they could not let him keep it.

"It's against procedure," the officer kept repeating.

Once they had arrived at the hospital, where Achille had been put in isolation, he had asked the social worker to return his things, especially his precious box. It was an unusual case. Without exception, prisoners, and especially persons in detention for reasons of mental health, had to part with all personal objects that might allow them to take their own life. Their belts were confiscated, as well as their shoelaces, jewellery, and clothing that could be made into a rope. Generally, the psychiatric patient was stripped and given one of those hideous hospital gowns. However, in Achille's case, it was not really the bag but the painstakingly wrapped package that he wanted to get back. The police had unwrapped the package and seen the iceberg made of varnished wood. The word *ADELA* had been burnt at the base. One of the officers had wanted to open the strange urn, but Sergeant Bonneau had prevented him from doing so. "Procedure" would have normally required him to open it and check its contents, and the young recruit did not hesitate to remind him of the fact. Naturally, Bonneau was aware of it, but the old policeman had been closely following the curious story of the "canoe man." The young officer seemed to feel the box might be filled with an illegal substance. Bonneau knew this was far from being the case.

Someone in Newfoundland had found an old photo of Adela, taken just after her sixteenth birthday. She had been photographed with her parents. The media had restored and enlarged the photo of the young girl. She was magnificent. Bonneau had seen the photo and the idea of opening the iceberg-shaped box revolted him. He would feel as if he were desecrating a grave. First he wondered whether he should ask the court for authorisation to open it, but in the end he had decided to do nothing, and the bundle was wrapped up again in the quilted bedcover. They took away the string and put everything else back in the backpack. The rope closing the top of it had been removed, as had the two shoulder straps. The smaller straps that closed the pockets on the outside of the bag had been cut. A policeman brought the bag into the room where Achille was being held. He carried the object at arm's length, as if it were a bomb that might explode at any moment. He carefully laid the bag on the bed and hurried out. The old man plunged his hands inside, touched the iceberg urn, and recovered his calm. Then he turned back to the woman sitting in front of him. She had to be forty-four or forty-five and had a serious weight problem. Her black hair, which was greying, was cut close to her head and made her look pear-shaped.

"So, my dear sir, can we talk?" she said, in lieu of an introduction.

She asked him all sorts of questions, questions he considered uninteresting and meaningless. She even asked him where Paris was located, as well as another city he had heard of but knew nothing about. She asked him questions on other subjects that were equally foreign to him. Finally they had talked about Adela and his idea of going to Newfoundland. There were doctors who came by as well. Achille could not remember their names. There were quite a few of them, and they all talked a lot but barely listened.

Then there was a man who claimed he was a lawyer. Michel Caouette had been working in legal aid for twenty years, and for twenty years he had hated his profession. He had chosen it by default, because his parents wanted him to be a doctor, or at least practise some kind of "noble" profession. For him, law had been the only acceptable option. He himself had wanted to do theatre. He had believed for awhile that he would be able to express his acting talent in court, but the judge had quickly put him in his place the first time he had tried to deliver a great oration.

He entered the room carrying a pile of files that almost collapsed onto the floor.

"I've been appointed by the court to represent you," he said. "So why don't you try and explain this business to me."

Achille could not have told him. He did not himself understand all that had happened, or why the police had wanted to arrest him. He had done nothing wrong. The interview had lasted ten minutes and the lawyer had told him that he would see him in court. When? Why?

He didn't know. Caouette had used a lot of words that the old man did not know the meaning of. He had cited laws that had no meaning for him. It all seemed to come from another world over which he had no control. The only thing the lawyer had explained was that the case, which was supposed to have been heard in Maniwaki, had been transferred to Montreal. This was "for the greater convenience of all," Caouette said, because now Achille was being held in a psychiatric centre in Montreal.

Several days later, Achille was taken to a big building with the words *Palais de Justice* engraved in big letters on the façade. Palaces were inhabited by kings, and kings did not have the reputation of being fair, or not as far as Achille recalled. Once inside the courthouse, they took the elevator. This was a first for the citizen of Sainte-Famille d'Aumond, who had never "travelled" in this kind of box. He insisted on keeping his bag, but at the entrance to the courtroom, he was forced to part with it. Adela would have to remain in the office of the court clerk.

Achille entered the room with an orderly on either side of him. There was a centre aisle and on either side were rows of chairs upholstered in black leather. All the chairs were occupied. Dozens of pairs of eyes were turned towards him, scrutinising him intently. Achille knew none of these people. Among the unknown faces, his eyes lingered on a young woman standing by the wall near the door, who stepped aside to let him pass. In the front of the room was a row of red leather chairs, again arranged on either side of the centre aisle. No one was sitting in those. These chairs were for the policemen, lawyers, witnesses and the accused. The fiery colour of the chairs gave one the impression that the people sitting in them were going to be grilled.

And in fact, it was to the red chairs, on the left side of the aisle, that Achille was led. There was a man seated at the very end of the row of red chairs to the right of the aisle. He was staring fixedly at the wall, his head turned away, as if he wanted to avoid meeting the old man's eyes. Achille had to lean forward to see the man's face. It was Paul. Paul was there! Finally, someone he knew! He started towards him but was quickly restrained by one of the orderlies. Uneasy, almost ashamed, Paul stammered: "It's for your own good I'm doing this, Pop," he said nervously. "I didn't want to let you do such a crazy thing."

Achille was taken back to his chair and forced to sit down.

"My own good? What's he talking about?" wondered Achille. Suddenly it all became clear. When the doctor in Maniwaki mentioned "someone" who felt he could be dangerous to himself, that someone had been Paul! But why? Paul had shown no interest in either Achille or Adela since the age of sixteen, except when he needed money.

Achille looked intently at Paul, who stared at the wall with renewed fixity. A group of four people made an entrance and headed for the row of chairs where Paul was sitting. Paul was relieved to no longer be sitting alone. He was relieved that he could drop his intent observation of the wall, which he had undertaken in order to avoid being seen by the old man. The people in the group greeted each other and shook hands, and engaged in a bit of private discussion before the proceedings began. Achille saw his lawyer arrive. He always seemed lost in his pile of files, as well as sick and tired of his job. Michel Caouette would be able to retire in four years, and he had no intention of making waves in the meantime. He greeted Achille and sat down beside him.

"I'll take care of everything," he assured him.

Judge Lionel Pelletier made his entrance and everyone rose. One of the orderlies pressed Achille's arm to make him follow suit. Achille could not help thinking that all this resembled a religious service. At a simple signal from the court clerk, everyone stood. The judge even looked like old Curé Perras. This image was far from reassuring. The court clerk read out the details of the court proceedings initiated by Paul, who it seemed, for the first time, was acknowledging that Achille was his father. In a nutshell, Paul was asking the Superior Court of Quebec to recognise Achille as mentally incompetent to manage his own affairs. Pierre Lanthier, the young lawyer representing Paul, got to his feet and spoke.

"By virtue of the law which aims to protect persons who could represent a danger to themselves or others, we intend to demonstrate to this court that Monsieur Achille Roy is an unstable person, and that he could represent a danger to himself and those around him."

Then it was Michel Caouette's turn to rise and speak.

"I've read the file," he said, as if to reassure himself, "and we do not plan to contest the facts. We judge that the client under the legal guardianship of his son for one year should enable us to confirm or dispel any doubt as to my client's mental health."

Achille leapt to his feet.

"I never said that! I don't even know you!" cried Achille, annoyed to hear this man he had only seen for a few minutes talking this way about him.

For Achille, there was no question of accepting he-didn't-know-what for a year. A year was a long time, and at his age, anything could happen.

"What's that? You say that you don't know this man, Monsieur Roy?" asked the judge, irritated by the interruption.

"I saw him for only a few minutes when they locked me up in that place, and I never saw him again."

"But do you know why you're here?" insisted the judge.

"No, I don't know why I'm here. I don't know anyone here. I don't know you and you don't know me. I only know Paul, but he hasn't really known us for quite a long time."

"I don't know you either, Monsieur Roy," said the judge, "but in a little while I will know you better. What interests me for the moment is that you seem to be telling me that this man is not representing you. Yet he is the lawyer who was appointed to your case…" The judge thought for a moment, searching for another word that the old man would be more likely to understand. "This man is the lawyer we asked to represent you."

"He's not representing me, that's for sure," replied Achille.

"Well, if there's no one to represent you, I'll have to postpone the proceedings."

The two lawyers rose in unison to protest. Lanthier, the young Montreal lawyer whose services Paul had retained, looked as if he had stepped out of a fashion magazine. The suit he was wearing was made to measure. He was wearing a peach-coloured shirt and a matching tie for which he must have paid a fortune. Right down to his impeccably new shoes, it was clear what kind of exorbitant fee he must have been charging. Lanthier protested, insisting that a judgement had to be handed down as soon as possible by the tribunal, for "certain decisions concerning Monsieur Roy had to be made."

Caouette was very affronted. In his rumpled suit, whose plaid pattern looked as if it came from another era, he looked like a used car salesman. The hem of his trousers was frayed and his shoes had probably travelled more than those of the poet Félix Leclerc.*

Caouette swore that he had met and talked at length with his client. He also claimed, as usual, that he was overworked and had other

---

* Reference to the Félix Leclerc song, *Moi mes souliers* :
 *Moi, mes souliers ont beaucoup voyagé, Ils m'ont porté de l'école à la guerre (etc.)*
 (My shoes have traveled widely, They've taken me from school to war (etc.))

cases to deal with.

"I even went to meet him at the hospital, which I don't do unless...," he said, his voice trailing off.

"Unless the court forces you to do so. I see," said Judge Pelletier, finishing the lawyer's sentence for him. "Monsieur Roy, I understand that you have not been properly informed about what is happening today and about your rights. You tell me this man does not represent you. I believe you. But you'll have to find someone to represent you before this court. Do you know a lawyer?"

Achille did not know any. He had never needed one. He was about to answer no when, from the back of the room, someone cried: "I want to. I'll represent this gentleman!"

Achille looked at the woman coming towards him. She was young, she could not be more than twenty-four or twenty-five, and she wore the kind of clothing students did: an above-the-knee jeans skirt and a white blouse embroidered with a spray of roses. Fairly tall, she walked with an assured step, the step of someone who knows what she wants and where she is going.

Anne Blais had just been admitted to the Quebec Bar and had come to the courthouse to deliver the documents that would make her status official. Finally she could start practising the profession of her dreams. From a young age, she had been enchanted by the Perry Mason films, in which the lawyer managed to untangle the most complicated plots and make the bad guys confess to save his innocent clients. It seemed to her the most wonderful profession in the world: to defend the innocent, save the widow from the clutches of villains, pursue the powerful who abused the weak. Of course, she had learned from her law courses that nothing was totally black or white. Things were often grey. And a lawyer did not always defend the innocent. Moreover, in general, it was rarely innocent people who appeared before the courts. Most of the regulars at the law courts were petty criminals, and not big wily industrialists. Even the so-called innocent were not completely innocent. Anne had finished her studies with panache and did not have to look long for a job. Even before she was admitted to the Bar, the firm of Latouche, Bernstein and Associates had approached her to join its practice. It was one of the biggest law firms in Montreal and all new graduates dreamed of getting a call from them. Generally there was only one person per graduating class who got their call. Anne had been flattered, but did not know yet whether she was going to accept. To say yes would ensure her a brilliant future, free of financial worries. But she was not sure this was what she wanted. She had promised to give her answer that day.

She had arrived at the courthouse and learned from the clerk that this very day the case of the *old man in the canoe* was being heard. This affair had fascinated her so she had decided to slip in among the crowd of curious onlookers waiting at the doors of the courtroom. Several journalists were hanging around, looking for new information. Anne had managed to slip into the back row. She had seen the man enter. He reminded her of her late grandfather. He gazed into the eyes of the people standing there, his eyes resting on her for a few moments, as if he had recognised her. His direct and penetrating gaze had made her panicky for a second; it seemed as if he could see right into her soul. When the judge had challenged the legal aid lawyer, she could not hold back any longer. She wanted this case. It was the kind of case she had dreamed about as a little girl watching Perry Mason. "I'll represent him!" she had cried with no hesitation. At first she had been embarrassed when all heads in the room turned in her direction, but resolutely, she stepped forward to address the judge.

"Mademoiselle…or should I say Counsel?" asked the magistrate.

"Counsel, Your Honour, since nine o'clock this morning. I just delivered my Bar authorisation to the office of the courthouse."

"Fine. But that does not mean this gentleman wants you… Counsel."

She turned towards the old man. He was looking at her intently again. She reminded him of someone with her long curly hair that tumbled over her shoulders, and her dreamy smile. She took his hand.

"Trust me," she said, almost imploring him.

"It's her," Achille had said unhesitatingly, turning to the judge.

"All right. I hope you know what you're doing, sir."

The date of the hearing was put ahead a week, to give the lawyer time to study the dossier. The judge would have to have a little more time, but Achille had insisted that the case should be heard as quickly as possible. Anne followed her client out of the courtroom, talking with him, questioning him, looking for information. From a public telephone at the hospital where Achille was being held, she contacted her adversary, Paul's lawyer, to find out the details of his presentation and sound out his intentions.

"I don't think you should take this case, Counsel, it could work against you in future," he said with a tone of superiority and arrogance that made Anne furious.

"What a pretentious jerk!" she said to herself.

But she could not help thinking about what Lanthier had said to her. What did it mean? Why would her future in law be jeopardised because she defended an old man with no criminal record and no money? She put the thought out of her head, telling herself it was some sort of lawyer's tactic that Lanthier was using on her. But clearly there was something she did not understand. Or maybe it was just her lack of experience? From what her client had said, the man who demanded that Achille be put under guardianship had shown little consideration for his parents in the past fifty years. In fact, he had almost completely stroked them from his life. Why was he suddenly so interested in the health of the adoptive father he had disowned? Achille Roy owned nothing. In his pocket he had about three thousand dollars that had recently been loaned to him and a piece of worthless land north of Maniwaki. Why make so much fuss over so little? Why would anyone want to administer Achille Roy's possessions when the man owned almost nothing?

The adversary meant to demonstrate that Achille Roy was mentally incompetent to make appropriate decisions on matters that concerned him, and that he could even be dangerous. A psychologist and a social worker were quoted. This idea of going from Sainte-Famille d'Aumond to Newfoundland by canoe was totally out of the ordinary. Anne had done a bit of canoeing when she was a student at the University of Ottawa and feared these boats, which capsized so easily. As for the Gatineau River, she had heard about it from some of her thrill-seeker friends. A big white-water canoe expedition was organised each year. If she had ever attempted such an adventure, she would surely have drowned. So there was, in this strange expedition, an obvious and undeniable element of danger. She would need to find someone who knew about white-water canoeing and who could explain and play down the dangers of an activity that she personally considered suicidal.

Anne resolved to go to Aumond immediatel to get a better idea of who her client was. It was quite a trip and she would probably have to stay for a few days. But all she had was seven days, and in that time she also had to find a psychiatrist who would come testify on their behalf. She suddenly thought of the professor who had taught her in Criminal Psychology.  Doctor Harvey was a venerable man. He had taught at the university for years, and she had loved his courses. But she also knew that he refused to testify for anyone, saying that he wanted to keep his objectivity. But she was in a tight spot and decided to try her luck. She called him immediately.

"Doctor Harvey, this is Anne Blais. Do you remember me?"

"How could I forget you? You always had twenty questions to ask me every class, and each time I asked myself how I was going to be able to cover all the course material before the term ended. I have a hunch that you're calling me with another question today," the professor said mischievously.

Anne decided to get right to the point, explaining the case, while insisting on the fact that she did not have much time. And there was no question, either, of remunerating him for appearing in court.

"You know that I refuse to act as an expert witness," he replied, leaving Anne feeling desperate, "but for you, I think I'll make an exception. You were one of the rare students I've had who was really interested in human psychology and not just points of law. Besides, I've been following this story myself a little and it would not displease me to meet this canoe man."

Anne thanked him profusely, and told the doctor where her client was being held so he could meet him. She told Achille, and informed him that she would be gone for a few days. She hoped her old Ford Tempo would hold up in spite of its twelve years. It would be a long trip. She was about to leave her room when the phone rang in the hallway. She answered, recognising the voice of Counsel Marc-André Latouche, remembering she had promised to call him that day.

"I'm sorry, sir, I know I was supposed to call you today but I sort of got tied up. You know what, I already have a client!" she said proudly.

"Actually, my dear, that's just what I wanted to talk to you about. If you wish to be associated with our firm, you're going to have to withdraw from this case. This client is, how shall I put it, troublesome for our firm, and it would be best if you drop him immediately. If not, we will have to withdraw the proposal we made you."

Anne was so surprised that for a moment she was speechless. What could this old man from Sainte-Famille d'Aumond possibly represent for the big Montreal firm? And how could they have found out about it so quickly?

"I don't see how my client –" she began.

"You don't have to see. Leave it for us to judge. I advise you, for your own good, to withdraw from this affair."

That know-it-all Lanthier had said the same thing to her. There must have been collusion between Lanthier and the Latouche firm. She was furious.

"Well if that's how it is, you can keep your proposal. Achille Roy is my client and that's how he's going to stay," she said angrily, slamming down the phone without waiting for a reply.

"It's not the best decision I've ever made in my life, but I'm still happy we got it over with right away," she thought.

Several hours earlier she had still been thinking of accepting the proposal, though she was not particularly drawn to these big firms full of self-satisfied people. What she wanted was to defend people and not the business capital of some big firm.

She started out for Maniwaki. The trip would be a long one. It would take four hours to get there. When she reached Maniwaki, first she looked for a hotel room, and then started hunting for her first contact person. Who could tell her something about this affair? In the lobby of the *Auberge du Draveur* were newspapers and magazines that had been made available to the hotel guests. She picked up a copy of the local newspaper and leafed through it. She stopped at an article by the journalist Martin Éthier. The story was low-key but well researched, and it presented her client honestly, at least from what she could tell. There were also a few details that seemed to have escaped the notice of the national press. She decided to contact the journalist. Maybe he would be able to give her some useful information.

Martin was surprised by her call. The affair of *the old man in the canoe* had gotten away from him since *Le Droit* had taken it over. He had almost been a direct witness to Achille Roy's arrest, and had learned that the case would be tried in Montreal. He had no more part of the story. He would just have to follow its progress like anyone else, on the television networks and in the tabloids. *Le Droit* would no doubt give major coverage to the trial. Moreover, he had received a call from the editor of the Ottawa daily, who wanted to see him. He wondered why. No one called up a journalist just to say hello. Maybe he would be offered a job. That would involve a lot of things. He had not expected to have anything to do with the old man again, but the lawyer's phone call brought him back to the story.

When Martin met her, at first he mistrusted her but soon changed his mind. He told her what he had seen and heard, what he had written, and most of all, what he had *not* written about the story, notably the mortgage Achille had taken out on his land, which a stranger had wanted to buy at twice the price. Anne listened carefully, taking notes, asking for names, phone numbers and personal comments. She wanted to know everything about the man. If possible, she wanted to know about his life, and not just from the time he got into his canoe and headed for Newfoundland. The journalist promised his support and suggested she meet the notary, Lafleur.

"He's the one that can tell you the most about Achille's youth and past."

They exchanged phone numbers. The lawyer walked around Sainte-Famille d'Aumond and spent an entire day in the company of the notary. When she met anyone whose contribution could bring something to the case, she asked him or her if they were prepared to go to Montreal to testify. Everyone said yes. Anne estimated that she could probably present a fair and equitable defence for her client. She had learned a great number of things, but knew she was still missing some important elements.

A week later, Achille entered the courtroom for the second time. The young lawyer had insisted that the orderly not hover over Achille. He did not need help. The police feared that the old man would escape again. As on the day of the first court appearance, Paul stood on the right side of the room, accompanied by several people, including his flamboyant lawyer. When the judge had mounted his throne (that's how Achille saw it), Lanthier started the proceedings by calling Paul to the stand. After swearing to tell the truth, he was asked by the lawyer to describe how he was related to the defendant.

"Achille is my father...," he said hesitantly, "my adoptive father."

The old man reflected bitterly that Paul had not said anything like this since his early childhood.

"Could you explain what has motivated you to ask the court for guardianship of your father's affairs?" asked Lanthier.

"Well, listen, I've known for awhile now that things aren't going too well with him. To tell the truth, he's always been a bit... disturbed. You know, he and my mother lived a bit like animals on their land. No one ever came to that house and they refused to see anyone. For a long time, they didn't even have electricity. It was only in the past few years that they agreed to get the house hooked up. No wonder my mother died. They lived the way people did a hundred years ago," he said, turning to the judge. "They never had a television or telephone. My mother was ill and she couldn't even call a doctor. When she died, I could see he had lost his mind. For one thing, this idea of taking the ashes out of the urn and putting them in that strange box...ridiculous!

I was ashamed. Then he starts raving about how he has to go to Newfoundland. He's never been to Newfoundland. When I saw he was going to leave in his canoe, I realized he'd gone childish in the head. A case of Alzheimer's, if you ask me."

"Did you fear for your father's life?"

"For sure. At his age, it's suicidal to canoe down that river. Every year people drown in it. You don't know what the Gatineau River is like. Millions of tons of water rushing towards Gatineau and Ottawa. No wonder there's so many hydroelectric dams along the river."

"Did you have the impression that your father wanted to put an end to his days?" asked the lawyer, each time insisting on the words "your father."

This time, the young woman lawyer got to her feet: "Objection, Your Honour! Monsieur Lanthier is asking a witness to give his opinion on my client's mental health. Monsieur Cole is not a psychologist."

"Objection sustained," answered the judge. "Please restate your question," he said to Lanthier.

"Did your father say anything that would be consistent with suicidal behaviour?"

"When my mother died, he said it was all over, that he'd lost his reason for living. He did not want to live any more. You could see it."

"Objection! The witness is giving us an unsubstantiated opinion."

"This time I'll have to reject your objection. The witness is the man's son. His opinion has a certain value," said the judge.

Paul saw his chance, and jumped at the opportunity.

"I know he was thinking of dying."

"Is there anything else that makes you say that he wasn't in his right mind?"

"Well, this story of going to borrow three thousand dollars on his land to finance this crazy trip. He could have asked me."

Achille made a gesture of impatience. He had told Anne that he had asked for his son's help. She put her hand on his arm to calm him. She knew how frustrating it was to listen to a witness lie without being able to react.

"And what's more, that's all he had, that piece of land. I was sure he was going to lose it because his pension cheque isn't going to help him reimburse that amount of money. You can see very well that it makes no sense."

Lanthier thanked him. Now it was Anne's turn to start the cross-examination. Paul had lied as much as a person could lie. When she asked him how many times he had seen his parents since he had left home, Paul claimed that he had not counted his visits but that he came to see them often.

"So could you tell us about Christmas at your parents' last year?"

Paul squirmed on the witness stand and said he could not remember the details. Anne insistently questioned him about this Christmas celebration, and finally he admitted that he had not gone the previous year, nor the year before that. As for the other years, he did not remember.

"Anyway, we weren't even allowed to go to church because he –" said Paul, pointing at Achille. "One day he beat up the parish priest."

Anne grew pale. This story was not going to help her case; she quickly passed on to another subject.

"Can you tell us how many times your wife, or your wives rather, met your father?"

"Well…"

"How many times?" Anne insisted.

"I don't know."

"I can ask your wife to appear in court if you wish," Anne threatened.

"Anything but that!" thought Paul. His wife would ruin everything.

"No, no. I don't think she ever met him. You know, she isn't in the best of health and to make the trip to Sainte-Famille d'Aumond was too much for her."

"And I suppose you thought your parents' home didn't offer the necessary comfort?"

"That's true enough. It made no sense at all. It was a real dump."

"A dump you say? And what about your colleagues and friends, did they ever go to Aumond?"

"No, they sure didn't."

"Why?"

"Well, for the same reason, and anyway I didn't want them to see what I came from."

"In other words, you were ashamed of the place?"

"That's right," acknowledged Paul.

"And you were also ashamed of your parents."

"Uh, no. Well, a bit," he said hesitantly.

"Is it not true that on several occasions you borrowed money from your parents?"

"Well, sure, it happened once or twice. You know, business was difficult and I needed a bit of cash to give me a leg up."

"According to the information I have here, you borrowed money on four different occasions, totalling $35,000."

"It's possible," said Paul, realising it would be difficult to deny it, for each time he borrowed from them, he had signed an IOU.

"Can you tell me, sir, how much of that money you reimbursed?"

"I don't remember."

"Is it possible that you never repaid a single cent?"

"It's…it's possible," he admitted.

"I have no more questions for the moment, but I may ask the witness to take the stand again," Anne said.

Next it was Officer Laflamme's turn to testify about the old man's arrest, and he did not miss his chance to conclude that the man was crazy.

"He wanted to go to Newfoundland. He was out of his mind," said Officer Laflamme. "At the age of eighty-eight, there he was with a canoe on his back. Totally out of his mind," he concluded.

While questioning him, Anne insisted on one point.

"Officer Laflamme, what is your educational background?"

"Well, uh, the police academy."

"Do you have any particular knowledge of psychology?"

"No."

"Have you any knowledge of psychiatry?"

"Of course not, but I'm used to seeing nutcases in my line of work."

"Have you ever worked in a psychiatric hospital?"

"No."

"How long did you stay with Monsieur Roy?"

"I guess about an hour."

"So how can you, with each of your answers, assure us this man has lost his mind?"

The officer did not reply, and Anne did not wait for him to do so. Next it was the turn of the social worker, Lyne Gagnon, who had been assigned the task of studying the Achille Roy case. Achille saw her sitting in one of the chairs next to Paul. While the first witnesses were being questioned, she devoured Lanthier with her eyes. His mid-length hair reminded her of the actor Hugh Grant. During the interrogation, each time the lawyer asked her a question, she sighed with pleasure. The simple fact that he was paying attention to her and showering her with kindness was balm for the scars of her soul, which was battered each morning by the unattractive image she saw when she looked in the mirror.

Right from the start, she said, she had noticed the patient showed deficits in terms of spatial and temporal identification.

"When I asked him where Paris is, he could not tell me its location. All he could tell me was that it was on the other side of the ocean. He didn't know where New York was, either. This demonstrates a certain decline in his ability to orient himself in relation to the rest of the world. Even in the case of Newfoundland, where he said he wanted to go, Monsieur Roy was not able to give the exact location of the province. All he could tell me was that it was near Fogo Island," she explained.

Moreover, according to the social worker, Monsieur Roy could not name the premier of Quebec nor the prime minister of Canada.

"He has forgotten everything that is instrumental to current events and everyday life. When I asked him what he had retained of the last television programme he had watched, he replied that Séraphin Poudrier had been severely lectured by Curé Labelle. The programme he is referring to has been off the air for years."

"Mademoiselle Gagnon, can you tell this court whether you detected suicidal impulses in Monsieur Roy?"

"Well, there's certainly a morbid obsession with his wife's ashes. He became aggressive when I tried to take his bag. I also noticed that he tends to talk to his bag as if he were talking to a living person. I sincerely believe that Monsieur Roy was very troubled by the death of his wife and wanted to join her in death. He seems to be living in the past."

Lyne Gagnon had only become a social worker recently. She had worked as an accounting clerk for almost fifteen years, then sunk into a deep depression from which she had never really emerged. For thirteen years she had tried all possible therapies, from consultations with a psychiatrist to group therapy and two sojourns in a psychiatric clinic. Now she saw a psychologist every week. In the same way as patients suffering from kidney failure are poisoned by their own blood and require dialysis, Lyne depended on her weekly appointment to purge all the ideas and images she had been poisoned with over the course of a week. It was a kind of dialysis of the mind. It was during this long process that she had got the idea that she could help people who suffered as she had.

Anne Blais wondered how this social worker had obtained the

right to practise. Her first questions related to the quality of her work with her client.

"How many sessions did you and Monsieur Roy have?" asked Anne.

"Well, let's say two," she replied, a little reluctantly.

She had spent more time with Lanthier preparing her testimony. Moreover, she viewed this young and inexperienced woman lawyer with certain condescension.

"And were these two sessions very far apart?" Anne continued.

"Well, let's say that...they were both on the same day. One in the morning and one in the evening."

"And you feel that's sufficient for you to make a diagnosis?"

Lyne was mortally offended. She sensed that this stuck-up young woman was trying to discredit her. Anger flared within her. She bit her lips, as she did each time she felt her blood start to boil, and her answers were punctuated with little nervous laughs.

"It was enough because Monsieur Roy did not want to talk anyway, and was muddled in his replies."

"You know where Paris is, don't you?" asked Anne.

"Paris? Of course, I've even been there."

"Do you know where Castor Blanc is?"

"Castor-what? Well, no...come on!" she said irritably, with another nervous laugh.

"Do you know the location of the Rapide-des-Six?"

"Of course not!"

"And what about Farley, could you locate it on the map?"

"Really, Your Honour, this is ridiculous!" she said, turning to the magistrate.

This time Lanthier rose and objected, pointing out that these questions had no bearing on the case.

"Your Honour, I ask for a little latitude. Mademoiselle bases her diagnosis of my client on the fact that he doesn't know where Paris or New York are. She checks on what my client knows by referring to her own baggage of knowledge. I am simply checking hers by referring to the knowledge of Monsieur Roy."

"Continue," said the judge.

"So about Farley; can you tell me where this place is?"

"No," she said coldly.

"And can you tell me, Mademoiselle, what was in the paper this morning?" asked Anne, crossing her fingers and hoping that the woman had not read the newspaper.

"I don't know, I had no time to read the newspaper."

"So if I said that you are not aware of the news of the day because you haven't read the newspaper, I would be correct, would I not?"

"Yes."

"Doesn't it ever happen to you to miss reading the newspaper for more than one day?"

"Often. I'm not a great reader of newspapers."

"So, following your reasoning, I could also cast doubt on *your* mental abilities because you don't know where Castor Blanc or Farley is, and you aren't aware of the latest news?"

Lanthier quickly got up to object, alleging that it was a leading question. The judge agreed, but the damage was done.

"I suppose, Mademoiselle Gagnon, that you have visited the residence of Monsieur Roy?"

"Of course not. He lives more than three hundred kilometres from here. I'd never have had the time to go. Besides, it wasn't necessary."

"So, if I understand correctly, you are able to make a diagnosis as severe as the one you are presenting today, based on two short sessions held on the same day, without doing any research on the milieu in which your patients live?" asked Anne sarcastically.

"I...I..."

"Thank you," said Anne, satisfied.

Next came the testimony of the expert witness in psychiatry, who gave a brilliant exposé on the degeneration of mental faculties among the elderly, and the symptoms of aging. He quoted numerous studies including statistics. The man frequently appeared in court. That was all he did, appear in court as an expert witness on behalf of different law firms. His fee was high and when the hoped-for conclusions were difficult to justify, his fee went up accordingly. In general, the expert recognised from reading the reports he had been given, notably the social worker's, that Achille Roy presented all the symptoms of a person who was losing his autonomy.

Anne simply asked him how much time he had spent with Achille Roy.

"That makes no difference. If the reports are well done, you can form an opinion," he said.

Anne insisted and he had to admit that he had never met Achille personally.

"And do you trust the quality of these reports?"

"Well, I suppose they are well done and I have no reason to doubt the work of Mademoiselle Gagnon."

"Ah, you suppose? So it would not be wrong to say that your report is based on supposition?"

The psychiatrist thought for a moment.

"When you put it that way, yes, I suppose you could make that claim."

According to the list Lanthier had submitted, there was to be another witness, but up until now, he had not revealed the identity of this witness. When the lawyer with the Hugh Grant hair got to his feet, Anne objected. Lanthier reminded the judge that Anne had been informed that he would be presenting other witnesses.

"We wanted to fax the list of our witnesses to Mademoiselle's office, but she only left us a phone number at the hospital where her client is being detained, and another at the student residence where she lives. We called the number five times to tell her and each time a different person answered the phone. Mademoiselle Blais seems to have a very active social life," said Lanthier smugly.

"Damn!" Anne said to herself. In her enthusiasm, she had not thought about this detail. The building where she lived had at least twenty-five rooms, most of them rented to students but also to some rather odd individuals. And since the tenants did not have their own phone lines, everyone used the telephone at the front door. The person who happened to be closest to the phone when it rang was supposed to answer it. Most of the time, messages were forgotten as soon as the call ended.

"My witnesses have come quite a distance and are no longer young. It would be detrimental to this case to postpone their testimonies," said Lanthier.

The judge agreed, and rejected Anne's protests.

"It is your responsibility, Counsel, to make sure you have not only the theoretical knowledge with which to ensure your client's defence, but also the technical facilities that are necessary to do so. That includes a telephone number where it is possible to reach you or leave you a message."

What a blow to the young inexperienced lawyer! It was clear that she was dismayed by her error. This time it was Achille who pressed her arm.

"The court calls Roméo Fortin."

Roméo Fortin. Achille had to search for the name in his memory.

"Roméo Fortin, son of Herménégilde Fortin. A great lout of a fellow," Achille whispered in Anne's ear, wondering what the bullyboy could have been up to for all these years.

But most of all, he was remembering Paul as a child and how Roméo had constantly harassed him. How dare he show up here and speak to him today!

Roméo was no longer the big braggart and swaggerer that he was as a youth. He was six years older than Paul and looked like an old man. Even Achille was in better shape than him.

He gave his name and the lawyer asked him a few questions to allow the court to identify Roméo's connection with Achille and his family.

"They were weirdoes. They lived in the woods and attacked anyone who stepped on their property."

"Could you give us some examples?"

"Well, there was the incident with Curé Perras that caused such a big stir. He kicked him around," he said, pointing at Achille. "That's why they never went to Mass. People used to say they were the Devil's family. Paul even got slapped in the face by the *curé* because he was the child of the Devil's family."

"And were you personally a victim of violence from this man?"

"For sure. One day he even grabbed me by the collar, just like that, for no reason. He came this close to suffocating me. I had marks on my neck for a long time after. He was the village madman, and no one went near him."

By the time it was her turn to question the witness Anne had lost some of her self-assurance. Achille whispered a few words to her, but certainly did not have time to describe the despicable being that Roméo had been. And now, it was the second time that the story of the *curé* had come up, and Anne had not even discussed it with her client.

"This poor man wasn't lucky, getting me as his defence counsel," she said to herself.

However, she took note of the fact that Paul had been Roméo's scapegoat. She started her cross-examination.

"What were your relations with Paul Cole?"

"We were at school together."

"All right. But were you friends."

"Well…we weren't really buddies. He was younger than me."

"Earlier you were talking about, and I quote, 'the Devil's family.' At that time, did you ever use this kind of expression to refer to Paul

Cole or Achille Roy?"

"I might have. Everyone said it."

"But did you have the habit of referring to Paul with this kind of name?"

"I may have."

"And did he like being called by those names?"

"He sure didn't, he was a real cry-baby. Always off in a corner by himself. A real savage."

"Did you ever have altercations with Paul?"

"What?"

"Fights, squabbles?"

"Not really fights, but squabbles, yes, it happened sometimes. He was always in the way, and I hated cry-babies."

"So you had 'squabbles,' as you say. How old were you at the time?"

"I must have been thirteen or fourteen."

"And Paul Cole, how old was he?"

"I don't know. Maybe six or seven."

"So you were twice his age. Do you think Paul Cole thought of these run-ins as mere 'squabbles'?"

"Well…I'm not sure."

"When you say that Monsieur Roy took you by the collar, was it not because of the abuse to which you subjected Paul?"

"I don't think so."

"Didn't he mention it?"

"What?"

"That you should leave his son alone?"

"Might've. I don't remember."

"You have a very selective memory, Monsieur Fortin."

"It was a long time ago."

"I have no further questions."

Lanthier got to his feet to announce one last witness. Anne protested again, though knowing the judge would serve her the same admonishment.

"Your Honour, it is imperative to hear this witness in order to demonstrate Monsieur Roy's dangerous temper. He has come all the way from Kingston to take the stand, and his health is fragile."

"You have my consent. Bring in your witness," said the judge.

"My name is Patrick McAllister."

Anne leaned over to ask Achille who the witness was. He had no idea. The name meant absolutely nothing to him. The man entered into the courtroom, leaning on a cane. His back was bent and he walked with difficulty. His head was bald except for two tufts of white hair on either side of his head. He moved with difficulty and looked as if he were about to collapse. Achille looked at him closely but still did not recognise him. The man made his way to the witness box, then looked up.

"The eyes, I recognise those eyes," murmured Achille, racking his memory.

He realised he knew this man and that the memory had nothing pleasant about it.

"Pat!" he said, loudly enough for the judge to order him to be silent. Anne wanted her client to tell him the identity of the witness, but he was overcome by an anger that had been buried in him for over seventy years. He could not explain to Anne. He could not talk to her about what had been so deeply hidden for such a long time. Painful memories, fraught with blood and violence. The sight of O'Brien, his penis erect, violating Adela came back to his mind, all those images he had never accepted and which now crowded into his head.

However, he had only a vague memory of Pat. Pat had been a mere bit-player in the drama that had occurred in the lumber camp. All he remembered about him was having wanted to push him out of the way. The following day, the guys in the lumber camp had told him what had happened. Pat had left the same day and Achille had never seen him again. He had never known his whole name. All he had known was that his name was Pat and that he had been O'Brien's sidekick.

Pat gave his identity and place of residence. The lawyer asked him to describe the circumstances in which he had known Achille Roy. Pat replied that they had both worked in the lumber camps in the northern Gatineau country in the beginning of the century.

"Could you tell us, Mister McAllister, if Monsieur Roy was a violent man at that time?"

"For sure he was! He killed a man," he answered, causing a stir in the courtroom. Anne leapt up to protest.

"Could you elaborate?" asked Lanthier.

"He killed a man with his fists. He hit him until he died."

Again the room was gripped with amazement and voices were raised. The judge had to intervene to restore order to the court.

"Are you sure of what you are saying, Mister McAllister?"

"I was there and I saw it. He was holding him by the neck and he hit O'Brien's face again and again until he was dead."

"Objection, Your Honour!" Anne almost shouted. "Monsieur Roy has never been accused of killing anyone. It appears in no report."

The judge partially sustained her objection, recognising that, indeed, there seemed to be no record of this purported homicide, but he invited Lanthier to ask for further precisions.

"The guy, O'Brien, was buried right in camp. No one ever heard about him again. The company pretended that a tree had fallen on him, and I was dismissed because I'd seen everything."

"And had you direct dealings with Monsieur Roy yourself?"

"Yes, he almost killed me too. If the other guys hadn't arrived, he would've killed me for sure. See, I still have the marks," he said, lifting his shirt.

One could still see the scar from the wood splinter that had pierced his body.

"He grabbed me by the collar and threw me through the wall. I've never seen a guy capable of that kind of violence."

"I have no further questions," said Lanthier, flashing a mocking smile at Anne.

Disconcerted, not knowing quite how to approach the cross-examination, Anne requested a break in the proceedings so she could talk to her client. Achille was shattered. The incident he had so wanted to forget was resurfacing that day. Seventy years later, he was going to have to pay for the death of O'Brien.

When she closed the door of the room where Achille had been brought, Anne barely recognised her client. The old man suddenly looked his age. Completely defeated, he stared at the floor. Even before she had asked him a question, he admitted: "It's true. What he said is true. For all these years I've wanted to forget, but it never left me. I regret so much not stopping in time. That bastard O'Brien!"

"Hold on a minute, I want you to tell me the story in detail," said Anne, as disconcerted as her client.

The affair was taking a turn she could not possibly have predicted. Achille told her about the circumstances in which he had met O'Brien, that is, when he had surprised him and Pat in the act of trying to rape Adela. He searched for the words to explain the scene he had seen that had so enraged him. He described how he had started to hit O'Brien, unable to stop, and then the attack from Pat.

"I don't think I hit Pat. I threw him against the wall."

Anne could well envisage the images Achille was describing. She could understand his anger. But the death of a man was the death of a man. When she asked if she could acknowledge the incident to the court, Achille replied: "Yes, because it's true."

The lawyer no longer knew quite how to approach the dossier. The incident was going to considerably damage her defence. The big-talking Lanthier would use it to prove that Achille could indeed be dangerous, not only to himself but to others as well. Even though the drama had occurred seventy years before, besides losing this case, Achille was now in danger of being accused of homicide as well. It made everything more complicated. The trial would have to be postponed to give her time to prepare a defence, but still Achille refused. He did not have time, he said.

"Listen, Monsieur Roy, when I met you, I asked you to trust me. I am going to repeat my request. As things stand now, what was said today in court could have huge consequences."

She hurriedly requested a report on Patrick McAllister from the police authorities of Quebec and Ontario. She hoped she would able to obtain the information quickly. Next, she appeared before the judge to request a delay. The judge granted her request but told her that beforehand, she should proceed to the cross-examination of the witness. Still, he agreed to suspend the hearing until three in the afternoon.

By the time the court was in session again, Anne had recovered her self-assurance. The police report she had in hand provided her with ammunition. She had also called the Maniwaki journalist to find out more about this story. Martin had never heard about it, but promised to look into it. Before the conversation ended, he added: "I think I could provide you with some interesting information about the son, Paul Cole. Information that could shed a lot of light on this affair."

They agreed to stay in touch. Pat returned, limping to the witness box. He was quite proud of the effect his testimony had had. He expected the woman lawyer to start questioning him about the events surrounding the death of O'Brien.

"Mister McAllister, can you tell us what you have been doing since the event you told us about earlier?"

He was surprised by the question.

"Well, I travelled here and there. A bit in the lumber camps in other places in Quebec and Ontario."

"Did you work steadily?"

"Pretty much."

"Can you tell us what you did in 1935?"

"I don't recall," he said coldly.

"Maybe if I show you this document, it will refresh your memory?"

Pat knew what she was talking about, but would have preferred not to answer.

"Well?"

"I was in prison."

"And can you tell us why?"

"It was all made up, that story. It was just a hooker."

"When you mention a 'made up story,' are you referring to the accusation of sexual assault for which you were judged guilty and condemned to twelve months in prison? Is that what you are referring to?"

"…Yes," he admitted with some hesitation.

"And now I'd like you to tell me what you were doing from 1940 to 1944."

"I don't remember," he said again.

"Wasn't that the time you spent in Kingston penitentiary on another sexual assault charge?"

"It wasn't sexual assault."

"Allow me to refresh your memory. You were accused and judged guilty of raping a woman in the building where you lived. She was savagely beaten and left for dead. Does that remind you of anything?"

"Yes," he admitted again.

"Now let's go back to the events you referred to earlier. Could you tell us where they took place?"

"In the cook house."

"For the benefit of the court, could you explain what a cook house is?"

It was a harmless question and Pat was quite happy to provide a detailed description.

"And what time would it have been?"

"I don't know. Maybe ten or ten-thirty at night?"

"But you said earlier that there must have been sixty people in this lumber camp. There must have been other loggers there to help you when, as you said, you were attacked by Monsieur Roy?"

"Of course not, the guys were in the sleep camp. After supper, the guys go to their sleep camps."

"But not you?"

"No. I mean, yes. I came back with O'Brien."

"Did someone live in the cook house?"

"No, no. But the cook was always there."

"And who was this cook?"

"I don't know, I never knew her name. She arrived at the camp at the same time as O'Brien."

"So it was a woman who lived in this place, am I correct?"

"Yes."

"So you and O'Brien came back to the cook house around ten or ten-thirty in the evening. Could you tell us what you intended to do?"

Pat hesitated. He searched for words that would prevent him from incriminating himself.

"Uh...O'Brien had something going with the woman in the cookery and he wanted to see her."

"He wanted to go see her? With you?"

"No...well, yes...he asked me to come along to keep watch."

"To keep watch? Why in heaven's name would O'Brien need someone to keep watch if he had already had relations with this woman?"

"Well, you couldn't really say it was real relations. He'd known her during the trip to the camp."

"And you were responsible for keeping watch on what, exactly?"

"The others, of course!"

"The other lumberjacks?"

"Yeah, that's it."

"I guess he was afraid they would arrive."

"You got it."

"But why would he be afraid of the other lumberjacks?"

"Well, you never know how...how..." Pat hesitated, again searching his words.

"How they might react?" suggested Anne.

"Yeah, that's it."

"And why would they have reacted badly?"

"Well, he wanted to go meet the girl and he was afraid...they'd be jealous."

"Isn't it actually that you and the said O'Brien had made a plan to sexually abuse this woman?"

"No, that's false. We just wanted to see her and talk to her."

"And what was this O'Brien doing when Monsieur Roy arrived?"

"I don't know. I think he was talking to her, and Roy, he arrives crazy with anger and picks him up by the back of the shirt and starts punching."

"Strange. Earlier you told us you hadn't seen what O'Brien was doing."

"Well, I could see a little."

"You claimed you were attacked without provocation. Did you not try to hit Monsieur Roy with an object?"

"I had to, he was nuts. I picked up a cast-iron frying pan that the girl had knocked down with her foot and –"

"With her foot? How could she make a frying pan fall with her foot?"

"Um, she was lying on the table and she kicked the shelf where the pots and pans were kept."

"And what was she doing on the table?"

"Um, I think she was fooling around with O'Brien."

"And she was struggling so hard that she knocked the shelf with her foot?"

"I don't know."

"Wasn't it because you and O'Brien were raping her, Mister McAllister?"

"No, that's false. He's the dangerous one," he said pointing at Achille.

"So explain to me why it was you who was sent from the lumber camp and not the man you are accusing of murder? Isn't that a bit strange for someone who says he's innocent?"

"I don't know. Achille was a damn good river driver and lumberjack. Maybe the company preferred to keep the best man, even if he was a murderer. Me, I wasn't so good…"

The cross-examination ended there. It was clear that Anne would not be able to get more out of him. The only people who could relate this event were Pat McAllister and Achille, and she knew her client would openly acknowledge what he had done. It looked as if things were coming to a bad end for the *old man in the canoe*. He would be declared mentally incompetent and locked up for a homicide that had occurred seventy years before.

Tears came to her eyes. This man, her first client, this exceptional man, would be the lamb sacrificed on the altar of her inexperience and stupidity.

## Fifteen

Anne had interpreted the call of the big-talking Lanthier as an ultimatum. She knew that in the legal milieu, negotiations between lawyers made it possible to shorten proceedings and reduce the sentences of the accused. In the case of Achille, it was an odious proposition, but she could not afford to reject it.

"Defence Counsel Blais," said Lanthier, exaggeratedly formal. "Your client has a choice: either he agrees to be put under guardianship and be recognised as mentally incompetent, which could spare him a murder charge, or he digs his heels in, and the Crown will most certainly pronounce him guilty of that man's death. I think the first option is his best bet."

In either case, Achille was likely to be incarcerated, either behind bars or in a padded cell. For Anne, this was more or less a failure, a setback – at the professional level, of course, but also a hard knock for her pride. For it was her pride that had made her plunge headlong into this case like a diver into the water. She could not stop thinking of how another lawyer would have done better, would have foreseen the undercut coming and known how to parry it. She should have protested against a number of different things, but had not done so.

She was ashen when she entered the room where Achille was being held. She explained the delicate situation he was in, due to this late-breaking denunciation. She apologised every second sentence and suggested he find a more experienced lawyer.

"What's happening is not your fault, young woman, it's mine. That man's death was my fault, and in a way, Paul's behaviour is my fault too," Achille assured her.

Then, as if he were totally changing the subject: "You know, you're almost the same size as her?"

"As who?" she asked, surprised.

"Adela," he said, pointing to the urn, which he had taken out of the quilt that was wrapped around it. "She was about your size, and had your hair, though she put a red tint in hers, but the curls are the same. You've got the same shape of face, too. Her eyes belonged to her and her alone, but you really look a lot like each other," Achille repeated, looking her up and down. Anne blushed.

His eyes met hers. There was so much gentleness and affection in this man's gaze that looking at him felt to Anne like drinking a big glass of cold milk, tasting its sweetness, feeling its soothing action in the stomach. There was an entire ocean of tenderness in these eyes, and she felt calm again. She imagined that it must have been like this in the old general store in Aumond when Achille and Adela exchanged a look of complicity. Total communion and communication, just in the gleam of their eyes.

"When we started to share our life, Adela did not speak a word of French and I not a word of English," he said. Anne noted that he never said "our lives" but "our life," as if their two existences had formed only one. "And you know, I'll never forget the first word she said to me in French. You know what that word was?"

Anne shook her head, captivated by his story.

"*Confiance*. And that remained true always. I trusted her, she trusted me. We never regretted it," he said, turning to the urn. "Except the time when she said she wanted to show me a flower growing by the river and pushed me in with all my clothes on," he added, laughing.

Then, turning to Anne, he said: "That's also the first word you said to me in front of the judge. I don't know you, but I know there is good in you. And for me, that's enough."

She was there to give her client bad news and try to cheer him up, but here it was Achille who was reviving her!

"So what do I tell this lawyer?" asked Anne, though she knew what the answer was.

"Tell him I'll fight it to the end."

The media had been following the Achille Roy trial minute by minute. The story had been given vast coverage. A journalist from the *Evening Telegram* had even been sent to the scene to talk about this curious lawsuit and particularly about the ashes of the exile from Fogo Island. When it was learned that one of the witnesses had accused Achille Roy of having killed a man seventy years earlier, it had caused great consternation. The image of the hero bringing his sweetheart back to her native land had paled. But the story continued to feed public opinion. Each detail became a new source of rumour, extrapolation and speculation.

When the court reconvened, Anne was nervous. She had

thoroughly researched the story and thought herself capable of presenting a good defence of her client's mental state. She had done everything so her client would not have to testify, but was at the same time tormented by the desire to have him do so. Achille Roy was an impressive man. His view of life was simple. His kind had disappeared a long time ago. When he spoke, it was with total calm and frankness. That was just the problem. To have Achille testify was to expose him to the Question. It was to deliver him into the hands of the prosecutor, Paul's attorney, the arrogant Lanthier, who would do anything to destroy Achille's credibility, and most of all, ask him if in fact he had killed John O'Brien. Achille would answer "yes," because lying revolted him, and because he felt that the crime had to be confessed.

The first witness she had chosen to call to the stand was the notary, Lafleur, who in spite of his advanced years still had a very lively mind. First, she questioned him on what his relationship had been to Achille Roy over the years. He talked with emotion of how the young lumberjack had taken in Adela and her child, buying them a house and providing for them. He also told the court of how Achille had come to see him and borrowed three thousand dollars to finance his expedition.

"Did it not seem strange to you, even a little disturbed, that a man of his age would want to go off in a canoe like that?" asked Anne.

"Mademoiselle Blais, I thought I'd bring you something that can tell you more than I can about Achille Roy's relationship with the river."

Two men entered the courtroom, carrying an impressive birch bark canoe on their shoulders. They took it to the front of the room. Their spectacular entrance had provoked a certain commotion, and Lanthier stood, drawing himself up to his full height to show his indignation.

"Your Honour, this court is not a circus!"

"I have to say, Counsel, that you are going a little far. What is this…this…boat doing in my court?"

"I ask you for a bit of latitude, Your Honour, it is an important exhibit if we are to understand my client's personality and his intimate relationship with nature, particularly the river, which was his whole life."

"So be it, but I wish to warn you that I will not let you ridicule this court," said the judge severely.

The last thing Anne wanted was to turn the judge against her, but she had agreed to the notary's idea, for she too was struck by the beauty of this work of art. Like a true expert, Norbert Lafleur presented the magnificent canoe that Achille had made for him, describing in detail the technique that had gone into its fabrication, emphasising its lightness and many qualities, explaining the Native Indian signs and symbols etched in the bark. Everyone could admire the quality of the workmanship. Judge Pelletier got up to take a closer look.

"Why did you consider it so important to bring this canoe here all the way from Sainte-Famille d'Aumond, Monsieur Lafleur?" asked Anne, remembering their difficulty in bringing the object into the courthouse, and up the stairs to the courtroom.

"Achille Roy handled canoes as well as he made them. We often used to go fishing together, and I've never seen anyone so good at reading the river, understanding currents, getting around its trouble spots. And then there was his reputation for shooting rapids. Once, in order to save a man's life, he shot the Devil's Rapid, the most dangerous part of the Gatineau River."

"When Monsieur Roy came to borrow three thousand dollars from you, weren't you afraid of losing your money?"

"Not for a moment. When Achille Roy said he'd be back to pay me, I had no doubt about it. His word was a contract."

"And did he seem suicidal to you?"

Lanthier objected, judging that Anne was asking the notary for a psychiatric opinion that he was not qualified to give. The judge acknowledged the objection, but reminded Lanthier that he had shown a great deal of latitude with his own witnesses, and that the opinion of this man who seemed to know Achille well might have a certain value.

"So, Monsieur Lafleur, did Achille Roy seem to you like someone who wanted to end his life?"

"On the contrary, Mademoiselle. If Achille Roy had wanted to kill himself, he would not have spent days and days in physical training, preparing for this trip and getting himself re-accustomed to the canoe. Achille Roy's life had meaning. He had a goal, which was to honour a promise he had made."

Paul's lawyer began his cross-examination, emphasising the fact that the notary did not have the competence to judge a person's mental health.

"No, I certainly do not possess this skill, but as a man of law, Mr. Prosecutor, I know the law on mental incompetence," said the notary. "And Achille Roy poses no danger to himself or others."

Lanthier did not insist. This witness's replies could only damage his case. Next, Anne called on Edgar Crytes, the owner of the *dépanneur* of Sainte-Famille d'Aumond. He explained that he had known Achille Roy as a customer of the store since childhood, and that his own father had held him in a great deal of esteem.

"And how has Monsieur Roy been with you for all these years?"

"He was a charming man, always calm and reasonable."

"And what about his mental faculties?"

"I have never had any doubts about him in the past, and I have no doubts about him today. Each time I've had to make a difficult decision, he was the one I always asked for advice. And even on subjects where I don't suppose he was qualified to answer me, he always came out with an opinion full of common sense. I don't know anyone with such sound judgement."

"Your father, Monsieur Crytes, witnessed the altercation with the parish priest cited by my colleague. Could you tell us about that?"

"Objection, Your Honour!" cried Lanthier. "This is just hearsay. This gentleman was not a direct witness to the event in question."

"Objection sustained," pronounced the judge, without waiting for Anne to protest.

"Your Honour, you accepted the testimony of Roméo Fortin, who wasn't a witness to the altercation either and who referred to it in this courtroom."

"The objection will be sustained anyway, Counsel. Restate your question," the judge said sharply.

Anne was about to reply when Edgar Crytes spoke.

"I did not witness the altercation. But what I did witness was the sermon Curé Perras had given the Sunday before. I was young, but it left an impression on me like it did on everyone who heard it."

Edgar Crytes related as precisely as possible the priest's pitiless sermon, his hateful words about this man who had welcomed an Anglican woman under his roof, though they were not married, and the extremely harsh words he had to say about her son "the bastard." Achille Roy had been very dignified. He had stood up with his family and left the church in the middle of the sermon.

"Your Honour, I was young and I was afraid of Curé Perras like everyone else in the village, but I had never seen such cruelty."

"You say your father was the only witness to this altercation with the priest and what it was about. If we are to base our judgements on the subject on the testimony presented to the court by Mr. Roméo

Fortin, Mr. Roy was a violent man. In that case, your father, who was on the church board, must have warned you about him?"

"Not at all! Quite the contrary. I think he admired him for putting the *curé* in his place."

"Objection, Your Honour. The gentleman is stating an opinion."

"Objection sustained."

"It wasn't an opinion. He said that the priest deserved worse than kicks in the backside, and having heard what he said in church, I agree."

"Objection, Your Honour," said Lanthier without a great deal of conviction.

Once the words were out, despite the objection, they still had an effect. In cross-examination, Lanthier had put special emphasis on the purchases Achille made in Crytes' store, and his way of going through him to acquire certain goods that the store had not kept in stock for years. That way he hoped to prove that Achille had long since lost his sense of time, even forgetting that the store was no longer a general store but just a *dépanneur*.

"Is it true that Monsieur Roy insisted on buying his building supplies from you, though you hadn't sold any for thirty years?"

"That's true. But I have to explain that –"

"That's all I was asking, sir," the lawyer cut him off, leaving him no opportunity to go into detail.

Next, Anne called Dr. James Whiteduck to the stand. When she had contacted him and discussed the state of her client with him, the young woman had quickly discerned that Achille had left a big impression on the Algonquin doctor, and she had asked him to testify on his behalf. The doctor had refused. He hated this kind of circus, the lawyers who put words in your mouth and twisted all your words. He had hung up the phone, thinking about the old man he had seen at the Maniwaki Health Centre and whom he had helped escape. He had done it because he felt it was fair.

A few minutes later, he called Anne back: "I'll be there."

Anne first asked him to explain the circumstances in which he had met Achille. Dr. Whiteduck explained that as an emergency room doctor, he often came into contact with patients admitted to Psychiatry in a state of crisis.

"Achille Roy wasn't like that at all," he said.

"In your opinion, was Achille Roy in full possession of his mental faculties?"

"Objection, Your Honour, Dr. Whiteduck is not a mental health specialist," cried Lanthier.

"Dr. Whiteduck has practised in the Emergency for many years, and must on countless occasions have treated patients suffering from mental problems," said Anne. "In this context, his opinion is not only that of a doctor but of a specialist for people in crisis situations."

"Objection overruled. Continue," said the judge as Lanthier sat down again, disappointed. "I have rarely seen such a mentally healthy elderly person. In fact, I've rarely seen anyone of any age who is so sane, including myself," added James.

"And his physical health?"

"Impeccable. He has no medical record. In eighty-eight years, he has never set foot in a hospital, as incredible as that may seem, except when his wife, or his common-law spouse, gave birth."

"Were you able to examine him yourself?"

"Of course. Physically, I couldn't believe he could be so old."

Dr. Whiteduck's statement had just discredited several witnesses from the opposite side. Anne left him to Lanthier, who started by attacking his medical diploma.

"I see here, Doctor, that it took you several years to be admitted into medical school. It even says here 'high school not completed.' Is that true?"

"Yes... no... There's an explanation...," replied James.

"Answer my question, yes or no. Is this true?"

"Yes, but..."

"I am not asking you to tell us all the vagaries of your academic life, Doctor, answer yes or no."

"Yes."

"Is it not true that you had to apply three times before being accepted into medical school."

"It's true, but only because the university did not want to recognise the diploma for the high school of Kitigan Zibi," he managed to say.

"Is it not true that you had to repeat high school to finally be admitted?"

"Well...I had to redo the high school graduation exams, it's true, but only because they refused the diploma from my high school," repeated Dr. Whiteduck, disconcerted by the cross-examination.

"If I understand correctly, in spite of all the funding the government grants universities to finance the education of Native students, you were not able to get yourself admitted into a teaching establishment?"

Anne objected to the disdain in Lanthier's question and the judge sustained her objection. In any case, Lanthier did not expect a reply.

This was just what James hated in the White courts of justice. The meaning of words could be twisted; events could be modified and given another meaning, the truth distorted. Now he regretted that he had agreed to come and relive years of frustration and racism. Here, he was nothing but a savage.

"You claim that this man is mentally sound. So tell me, how do you arrive at such a verdict and read a man's mind in only a few minutes?"

James Whiteduck thought about it. The lawyer was a bastard, but the question made sense. He remained silent and it was clear that he was giving it serious thought. Everyone waited with bated breath for his reply. Anne started to fear that his entire testimony was about to fall apart. James was tormented. Slowly he began to speak, almost in a whisper.

"I didn't read his mind, he read mine. Twice during our conversation, he brought me back to my Native origins. He brought up things that are part of my deepest roots. In words that were simple but so true, not only did he answer each of my questions but also really he made me think. I saw the same thing in Nunavut among elderly people whose ages you could never guess and who you could have sworn had stepped right out of the novel *Agaguk*.* They'd never known anything but the nomadic life of northern peoples. That's what I discovered in this. A reality that was different from mine, or from yours, of course – as different as the life of a wolf is from the life of a dog. Would you call a wolf crazy because it doesn't behave like a dog? No, because the wolf belongs to another world. And today, we thank heaven that there are still wolves on earth to make us understand nature, to admire it in its freedom."

"No more questions," said Lanthier, who wanted to be over and done with this witness who was a little too talkative.

"I'd like to add something, Your Honour," said Dr. Whiteduck.

"Go ahead."

---

* *Quebec literary classic (1958), by Yves Theriault, about the life and destiny of an Inuit man.*

"I was responsible for Monsieur Roy's escape from the Maniwaki Health Centre."

"What are you saying, Doctor?" asked the judge.

Anne was thunderstruck. Her client had never mentioned anything about the doctor participating in his escape.

"I made an oath to treat those who need it. I also swore to do the right thing as far as it was possible to do so. When I asked Monsieur Roy why he wanted to go to Newfoundland and why it was so important to go by canoe, his answer seemed so logical that it became impossible for me to obey the court order, for then I would be going back on my two oaths."

The courtroom had fallen silent. By admitting to his participation in Achille's escape, Dr. Whiteduck could face severe disciplinary measures. Anne was still stunned by this avowal, as she was by his entire testimony.

"Doctor, I don't know if you are aware of the consequences of your admission," said the judge, "but I thank you for your honesty."

Anne sat down again. As the doctor stepped down from the stand, she looked at him with gratitude.

She had other witnesses to call, including the postmistress from d'Aumond. She had wanted to come testify and what she had to say was not without interest. Her testimony was primarily expected to define the couple's special relationship. Nicole Lyrette, aged forty-seven, had been postmistress for twenty-four years. She had known Achille and Adela when she was twenty-two.

"I met Madame Adela and Monsieur Achille at the general store. They'd come in to buy some things and I was there because I was looking for a way to get to Maniwaki and then Hull."

"And why did you want to go to Hull?" asked Anne.

"Because…because I was pregnant. I didn't know what to do. I wanted to get an abortion," she said hesitantly.

In the courtroom, there were murmurs from the people from Aumond who had been called as witnesses and those who had accompanied them. Everyone knew that Nicole had had a child; she had disappeared for a year and reappeared with the baby. No one had ever known anything about the father or the pregnancy, nor where she had gone.

"I watched them look at each other and I envied them. Then the lady looked at me, and I think she saw my distress. She came over to me and asked me to go outside with her. We went out and she asked me immediately: 'How many months?' I was so surprised. No one knew. I told her, simply. She had also seen my bag and knew I was going to leave. She told me not to do that, and asked me to come to her place. I had no other place to go."

"And how did Monsieur Roy take it?"

"He came out of the store. She looked at him a few seconds and he helped me put my things in the cart. I was so afraid he was going to ask me questions right there, in front of the store. I was terrified. But no, nothing. I think he had understood everything too. I don't know if his wife told him later, but he always acted as if he knew and that there was nothing unusual about it."

"What happened after?"

"I went to live with them for almost a year."

"You lived with them for a year and no one knew?"

"No, I didn't want anyone to know. I had my baby there and she helped me give birth. After that, they took care of me and the baby."

"Well, I'll be damned! That's what all that baby formula was for!" exclaimed Edgar Crytes. The judge called for silence.

Edgar had been surprised when Adela had put in the order with him, for she had to be almost sixty. She explained that it was to feed an abandoned fawn they had found. There were murmurs in the courtroom from the people of Aumond.

Nicole Lyrette explained that she had returned to the village afterwards and the couple had never divulged the secret. Later, Adela had come to her assistance when she had decided to apply for the job of postmistress, a job that everyone wanted. She did not speak a word of English, and the person in charge of hiring required candidates to have a working knowledge of the language. The lady had given her an intensive language course and during her interview, Nicole was the only person who could express herself in English.

"Would you say that Monsieur Roy is in his right mind?"

"Those people had more Christian values, goodness and fairness than anyone I've ever known."

"Thank you," said Anne in conclusion.

Pierre Lanthier found few questions to ask the witness. Nicole's testimony had been clear, without contradictions or weak points. Lanthier opted for a line of questioning that would allow him to slightly discredit the witness. The sentence fell like a bomb on the court when he questioned her on her life before meeting Adela and Achille. He wanted to expose her as a woman of suspect morality, so oriented his questions around the father of the child. Did she go out with a lot of men? Had the father been told about the baby? She simply replied no.

"Why? Why? Why?" the lawyer harassed her.

"Because the man said all sorts of nice things to me, he made me believe he loved me and wanted me. After we made love, he rejected me and threatened me if I revealed what had happened. I never saw him again except recently, and he never tried to contact me."

Lanthier did not really know how to attack her, so focussed his questions on the father of the child.

"This man must not have a very good reputation, if after all these years, you still refuse to name him."

"Maybe you're right, sir," she said, exasperated, "for this man is your client."

The bomb had been dropped. Lanthier was not able to make the connection at first. He turned to the red chairs behind him and saw Paul's livid expression. Clearly he was as surprised as everyone in the room, where people were murmuring more than ever. Achille was astounded. He looked at Nicole Lyrette, then Paul, then back at the woman. All the times he had played with Nicole's child, he had been playing with Adela's grandson! His grandson. He regretted that Adela had never known.

No matter how hard the judge hit the table to call for order, the room remained in an uproar. He had to call a halt to the proceedings. Anne was as surprised as the others. She knew the woman's history, but had not known the name of the child's father. She was stunned and could not evaluate the impact this admission would have on the rest of the proceedings. Of course it put Paul in a bad light, but the revelation also raised doubts about Achille's own honesty. Was it possible he had been unaware of such a thing? Was it because the baby was his grandson that he had come to the girl's rescue? But no. Achille had looked more surprised than anyone, and Achille Roy did not lie. He could only prevent himself from saying something if no one asked him any questions. He was even capable of cleverly returning a question to the person who had asked it, but never would he have lied. There was no reason he would he have done so; he would have been so happy to know that he had a grandson.

Now the only witness who had yet to testify was Anne's former psychology professor, Dr. Harvey. She scored a few points and cast doubt on certain parts of the prosecution's arguments in favour of mental incompetence, but Lanthier had been rough on some of her witnesses. The credibility of Dr. Whiteduck, among others, had been called into question, and Anne regretted having put him through the ordeal. Moreover, Achille still had the murder of John O'Brien hanging over his head like the sword of Damocles, and she knew that Lanthier would take full advantage of this.

Dr. Harvey was perfect. His reputation could not be attacked, and he was very knowledgeable about the practice of law. Lanthier could not manipulate him as he had tried to do with Anne's other witnesses. The doctor had met and talked with the old man during his hospital stay. When Anne asked if he thought Achille Roy was mentally sound, Harvey replied with a question of his own: "Would it occur to you to say I'm disturbed because I'm still practising at eighty years old? Of course not," he answered. "On the contrary, people usually respect me because of it. So why should a man who is considered an expert canoeist be treated like a disturbed person because he undertakes an expedition by canoe? To me, those are grounds for respect."

Anne was satisfied. No one would have dared question Dr. Harvey's competence. Even Lanthier would not attempt it. When his turn came, he asked Harvey a few harmless questions, then attacked.

"I liked the example you gave, but you do admit that there is a higher degree of danger involved in going down the Gatineau by canoe than in doing what you do at your age, and I hasten to add that I have a great deal of respect for you."

"Are you so sure about that? For you and me, the simple fact of stepping into a canoe is dangerous, but for Achille Roy, the danger is negligible and controlled. I'm not saying he couldn't have an accident, but for him it is a normal act that depends on a certain number of variables. And I believe that this man's judgement is as good as mine…or yours."

Lanthier did not insist, Dr. Harvey was liable to put him in a bad spot.

Meanwhile, Anne had finished; she had no more witnesses to call. She would have wished more for her client.

The judge pronounced the words that she did not want to hear.

"We have finished with the presentation of the evidence. On Monday we will hear the closing arguments."

Leaving the courtroom, she was trying to evaluate her chances of winning when the head of the court office informed her she had received a call from the journalist Martin Éthier. He had promised to help her, but she had not had any sign of life from him for awhile and she had ceased to hope that she would hear from him. She hurried to find a telephone to call him back.

"Anne, I think I've found something good for you."

# Sixteen

The Quebec media had been closely following the affair of the *old man in the canoe*, but they were not the only ones interested in him. The reporter from the *Evening Telegram* had been thriving on the details he had been able to glean about the hearing. The story of Achille and the lovely Adela had become a real-life serial that Newfoundlanders were following with great interest. Though some of the information was true, some of it was pure invention. Achille's popularity had significantly decreased when it was learned that he had killed a man. Some people wondered if, after all, the man was not *mentally disturbed* as his son claimed. But there was a new wave of sympathy for him when it was reported in the media that the murder had been committed to protect Adela from the clutches of a vile rapist. Then some people had embellished on the story, claiming that Achille had fought an entire horde of men in order to defend her. Later their hearts were touched when they learned that Achille and Adela had taken Nicole Lyrette into their home, assisted her in giving birth to her child, and supported her without knowing that the baby was their grandson.

In Fogo Island, the local residents committee was ready to receive the ashes of its daughter Adela Cole, but the news of Achille's arrest had caused great consternation among the citizens. The *Evening Telegram* had sent a reporter to the island to follow developments in the community. John Owen, a Tilting fisherman, proposed to go meet Achille and his canoe when they arrived on the coast of Blanc-Sablon, and escort him across the arm of sea that lay between Quebec and Newfoundland. There were at least eight fishermen who wanted to do the same. But now, no one knew whether the ashes would ever make it to their destination.

"Seems to me the government could do something. After all, she's a Tilting girl," said Rose Leate, president of the committee, pacing back and forth, disappointed to see that the heroine's return might be compromised.

"Stop pacing around like that! That's not the way it's going to happen. In the eyes of the law, she's from Quebec. She doesn't belong to us. The only person who can decide what to do with her is her man, and as it stands, he's in lock-up," said John Owen.

"But it could also be that great wretch Paul who decides, if the court decides in his favour. From what I understand, his mother isn't about to get anything from him, especially now that she's dead," added Horace Cobb.

"Nothing to do but wait for the judge's ruling."

"But what if he can't get here?"

"You've got a point. We're all going to look foolish, with all that money we collected to build a monument," acknowledged Rose Leate.

"That's not the way it's going to happen!" exclaimed John Owen. "I haven't gone to sea in a dog's age because there's nothing more to fish. Someone in Ottawa's gone and decided that we can't fish any more. But this is someone of our own blood, it's our honour at stake. I intend to take my boat and go up the current to Montreal and get him…get *them*," Owen corrected himself.

Everyone looked at Owen, smiling, but John Owen was not the type to make jokes. He had become quite passionate about the whole affair. His mother was the granddaughter of Adela Cole's sister. The family tie had more or less given him the status of nobility on the island. And when he said he was to go up to Montreal, it was because he had every intention of doing so.

"You're not serious about this?" demanded Cobb, trying to determine how serious he was.

"I've never been so serious in my life. Tomorrow I'm even going to load up my boat. I've still got some fuel left, and I've got to clean my motor. What a beautiful sight it would be, a handful of boats from Fogo Island in the port of Montreal. That'd show them we're determined to bring Adela back to her island," Owen had replied.

"If Owen goes, I don't see why my boat should sit idle. We'll go too!" cried Ben Lester, another fisherman.

One more fisherman spoke up, then another. By the end of the meeting, five boats had enlisted in the trip up the Saint Lawrence. When the *Evening Telegram* reported the news, the numbers doubled, then tripled, and continued to rise.

In Montreal, the hearing was taking a strange turn. Anne had requested an urgent meeting with Judge Pelletier to get his authorization for new witnesses to appear before the closing arguments. The old magistrate had displayed, or rather grumbled, his displeasure and ill humour. Lanthier, who had been informed of the young woman lawyer's request, had naturally wanted to be present at the meeting, and had vigorously objected. The affair was starting to weigh on the judge. At first he had thought it was a simple request for guardianship on the basis of mental incompetence, the kind of case he was used to hearing. No one was interested in this kind of thing. But instead he found himself in the middle of a media circus. The judge's photo had appeared in various newspapers, and pseudo-specialists had dissected his past to try and predict how he would rule. And the media were always dangerous, even quite corrupt. He had seen two judges, respected colleagues, dismissed or suspended on the basis of certain clumsy remarks that had ended up in the newspapers. The *old man in the canoe* affair was so highly publicised that each of his comments was monitored. He no longer had the freedom he was used to having in his court. All this publicity made him very unsettled. He was anything but enthusiastic at the idea of prolonging the proceedings. The judge did not like surprises and the young lawyer had already sprung quite a few on him. Since that morning, the media were all talking about the armada of Newfoundland fishing boats anchored in the port. There were a dozen of them, all flying the flag of Newfoundland and the colours of their villages. Some had left Fogo Island a few days before, others had gathered at Port-aux-Basques to join the flotilla. They had arrived in the port of Montreal and caused enough of an uproar to attract attention. That was all it took for all the cameras and microphones in Montreal to be turned on this damn hearing.

Martin had not lied. The witnesses he had tracked down had quite a lot to say, and what they had to say was interesting. But Anne did not trust Lanthier. Doors of opportunity had opened, but she needed time. She had to lay some kind of trap for her adversary.

"Counsel, if you have not had time to prepare your defence and call all your witnesses, there's no one but yourself to blame," lectured the judge.

"Your Honour, I only learned of the existence of these witnesses a few hours ago, and I sincerely believe their testimonies are absolutely necessary to my client's defence," replied Anne.

"If you produce new witnesses, then I want to hear your client talk. Until now he hasn't said a word and it seems to me this court needs a few things clarified," said Lanthier with his usual arrogance.

"Monsieur Lanthier is right. If you produce new witnesses, you have to allow him to interrogate your client," the judge acknowledged.

Anne was in a tight spot. She would have liked to spare Achille having to testify and especially having to answer the questions of the pedantic Lanthier, but she had no choice.

"I accept," said Anne reluctantly. "But my client will be heard after my witnesses."

She informed the bailiff that she had three important summonses to dispatch. Some of the information Martin had given her had been illuminating, but to know how to use it was another matter. The first subpoena was delivered to Julie Lazure, the second to Pierre Dagenais and the third to Clifford Stanley.

When the hearing finally resumed two days later, Anne was ready. Or so she thought. "Your Honour, I would like to call Mademoiselle Julie Lazure to the stand."

Paul had not recognised the girl's name, but when he saw her enter the courtroom, certain images he had forgotten came back to his mind. He grew pale. Anne took note of the change in him. She asked the woman to give her name and profession.

"I'm a dancer," she said.

"When you say 'dancer,' could you be more precise?"

"I'm a topless dancer. I dance nude in bars," she said without mincing words.

Anne had asked her to dress plainly, but even a plain outfit looked provocative on her, and left no doubt as to the truth of her affirmation. Her pants were so tight that even a tattoo would probably have left a bump.

"And could you tell us where you're dancing now?" asked Anne.

"At the Four Stars Bar...in Maniwaki," she added, realising that no one in Montreal knew the place.

"And do you ever do more than just dance in this bar?"

"Well...I sometimes go upstairs with customers."

"You go upstairs with customers?" asked Anne, pretending not to understand, to incite her to be more specific.

"Well, yeah, sometimes we turn tricks with customers. You know, we have sex!" she said with no false modesty.

Julie Lazure had long since ceased trying to hide the nature of her work.

"Are there customers who also pay you for...how shall I put it...to have sexual relations with other men?"

"Well, there's the president who often comes to the bar with friends and asks me to take them upstairs."

"When you say 'president,' who are you referring to?"

"The president of the Regional Committee on Industry, Pierre Dagenais."

"And does that happen often?"

"Quite often, sometimes it's just him and sometimes it's someone he wants to get on his side."

"Tell us about last April 14. Were you working that evening?"

"Yes. Dagenais arrived with a guy I'd never seen before. He was in a pretty good mood. The cognac was flowing and he insisted I spend the evening at their table."

"And what was your role?"

"Dagenais asked me to be their hostess. I had to serve them and get cosy with the guy who was with them, then take him upstairs."

At this moment, Lanthier stood and vigorously objected.

"Your Honour, I object to this testimony. This woman of more than doubtful morality has nothing to do with the present case. We're wasting our time with stories and idle gossip that do not concern us."

"I have to admit, Mademoiselle Blais, that I don't see where you're going with this testimony," said the judge, who was becoming increasingly irritated.

"I'm getting there, Your Honour, and I assure you that you'll soon be enlightened as to the reasons for this testimony."

Judge Pelletier begrudgingly allowed her to continue.

"You spent the evening in the company of Monsieur Dagenais and his guest. I suppose you heard their conversation?"

"Of course. They were talking about just one thing. They were talking about some agreement they'd just signed, which meant they could split almost a million dollars. It was a lot of money, you better believe I was all ears."

"Did you understand what it was about?" inquired Anne.

"It was something about a big company, you know, those companies who cut wood and make boards, that kind of thing. That's what it was about. The company was supposed to be coming to build a factory. And these two signed an agreement with them to give them the land to do it."

"But wasn't there something that seemed to be blocking their plan?"

"Yes. Dagenais kept saying to the other guy: 'You gotta get rid of the old man.'"

"Could you identify the man who was with Monsieur Dagenais that night?"

"For sure I can. He's here. That's him sitting next to Mr. Handsome," said Julie, pointing to Paul and his lawyer.

The information caused a stir in the room. Paul pretended to be shocked by this disclosure. Lanthier was on his feet, demanding that the witness be excluded.

"Not only will she not be excluded, but as Mademoiselle Blais seems to have finished, you may speak," replied the judge.

"So you work in prostitution?" asked Lanthier with a tone of disdain.

"I wouldn't put it like that. Let's say I earn a bit of cash on the side with men who need sex."

"You said earlier that your role during these evenings is to act as a hostess, but do you consume alcohol with the clients?"

"Of course, it's part of the deal we have with the bar owner."

"And that evening, had you consumed a great deal of alcohol?"

"I'd had…quite a bit…but not enough so I didn't know what was going down."

"How can you remember so many details? I wouldn't be able to."

She was about to answer, but the lawyer did not let her speak. He steered his questioning towards the subject he wanted to address.

"And you take drugs, don't you?"

"No," Julie Lazure replied sharply.

"Mademoiselle, don't forget that you are under oath and I have your criminal record in front of me."

Julie changed her tune. She admitted that she had consumed cocaine from time to time, which was why she had been arrested in the past. Lanthier rested his case. He knew the judge had no liking for drug addicts, especially when it came to cocaine. The magistrate had seen countless young people come through his courtroom after committing the worst kind of crimes to procure the drug.

When Anne announced Pierre Dagenais as the upcoming witness, the last bit of colour flooded out of Paul's face. Dagenais came forward. He was obviously furious to be there, and had threatened the young woman lawyer that he would call on some of his friends in high places if she did not give up on making him appear in court. She had merely replied by telling him the date and time of the hearing, and the courtroom number.

"Monsieur Dagenais, you have been president of the Regional Committee on Industry for ten years, is that correct?"

"Yes," growled Dagenais.

"I see here, in articles from your regional newspaper, that you were the principal instigator of a plan to build a factory in your area."

Dagenais hesitated, feeling that every one of his words could be turned against him. On the other hand, he could not resist the idea of making himself out to be the saviour of his region.

"Of course."

"It must represent a big advantage for your region?"

"It means the creation of two hundred jobs, right off the top. You can imagine people are happy about it."

"I imagine it's a nice project for you as president of the Regional Committee on Industry?" asked Anne, assuming a flattering manner.

Put that way, the question pleased Dagenais who thrust out his chest before replying.

"It's very rewarding to see people happy, and be able to say I did something for my community," affirmed Dagenais, who was about to launch into an oration that would draw tears from a heart of stone.

"I imagine you're the kind of man who leaves nothing to chance?"

"You've got that right. When I take on something new, I want to know everything that's going on."

"I suppose that the Forestech Company had enough confidence in you to show you everything in detail, such as the blueprints for the factory?"

"They didn't just show them to me, I directly participated in having them drawn up."

"So I am led to understand that you were also involved in choosing the site?"

This time, Dagenais bristled.

"Oh, you know, there were a few sites they had in mind," he replied.

"Is it possible that they included the land belonging to Monsieur Achille Roy?"

"I don't know, I don't remember. You know, I didn't see all of them."

"That's funny, a moment ago you said you knew everything in detail."

"Not that detail."

"Do you know Monsieur Robert Blanchette?"

"Of course, he's my lawyer."

"Then explain to us how your lawyer happened to go consult the land registry records on your behalf, and inquire into the property in question? See, I have a copy of the receipt."

Dagenais had started to perspire. He no longer knew how to answer.

"I don't think he mentioned it."

"So explain how you were able to sign a cheque of six thousand dollars, which this same lawyer wanted to give the notary Lafleur in exchange for the mortgage debt which Achille Roy had contracted on his land? Would you have written a cheque like that without being familiar with this piece of land or without knowing that this lawyer was acting in your name?"

Dagenais was cornered.

"Oh, yes, that's right, I think I asked him to find me a little piece of land to buy. Just for fun…so I could be a kind of gentleman-farmer," he said with a nervous laugh.

He was lying and it was obvious.

"Monsieur Dagenais, do you know this man?" she said, pointing to Paul.

"Slightly. We met one or two times."

"You met at the Four Stars bar last April 14?"

"It's possible. I don't remember."

"But were you at this establishment on the evening of April 14?"

"It's possible. I go there sometimes, but I can't be sure."

"Yet you ought to remember. Did you not have a little brush with the law over the course of that evening?"

"No," replied Dagenais icily.

Martin had confirmed to Anne that no charges had yet been laid against Dagenais.

"So you'll have no objection to listening to this tape with us."

A tremor passed through Dagenais' body and his self-assurance crumbled all at once. His face fell as the court listened to the crackling of the police radio conversations. He heard himself insult then hit the police officer.

"It's true. I was there," admitted Dagenais.

"Were you there with the gentleman present?"

"Yes."

"Can you tell us why?"

"Nothing special. I meet a lot of people when I do business."

"Are you sure you weren't discussing anything important? I have here an agreement you signed with the Forestech Company in which the company commits to buying Monsieur Roy's land from you. The agreement stipulates that you commit yourself to acquiring the said land before construction begins."

Dagenais looked at the document he had signed. He was in a tight spot, but there was no way he was going to take sole responsibility for this affair.

"*He* was the one who came to see *me*," he said, pointing at Paul. "He told me he could get that land for the new factory, no problem, but first he had to become the guardian of his father, who would never want to sell. He asked me to lend him money against a percentage of the land sale."

"And can you tell us to what use the money you advanced him was supposed to be put?"

"To pay the legal fees that were necessary to get his father declared senile," Dagenais finally blurted.

Outraged, Paul jumped to his feet, and would have gone for Dagenais if his lawyer had not blocked him. Paul and Dagenais were screaming at each other, each accusing the other of being a liar and a sell-out. Both were right. The judge shouted and called for silence, but in vain. Dagenais' admission had provoked pandemonium in the courtroom. Lanthier was dismayed. He felt the case slipping through his fingers. Anne was satisfied, though still concerned for her client.

In all the commotion, no one had noticed the frail man approaching the stand. Most of the people in the room were on their feet. When Judge Pelletier managed to restore order and everyone had returned to his or her places, the frail man remained standing before the magistrate.

"Sir, I would ask you to sit down like the others," said the judge.

"I would like to address the court."

Everyone stared at him. The man had to be eighty or eighty-five years old. He was well groomed, wearing a suit that must have been made by a very good tailor. His elegance stood out in the courtroom. Even Lanthier with his flamboyant suit and stylish tie could not compete with such distinction.

"You cannot approach the stand, sir, you are not one of the witnesses."

"I should be, because I witnessed the alleged murder that Achille Roy was accused of committing."

The courtroom noisily expressed its astonishment.

"Who are you, sir?"

"My name is Luc Larivière and I am president of the Produits Rivière Company. We make beauty products."

"My God!" Anne blurted.

Anne had been using Rivière products for years, and this prosperous company was well known for its success in the stock market. Luc Larivière was the company president. She was so surprised that she did not even hear Achille, next to her, murmur, "It's the cookee!"

"I heard about what McAllister came to tell the court and I felt I had to come here in person, so the truth would be known."

Lanthier got up to protest, but had lost his nerve.

"No one called this witness, not I or my colleague either. I vigorously oppose his testimony."

"Keep your vigour to yourself, Monsieur Lanthier," said the judge. "This is my court and I can hear any witness who could prove useful to this case. I'll be the one to judge whether what he has to say may pertain to this case or not."

Lanthier started to object again, but the judge signalled to him to be seated.

"What have you to tell us, sir?"

"At that time, I must have been thirteen, and Adela, the woman who would become the spouse of Monsieur Roy, had arrived with a truckload of Irish immigrants. I worked in the kitchen as the 'cookee' and she was the cook. She was pregnant before she arrived and had made me understand that. I soon realised that she was afraid of those two men, John O'Brien and Pat McAllister."

"So tell us what happened," said the judge, curious to hear what the man had to say.

"O'Brien had tried to take her by force during the trip to the lumber camp and he and Pat had decided to rape her when she was alone in the kitchen. I saw everything, because I was behind the kitchen wall. I was too afraid to intervene. She struggled, but O'Brien was holding her down and prevented her from crying out. He had pulled down his pants and I believe he was about to…penetrate her, when Achille came in. He grabbed hold of him," he said, imitating the gesture. "O'Brien started hitting him. Achille hit him a few times in the face while the other struggled, and Pat attacked him with a cast-iron frying pan. I think Achille had a few ribs broken in the fight. He took hold of Pat and threw him against the wall. Pat went right through the wall, and that's how he got his scar. At the time, Your Honour, we all considered it an act of self-defence. Achille had come to the assistance of a person in distress."

"It is not up to me to make any kind of pronouncement on this question, sir, that is for another court to decide. My job is to decide whether this man is of sound mind, but I thank you for your sincere testimony."

"Life is not a shelf divided into sections," Luc replied. Anne held her breath before such audacity. "You can't say it doesn't concern you. This trial is unjust and this man did not deserve it. It *is* your role to give justice where justice is due, so for the love of God, do it!"

Anne thought the judge would explode in the face of this lesson in morality that the frail little man had dared to give him. She also expected the judge to announce the beginning of the closing arguments, but he did not, to her great surprise and the even greater surprise of her adversary.

"In the face of the evidence and testimonies presented before this court, and though the lawyers have not presented their closing arguments, I am ready to deliver my decision."

Lanthier again rose to his feet to protest, insisting that he should be allowed to present a synthesis of his arguments, but he had lost even the conviction to object.

"That's enough, Monsieur Lanthier! I've heard enough. This court acknowledges Achille Roy to be a person of sound and balanced mind, and suspends all measures intended to restrict his freedom. And in light of all the facts that have been presented to us, we strongly suggest that the Crown not undertake proceedings against Monsieur Roy in relation to the death of John O'Brien, which occurred seventy years ago. However, we do recommend that the Ministry undertake proceedings against Monsieur Paul Cole and Monsieur Pierre Dagenais for attempted fraud."

The courtroom noisily expressed its satisfaction at the ruling. Achille was free. Free to get back on the river again.

# Seventeen

Achille was immediately set free. It was a big shock. There he was in the heart of Montreal, with hundreds of cars passing in every direction, the sky obstructed by skyscrapers. Anne, who had hooked her arm through his, noticed his hesitation and lightly pressed his hand.

"You've trusted me until now, let me be your guide."

He looked at her and gave her a big smile. In front of them, a barrage of television crews and photographers waited for them to emerge. Anne thought about the president of the law firm Latouche, Bernstein and Associates. This firm represented the Forestech Company, who had closed the land deal with Dagenais. To gain access to company information, Anne had sent a summons to the company president. To avoid having to appear, he had given orders to the law firm to send her the information. This included a copy of the agreement between Dagenais, Paul and Forestech for the purchase of Achille's land.

Anne may not have obtained a position in the firm, but she had certainly gained their respect. The affair had made her so well known that she could now think of opening her own law office, for she was the lawyer for the *old man in the canoe*. Anne derived a great deal of pride from this, and had discovered an extraordinary human being in the process. She clung like a little girl to Achille's arm.

"The journalists are like a pack of young dogs," thought Achille, watching them milling around them. Each wanted to ask his or her question first. It took them a few minutes to answer all the questions and give the dog-pack enough material to feed their news bulletins. When one of them asked Achille what his plans were, he simply answered: "To get back on the river and do what I promised."

Several Newfoundland fishermen whose boats were moored in the port had come to the courthouse to find out what was going on. They offered to put Achille's canoe on board one of the boats and take him to Fogo Island. Achille politely refused, just as he had refused the offer of Luc Larivière, who had wanted to charter a plane to transport him. Achille had long since decided that things were going to go the way he had planned. He had imagined this journey so many times, and was already savouring the pleasure of paddling on the big river, feeling the tides rise and fall, tackling the sea waves. However, he accepted the fishermen's offer to act as his escorts on the trip to Newfoundland. He would benefit from their knowledge of sea navigation and could talk to them about this island that he knew so well and yet so little.

Achille accepted Anne's invitation to provide him with lodgings for as long as he needed them. However, he wanted to get on his way the next day. He spent the evening talking with the young woman and answering her many questions.

"And what about Paul?" asked Anne.

Achille's face fell. He had always believed, since the time Paul had left Sainte-Famille d'Aumond, that time would calm his thirst for wealth and that he would return to his roots. The old man's recent experience showed him that time had only exacerbated Paul's desire for money. He admitted that even just hearing his name gave him a sense of failure.

"He was my son," he said.

The young lawyer noted his use of the past tense when talking about Paul. Achille took advantage of the occasion to ask her to prepare a will in which he left everything he had to his newfound grandson. She wrote it up on the spot and promised to register it the next day. Despite Achille's protests, Anne gave him her bed for the night. She needed to make a few calls and the couch would suit her fine.

"I would not let my *roi* sleep anywhere but in a good bed!" she said, bowing down before him like a valet before a monarch, and showed him the door to the bedroom.

She phoned Martin Éthier. She had become friends with the journalist and they had planned to see each other again. Anne quite liked this forgotten region that still lived in another time. She learned that the Forestech Company had found another piece of land in the village of Bois-Franc, a few kilometres from Achille's farm, on the other side of the Gatineau. The journalist had also found out about the measures with which the Crown intended to follow up Pelletier's judgement. Dagenais was not going to be able to escape his drunk driving charge, and the officers involved had suddenly recovered the use of their memories, so Dagenais would also face assault charges. He and Paul would be questioned for attempted fraud. In a curt letter, Pierre Dagenais had submitted his resignation for "personal reasons" from the Regional Committee on Industry. As for the police chief, there was question of him being transferred, but his departure was said to be unrelated to the Dagenais affair.

"And what about you? How are you doing?" asked Anne.

"Okay. I've been studying the job offer from *Le Droit*, but you know, I kind of enjoy my freedom and my part of the country."

He and Anne decided to meet over the weekend to spend some time in the great outdoors. They were thinking of going canoeing on the Joseph River. They made a date for the following Saturday, "maybe even Friday," Anne added just before hanging up the phone.

The next day, Achille was up bright and early. For Anne, the thrill of victory was now replaced by sadness. She regretted that the old man was leaving and had the feeling they might never see each other again. She had asked Achille what he planned to do after he had completed his expedition. Was he going to stay in Newfoundland or would he come back to Aumond? Achille had no idea at the moment, for he was concentrating all his attention on the next leg of his odyssey.

Achille's canoe had been brought down into the port. Among the motley assortment of boats, some of which were bigger than houses, Achille's canoe looked like one of those little boats that children make out of paper and set afloat on streams in the spring. A crowd had gathered on the dock to welcome Achille and wish him a good trip. Naturally, there were journalists on hand, for they all wanted to cover the moment of Achille's departure. The Newfoundland fishing boats lined up, and as Achille plunged his paddle into the dirty water of the port, they gave him an honorary salute with their sirens.

The fishermen had agreed to follow Achille to Fogo Island, taking turns. Achille appreciated their presence. They had a certain accent that had always charmed him. Each boat followed or went ahead of the canoe, and when it was time for a break, the fishermen got together and hoisted the little canoe onto the deck. A meal was always ready on the crew's table, and the old man delighted in tasting their catch of the day. At night, the boat dropped anchor and he climbed on board for the night. Early the next morning, he resumed his voyage. The fishermen who were used to the sea, warned him about the shifting tides. They would head to shore and wait there until the tide was more favourable. Twice, Achille had had to scold them because during the night they had taken advantage of his sleep to take him a few kilometres farther. He explained to them what this journey represented and asked them to respect his wishes.

※

Sometimes they ran into rough weather, and the old canoeist was very happy to take shelter on the boat, even though it bobbed like a cork on the waves. The calm the fishermen displayed at such moments inspired his trust.

Because he never went far from the coast, Achille passed all the cities and villages on the north shore of the Saint Lawrence. Sometimes a group of people was waiting for him, honking their horns as he passed. There was always an amateur photographer wanting to immortalise Achille's passage.

He had rapidly learned to adjust his days on the water to the rhythm of the tides. He tried to take full advantage of the current's strength to make faster headway. Sometimes the water retreated so quickly that he felt as if he were flying along one of the rapids in the Gatineau River.

According to his travel companions from Newfoundland, the media were all following the traveller's progress. Each day, a newscaster retraced the day's trajectory on a giant map. Much as people told him he had become a celebrity, Achille could not understand what it was that fascinated them. After all, he was just an old man travelling by canoe. There was nothing extraordinary about it.

"There are a lot of people who do not have the courage and determination to do what they believe they have to do. You've done it," James Owen told him.

Slowly but surely, day after day, the strange procession made its way towards the Côte-Nord. When they arrived across from Newfoundland and Achille prepared himself to confront the sea, many boats were waiting for him. There were so many of them, the old man said to himself, that if they were put end to end he could probably cross the arm of the sea without getting his feet wet. As he advanced into the sea, new faces on new boats made signs at him. All seemed as if they knew him, but he did not know any of them.

For this final crossing, Achille had taken the urn out of his bag. It was the first time that the Newfoundlanders had got a glimpse of the urn. They were surprised to see that the thing was a miniature replica of an iceberg. He had taken the urn from its quilt and solidly attached it to the seat made of strips of rawhide, called *babiches*, the place where Adela used to sit. He knew very well that she could not see, at least not in the way she had when she was alive, but Achille was profoundly convinced that there was still a bond between them. Sometimes, he could still feel her presence and he easily imagined how she would have answered his questions. He could hear her say: "*That's the sea!* The real sea..."

She would have deeply inhaled the salt air, detecting the different scents of flowers, fish and marine algae. She would have heard the faraway moan of a whale and known if it were a mating call or a mother calling her calf. She had told him this a very long time ago. Achille had recorded Adela's words, images and explanations. The words had been repeated for seventy years, to be heard again at this precise moment. He was sure that she could see what he saw. He heard her in his head and repeated the words that had been spoken so many times. She had described the sea's movement to him as the fluttering of a tablecloth in the wind, that constant, strong and salty wind.

The presence of the many boats greatly helped him to progress by blocking the wind that could have carried his small boat away. But Achille had learned to manoeuvre with the breeze, tacking to keep the canoe at the right angle. The big waves were just as Adela had described them. Of the entire expedition, this was the part he feared most. A veteran of lakes and rivers, Achille had had to deal with sudden storms that lifted the waves to over one metre high. He had been afraid a number of times, but had known how to hold to his course without panicking. On a lake in a fury, the breakers came in such rapid succession that most boats overturned or sank. Overconfident travellers had perished in the tormented waves of lakes caught in sudden storms. But on the sea, though the waves were much bigger, it seemed to Achille that the immensity also made them seem farther away. One after another they came, sometimes lazily, in a predictable order and at predictable intervals. He immediately liked the feeling he got when he was on top of a wave and could see the island far, far off in the distance.

The canoe arrived at the Rock late in the evening. Achille had decided he would do this part all at once. He allowed himself a few breaks and had eaten, but arriving at the wharf of St. Barbe, the first Newfoundland village, he was exhausted as he had never been before. Each stroke of the paddle had become a torture, a colossal effort. He had cramps in his arms and shoulders. The sun and salt had wounded his hands, which were now covered in blisters, some of which had burst. His face burned, despite the efforts of the fishermen who had applied balm to his cheeks and treated his hands each time he took a break. They begged him not to continue until the next day, but Achille had kept going.

On the wharf of St. Barbe, the people of the village were waiting for him. Several journalists from Newfoundland too, even one who had been sent from the Canadian Press. A number of big television networks had also made the trip, but the journalists, cameramen and technicians had complained the whole way about the road between St. John's and this tiny village. What's more, there were not enough rooms in this remote little village for the hordes of curious onlookers to stay in.

Achille had to give himself a forty-eight hour rest. He was exhausted and needed to get his wounds looked after. He took advantage of the hospitality of the local people, who fought one another for the honour of receiving him. However, two days later, he took to the sea again. In the port, the boats noisily saluted the event. Even the ferry that linked St. Barbe to L'Anse-au-Clair cut its motors to allow its passengers to see the *old man in the canoe* take to the sea.

The passage to L'Anse-aux-Meadows was difficult. It took several days. The island of Newfoundland advanced northwards, forming a point, and Achille had to go around it then come back down again in the direction of Fogo. The wind was blowing hard, and to keep the canoe going in the right direction was not easy. Luckily his travel companions, who knew the sea well, positioned their boats in front of him to block the wind. If Vikings, the boldest of all sailors, who had settled in this place a thousand years earlier, had seen this old man in his little bark canoe, they would probably have welcomed him as one of their own.

After L'Anse-aux-Meadows, Achille had to go all the way back down the coast, taking advantage of a rear wind that pushed his canoe along more rapidly. He reached Jackson Arm, and then crossed White Bay. Every kilometre of the coast offered a unique panorama, an unfinished sculpture begun millions of years ago. There were little bays everywhere.

Fortunately, the fishermen accompanying him showed him the route to take. In spite of his compass, Achille would have had trouble finding his way through this meandering course. He passed a place called Fleur-de-Lys. He thought of Adela, who had told him about the frequent battles between the French and English fishermen four hundred years earlier. Was this a former French fishing port? He passed close to the islands of Little Bay, then Long Island, Triton, Leading Tickles and Fortune Harbour. Each time, the fishermen came out to greet him and cheer him on. When he landed for the night, he had a choice of many possible lodgings. He was embarrassed by all the attention and the disturbance he created in each place. Achille had wanted to refuse these invitations and spend the night in the cabin of Owen's boat, but the captain advised him that this kind of gesture would be considered an insult. So Achille graciously yielded to the pleasant obligation. He had seen hundreds if not thousands of faces by now, of kind people, proud and unpretentious people. For the Newfoundland villagers, to share their home and their table was nothing out of the ordinary, it was a way of life. Left for a long time without resources, forgotten on their isle of rock, they had acquired in their genes an innate sense of enterprise, hospitality and sharing.

When he arrived at Twillingate, Achille understood that his voyage was nearing its end. He zigzagged in and out between a series of little islands until he got to Little Harbour, then crossed at Farewell. All he had left to do was cross a bit of sea before getting to Fogo Island and Tilting. Once again, he felt this stage must be done all at once. There were many boats around him and he had been paddling very intensely so far. He had no idea how long it would take to get to Tilting, but he remembered how difficult the crossing had been between Quebec and Newfoundland. When he arrived within view of the port, Achille started to feel he was not going to make it. On the wharf were dozens of curious people waiting for him, waving their hands or white handkerchiefs in welcome. The old man did not even have the strength to climb out of his canoe and the men of the village had to carry him. Totally exhausted, he was hardly aware of the last moments of his voyage. The images in his head were less like a film than a series of photographs. Between each print was utter darkness.

※

When he woke up twenty-four hours later, Achille looked around. Naturally he did not know the house, but at first glance, it looked oddly like the kind of Quebec house he was used to. The room was under the eaves. The ceiling followed the angle of the roof so it was difficult to stand up straight except right in the middle of the room. A sash window looked out onto the back yard.

Achille found it difficult to move and his hands still hurt. Every one of his old muscles was aching. Someone had treated his wounds while he was in a semi-conscious state, before he fell asleep. His hands had been bandaged and a balm applied to his face. When he tried to get up, his knee joints were so stiff that he fell back heavily onto the bed. He had to lean on a chair to get up. With great difficulty, he managed to take a few steps. When he had finished washing and put on a clean set of clothes, Achille had to make another painful effort in order to walk down the stairs. He gripped the banister with one hand, holding the precious urn against his chest with the other.

A woman was waiting for him at the foot of the stairs. She told him she was happy to have him as her guest in this historic house that had been converted into an inn. On the first floor were a living room and kitchen. In the middle of the kitchen was a big table with long benches on either side. Several people were already sitting there, obviously waiting for Achille to appear. Normally the place only offered breakfast, but Achille had slept for many hours and needed to restore his strength. The hostess knew it, and served him a generous portion of Jigg's Dinner, which he devoured with great appetite.

Though he was used to Adela's quick way of talking, Achille had trouble making out what the people at the table were saying. "Over the years, Adela must have slowed down her speech," he reflected. "I hadn't remembered that Newfoundlanders could talk so quickly." He recognised certain familiar expressions, but their English was not the same as that of his companion. However, they ended up understanding each other, as he and Adela had done. Achille realised that these people were Fogo Island citizens and had decided to erect a monument to the memory of Adela. She had become a symbol of all Newfoundland's children who had left and been unable to return to their native land. The monument was in the process of being built. They had thought of placing the urn inside the monument. Achille was stunned. They had never known Adela, not even laid eyes on her! They had heard about her for just the past few weeks, and they already wanted to erect a monument to her!

There was something about the idea that offended the simple man that Achille was. He asked if he could think about it. He had made the plan to take her back home, but he had not thought it through much farther than that. What should happen next? What should he do with the ashes? He had not pondered the question for even a minute. His goal had been to take Adela back to her birthplace. But now that he was there, he did not know quite what to do. Adela did not belong to anyone. She did not belong to this group of people who, though they were all very nice, had taken charge of her because she was born here. She did not belong to the Owen clan, either, despite the fact that they were related. Nor did she belong to Achille, though she had always said the opposite. Adela had been herself. She had not become Adela Roy. Though she would have, if ever she had felt it was important to him.

Over the following days, Achille walked around the village several times, visiting such and such a site that Adela had told him about, walking on the pier where she had hidden, guessing the probable mooring place of the boat she had sneaked inside in order to flee seventy years before. He also saw the Dwyer General Store and imagined all those fishermen who became slaves of the companies who owned the store. He admired the rocky coast that Adela had so often described. He went to Sandy Cove and watched whales dancing on the waves. He looked out to sea as far as he could see. The completely unimpeded horizon made him feel uneasy, he who was used to the forests of the Gatineau, where one had to look up to see the sky through the tree branches. Here the sea was queen. He saw it from the way it had sculpted the coastlines over several million years. How many waves had it taken to round and smooth those immense slabs of rock?

He was looking far out, beyond the horizon, when he first saw it emerge from the rock point to his right. A huge iceberg gradually appeared, like an enormous ship. The mountain of ice surpassed anything that Adela had been able to describe to him. Of course, he had admired the photos and had always kept the one from the calendar that he had used as his model for the box, but it could not possibly compete with reality. The thing was so huge, so majestic, that it was difficult to imagine that such a block could have suddenly broken off a continent of ice. The sun shone on the iceberg, bringing out its many different colours. Adela was right, an iceberg was not white, contrary to what people from the mainland imagined. The top of it was crystal white, but the lower down one looked, the more shades of green and blue one saw. "Wow!" Achille exclaimed.

The mountain of ice had travelled down here from the Great North and it was probably smaller now than it was when it first left.

It was a spectacular sight. The mass advanced slowly, very slowly, pushed by the movement of the water and the wind. Sometimes it took only a few hours for an iceberg to travel across the horizon, but sometimes it would run aground and remain in the same place for several weeks. In the distance, other icebergs started to appear. It was at this moment that Achille suddenly knew what he had to do.

When he returned to the village, he asked to meet with the people who had welcomed him. He wanted to inform them of his decision. When everyone was assembled in the main room of the little inn, Achille said a few words to them.

"Adela Cole was a child of this country. She told me so often, and the images of the country she related to me were so clear that I have no doubt that her roots were here. I have walked on the earth of her childhood. I've seen what she saw. But Adela does not belong to you, no more than she belongs to me. She was always a child of the sea. And this morning I realised what she would have wanted, because I saw my first iceberg. It's on this iceberg, face to the wind and the sea, that she would have wanted to depart in peace."

Everyone started to protest at once, searching for reasons that Achille should not carry out his plan, but it was Owen who put an end to the discussion.

"That devil of a Quebecer is right," he said. "Adela Cole does not belong to us. If anyone has a claim to her, it's he. But it's also he who's given the best definition of what it is to be a Newfoundlander: a child of the wind and sea."

With regret, the members of the committee had to admit that this idea probably corresponded better to what Adela Cole would have wanted than their plan to build a monument to her memory.

Owen even offered to take Achille to one of the icebergs himself. If they had to forget about the idea of putting the ashes in the monument, it was out of the question for them to miss out on such a ceremony. The fishermen from Tilting would take to the sea the following Sunday to witness the event. Owen had agreed to pilot the boat that headed the procession, for he was familiar with icebergs. Gigantic, extremely dense, almost motionless, these floating ice floes could be treacherous. Each year, fishermen or tourists who got too close to them lost their lives. Because the water in the icebergs had been frozen millions of years before, people believed they possessed mysterious, almost magical properties. A boat would get close enough to the cliff of ice so that people could break off a few pieces with a few blows of an axe, and suddenly a huge section of the iceberg would break away. A block of ice of such great diameter could pierce the hull of a boat as easily as a toothpick piercing a cake. Sometimes boats that appeared to be a good distance from the icebergs would run aground on the icy base hidden beneath the water. Moreover there was the even greater risk of the iceberg overturning. Such a mass suddenly turning over created such turbulence that a boat could capsize. The famous and tragic wreck of the "unsinkable" *Titanic*, which occurred close to Newfoundland, was the most notable example of the danger of the ices of the north.

It had been agreed that everyone would keep an eye on the icebergs' movements. The fishermen's weather channel always provided precious instructions on the subject of the movement of the ices. But they had to act quickly, for the iceberg season was nearing an end. From the end of April to the end of July and even until the beginning of August, there were often many of them on the Newfoundland horizon. Sometimes an iceberg was there one day and gone the next, as if by magic. It also happened that no one saw a single iceberg over the entire season. The currents and winds had borne them elsewhere. At these times more superstitious fishermen would say, "Fishing won't be good." The icebergs had returned, but not the fish.

Owen had located a group of icebergs a little to the north of Tilting. He headed towards them. Achille was holding his precious box. The day before, he had bid farewell to Adela. He had told her of his love for her, seeking the words that he had not had time to say to her, even in all the years he lived with her. He had wept in silence, for he knew that soon they would be parted forever.

Owen passed close to an iceberg, but it was not a good one for Achille's purposes. The sides were as steep as those of a cliff and there was no place to deposit the urn. They had to be able to deposit the box and be certain it would stay there, at least long enough for Achille's will to be done and for Adela to float as long as possible on the waves, wherever the sea and wind wanted to take her.

The sun was breaking through the clouds; the breeze was good and the sea calm. Owen turned his boat to portside, followed by the twenty-odd fishing boats that had come out to witness the ceremony.

"The churches must be empty today," thought Owen with a smile.

He headed towards a second iceberg, whose giant face reared up before them. Owen first believed that it would not be suitable either, but in circling it, he saw that at its centre, the sun had dug a sort of basin that was just at sea level. On either side, the iceberg proudly reached for the sky. The place was ideal. All he had to do was approach the block of ice directly, heading for this central hollow. They had to be careful, for the two great peaks of ice could collapse without warning. Once they were close to the iceberg, a man could get out of the boat onto the ice, and set the urn down in a secure spot. The boat was now only about fifty metres from the iceberg.

Owen went from drive to reverse, keeping a close watch on either side of the boat so as to avoid getting stuck in the ice. That way he managed to find the ideal angle with which to move his boat into the central cavity of the iceberg.

Achille was standing at the prow of the boat, still holding the urn tightly. The fisherman thought of how important this moment must be for him. He admired him. "A devil of a good Quebecer," he reflected, he who had never had much affection for French speakers. He wondered if he would have had the same determination to bring his sweetheart back to her native land after so many years. He asked Achille to come into the cabin, where he would have been more comfortable, but the old man declined. He had agreed to letting someone else step onto the iceberg and lay the box down, but he would not give up the urn until the person was actually standing on the ice.

The wave hit the boat from the side, forcing Owen to correct his steering to get the boat back to the right angle. He wanted the moment of contact to be gentle, but most of all he wanted to avoid getting stuck in the ice. Achille was leaning on the boat's gunwale. He was anticipating the shock as the boat hit the ice and did not want to be thrown forward. Each time the boat arrived at less than a metre from the ice, the wave turned it around and Owen had to reverse again to correct the angle. This time, he had managed to do it. At the last moment, he turned on the motors so the prow of the boat could edge onto the ice. The occupants of the boat were jostled forward when the boat entered into contact with the iceberg. A fisherman was already moving forward to step out onto the iceberg when Owen heard the cracking sound. It was not the crack of splitting wood. It was something else, and Owen had heard the sound before, like a clap of thunder. The ice had just broken.

He looked at the left part of the iceberg, where it was tallest. For a few seconds, time seemed to stand still. Owen was alert to the slightest movement. His heart had stopped, yet it seemed it was only an inconsequential cracking noise, the kind that icebergs quite often produce. For a fraction of a second, his brain refused to comprehend what his eyes had already taken in. The peak at the left side of iceberg had shifted. He turned to the right. It had also begun to list towards the outside. The iceberg had broken right down the middle, just under the hull of the boat, and the two halves were tipping over. He wanted to reverse, but he did it so quickly that the motor stalled. In the time it took to turn on the ignition and for the motor to start up again, the prow of the boat had already raised a metre higher. Tipping towards the outside, the parts of the iceberg that were underneath the boat turned and suddenly shot upwards. He saw Achille holding on as tightly he could to the rail.

The boat was almost vertical now and Owen desperately clutched at the bar he was holding onto. Water was entering the deck in the stern. Then the two parts of the iceberg collapsed with a deafening noise into the sea. The boat, suddenly liberated from its lever of ice, fell heavily back onto the sea.

Owen could see that Achille was still holding his own, the urn firmly tucked under his arm. His eyes met Owen's just as the wave caused by the fall of the iceberg washed over onto the deck of the boat. The old man let go of the rail for a moment to catch the urn, which threatened to slip out of his grasp. For several seconds, Owen saw nothing but water and wondered if the boat had overturned. But the wave receded from the deck. It was empty. The sea had washed everything overboard from the spot where Achille had been standing with his urn moments earlier.

The men on deck had gripped onto whatever they could when the wave hit them. Owen shouted, screamed orders to everyone. The men came hurrying from all directions, looking for the old man. Farther away, the people in the other boats had witnessed with horror the breaking of the iceberg. They had seen the two mountains of ice separate and topple over into the sea. Helpless to do anything, they had also seen the boat standing straight up in the water and had feared it would overturn.

Now all was chaos. After a few minutes, Owen yelled into his radio: "Man overboard…man overboard…"

Several boats sped to the rescue, forming a circle around what now had become two icebergs. After a few minutes, Owen knew it was all over. In this northern sea, a man could not survive very long. Another boat had come alongside Owen's, searching frantically. One of the men cried out: "The box! Look at the box there floating!" He pointed to the tiny wooden iceberg, rocked by the waves.

He leaned overboard to pick up the box.

"No!" shouted Owen. "Leave it there!"

The man hesitated, then pulled himself back into the boat without touching the box. It was better to leave it there, now that Adela was reunited with the man she loved. The boat sirens resounded in chorus as a final tribute to them, and the sound faded in the distance like the song of a "whale calling her love."